SO-ADI-842

Betty & Veronica® SPECTACULAR

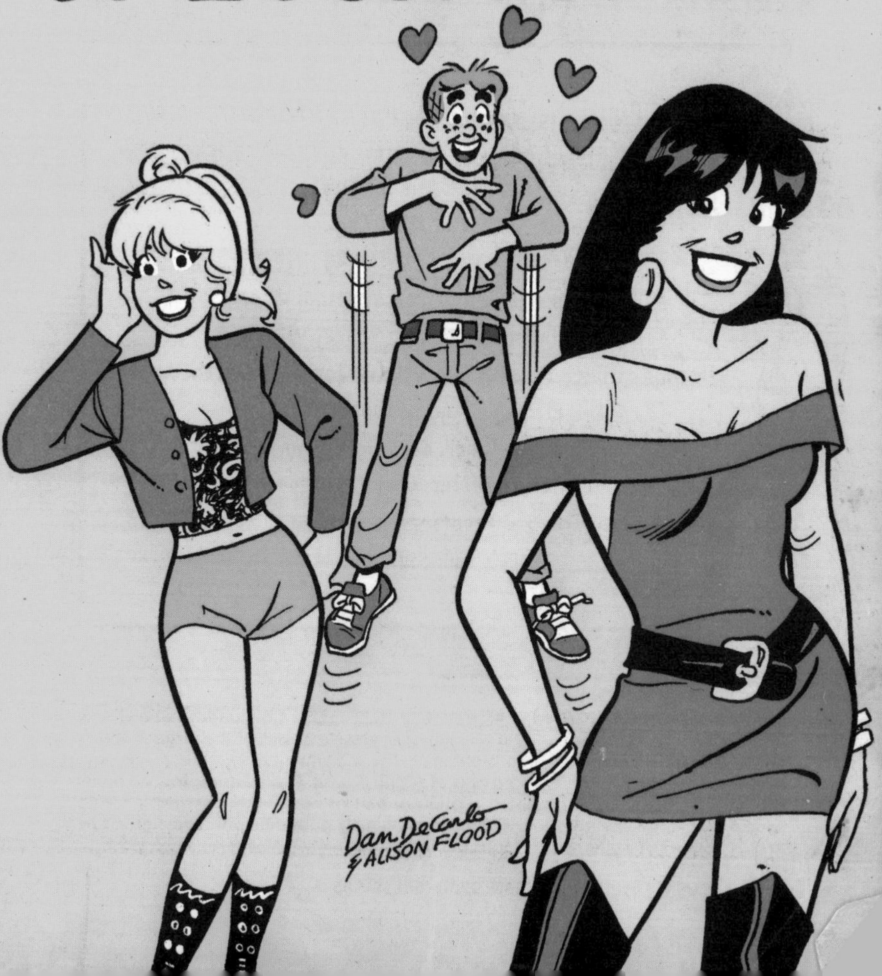
Dan DeCarlo
& ALISON FLOOD

Betty & Veronica SPECTACULAR

Publisher / Co-CEO: Jon Goldwater
Co-President / Editor-In-Chief: Victor Gorelick
Co-President: Mike Pellerito
Co-President: Alex Segura
Chief Creative Officer: Roberto Aguirre-Sacasa
Chief Operating Officer: William Mooar
Chief Financial Officer: Robert Wintle
Director of Book Sales & Operations: Jonathan Betancourt
Production Manager: Stephen Oswald
Lead Designer: Kari McLachlan
Associate Editor: Carlos Antunes
Assistant Editor / Proofreader: Jamie Lee Rotante
Co-CEO: Nancy Silberkleit

BETTY & VERONICA SPECTACULAR VOL 1 © 2018 Archie Comic Publications, Inc. Archie characters created by John L. Goldwater; the likenesses of the original Archie characters were created by Bob Montana. The individual characters' names and likenesses are the exclusive trademarks of Archie Comic Publications, Inc. All rights reserved. Nothing may be reprinted in whole or part without written permission from Archie Comic Publications, Inc. All stories previously published and copyrighted by Archie Comic Publications, Inc. (or its predecessors) in magazine form 1992-1994.

Printed in USA. First Printing. ISBN: 978-1-68255-905-5

WRITTEN BY

George Gladir, Bill Golliher, Dan Parent,
Mike Gallagher & Mike Pellowski

ART BY

Dan DeCarlo, Dan Parent, Stan Goldberg,
Alison Flood, Rudy Lapick, Henry Scarpelli,
Barry Grossman & Bill Yoshida

Betty & Veronica® SPECTACULAR

TABLE OF CONTENTS

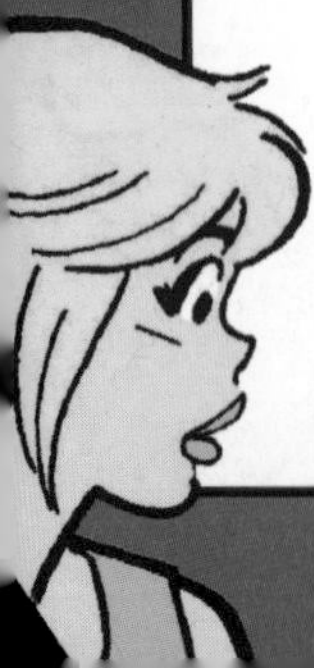

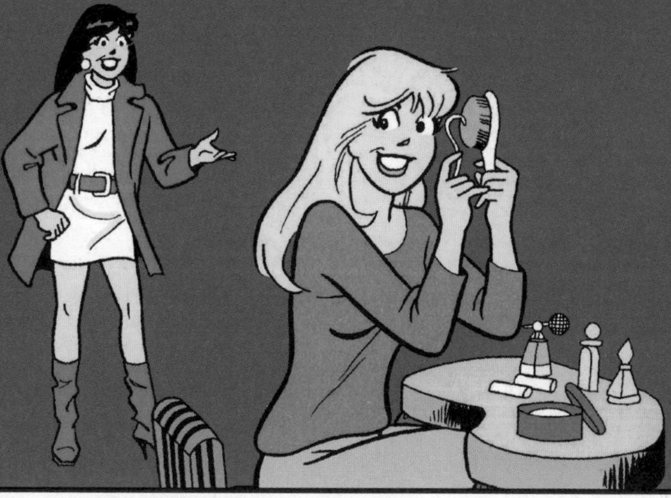

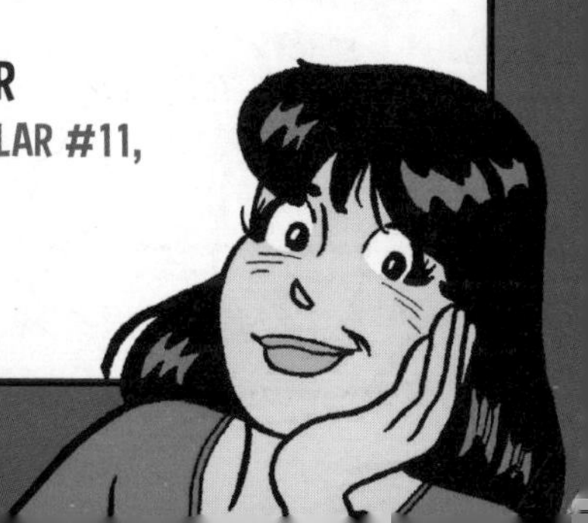

Betty & Veronica SPECTACULAR

Welcome to this SPECTAULAR collection of some of Betty and Veronica's finest and funniest moments!

The *Betty & Veronica Spectacular* series began in 1992 as one of the quarterly replacements for the *Archie Giant Series* that ran from 1960 - 1992. The *Archie Giant Series* featured ever-revolving subtitles, including a *Betty and Veronica Spectacular* among others. The new B&V series gave fans of the two BFFs even more stories to enjoy, and every issue saw each of the two characters starring in their own stories that further defined their distinct personalities and interests as well as gave a platform for other female characters to have their moments in the spotlight. As time went on, the series also introduced a few new female characters—one of which you'll see in this particular collection is Sugarplum, the teenage daughter of Santa Claus. Fans could also enjoy even more pin-ups and fashion pages.

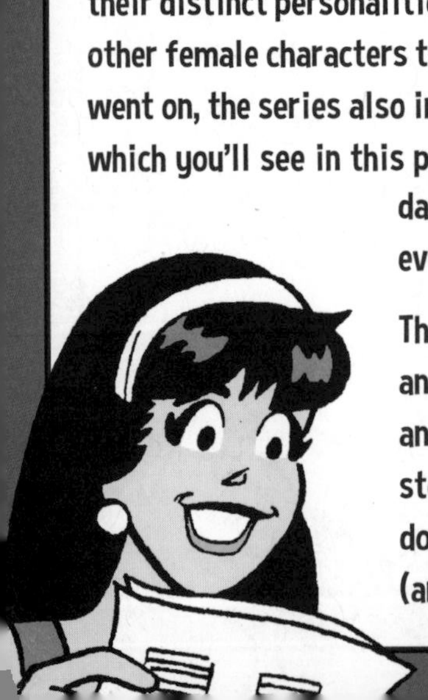

The series would later go on to change formats and presentation—but that's for another time and another volume! For now, enjoy all of these fun stories that feature the girls doing what they do best: taking on new challenges and having fun (and looking fashionable!) while doing it!

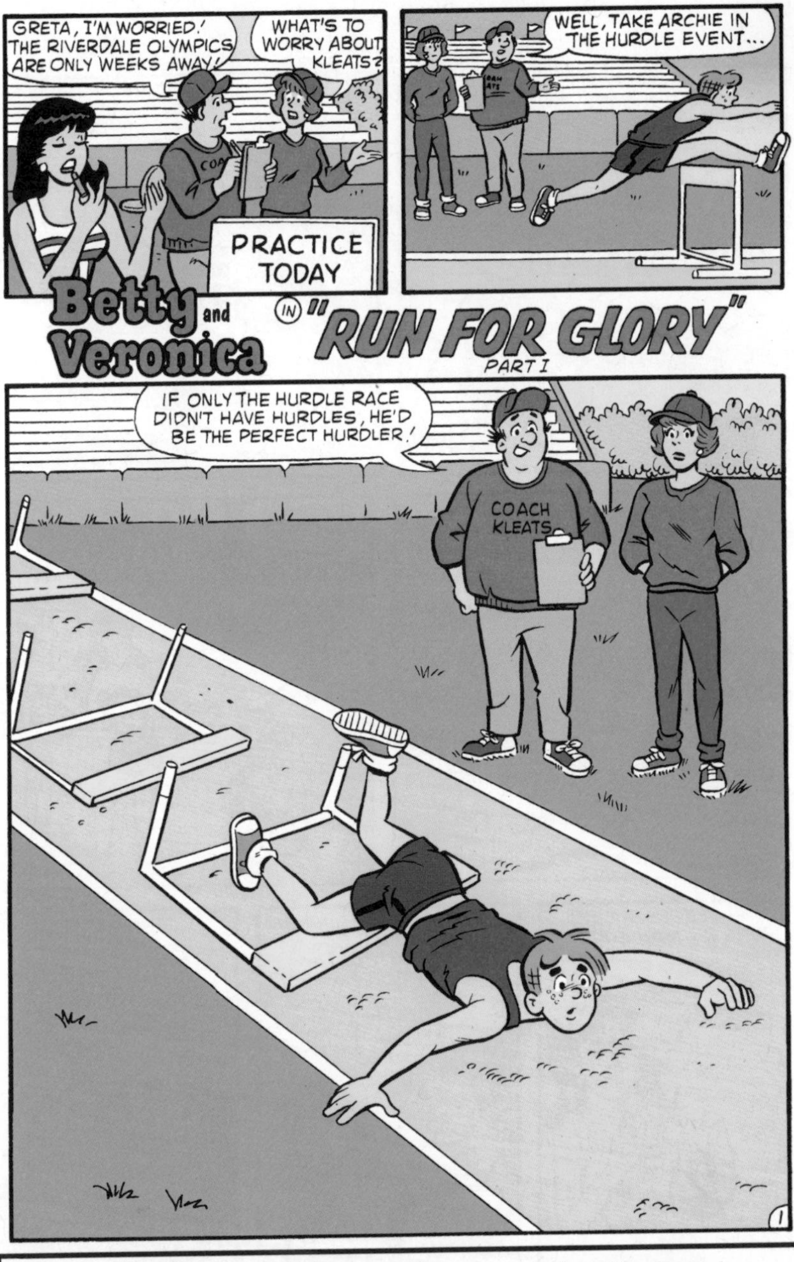
GRETA, I'M WORRIED! THE RIVERDALE OLYMPICS ARE ONLY WEEKS AWAY!
WHAT'S TO WORRY ABOUT, KLEATS?
PRACTICE TODAY
WELL, TAKE ARCHIE IN THE HURDLE EVENT...
Betty and Veronica IN "RUN FOR GLORY"
PART I
IF ONLY THE HURDLE RACE DIDN'T HAVE HURDLES, HE'D BE THE PERFECT HURDLER!
COACH KLEATS
1

Story: George Gladir Pencils: Dan DeCarlo & Dan Parent
Inks: Rudy Lapick Letters: Bill Yoshida Colors: Barry Grossman

Originally printed in BETTY & VERONICA SPECTACULAR #1, October 1992

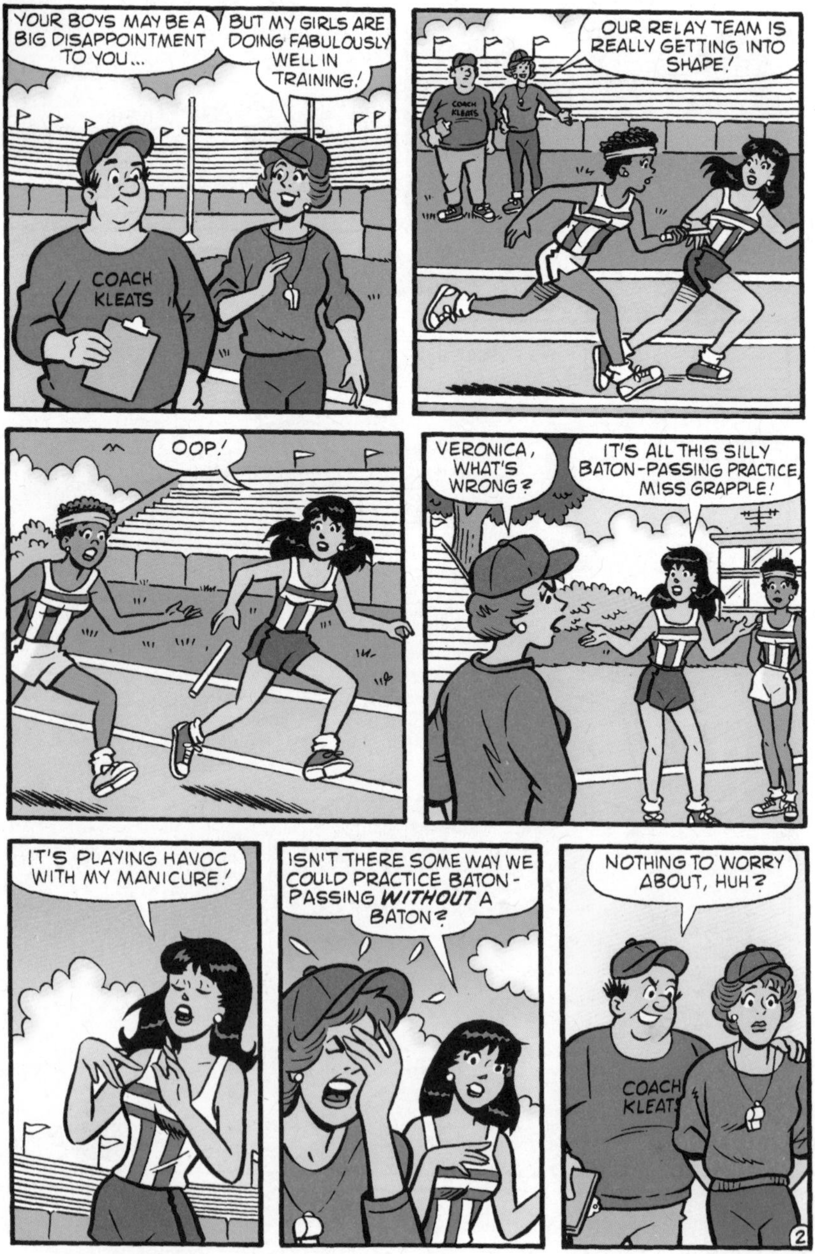

YOUR BOYS MAY BE A BIG DISAPPOINTMENT TO YOU...
BUT MY GIRLS ARE DOING FABULOUSLY WELL IN TRAINING!
COACH KLEATS
OUR RELAY TEAM IS REALLY GETTING INTO SHAPE!
COACH KLEATS
OOP!
VERONICA, WHAT'S WRONG?
IT'S ALL THIS SILLY BATON-PASSING PRACTICE, MISS GRAPPLE!
IT'S PLAYING HAVOC WITH MY MANICURE!
ISN'T THERE SOME WAY WE COULD PRACTICE BATON-PASSING ***WITHOUT*** A BATON?
NOTHING TO WORRY ABOUT, HUH?
COACH KLEATS
2

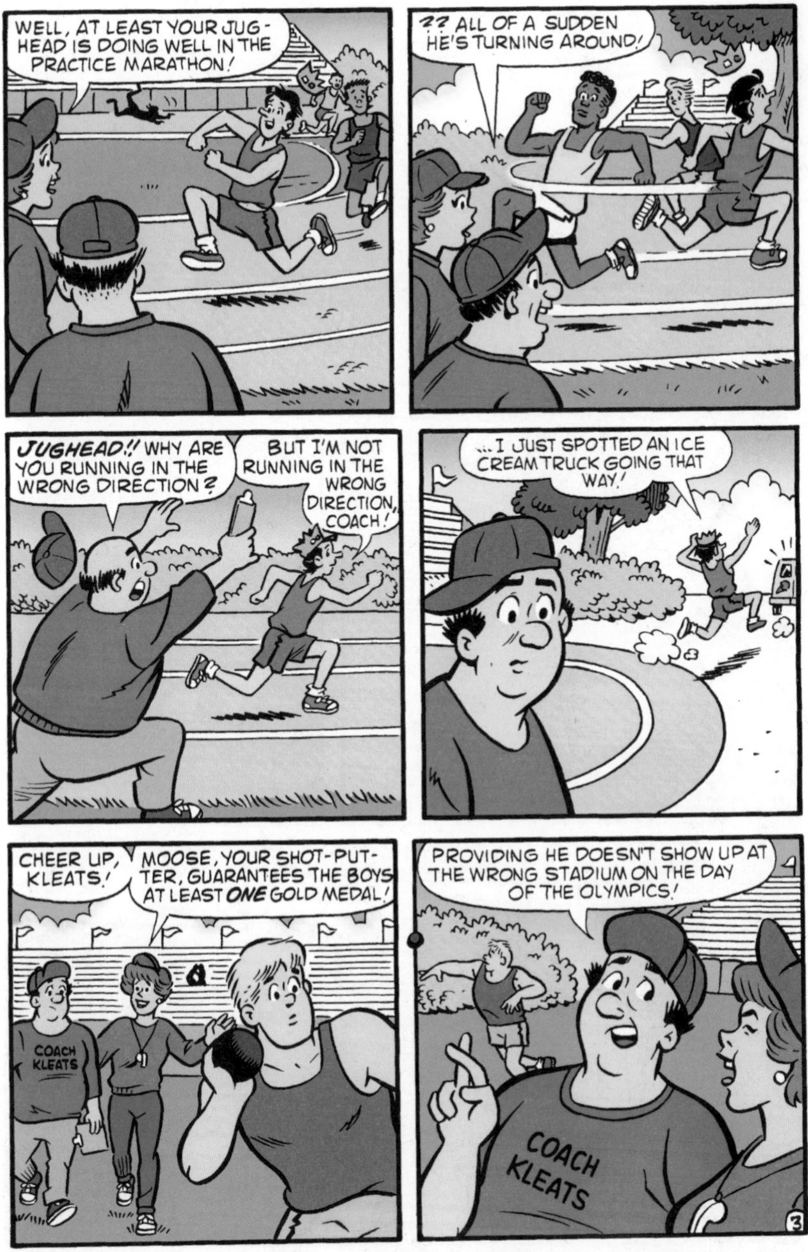
WELL, AT LEAST YOUR JUG-HEAD IS DOING WELL IN THE PRACTICE MARATHON!
?? ALL OF A SUDDEN HE'S TURNING AROUND!
JUGHEAD!! WHY ARE YOU RUNNING IN THE WRONG DIRECTION?
BUT I'M NOT RUNNING IN THE WRONG DIRECTION, COACH!
...I JUST SPOTTED AN ICE CREAM TRUCK GOING THAT WAY!
CHEER UP, KLEATS!
MOOSE, YOUR SHOT-PUT-TER, GUARANTEES THE BOYS AT LEAST ONE GOLD MEDAL!
COACH KLEATS
PROVIDING HE DOESN'T SHOW UP AT THE WRONG STADIUM ON THE DAY OF THE OLYMPICS!
COACH KLEATS
3

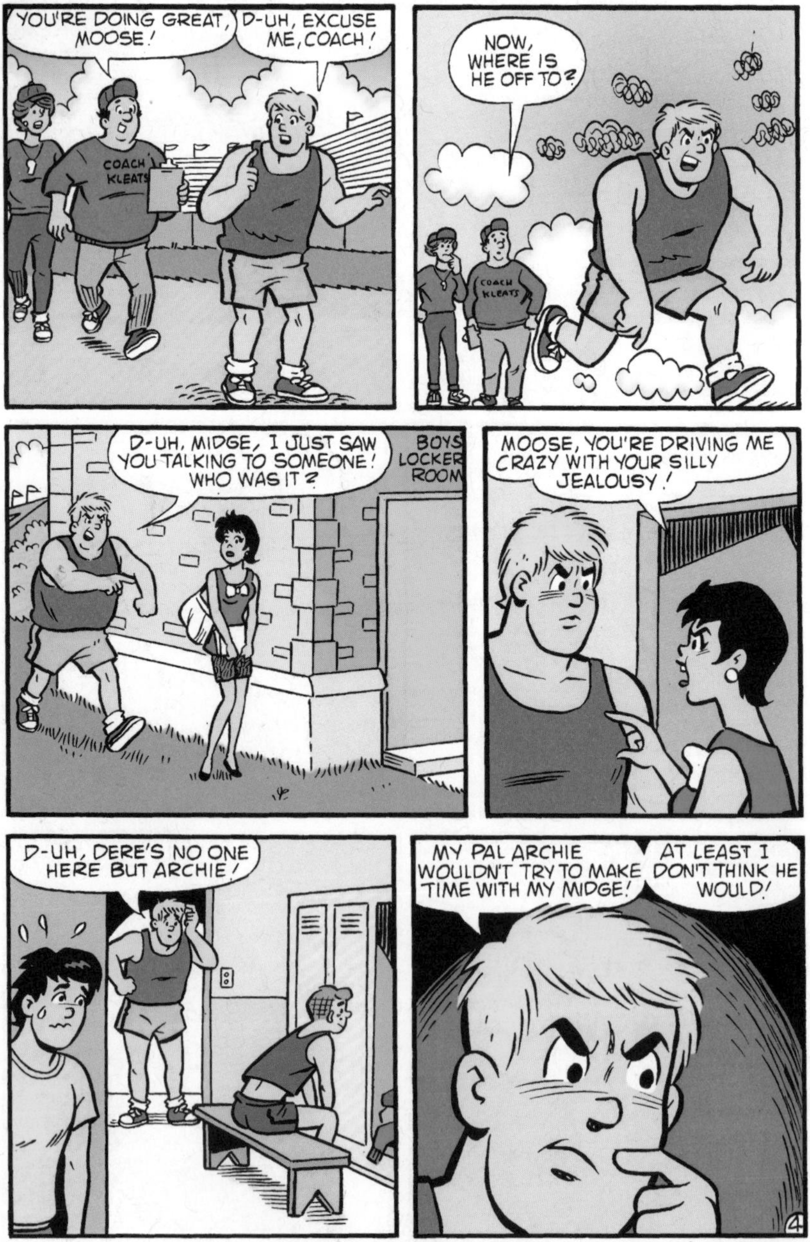
YOU'RE DOING GREAT, MOOSE!
D-UH, EXCUSE ME, COACH!
COACH KLEATS
NOW, WHERE IS HE OFF TO?
COACH KLEATS
D-UH, MIDGE, I JUST SAW YOU TALKING TO SOMEONE! WHO WAS IT?
BOYS LOCKER ROOM
MOOSE, YOU'RE DRIVING ME CRAZY WITH YOUR SILLY JEALOUSY!
D-UH, DERE'S NO ONE HERE BUT ARCHIE!
MY PAL ARCHIE WOULDN'T TRY TO MAKE TIME WITH MY MIDGE!
AT LEAST I DON'T THINK HE WOULD!
4

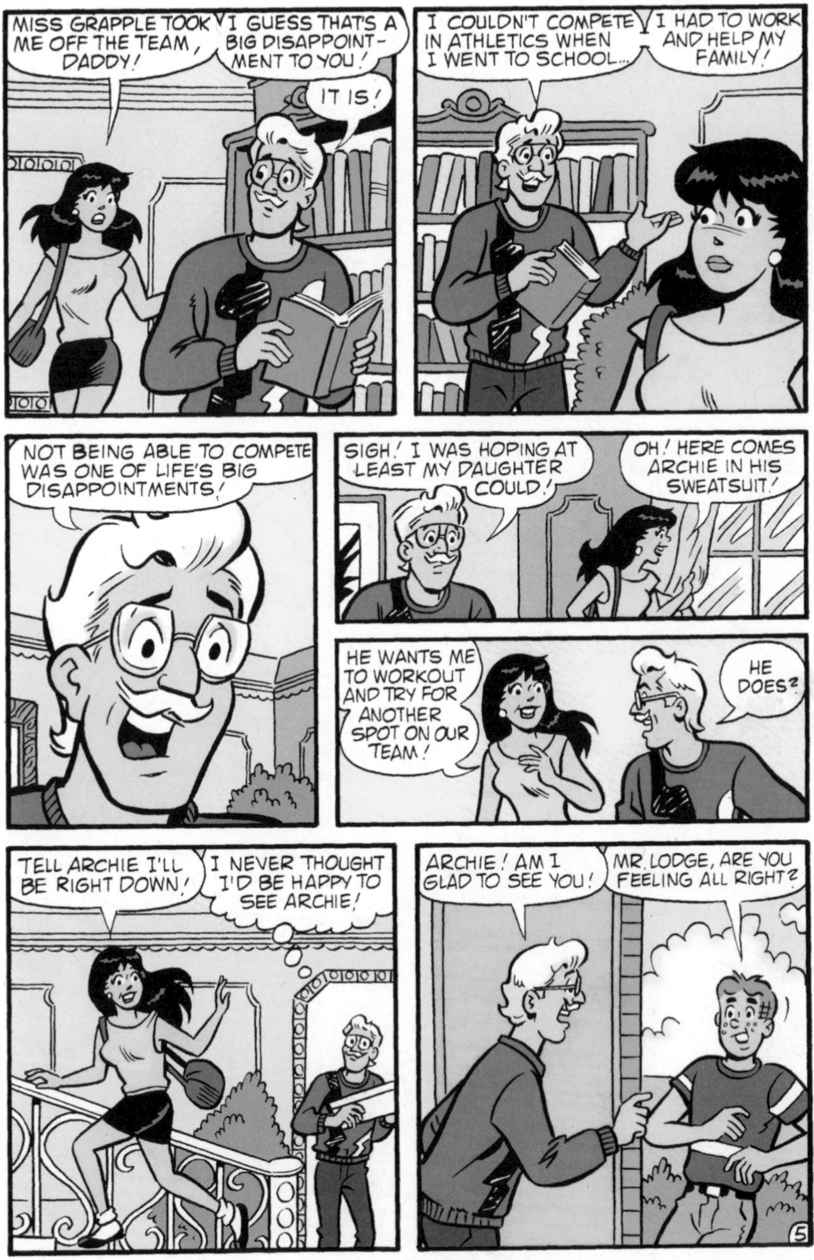
MISS GRAPPLE TOOK ME OFF THE TEAM, DADDY!
I GUESS THAT'S A BIG DISAPPOINT-MENT TO YOU!
IT IS!
I COULDN'T COMPETE IN ATHLETICS WHEN I WENT TO SCHOOL...
I HAD TO WORK AND HELP MY FAMILY!
NOT BEING ABLE TO COMPETE WAS ONE OF LIFE'S BIG DISAPPOINTMENTS!
SIGH! I WAS HOPING AT LEAST MY DAUGHTER COULD!
OH! HERE COMES ARCHIE IN HIS SWEATSUIT!
HE WANTS ME TO WORKOUT AND TRY FOR ANOTHER SPOT ON OUR TEAM!
HE DOES?
TELL ARCHIE I'LL BE RIGHT DOWN!
I NEVER THOUGHT I'D BE HAPPY TO SEE ARCHIE!
ARCHIE! AM I GLAD TO SEE YOU!
MR. LODGE, ARE YOU FEELING ALL RIGHT?
5

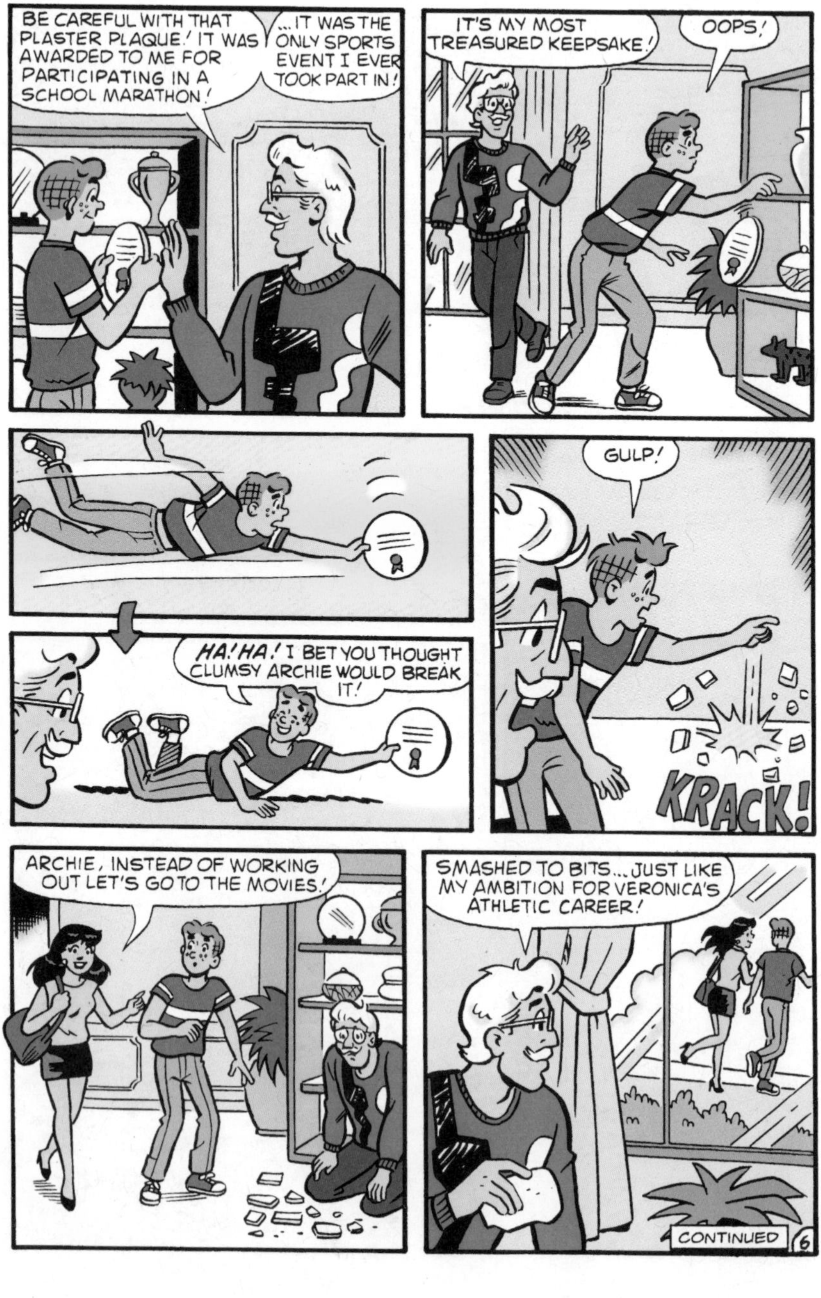
BE CAREFUL WITH THAT PLASTER PLAQUE! IT WAS AWARDED TO ME FOR PARTICIPATING IN A SCHOOL MARATHON!
...IT WAS THE ONLY SPORTS EVENT I EVER TOOK PART IN!
IT'S MY MOST TREASURED KEEPSAKE!
OOPS!
HA! HA! I BET YOU THOUGHT CLUMSY ARCHIE WOULD BREAK IT!
GULP!
KRACK!
ARCHIE, INSTEAD OF WORKING OUT LET'S GO TO THE MOVIES!
SMASHED TO BITS... JUST LIKE MY AMBITION FOR VERONICA'S ATHLETIC CAREER!
CONTINUED
6

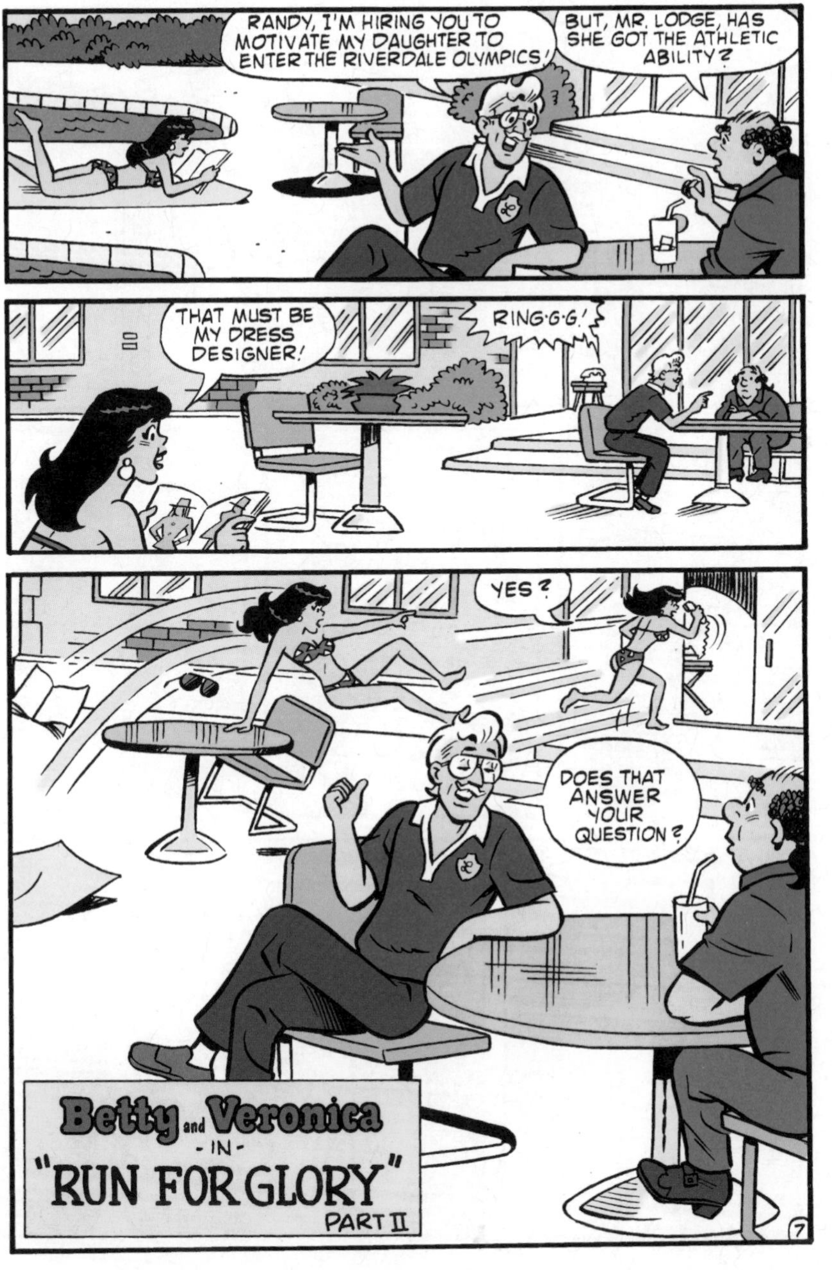
RANDY, I'M HIRING YOU TO MOTIVATE MY DAUGHTER TO ENTER THE RIVERDALE OLYMPICS!
BUT, MR. LODGE, HAS SHE GOT THE ATHLETIC ABILITY?
THAT MUST BE MY DRESS DESIGNER!
RING-G-G!
YES?
DOES THAT ANSWER YOUR QUESTION?
Betty and Veronica
-IN-
"RUN FOR GLORY"
PART II
7

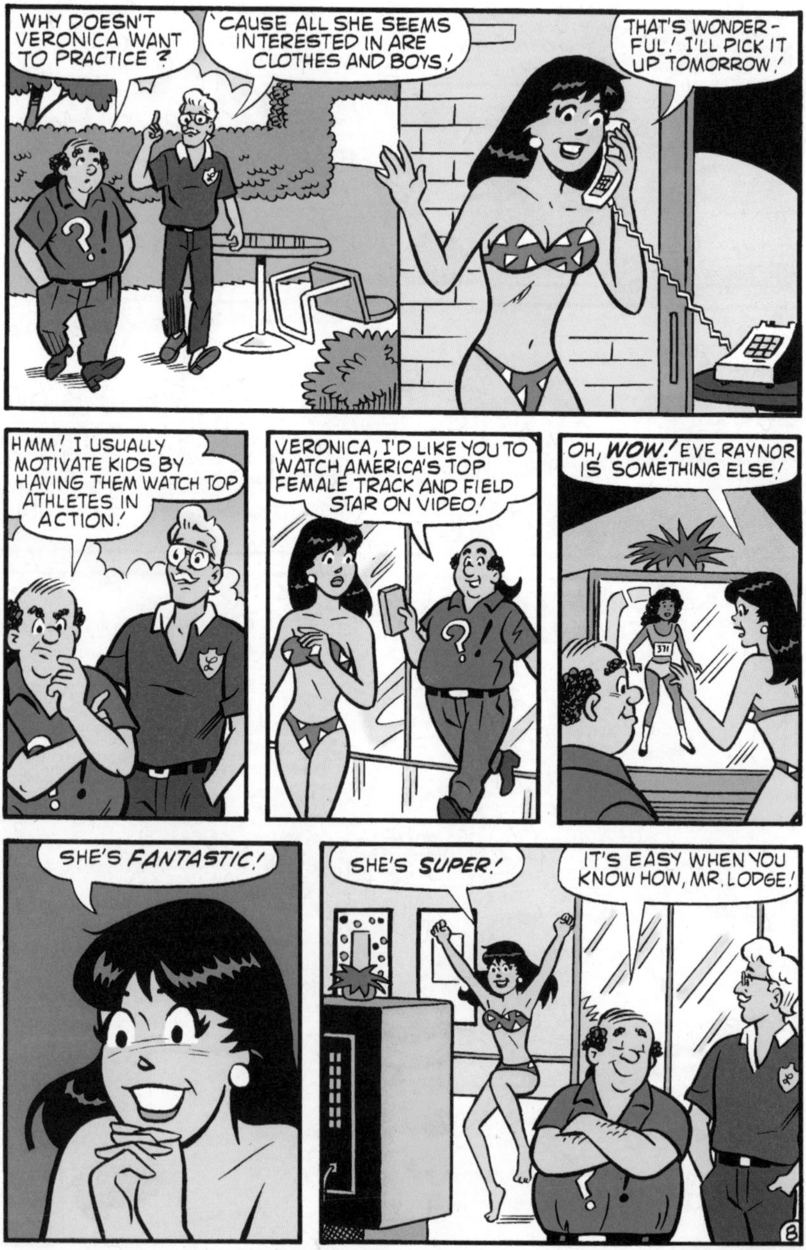
WHY DOESN'T VERONICA WANT TO PRACTICE ?
`CAUSE ALL SHE SEEMS INTERESTED IN ARE CLOTHES AND BOYS!
THAT'S WONDER-FUL! I'LL PICK IT UP TOMORROW!
HMM! I USUALLY MOTIVATE KIDS BY HAVING THEM WATCH TOP ATHLETES IN ACTION!
VERONICA, I'D LIKE YOU TO WATCH AMERICA'S TOP FEMALE TRACK AND FIELD STAR ON VIDEO!
OH, WOW! EVE RAYNOR IS SOMETHING ELSE!
SHE'S FANTASTIC!
SHE'S SUPER!
IT'S EASY WHEN YOU KNOW HOW, MR. LODGE!
8

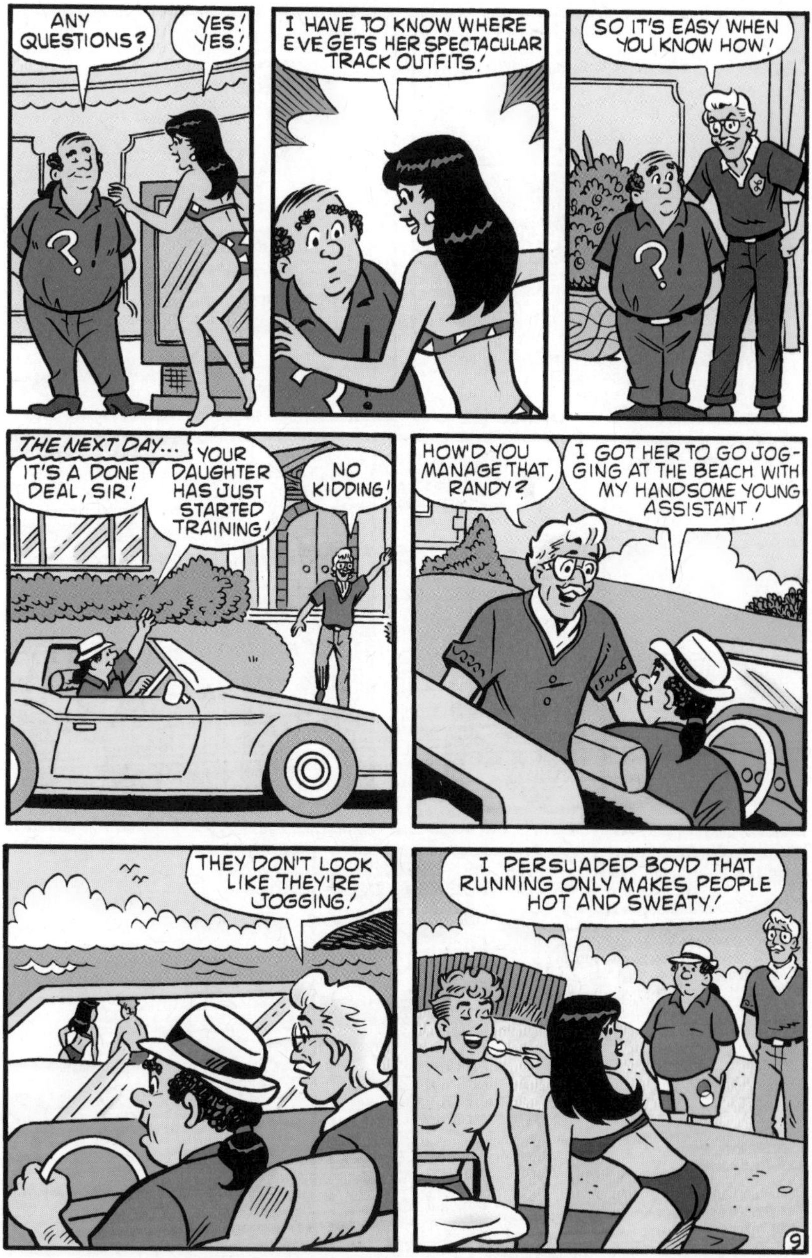
ANY QUESTIONS?
YES! YES!
I HAVE TO KNOW WHERE EVE GETS HER SPECTACULAR TRACK OUTFITS!
SO IT'S EASY WHEN YOU KNOW HOW!
THE NEXT DAY...
IT'S A DONE DEAL, SIR!
YOUR DAUGHTER HAS JUST STARTED TRAINING!
NO KIDDING!
HOW'D YOU MANAGE THAT, RANDY?
I GOT HER TO GO JOG-GING AT THE BEACH WITH MY HANDSOME YOUNG ASSISTANT!
THEY DON'T LOOK LIKE THEY'RE JOGGING!
I PERSUADED BOYD THAT RUNNING ONLY MAKES PEOPLE HOT AND SWEATY!
9

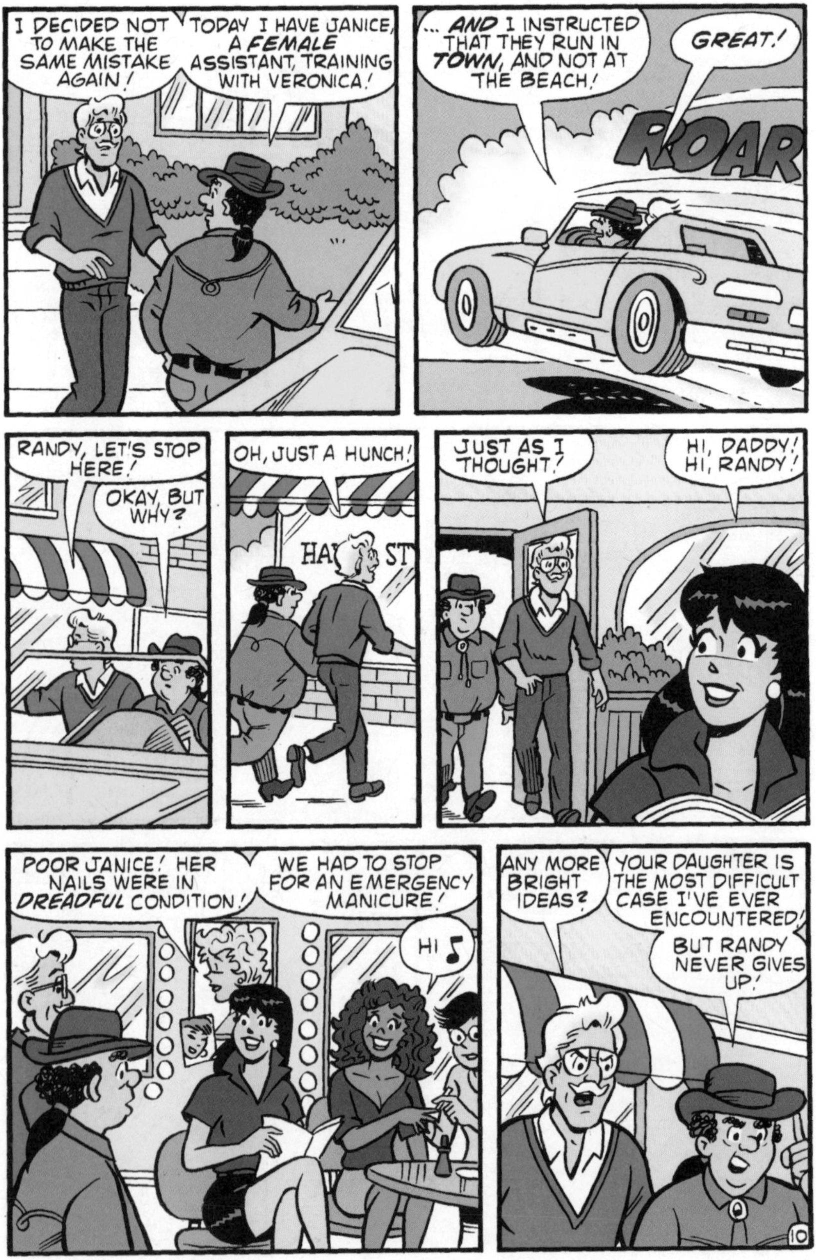
I DECIDED NOT TO MAKE THE SAME MISTAKE AGAIN!
TODAY I HAVE JANICE, A *FEMALE* ASSISTANT, TRAINING WITH VERONICA!
... *AND* I INSTRUCTED THAT THEY RUN IN *TOWN*, AND NOT AT THE BEACH!
GREAT!
ROAR
RANDY, LET'S STOP HERE!
OKAY, BUT WHY?
OH, JUST A HUNCH!
JUST AS I THOUGHT!
HI, DADDY! HI, RANDY!
POOR JANICE! HER NAILS WERE IN *DREADFUL* CONDITION!
WE HAD TO STOP FOR AN EMERGENCY MANICURE!
HI ♪
ANY MORE BRIGHT IDEAS?
YOUR DAUGHTER IS THE MOST DIFFICULT CASE I'VE EVER ENCOUNTERED!
BUT RANDY NEVER GIVES UP!
10

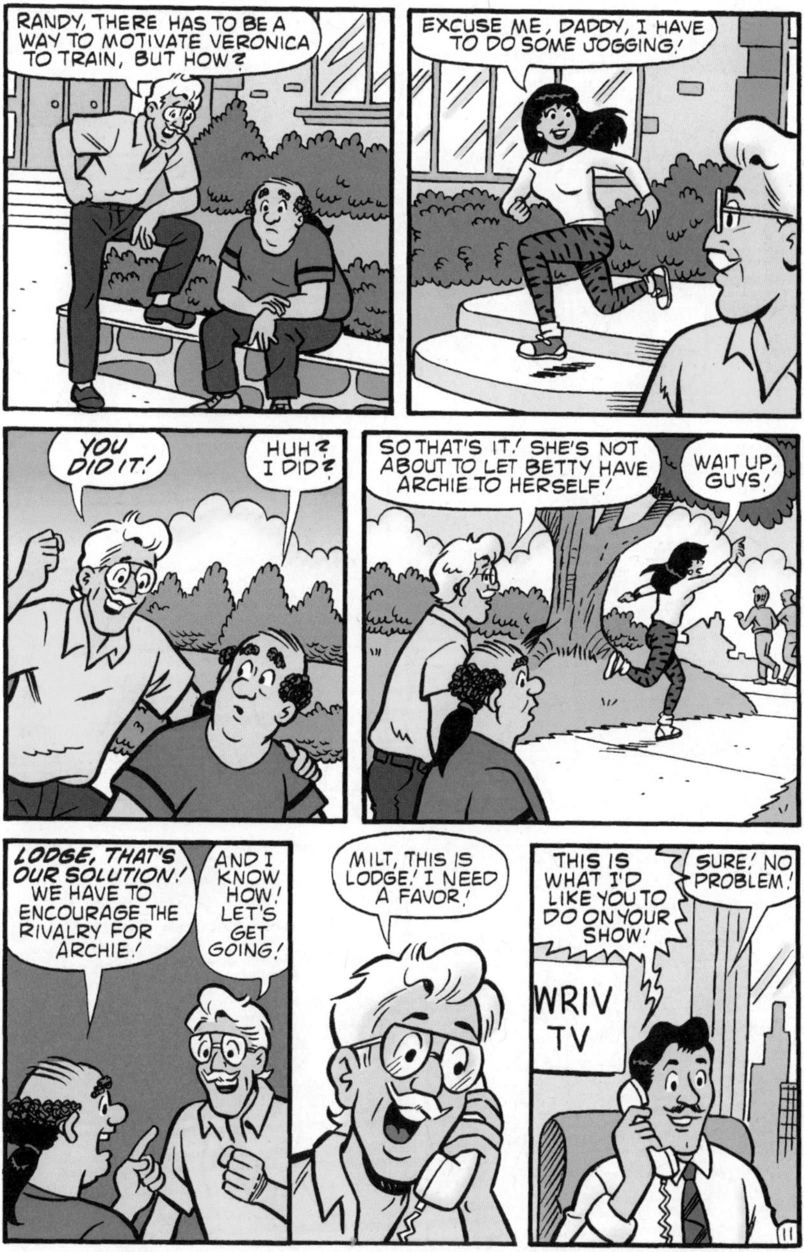
RANDY, THERE HAS TO BE A WAY TO MOTIVATE VERONICA TO TRAIN, BUT HOW?
EXCUSE ME, DADDY, I HAVE TO DO SOME JOGGING!
YOU DID IT!
HUH? I DID?
SO THAT'S IT! SHE'S NOT ABOUT TO LET BETTY HAVE ARCHIE TO HERSELF!
WAIT UP, GUYS!
LODGE, THAT'S OUR SOLUTION! WE HAVE TO ENCOURAGE THE RIVALRY FOR ARCHIE!
AND I KNOW HOW! LET'S GET GOING!
MILT, THIS IS LODGE! I NEED A FAVOR!
THIS IS WHAT I'D LIKE YOU TO DO ON YOUR SHOW!
SURE! NO PROBLEM!
WRIV TV
11

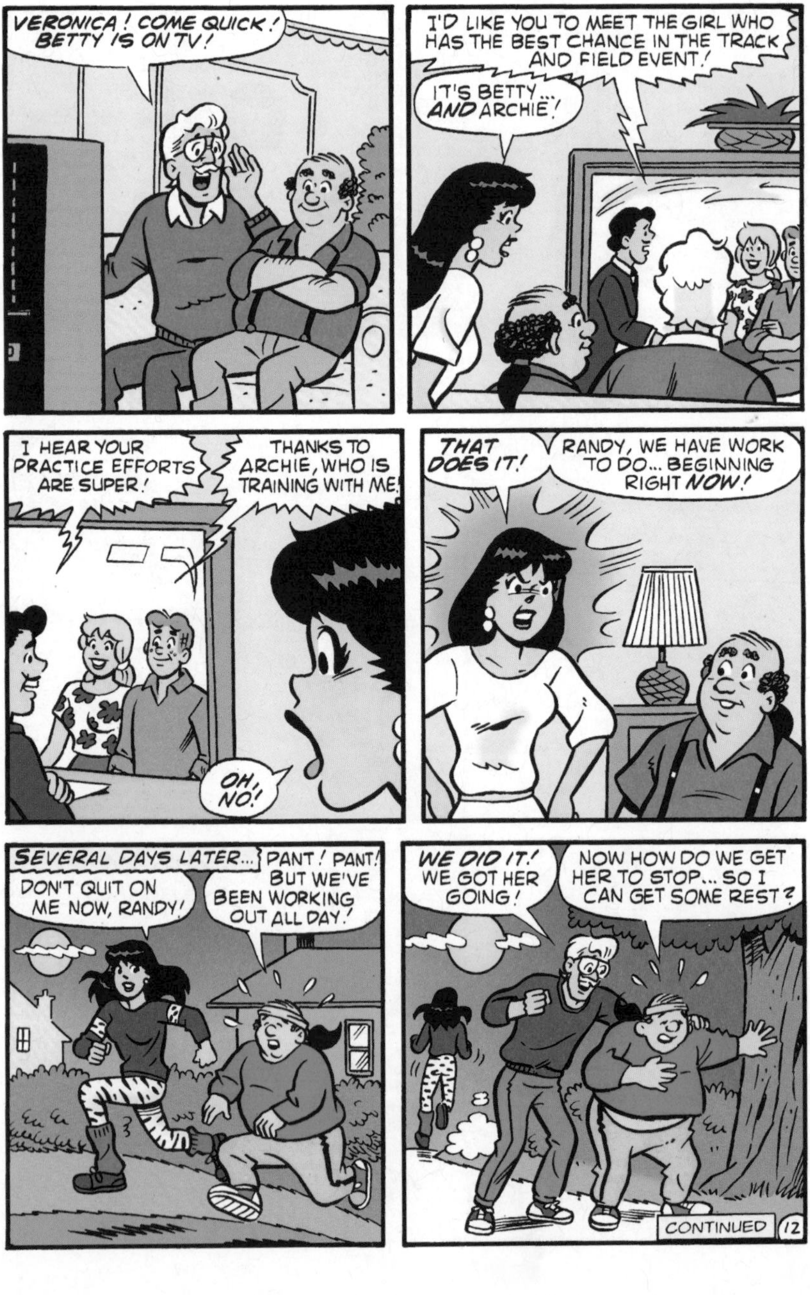
VERONICA! COME QUICK! BETTY IS ON TV!
I'D LIKE YOU TO MEET THE GIRL WHO HAS THE BEST CHANCE IN THE TRACK AND FIELD EVENT!
IT'S BETTY... AND ARCHIE!
I HEAR YOUR PRACTICE EFFORTS ARE SUPER!
THANKS TO ARCHIE, WHO IS TRAINING WITH ME!
OH, NO!
THAT DOES IT!
RANDY, WE HAVE WORK TO DO... BEGINNING RIGHT NOW!
SEVERAL DAYS LATER...
DON'T QUIT ON ME NOW, RANDY!
PANT! PANT! BUT WE'VE BEEN WORKING OUT ALL DAY!
WE DID IT! WE GOT HER GOING!
NOW HOW DO WE GET HER TO STOP... SO I CAN GET SOME REST?
CONTINUED
12

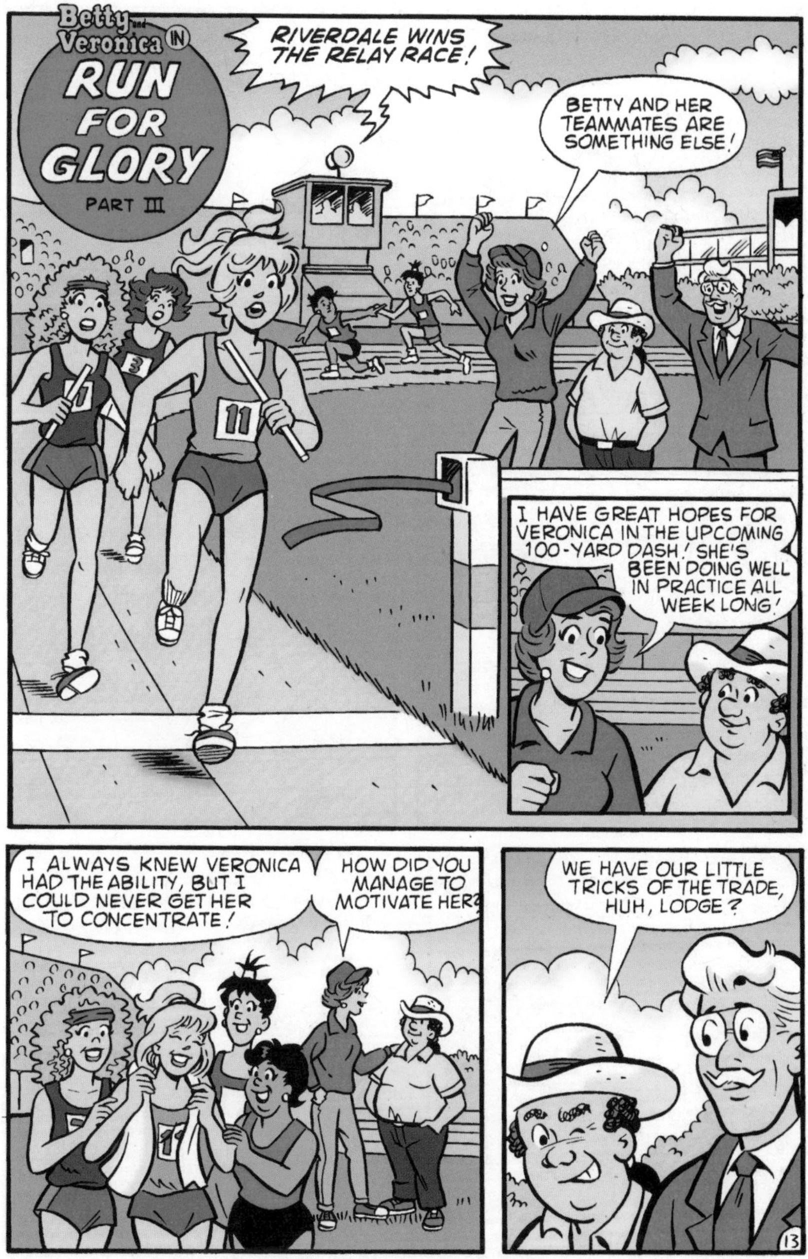
Betty and Veronica IN
RUN FOR GLORY
PART III
RIVERDALE WINS THE RELAY RACE!
BETTY AND HER TEAMMATES ARE SOMETHING ELSE!
I HAVE GREAT HOPES FOR VERONICA IN THE UPCOMING 100-YARD DASH! SHE'S BEEN DOING WELL IN PRACTICE ALL WEEK LONG!
I ALWAYS KNEW VERONICA HAD THE ABILITY, BUT I COULD NEVER GET HER TO CONCENTRATE!
HOW DID YOU MANAGE TO MOTIVATE HER?
WE HAVE OUR LITTLE TRICKS OF THE TRADE, HUH, LODGE?
13

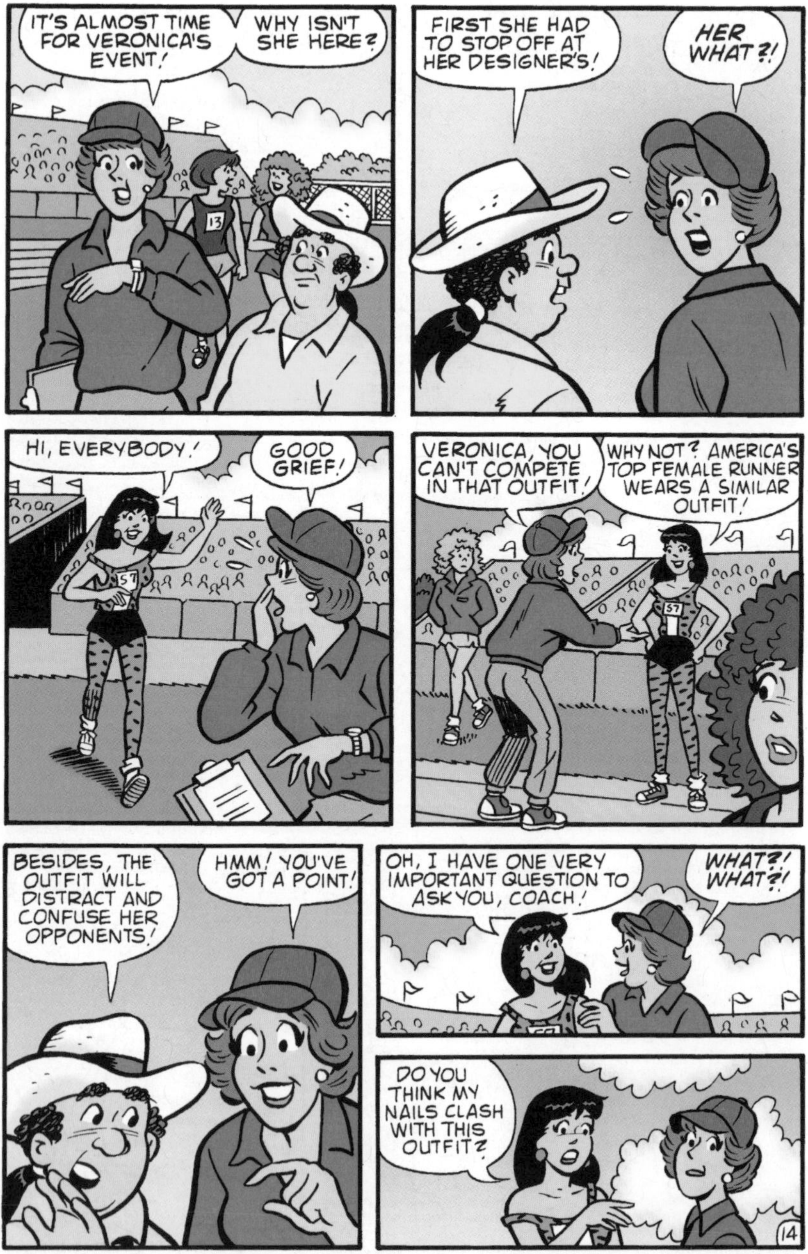
IT'S ALMOST TIME FOR VERONICA'S EVENT!
WHY ISN'T SHE HERE?
FIRST SHE HAD TO STOP OFF AT HER DESIGNER'S!
HER WHAT?!
HI, EVERYBODY!
GOOD GRIEF!
VERONICA, YOU CAN'T COMPETE IN THAT OUTFIT!
WHY NOT? AMERICA'S TOP FEMALE RUNNER WEARS A SIMILAR OUTFIT!
BESIDES, THE OUTFIT WILL DISTRACT AND CONFUSE HER OPPONENTS!
HMM! YOU'VE GOT A POINT!
OH, I HAVE ONE VERY IMPORTANT QUESTION TO ASK YOU, COACH!
WHAT?! WHAT?!
DO YOU THINK MY NAILS CLASH WITH THIS OUTFIT?
14

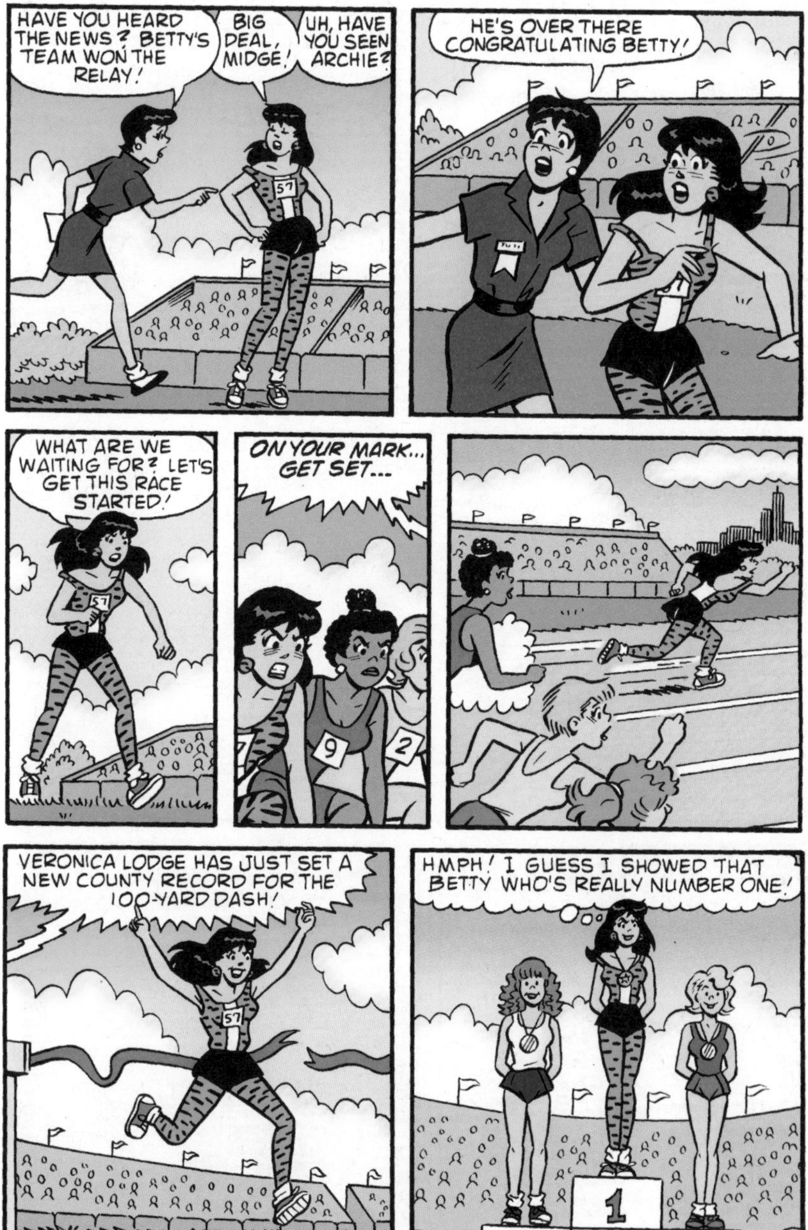
HAVE YOU HEARD THE NEWS? BETTY'S TEAM WON THE RELAY!
BIG DEAL, MIDGE!
UH, HAVE YOU SEEN ARCHIE?
HE'S OVER THERE CONGRATULATING BETTY!
WHAT ARE WE WAITING FOR? LET'S GET THIS RACE STARTED!
ON YOUR MARK... GET SET...
57
9
2
VERONICA LODGE HAS JUST SET A NEW COUNTY RECORD FOR THE 100-YARD DASH!
HMPH! I GUESS I SHOWED THAT BETTY WHO'S REALLY NUMBER ONE!
1
15

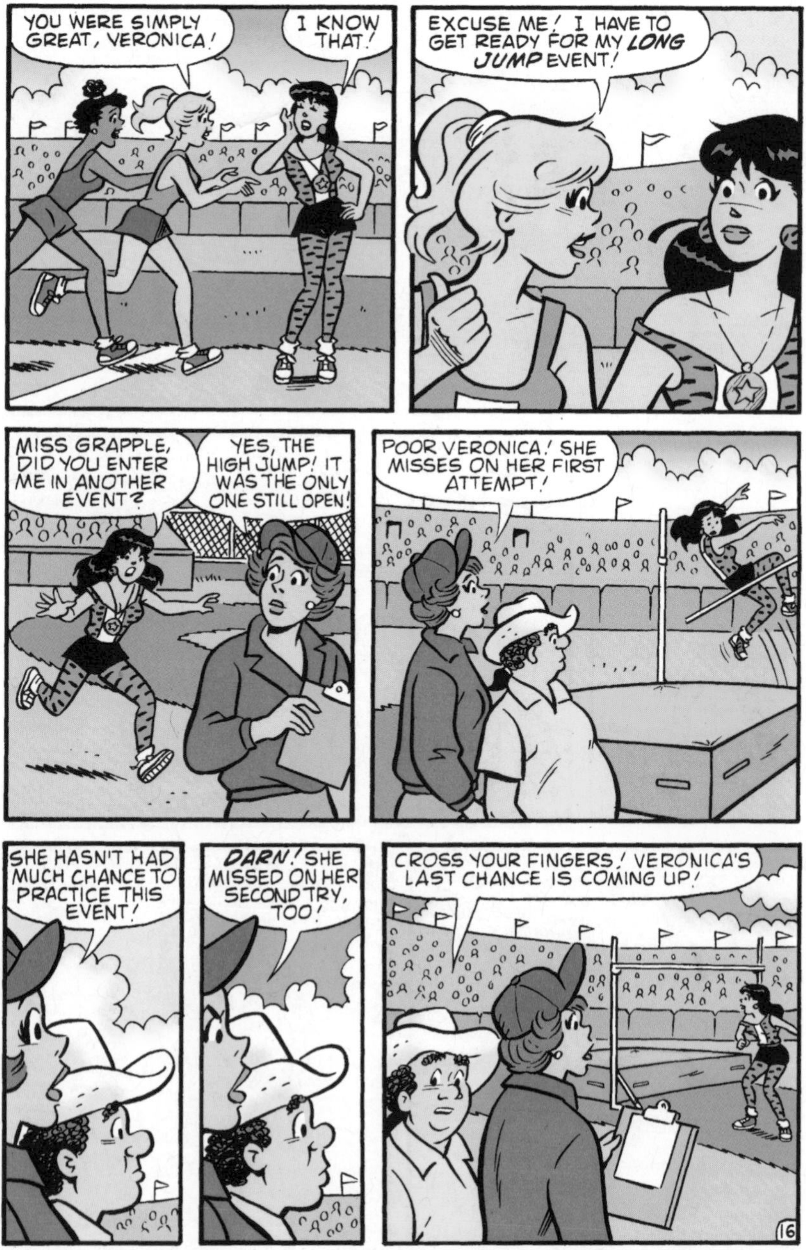
YOU WERE SIMPLY GREAT, VERONICA!
I KNOW THAT!
EXCUSE ME! I HAVE TO GET READY FOR MY LONG JUMP EVENT!
MISS GRAPPLE, DID YOU ENTER ME IN ANOTHER EVENT?
YES, THE HIGH JUMP! IT WAS THE ONLY ONE STILL OPEN!
POOR VERONICA! SHE MISSES ON HER FIRST ATTEMPT!
SHE HASN'T HAD MUCH CHANCE TO PRACTICE THIS EVENT!
DARN! SHE MISSED ON HER SECOND TRY, TOO!
CROSS YOUR FINGERS! VERONICA'S LAST CHANCE IS COMING UP!
16

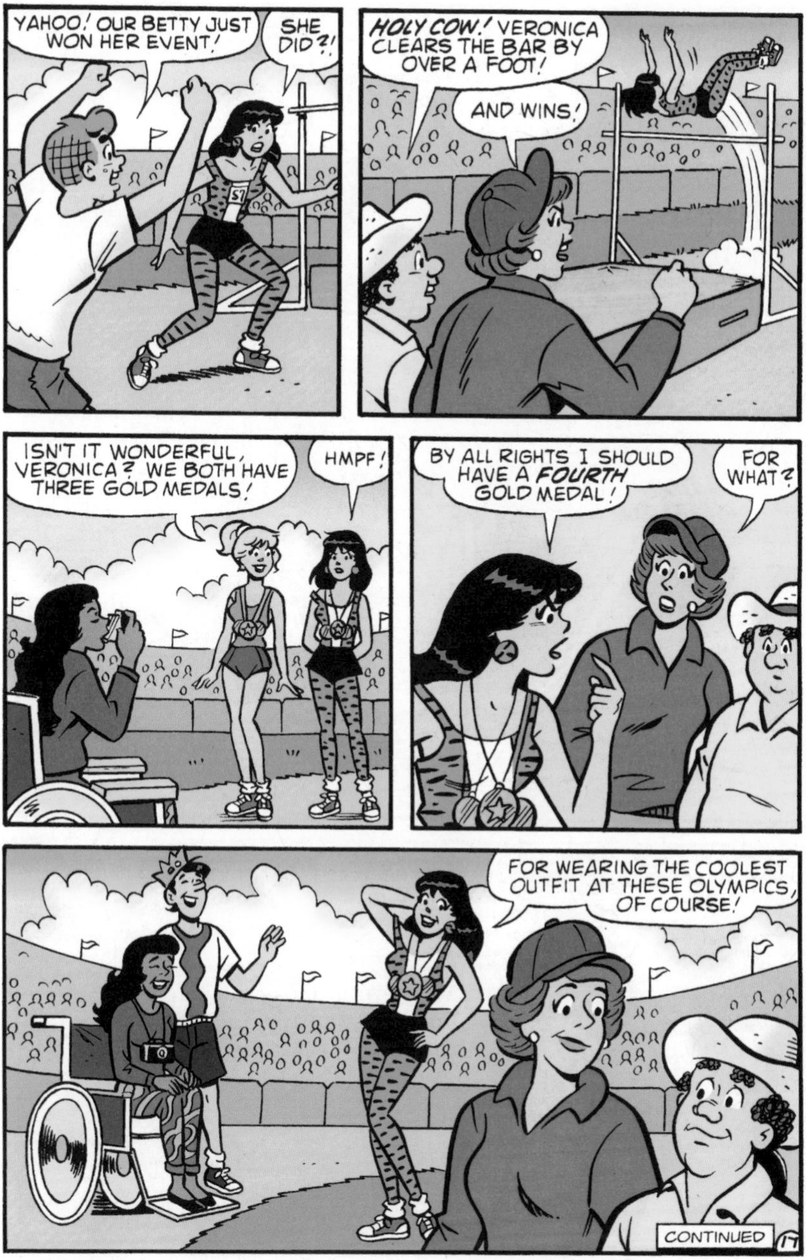
YAHOO! OUR BETTY JUST WON HER EVENT!
SHE DID?!
HOLY COW! VERONICA CLEARS THE BAR BY OVER A FOOT!
AND WINS!
ISN'T IT WONDERFUL, VERONICA? WE BOTH HAVE THREE GOLD MEDALS!
HMPF!
BY ALL RIGHTS I SHOULD HAVE A FOURTH GOLD MEDAL!
FOR WHAT?
FOR WEARING THE COOLEST OUTFIT AT THESE OLYMPICS, OF COURSE!
CONTINUED
17

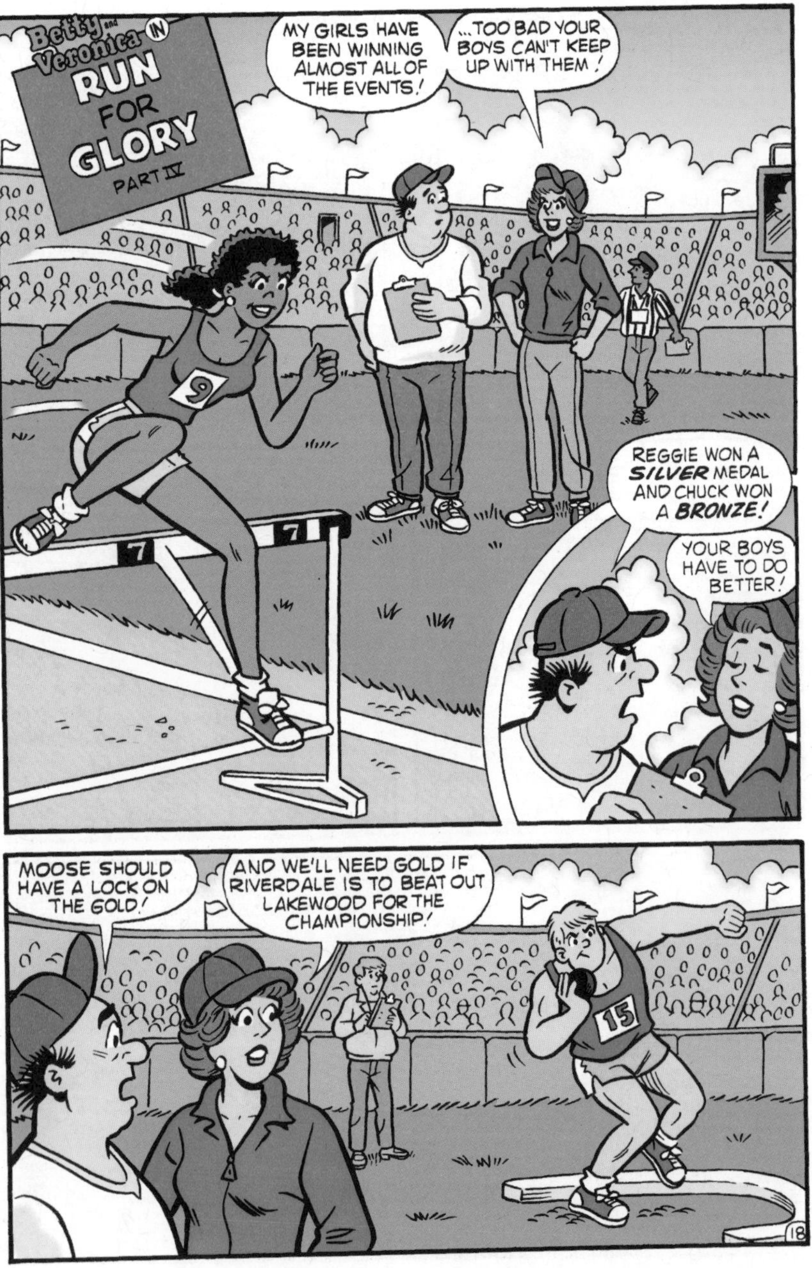
Betty and Veronica IN
RUN FOR GLORY
PART IV
MY GIRLS HAVE BEEN WINNING ALMOST ALL OF THE EVENTS!
...TOO BAD YOUR BOYS CAN'T KEEP UP WITH THEM!
9
7
REGGIE WON A SILVER MEDAL AND CHUCK WON A BRONZE!
YOUR BOYS HAVE TO DO BETTER!
MOOSE SHOULD HAVE A LOCK ON THE GOLD!
AND WE'LL NEED GOLD IF RIVERDALE IS TO BEAT OUT LAKEWOOD FOR THE CHAMPIONSHIP!
15
18

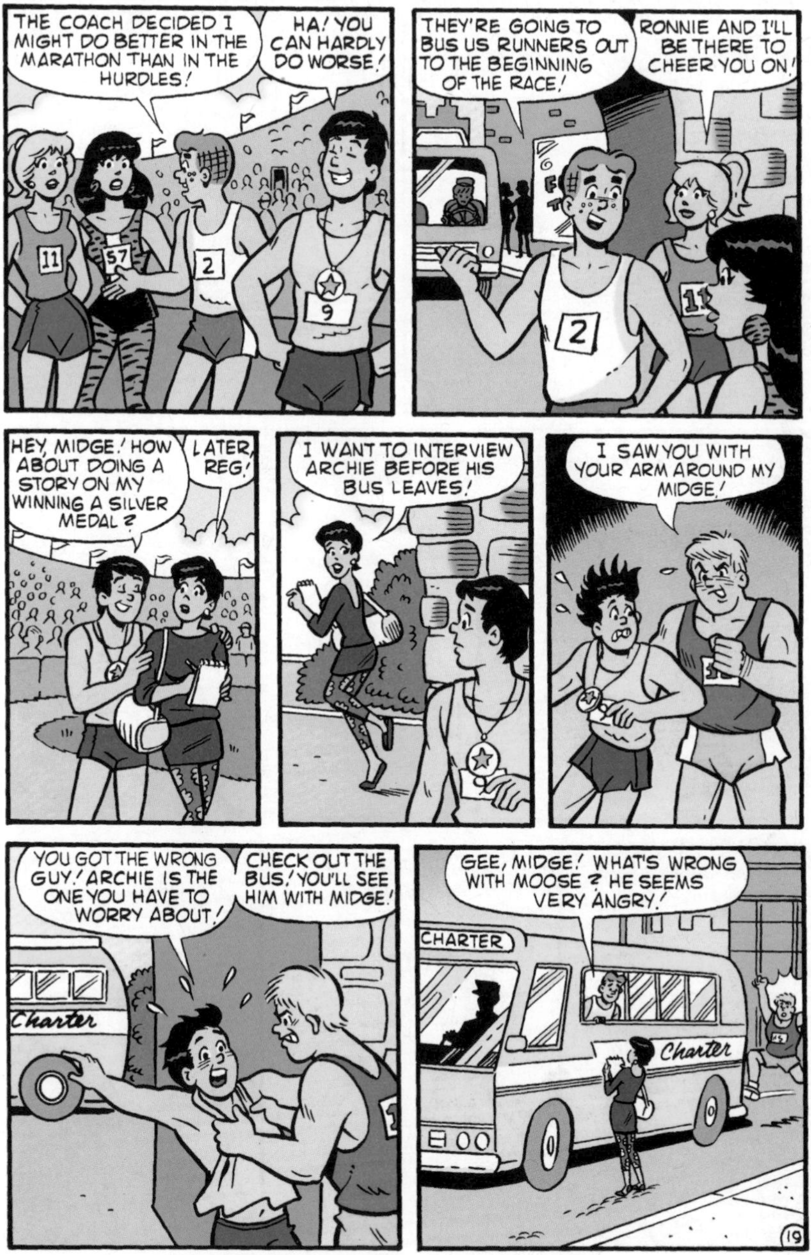
THE COACH DECIDED I MIGHT DO BETTER IN THE MARATHON THAN IN THE HURDLES!
HA! YOU CAN HARDLY DO WORSE!
THEY'RE GOING TO BUS US RUNNERS OUT TO THE BEGINNING OF THE RACE!
RONNIE AND I'LL BE THERE TO CHEER YOU ON!
HEY, MIDGE! HOW ABOUT DOING A STORY ON MY WINNING A SILVER MEDAL?
LATER, REG!
I WANT TO INTERVIEW ARCHIE BEFORE HIS BUS LEAVES!
I SAW YOU WITH YOUR ARM AROUND MY MIDGE!
YOU GOT THE WRONG GUY! ARCHIE IS THE ONE YOU HAVE TO WORRY ABOUT!
CHECK OUT THE BUS! YOU'LL SEE HIM WITH MIDGE!
GEE, MIDGE! WHAT'S WRONG WITH MOOSE? HE SEEMS VERY ANGRY!
CHARTER
Charter
19

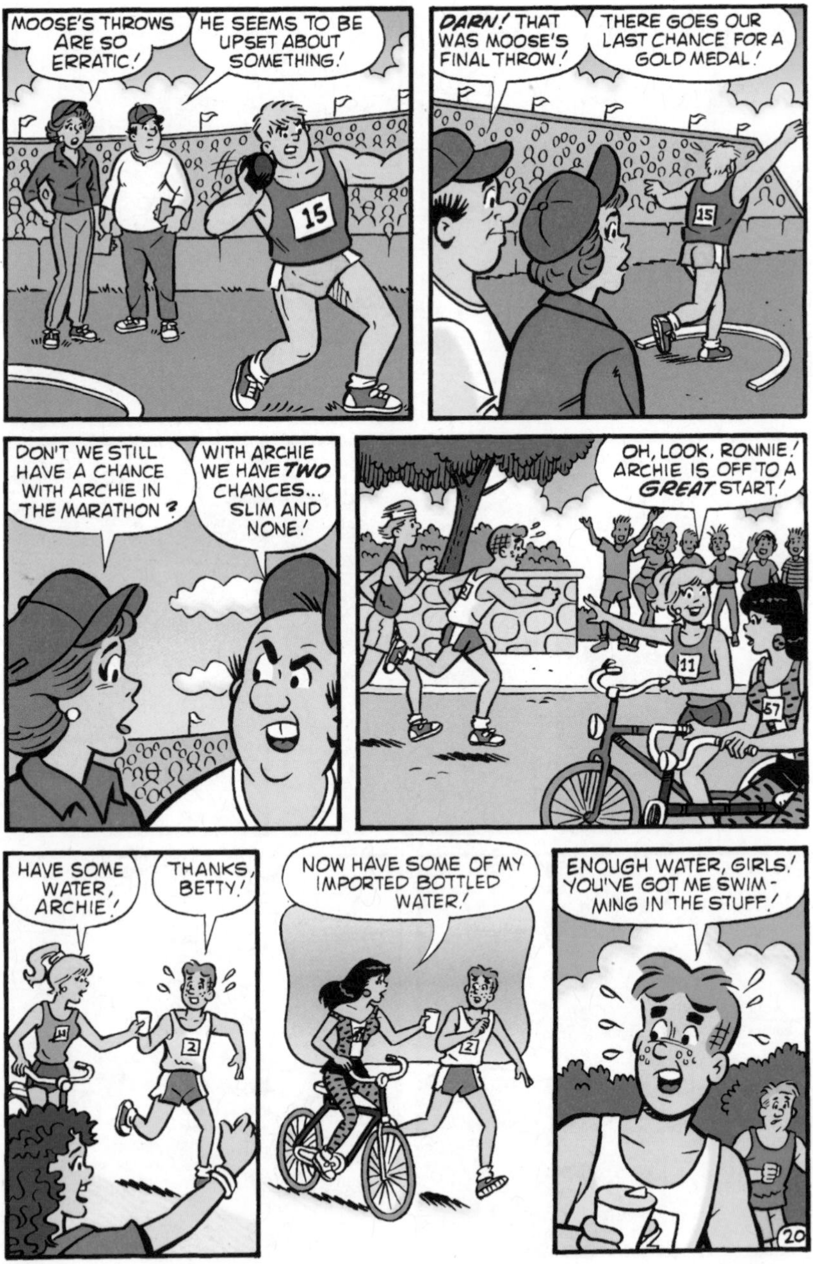
MOOSE'S THROWS ARE SO ERRATIC!
HE SEEMS TO BE UPSET ABOUT SOMETHING!
DARN! THAT WAS MOOSE'S FINAL THROW!
THERE GOES OUR LAST CHANCE FOR A GOLD MEDAL!
DON'T WE STILL HAVE A CHANCE WITH ARCHIE IN THE MARATHON?
WITH ARCHIE WE HAVE TWO CHANCES... SLIM AND NONE!
OH, LOOK, RONNIE! ARCHIE IS OFF TO A GREAT START!
HAVE SOME WATER, ARCHIE!
THANKS, BETTY!
NOW HAVE SOME OF MY IMPORTED BOTTLED WATER!
ENOUGH WATER, GIRLS! YOU'VE GOT ME SWIM-MING IN THE STUFF!
20

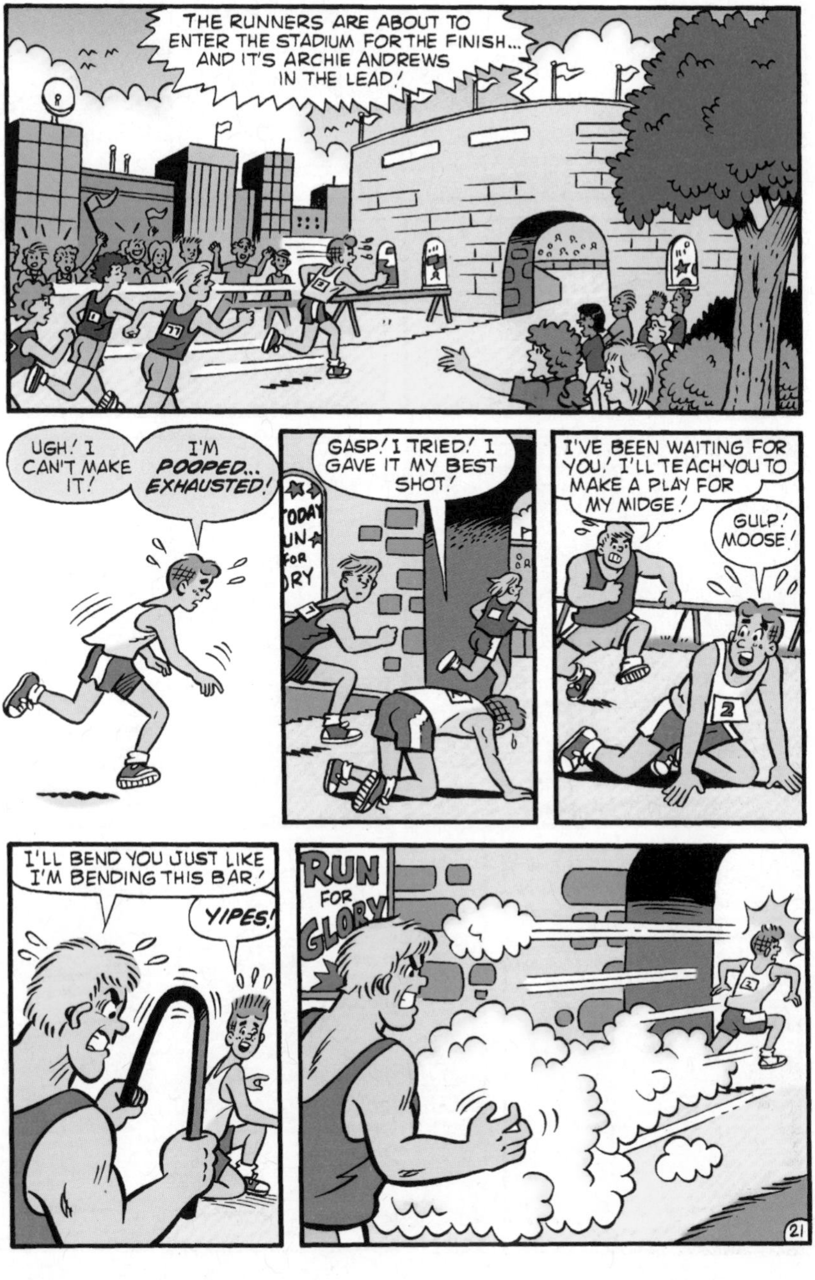
THE RUNNERS ARE ABOUT TO ENTER THE STADIUM FOR THE FINISH... AND IT'S ARCHIE ANDREWS IN THE LEAD!
UGH! I CAN'T MAKE IT!
I'M POOPED... EXHAUSTED!
GASP! I TRIED! I GAVE IT MY BEST SHOT!
I'VE BEEN WAITING FOR YOU! I'LL TEACH YOU TO MAKE A PLAY FOR MY MIDGE!
GULP! MOOSE!
I'LL BEND YOU JUST LIKE I'M BENDING THIS BAR!
YIPES!
RUN FOR
21

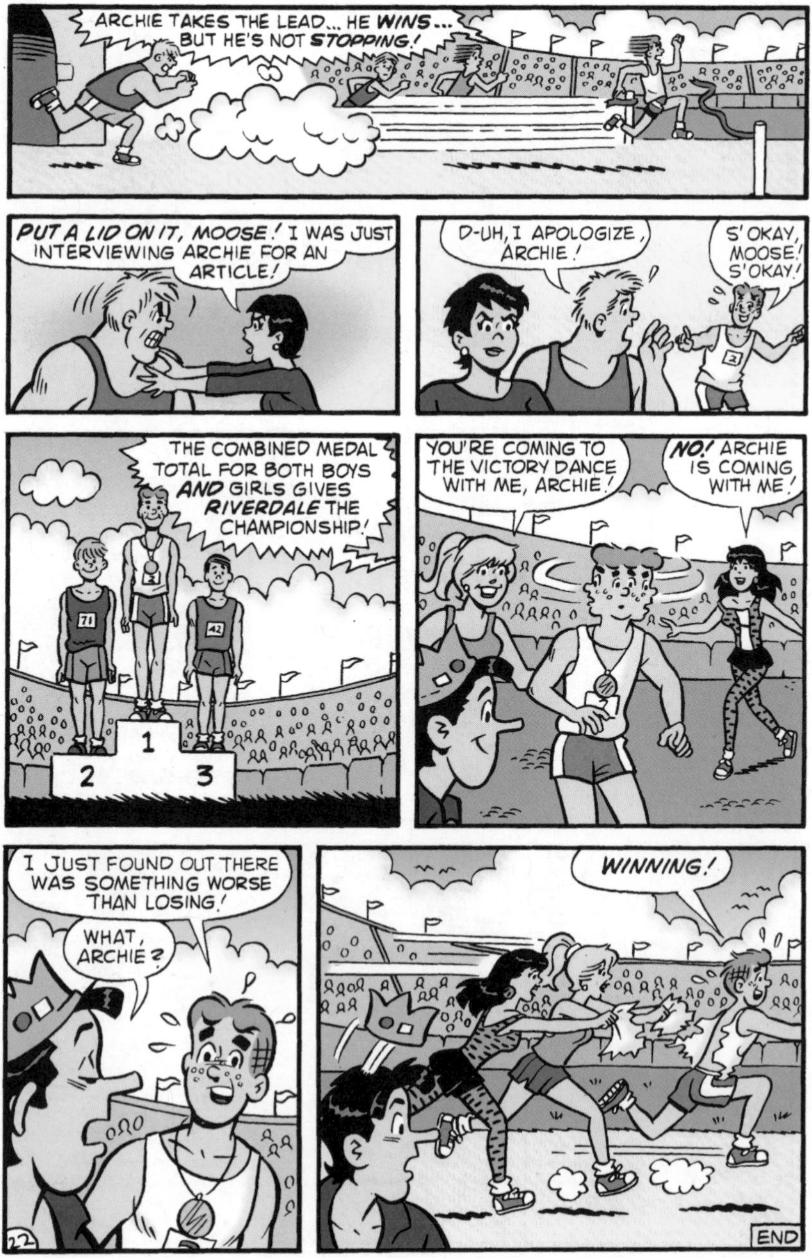
ARCHIE TAKES THE LEAD... HE WINS... BUT HE'S NOT STOPPING!
PUT A LID ON IT, MOOSE! I WAS JUST INTERVIEWING ARCHIE FOR AN ARTICLE!
D-UH, I APOLOGIZE, ARCHIE!
S'OKAY, MOOSE! S'OKAY!
THE COMBINED MEDAL TOTAL FOR BOTH BOYS AND GIRLS GIVES RIVERDALE THE CHAMPIONSHIP!
2
1
3
YOU'RE COMING TO THE VICTORY DANCE WITH ME, ARCHIE!
NO! ARCHIE IS COMING WITH ME!
I JUST FOUND OUT THERE WAS SOMETHING WORSE THAN LOSING!
WHAT, ARCHIE?
22
WINNING!
END

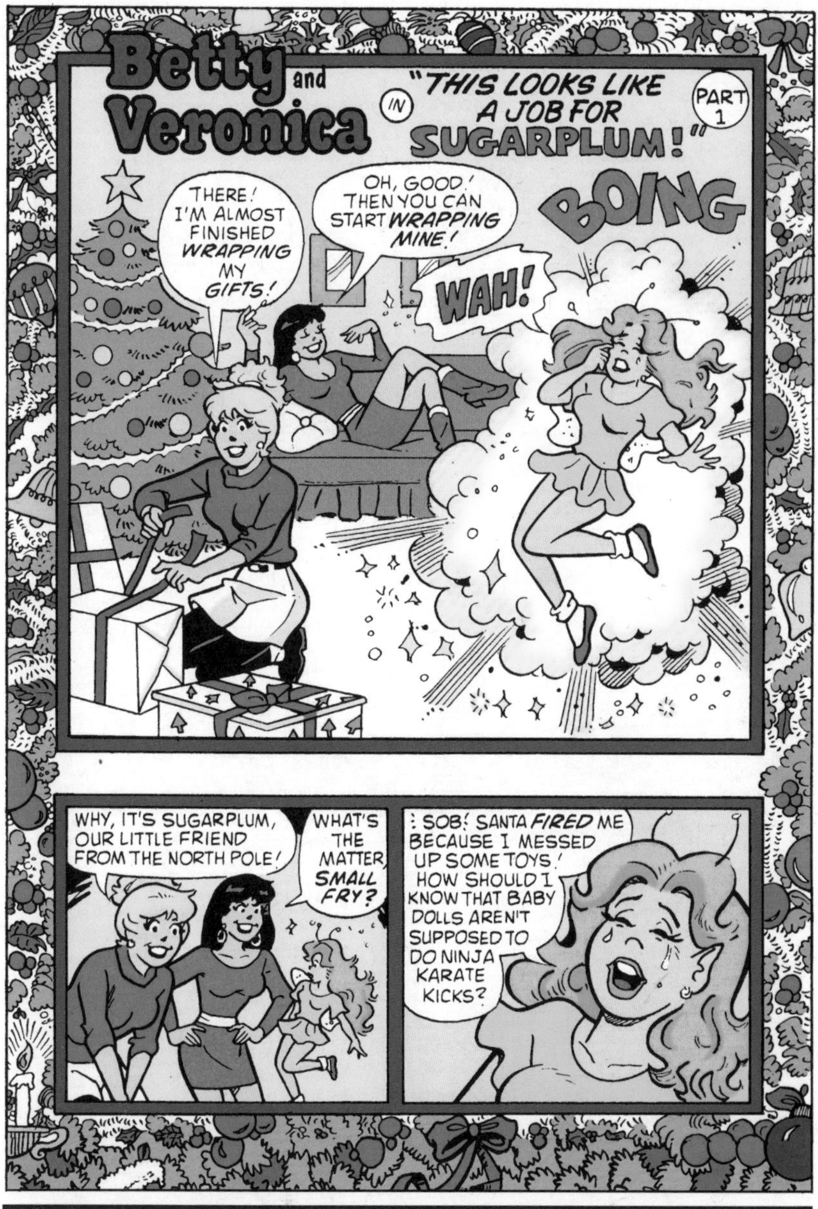

Betty and Veronica
IN
"THIS LOOKS LIKE A JOB FOR SUGARPLUM!"
PART 1
THERE! I'M ALMOST FINISHED WRAPPING MY GIFTS!
OH, GOOD! THEN YOU CAN START WRAPPING MINE!
BOING
WAH!
WHY, IT'S SUGARPLUM, OUR LITTLE FRIEND FROM THE NORTH POLE!
WHAT'S THE MATTER, SMALL FRY?
: SOB! SANTA FIRED ME BECAUSE I MESSED UP SOME TOYS! HOW SHOULD I KNOW THAT BABY DOLLS AREN'T SUPPOSED TO DO NINJA KARATE KICKS?

Story: Dan Parent & Bill Golliher   Pencils: Dan DeCarlo & Dan Parent
Inks: Alison Flood   Letters: Bill Yoshida   Colors: Barry Grossman

Originally printed in BETTY & VERONICA SPECTACULAR #2, February 1993

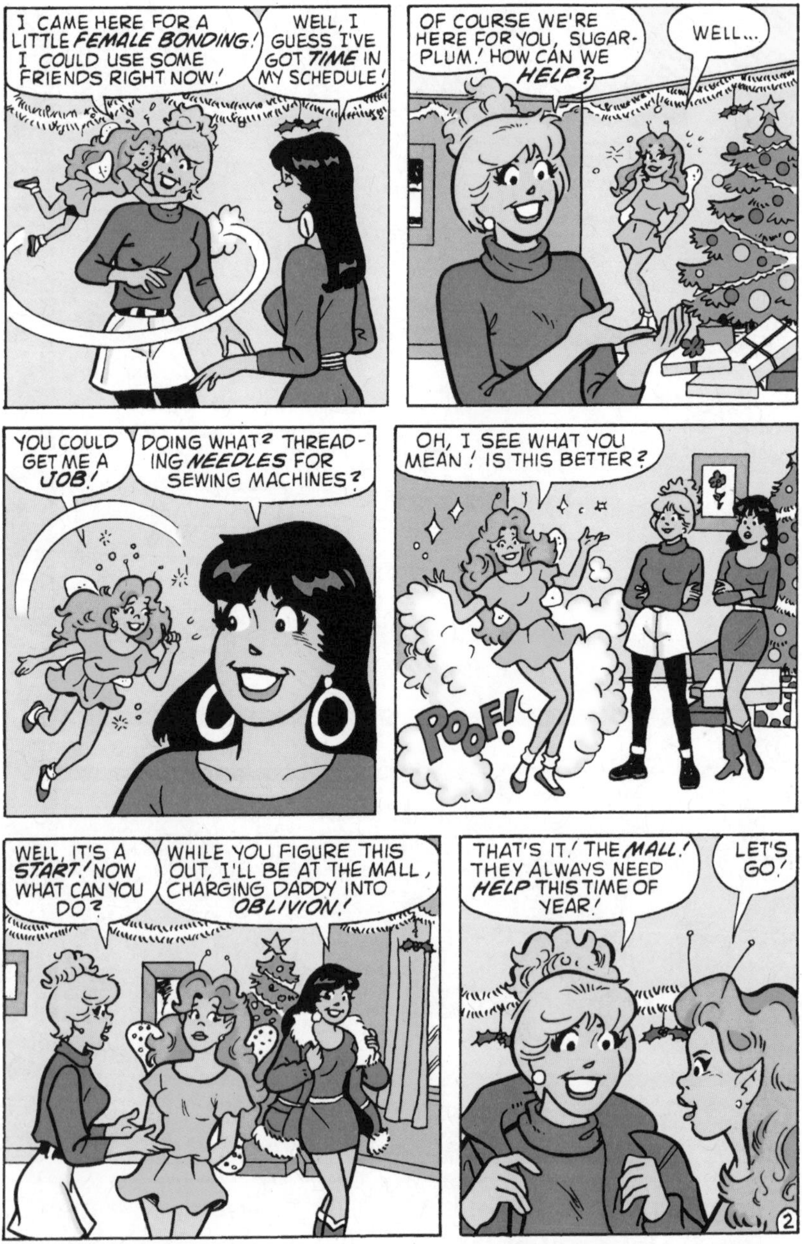
I CAME HERE FOR A LITTLE FEMALE BONDING! I COULD USE SOME FRIENDS RIGHT NOW!
WELL, I GUESS I'VE GOT TIME IN MY SCHEDULE!
OF COURSE WE'RE HERE FOR YOU, SUGAR-PLUM! HOW CAN WE HELP?
WELL...
YOU COULD GET ME A JOB!
DOING WHAT? THREADING NEEDLES FOR SEWING MACHINES?
OH, I SEE WHAT YOU MEAN! IS THIS BETTER?
POOF!
WELL, IT'S A START! NOW WHAT CAN YOU DO?
WHILE YOU FIGURE THIS OUT, I'LL BE AT THE MALL, CHARGING DADDY INTO OBLIVION!
THAT'S IT! THE MALL! THEY ALWAYS NEED HELP THIS TIME OF YEAR!
LET'S GO!
2

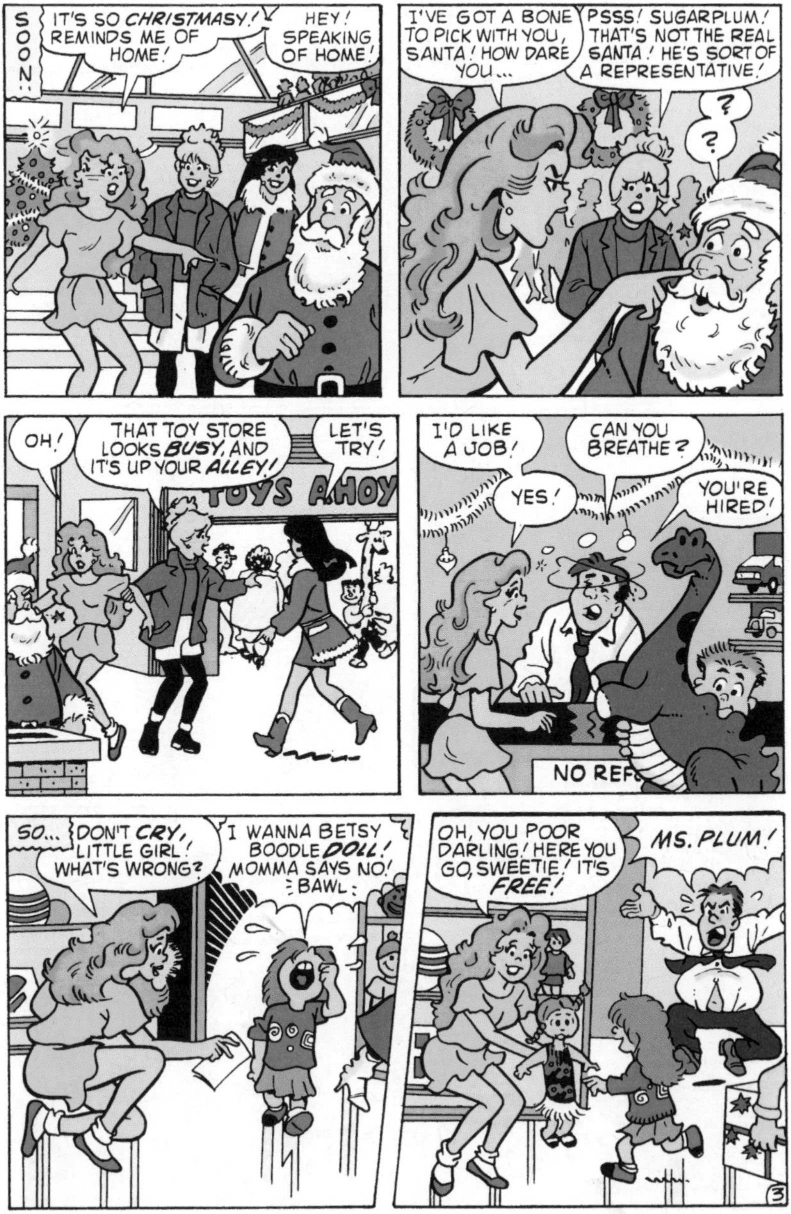
SOON!
IT'S SO CHRISTMASY! REMINDS ME OF HOME!
HEY! SPEAKING OF HOME!
I'VE GOT A BONE TO PICK WITH YOU, SANTA! HOW DARE YOU...
PSSS! SUGARPLUM! THAT'S NOT THE REAL SANTA! HE'S SORT OF A REPRESENTATIVE!
? ?
OH!
THAT TOY STORE LOOKS BUSY, AND IT'S UP YOUR ALLEY!
LET'S TRY!
TOYS AHOY
I'D LIKE A JOB!
CAN YOU BREATHE?
YES!
YOU'RE HIRED!
NO REF
SO...
DON'T CRY, LITTLE GIRL! WHAT'S WRONG?
I WANNA BETSY BOODLE DOLL! MOMMA SAYS NO! BAWL
OH, YOU POOR DARLING! HERE YOU GO, SWEETIE! IT'S FREE!
MS. PLUM!
3

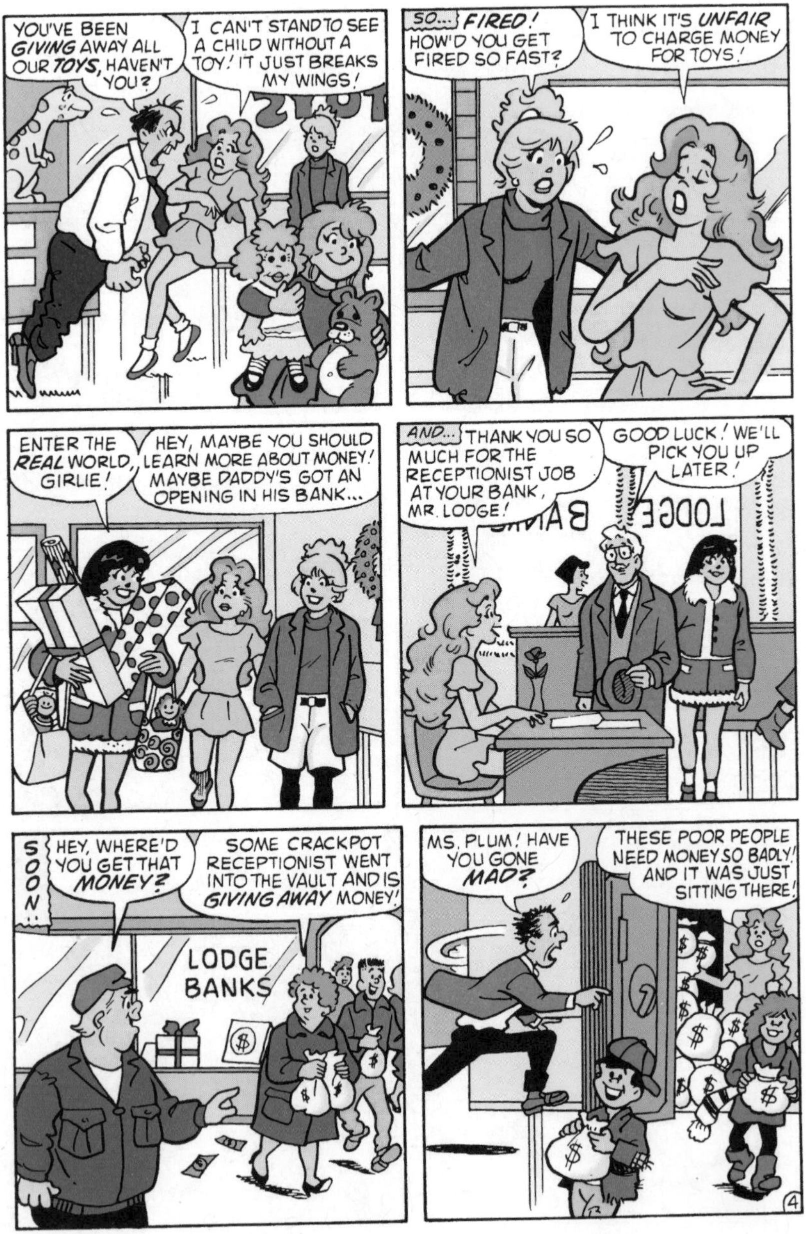
YOU'VE BEEN GIVING AWAY ALL OUR TOYS, HAVEN'T YOU?
I CAN'T STAND TO SEE A CHILD WITHOUT A TOY! IT JUST BREAKS MY WINGS!
SO... FIRED! HOW'D YOU GET FIRED SO FAST?
I THINK IT'S UNFAIR TO CHARGE MONEY FOR TOYS!
ENTER THE REAL WORLD, GIRLIE!
HEY, MAYBE YOU SHOULD LEARN MORE ABOUT MONEY! MAYBE DADDY'S GOT AN OPENING IN HIS BANK...
AND...
THANK YOU SO MUCH FOR THE RECEPTIONIST JOB AT YOUR BANK, MR. LODGE!
GOOD LUCK! WE'LL PICK YOU UP LATER!
SOON...
HEY, WHERE'D YOU GET THAT MONEY?
SOME CRACKPOT RECEPTIONIST WENT INTO THE VAULT AND IS GIVING AWAY MONEY!
LODGE BANKS
MS. PLUM! HAVE YOU GONE MAD?
THESE POOR PEOPLE NEED MONEY SO BADLY! AND IT WAS JUST SITTING THERE!
4

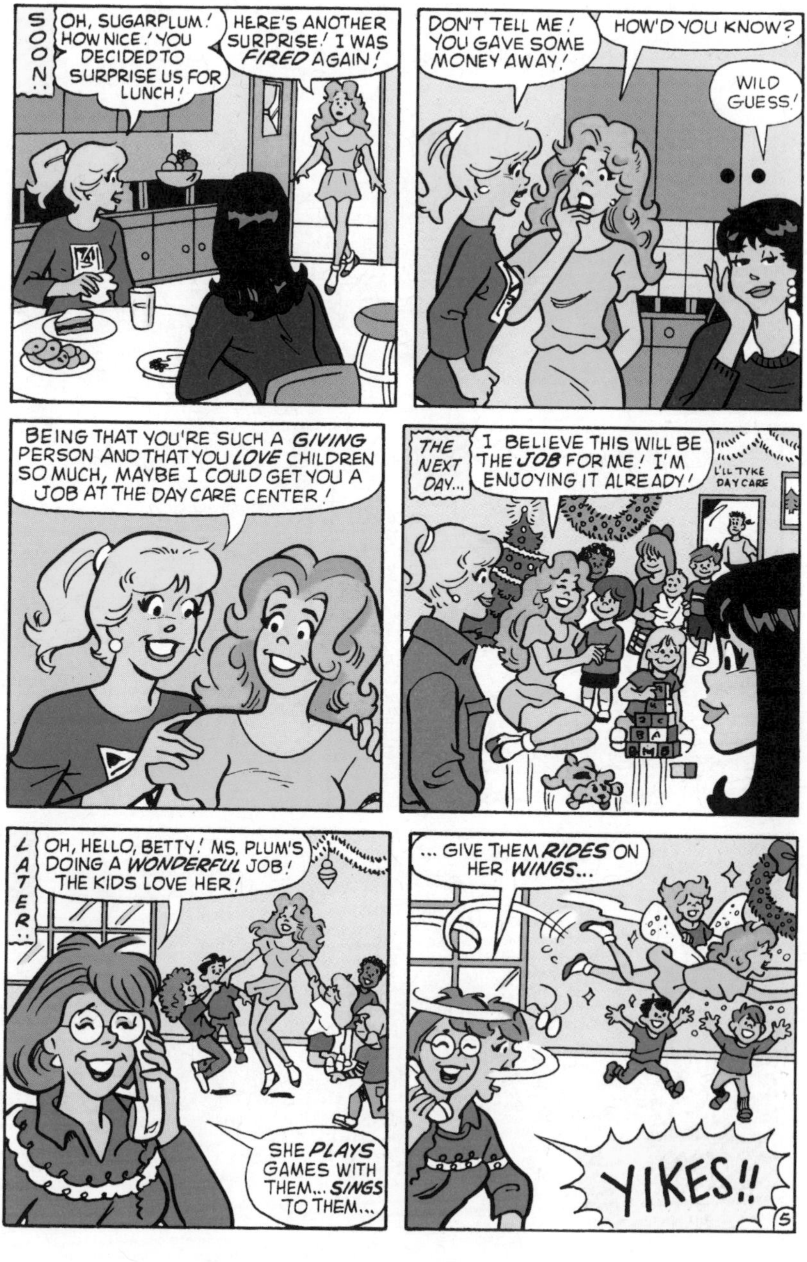
SOON:
OH, SUGARPLUM! HOW NICE! YOU DECIDED TO SURPRISE US FOR LUNCH!
HERE'S ANOTHER SURPRISE! I WAS FIRED AGAIN!
DON'T TELL ME! YOU GAVE SOME MONEY AWAY!
HOW'D YOU KNOW?
WILD GUESS!
BEING THAT YOU'RE SUCH A GIVING PERSON AND THAT YOU LOVE CHILDREN SO MUCH, MAYBE I COULD GET YOU A JOB AT THE DAY CARE CENTER!
THE NEXT DAY...
I BELIEVE THIS WILL BE THE JOB FOR ME! I'M ENJOYING IT ALREADY!
L'IL TYKE DAY CARE
LATER:
OH, HELLO, BETTY! MS. PLUM'S DOING A WONDERFUL JOB! THE KIDS LOVE HER!
SHE PLAYS GAMES WITH THEM... SINGS TO THEM...
... GIVE THEM RIDES ON HER WINGS...
YIKES!!

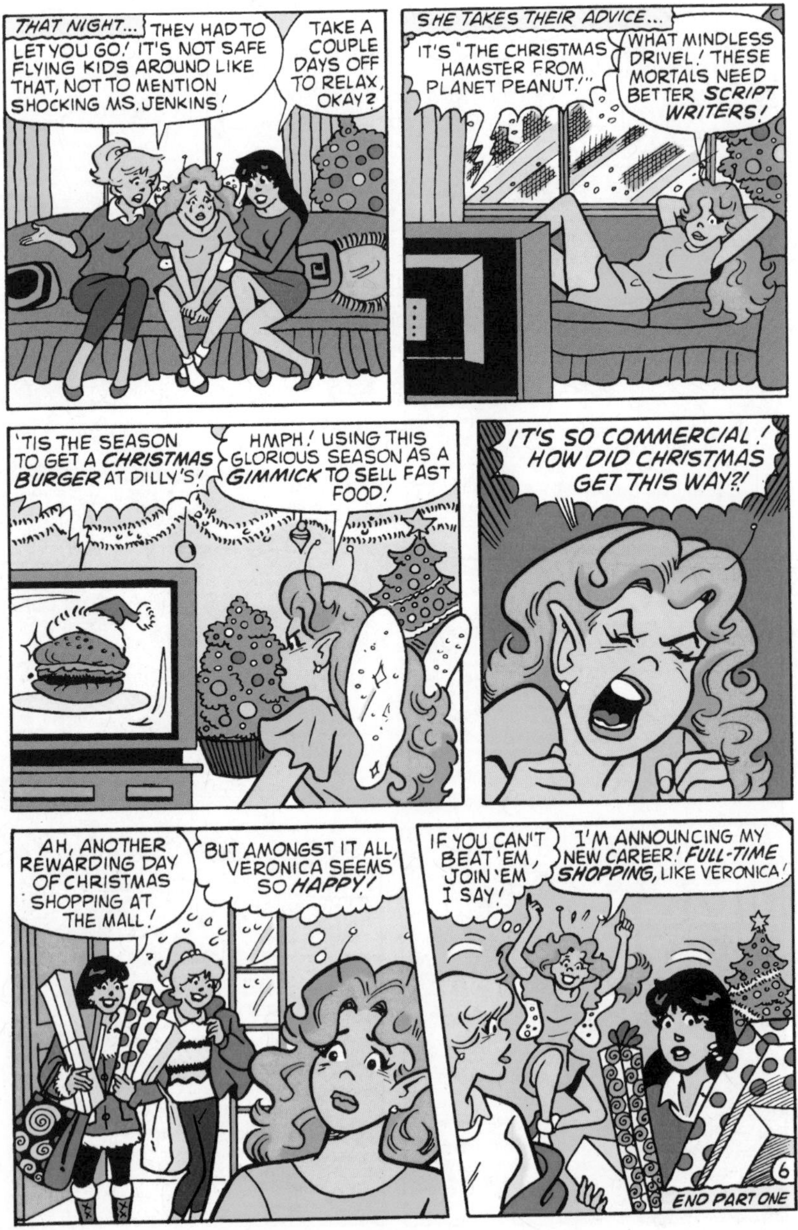
THAT NIGHT...
THEY HAD TO LET YOU GO! IT'S NOT SAFE FLYING KIDS AROUND LIKE THAT, NOT TO MENTION SHOCKING MS. JENKINS!
TAKE A COUPLE DAYS OFF TO RELAX, OKAY?
SHE TAKES THEIR ADVICE...
IT'S "THE CHRISTMAS HAMSTER FROM PLANET PEANUT!"
WHAT MINDLESS DRIVEL! THESE MORTALS NEED BETTER SCRIPT WRITERS!
'TIS THE SEASON TO GET A CHRISTMAS BURGER AT DILLY'S!
HMPH! USING THIS GLORIOUS SEASON AS A GIMMICK TO SELL FAST FOOD!
IT'S SO COMMERCIAL! HOW DID CHRISTMAS GET THIS WAY?!
AH, ANOTHER REWARDING DAY OF CHRISTMAS SHOPPING AT THE MALL!
BUT AMONGST IT ALL, VERONICA SEEMS SO HAPPY!
IF YOU CAN'T BEAT 'EM, JOIN 'EM I SAY!
I'M ANNOUNCING MY NEW CAREER! FULL-TIME SHOPPING, LIKE VERONICA!
6
END PART ONE

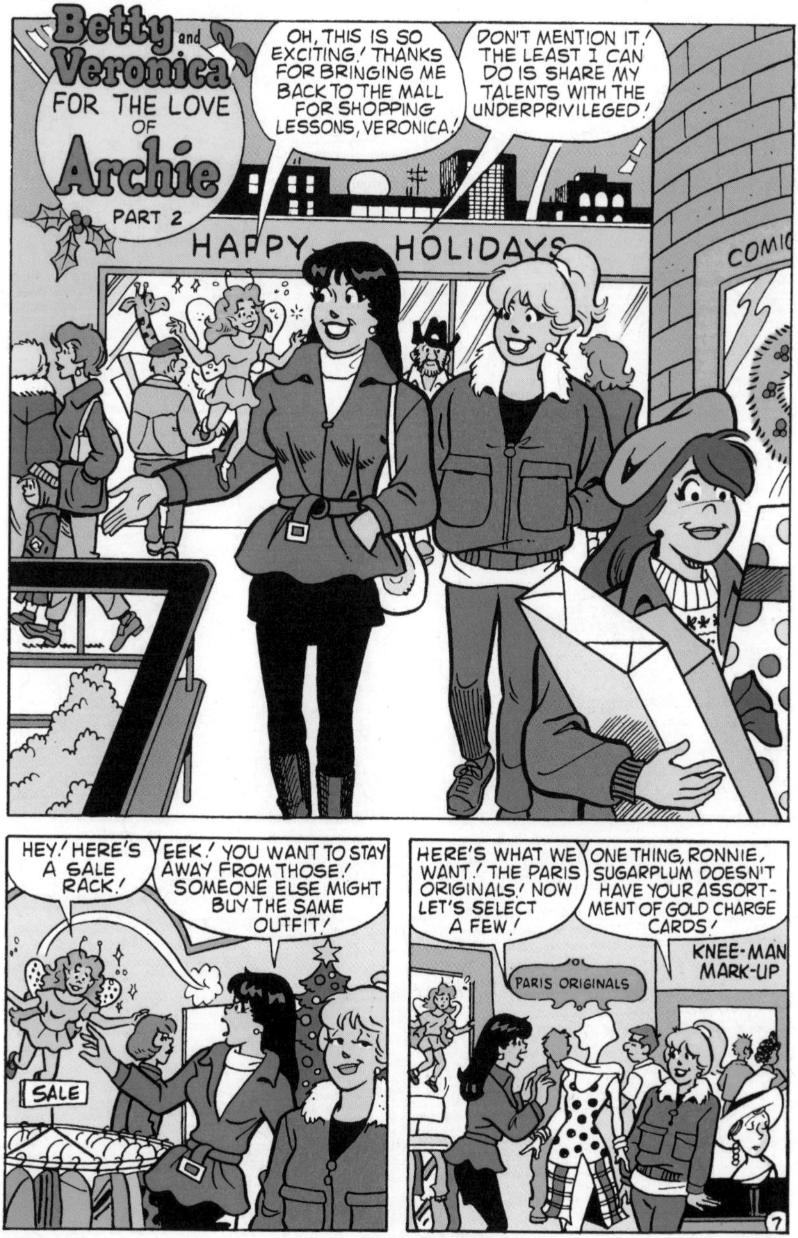
Betty and Veronica
FOR THE LOVE OF Archie
PART 2
OH, THIS IS SO EXCITING! THANKS FOR BRINGING ME BACK TO THE MALL FOR SHOPPING LESSONS, VERONICA!
DON'T MENTION IT! THE LEAST I CAN DO IS SHARE MY TALENTS WITH THE UNDERPRIVILEGED!
HAPPY HOLIDAYS
HEY! HERE'S A SALE RACK!
EEK! YOU WANT TO STAY AWAY FROM THOSE! SOMEONE ELSE MIGHT BUY THE SAME OUTFIT!
SALE
HERE'S WHAT WE WANT! THE PARIS ORIGINALS! NOW LET'S SELECT A FEW!
ONE THING, RONNIE, SUGARPLUM DOESN'T HAVE YOUR ASSORTMENT OF GOLD CHARGE CARDS!
KNEE-MAN MARK-UP
PARIS ORIGINALS
7

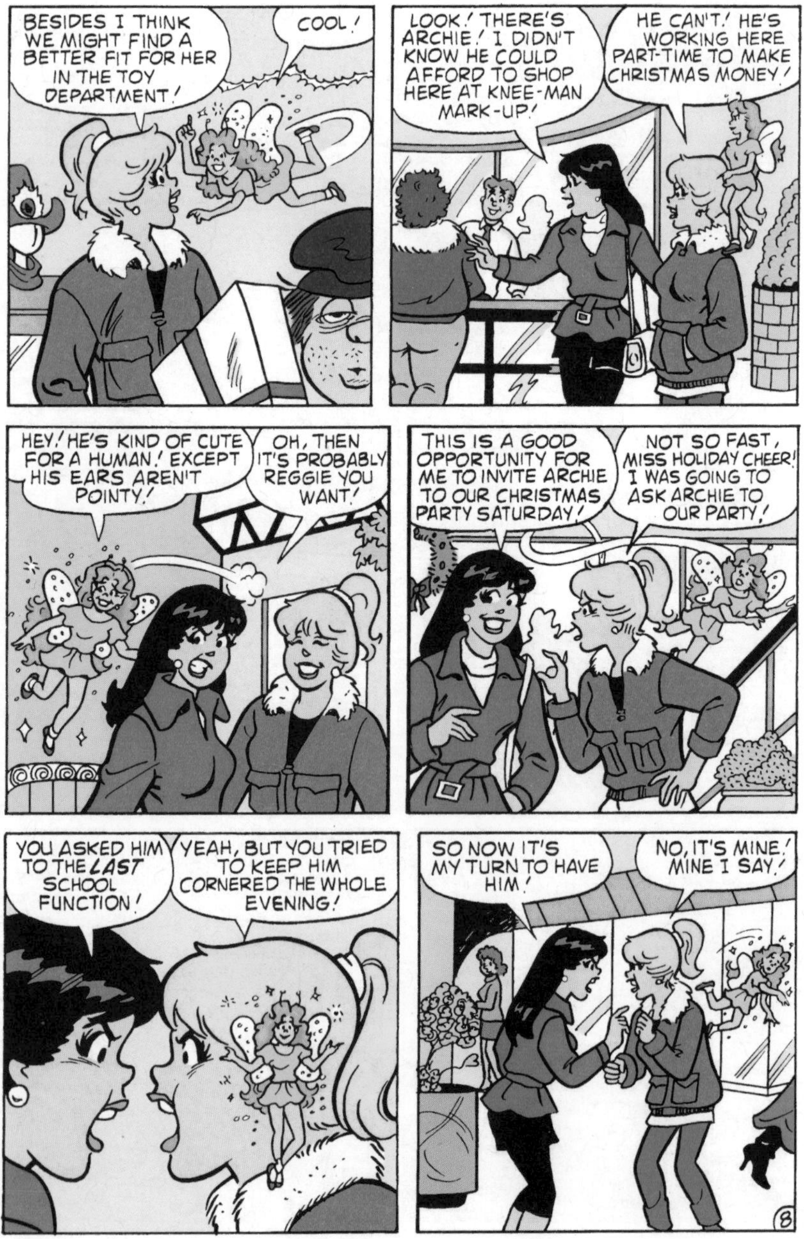

BESIDES I THINK WE MIGHT FIND A BETTER FIT FOR HER IN THE TOY DEPARTMENT!
COOL!
LOOK! THERE'S ARCHIE! I DIDN'T KNOW HE COULD AFFORD TO SHOP HERE AT KNEE-MAN MARK-UP!
HE CAN'T! HE'S WORKING HERE PART-TIME TO MAKE CHRISTMAS MONEY!
HEY! HE'S KIND OF CUTE FOR A HUMAN! EXCEPT HIS EARS AREN'T POINTY!
OH, THEN IT'S PROBABLY REGGIE YOU WANT!
THIS IS A GOOD OPPORTUNITY FOR ME TO INVITE ARCHIE TO OUR CHRISTMAS PARTY SATURDAY!
NOT SO FAST, MISS HOLIDAY CHEER! I WAS GOING TO ASK ARCHIE TO OUR PARTY!
YOU ASKED HIM TO THE *LAST* SCHOOL FUNCTION!
YEAH, BUT YOU TRIED TO KEEP HIM CORNERED THE WHOLE EVENING!
SO NOW IT'S MY TURN TO HAVE HIM!
NO, IT'S MINE! MINE I SAY!
8

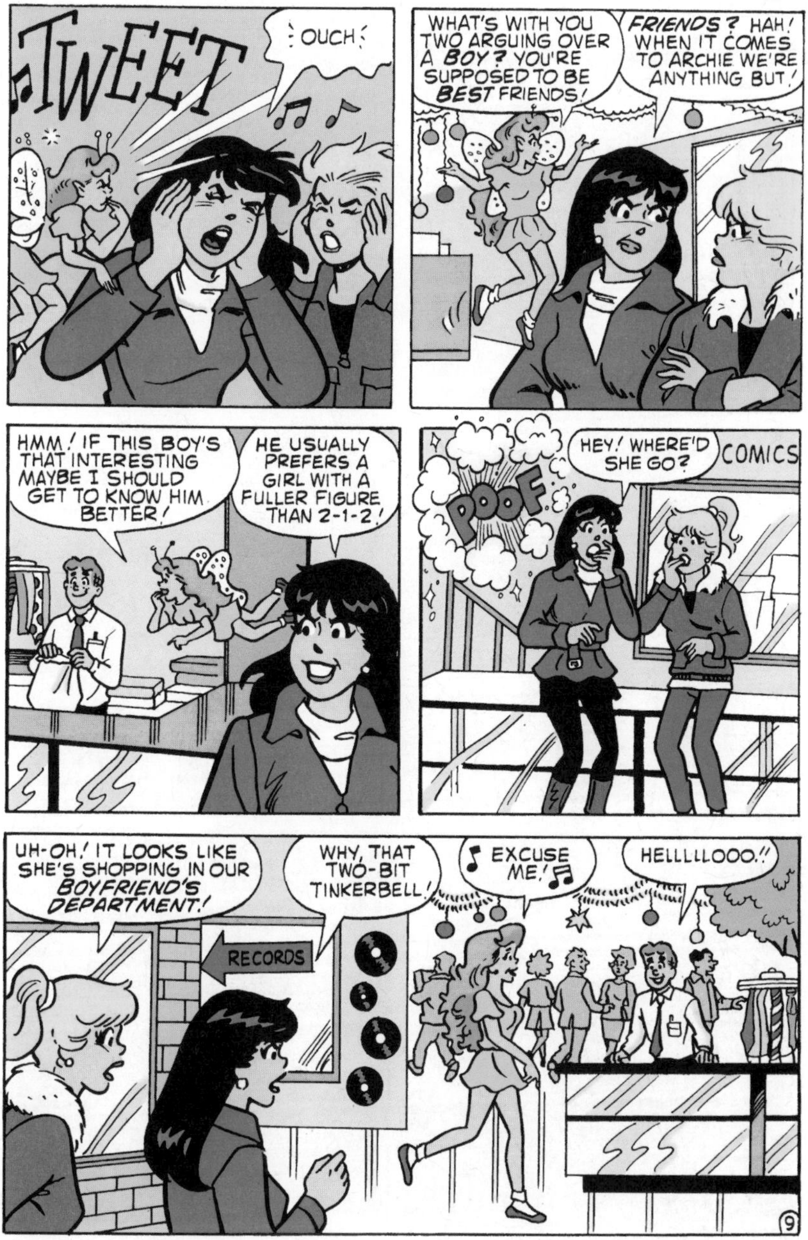
TWEET
OUCH
WHAT'S WITH YOU TWO ARGUING OVER A BOY? YOU'RE SUPPOSED TO BE BEST FRIENDS!
FRIENDS? HAH! WHEN IT COMES TO ARCHIE WE'RE ANYTHING BUT!
HMM! IF THIS BOY'S THAT INTERESTING MAYBE I SHOULD GET TO KNOW HIM BETTER!
HE USUALLY PREFERS A GIRL WITH A FULLER FIGURE THAN 2-1-2!
POOF
HEY! WHERE'D SHE GO?
COMICS
UH-OH! IT LOOKS LIKE SHE'S SHOPPING IN OUR BOYFRIEND'S DEPARTMENT!
WHY, THAT TWO-BIT TINKERBELL!
RECORDS
EXCUSE ME!
HELLLLLOOO!!
9

WHAT CAN I HELP YOU WITH?

LET'S SEE! MAYBE I'LL TAKE A NECKTIE FOR MY OLD BOSS!

SOMETHING IN A RED AND GREEN WITH REINDEER PRINT IF YOU HAVE IT!

FOR YOU, BEAUTIFUL! I'LL SEE WHAT I CAN DO!

HOW'S THIS?

OH, IT'S BEAUTIFUL! ¡SNIFF!

WHAT'S THE MATTER?

I JUST MOVED HERE AND WITH THE HOLIDAYS COMING UP I FEEL SORT OF LONELY!

HE'S NOT ACTUALLY FALLING FOR THIS DRIVEL, IS HE?

GET REAL! THIS IS *ARCHIE!* OF COURSE HE IS!

TAKE SATURDAY NIGHT, FOR INSTANCE! I DON'T HAVE A SINGLE THING PLANNED!

SOME FRIENDS OF MINE ARE HAVING A PARTY THAT NIGHT! WHY DON'T YOU COME WITH ME?

10

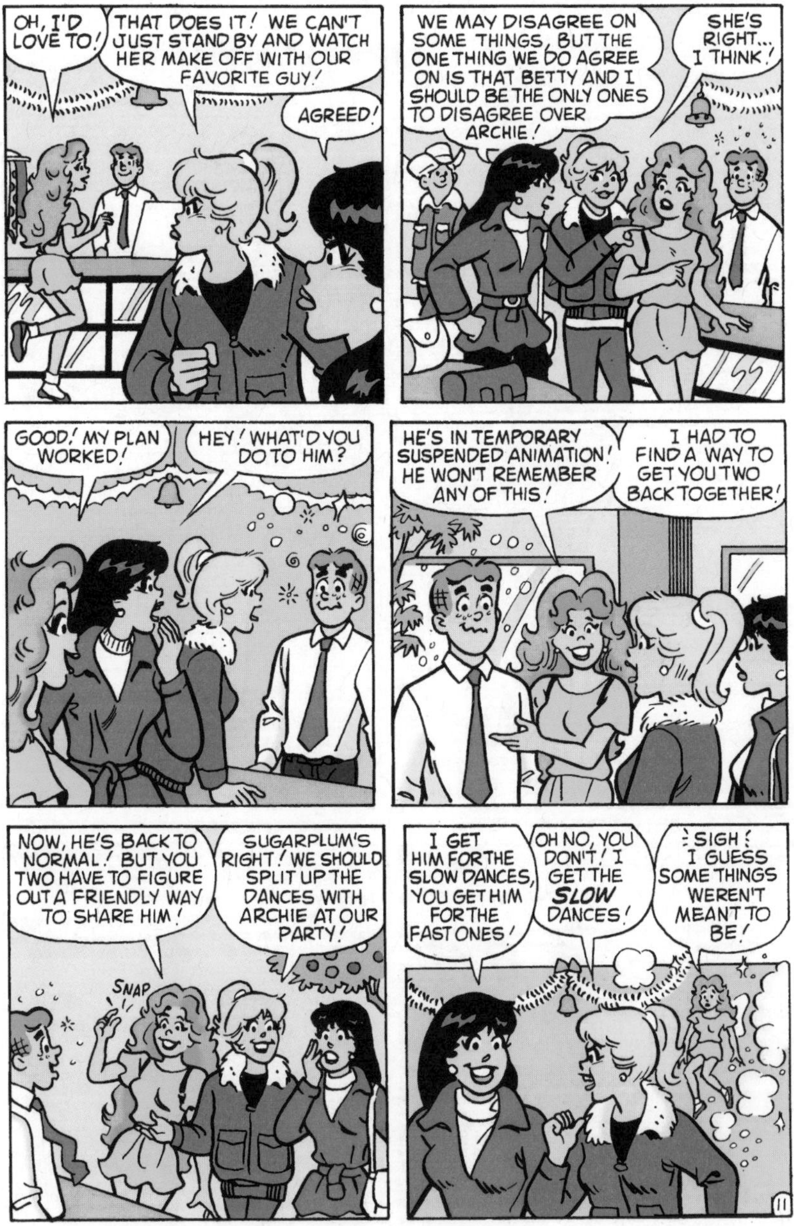
OH, I'D LOVE TO!
THAT DOES IT! WE CAN'T JUST STAND BY AND WATCH HER MAKE OFF WITH OUR FAVORITE GUY!
AGREED!
WE MAY DISAGREE ON SOME THINGS, BUT THE ONE THING WE DO AGREE ON IS THAT BETTY AND I SHOULD BE THE ONLY ONES TO DISAGREE OVER ARCHIE!
SHE'S RIGHT... I THINK!
GOOD! MY PLAN WORKED!
HEY! WHAT'D YOU DO TO HIM?
HE'S IN TEMPORARY SUSPENDED ANIMATION! HE WON'T REMEMBER ANY OF THIS!
I HAD TO FIND A WAY TO GET YOU TWO BACK TOGETHER!
NOW, HE'S BACK TO NORMAL! BUT YOU TWO HAVE TO FIGURE OUT A FRIENDLY WAY TO SHARE HIM!
SUGARPLUM'S RIGHT! WE SHOULD SPLIT UP THE DANCES WITH ARCHIE AT OUR PARTY!
SNAP
I GET HIM FOR THE SLOW DANCES, YOU GET HIM FOR THE FAST ONES!
OH NO, YOU DON'T! I GET THE SLOW DANCES!
SIGH! I GUESS SOME THINGS WEREN'T MEANT TO BE!
11

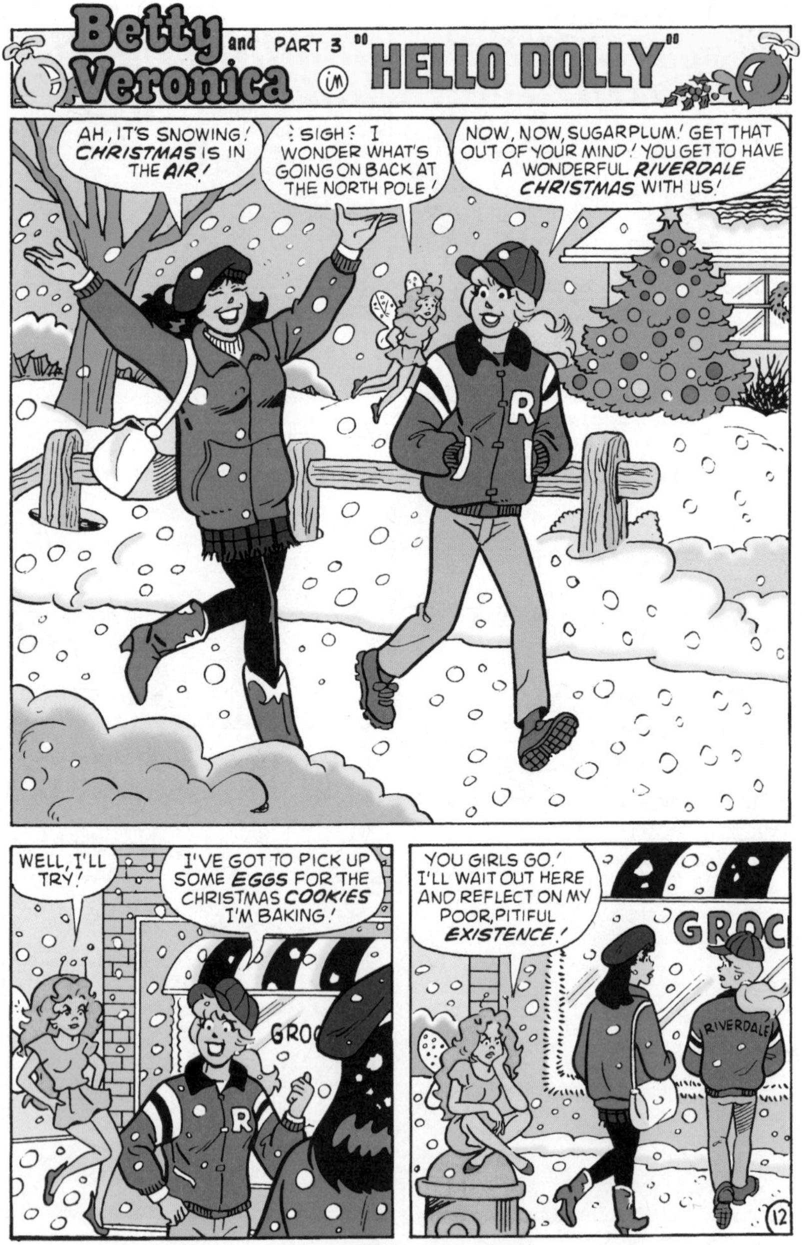
Betty and Veronica in
PART 3
"HELLO DOLLY"
AH, IT'S SNOWING! CHRISTMAS IS IN THE AIR!
: SIGH : I WONDER WHAT'S GOING ON BACK AT THE NORTH POLE!
NOW, NOW, SUGARPLUM! GET THAT OUT OF YOUR MIND! YOU GET TO HAVE A WONDERFUL RIVERDALE CHRISTMAS WITH US!
WELL, I'LL TRY!
I'VE GOT TO PICK UP SOME EGGS FOR THE CHRISTMAS COOKIES I'M BAKING!
GROC
YOU GIRLS GO! I'LL WAIT OUT HERE AND REFLECT ON MY POOR, PITIFUL EXISTENCE!
GROC
RIVERDALE
12

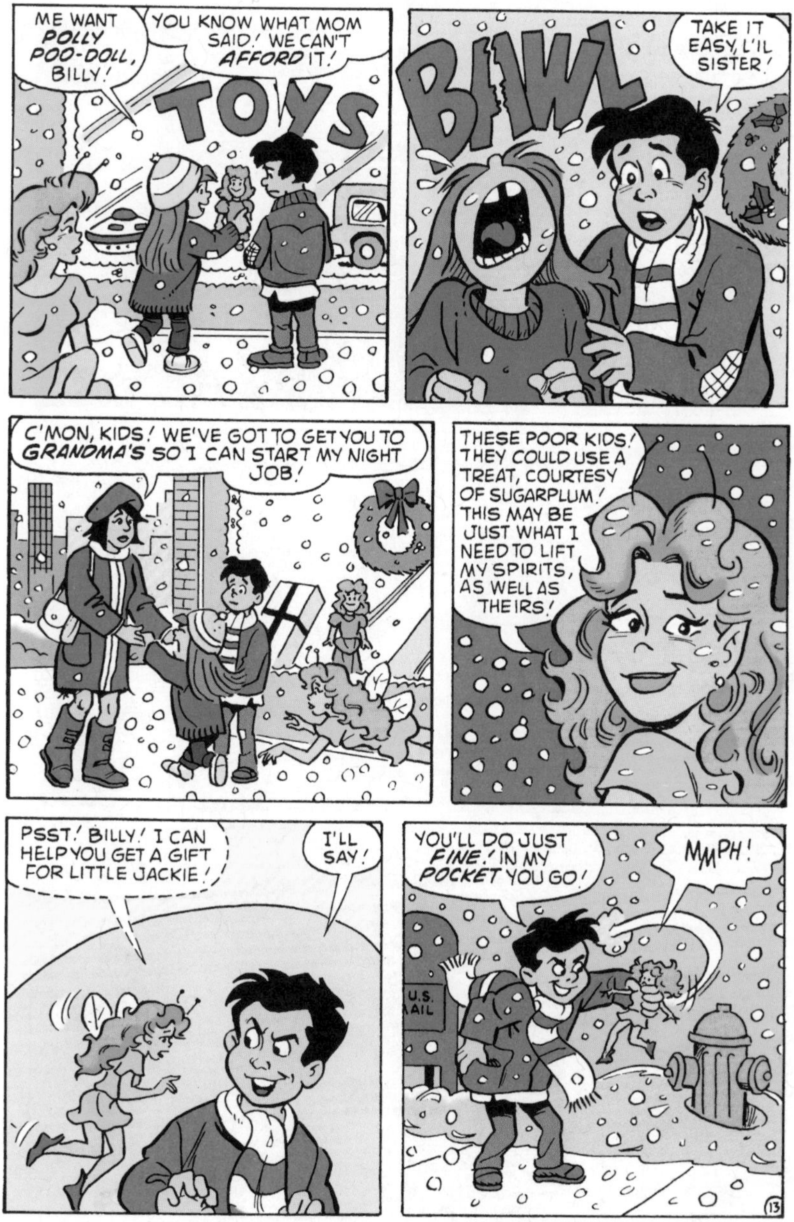
ME WANT POLLY POO-DOLL, BILLY!
YOU KNOW WHAT MOM SAID! WE CAN'T AFFORD IT!
TOYS
BAWL
TAKE IT EASY, L'IL SISTER!
C'MON, KIDS! WE'VE GOT TO GET YOU TO GRANDMA'S SO I CAN START MY NIGHT JOB!
THESE POOR KIDS! THEY COULD USE A TREAT, COURTESY OF SUGARPLUM! THIS MAY BE JUST WHAT I NEED TO LIFT MY SPIRITS, AS WELL AS THEIRS!
PSST! BILLY! I CAN HELP YOU GET A GIFT FOR LITTLE JACKIE!
I'LL SAY!
YOU'LL DO JUST FINE! IN MY POCKET YOU GO!
MMPH!
U.S. MAIL
13

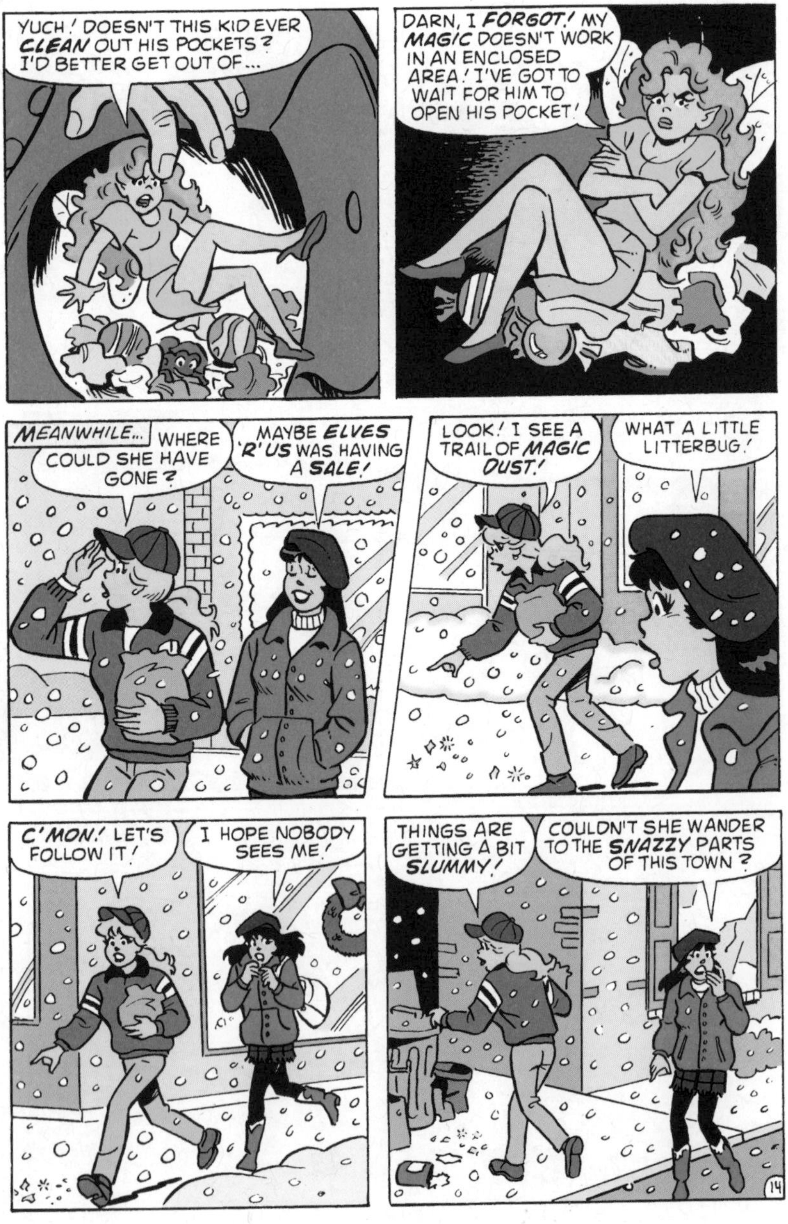
YUCH! DOESN'T THIS KID EVER CLEAN OUT HIS POCKETS? I'D BETTER GET OUT OF...
DARN, I FORGOT! MY MAGIC DOESN'T WORK IN AN ENCLOSED AREA! I'VE GOT TO WAIT FOR HIM TO OPEN HIS POCKET!
MEANWHILE...
WHERE COULD SHE HAVE GONE?
MAYBE ELVES 'R' US WAS HAVING A SALE!
LOOK! I SEE A TRAIL OF MAGIC DUST!
WHAT A LITTLE LITTERBUG!
C'MON! LET'S FOLLOW IT!
I HOPE NOBODY SEES ME!
THINGS ARE GETTING A BIT SLUMMY!
COULDN'T SHE WANDER TO THE SNAZZY PARTS OF THIS TOWN?
14

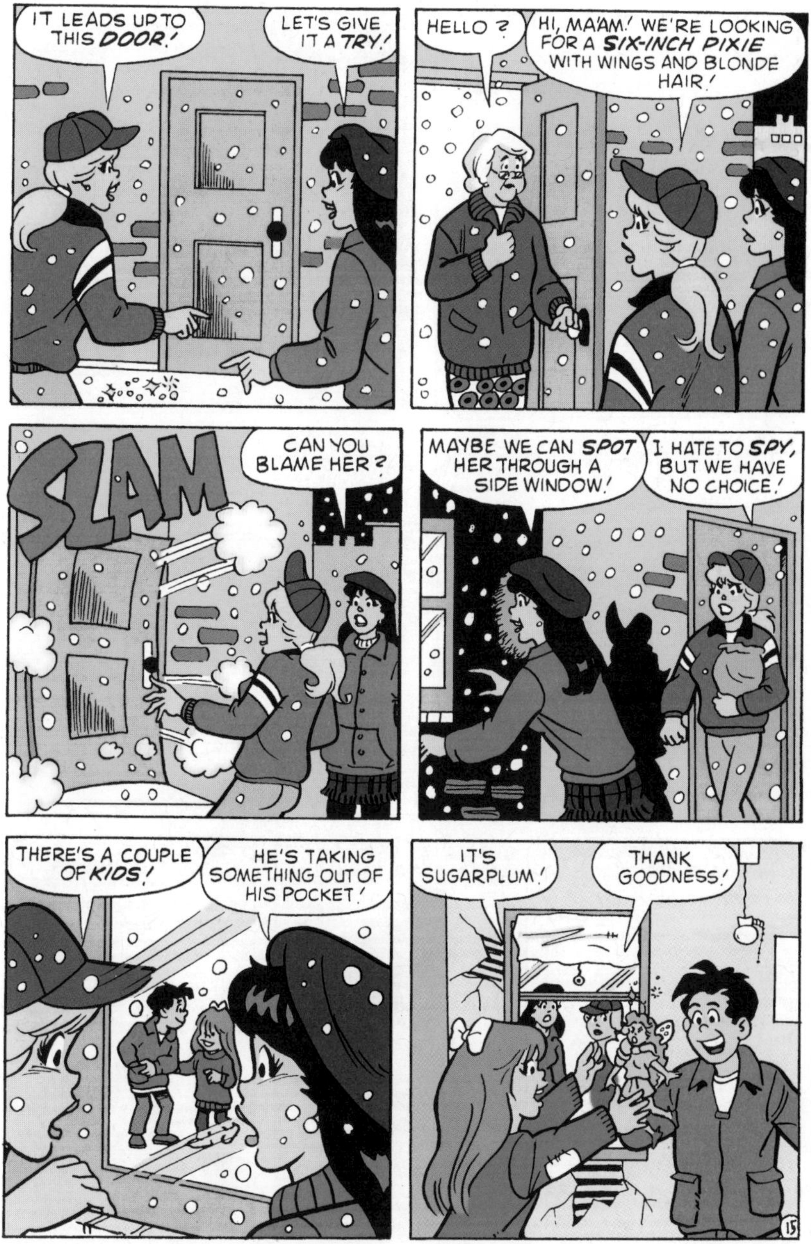
IT LEADS UP TO THIS DOOR!
LET'S GIVE IT A TRY!
HELLO ?
HI, MA'AM! WE'RE LOOKING FOR A SIX-INCH PIXIE WITH WINGS AND BLONDE HAIR!
SLAM
CAN YOU BLAME HER ?
MAYBE WE CAN SPOT HER THROUGH A SIDE WINDOW!
I HATE TO SPY, BUT WE HAVE NO CHOICE!
THERE'S A COUPLE OF KIDS!
HE'S TAKING SOMETHING OUT OF HIS POCKET!
IT'S SUGARPLUM!
THANK GOODNESS!
15

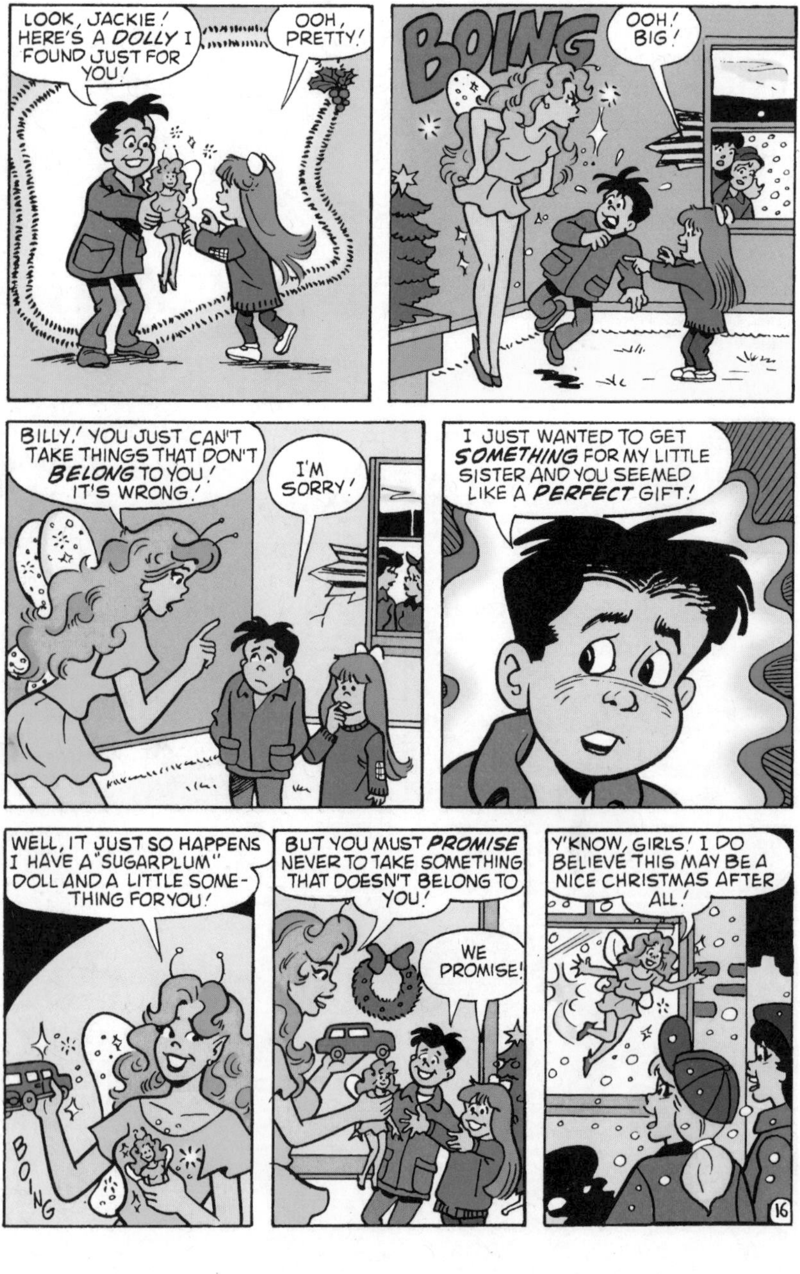
LOOK, JACKIE! HERE'S A DOLLY I FOUND JUST FOR YOU!
OOH, PRETTY!
BOING
OOH! BIG!
BILLY! YOU JUST CAN'T TAKE THINGS THAT DON'T BELONG TO YOU! IT'S WRONG!
I'M SORRY!
I JUST WANTED TO GET SOMETHING FOR MY LITTLE SISTER AND YOU SEEMED LIKE A PERFECT GIFT!
WELL, IT JUST SO HAPPENS I HAVE A "SUGARPLUM" DOLL AND A LITTLE SOME-THING FOR YOU!
BOING
BUT YOU MUST PROMISE NEVER TO TAKE SOMETHING THAT DOESN'T BELONG TO YOU!
WE PROMISE!
Y'KNOW, GIRLS! I DO BELIEVE THIS MAY BE A NICE CHRISTMAS AFTER ALL!
16

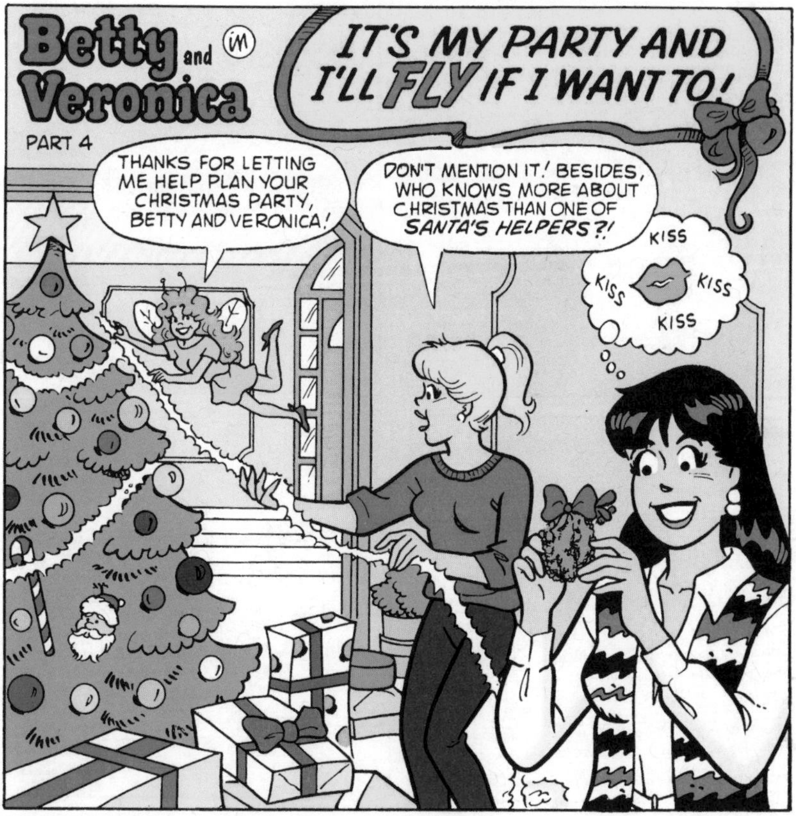
Betty and Veronica in
IT'S MY PARTY AND I'LL FLY IF I WANT TO!
PART 4
THANKS FOR LETTING ME HELP PLAN YOUR CHRISTMAS PARTY, BETTY AND VERONICA!
DON'T MENTION IT! BESIDES, WHO KNOWS MORE ABOUT CHRISTMAS THAN ONE OF SANTA'S HELPERS?!
KISS KISS KISS KISS

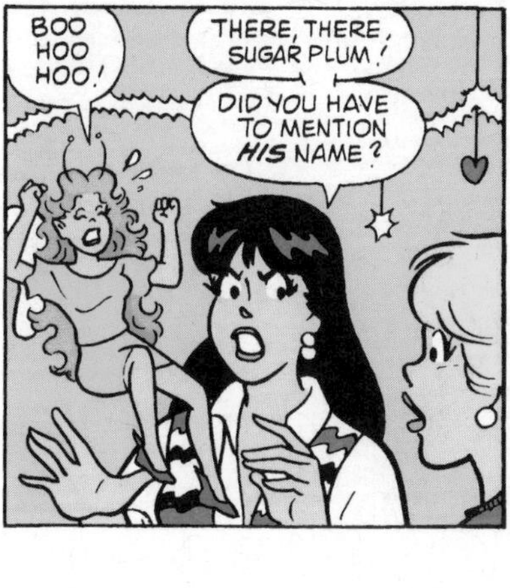
BOO HOO HOO!
THERE, THERE, SUGAR PLUM!
DID YOU HAVE TO MENTION HIS NAME?

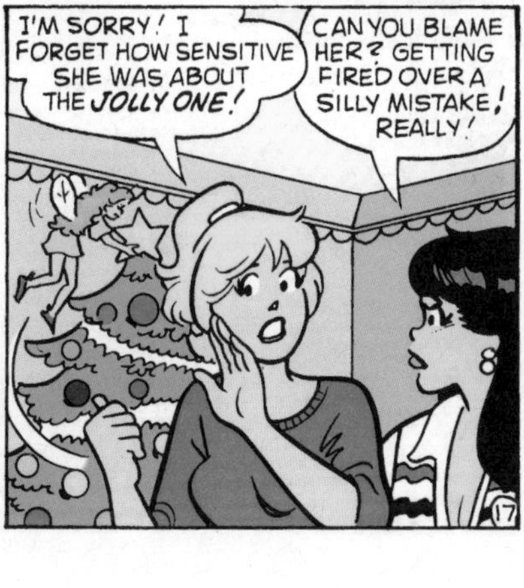
I'M SORRY! I FORGET HOW SENSITIVE SHE WAS ABOUT THE JOLLY ONE!
CAN YOU BLAME HER? GETTING FIRED OVER A SILLY MISTAKE! REALLY!
17

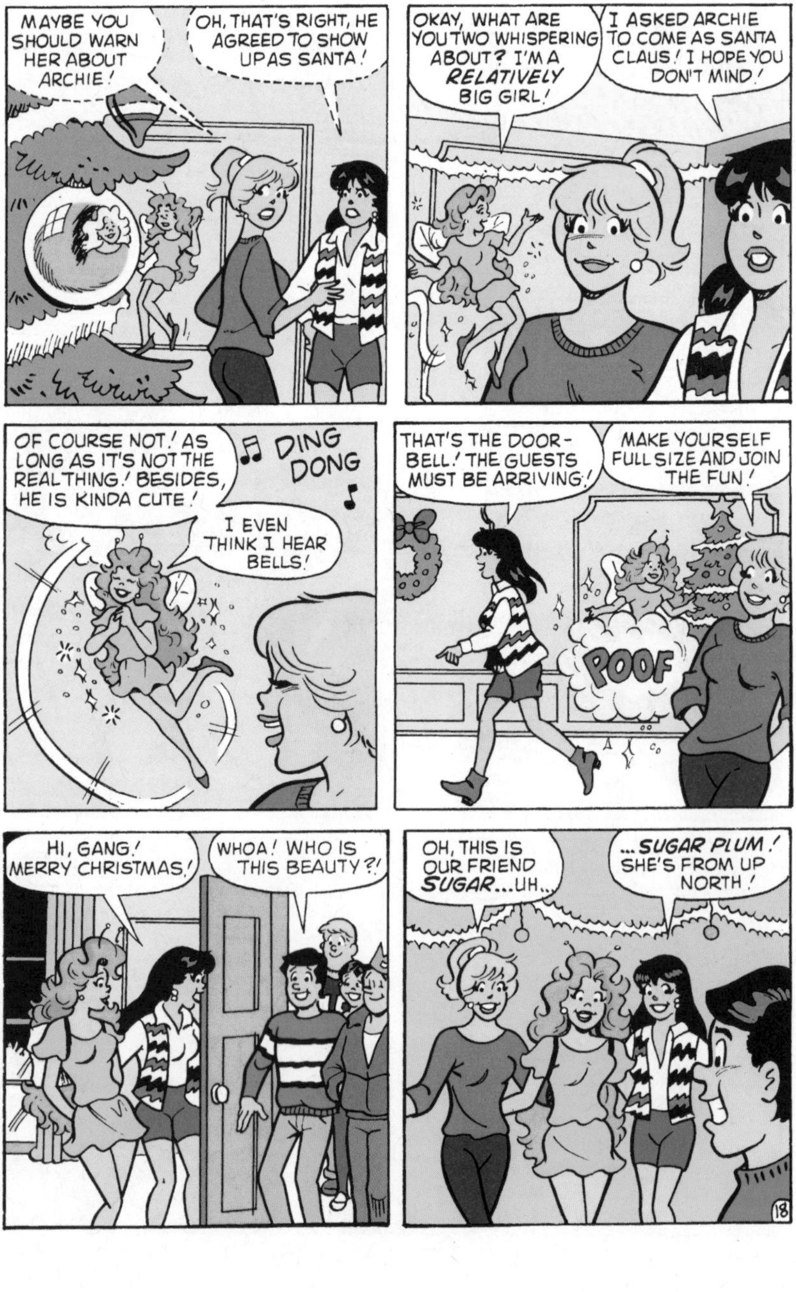
MAYBE YOU SHOULD WARN HER ABOUT ARCHIE!
OH, THAT'S RIGHT, HE AGREED TO SHOW UP AS SANTA!
OKAY, WHAT ARE YOU TWO WHISPERING ABOUT? I'M A RELATIVELY BIG GIRL!
I ASKED ARCHIE TO COME AS SANTA CLAUS! I HOPE YOU DON'T MIND!
OF COURSE NOT! AS LONG AS IT'S NOT THE REAL THING! BESIDES, HE IS KINDA CUTE!
DING DONG
I EVEN THINK I HEAR BELLS!
THAT'S THE DOOR-BELL! THE GUESTS MUST BE ARRIVING!
MAKE YOURSELF FULL SIZE AND JOIN THE FUN!
POOF
HI, GANG! MERRY CHRISTMAS!
WHOA! WHO IS THIS BEAUTY?!
OH, THIS IS OUR FRIEND SUGAR...UH...
...SUGAR PLUM! SHE'S FROM UP NORTH!
18

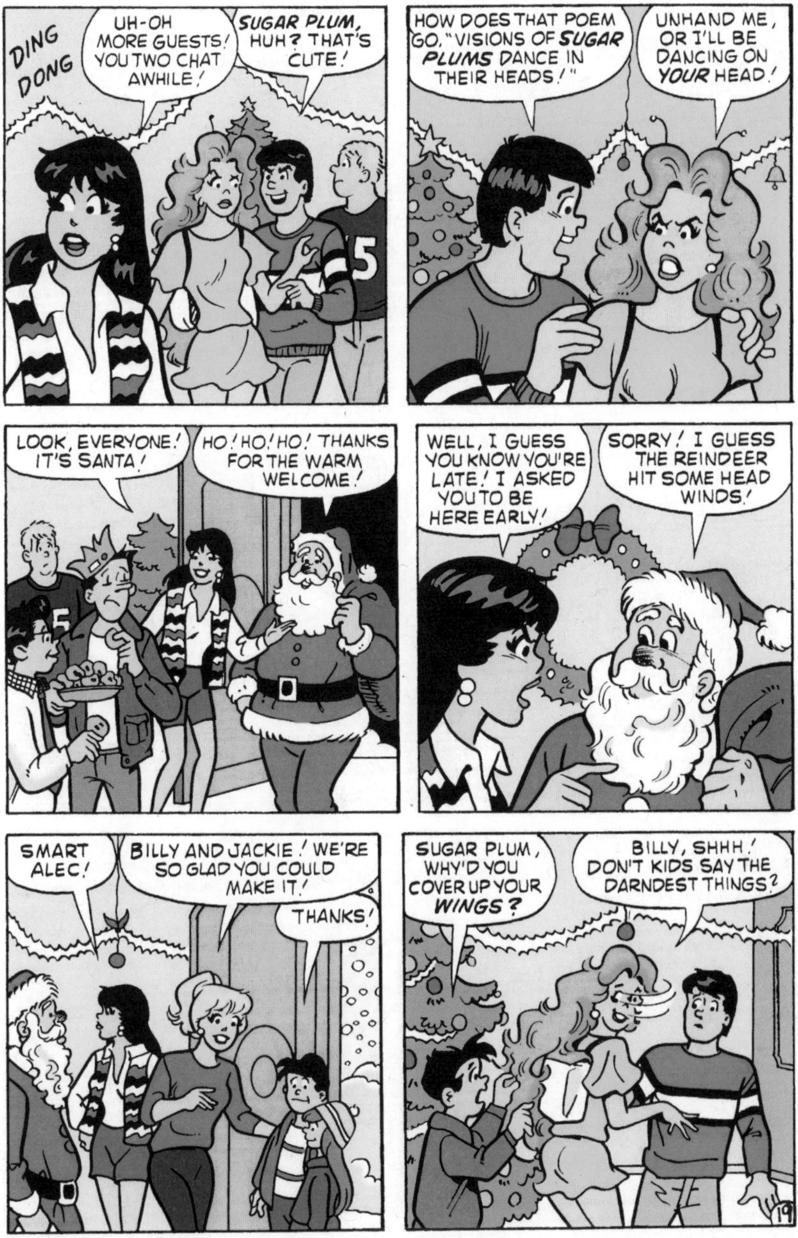
DING DONG
UH-OH MORE GUESTS! YOU TWO CHAT AWHILE!
SUGAR PLUM, HUH? THAT'S CUTE!
HOW DOES THAT POEM GO, "VISIONS OF SUGAR PLUMS DANCE IN THEIR HEADS!"
UNHAND ME, OR I'LL BE DANCING ON YOUR HEAD!
LOOK, EVERYONE! IT'S SANTA!
HO! HO! HO! THANKS FOR THE WARM WELCOME!
WELL, I GUESS YOU KNOW YOU'RE LATE! I ASKED YOU TO BE HERE EARLY!
SORRY! I GUESS THE REINDEER HIT SOME HEAD WINDS!
SMART ALEC!
BILLY AND JACKIE! WE'RE SO GLAD YOU COULD MAKE IT!
THANKS!
SUGAR PLUM, WHY'D YOU COVER UP YOUR WINGS?
BILLY, SHHH! DON'T KIDS SAY THE DARNDEST THINGS?
19

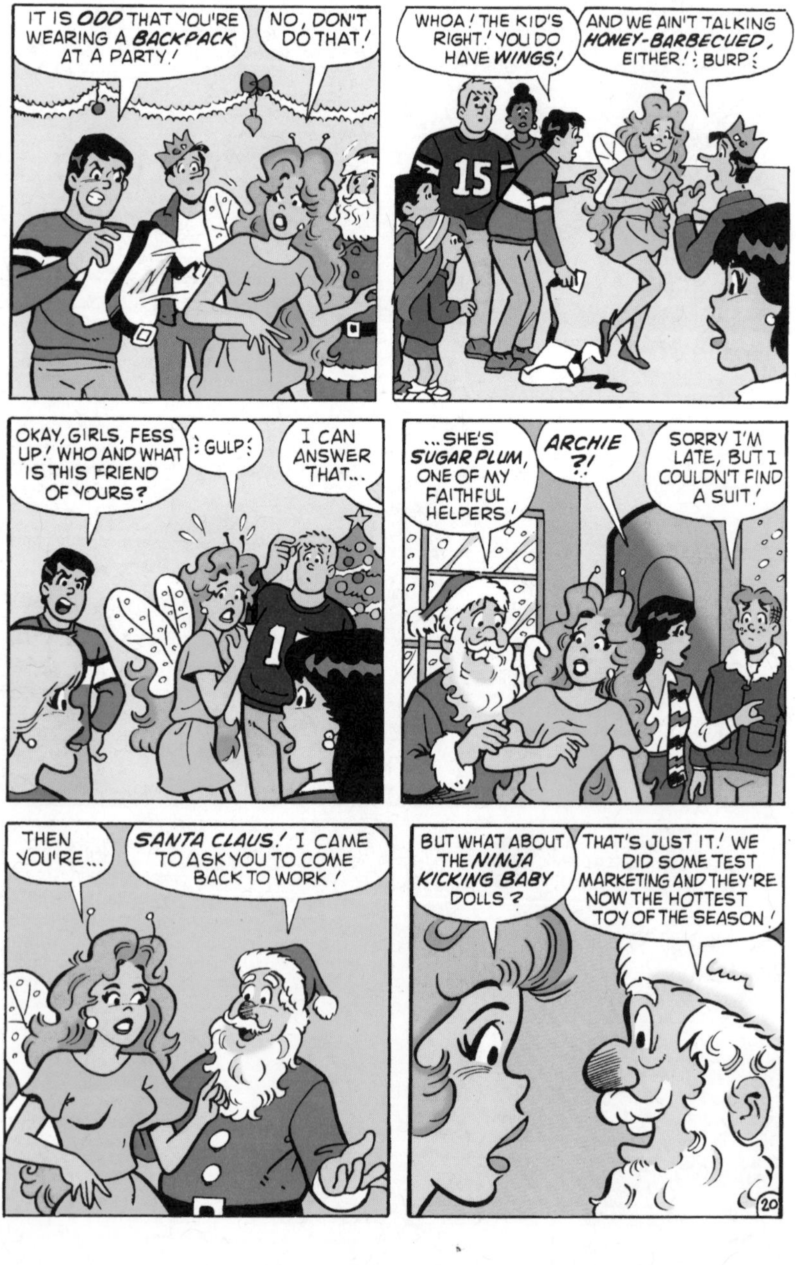
IT IS ODD THAT YOU'RE WEARING A BACKPACK AT A PARTY!
NO, DON'T DO THAT!
WHOA! THE KID'S RIGHT! YOU DO HAVE WINGS!
AND WE AIN'T TALKING HONEY-BARBECUED, EITHER! BURP
15
OKAY, GIRLS, FESS UP! WHO AND WHAT IS THIS FRIEND OF YOURS?
GULP
I CAN ANSWER THAT...
...SHE'S SUGAR PLUM, ONE OF MY FAITHFUL HELPERS!
ARCHIE?!
SORRY I'M LATE, BUT I COULDN'T FIND A SUIT!
THEN YOU'RE...
SANTA CLAUS! I CAME TO ASK YOU TO COME BACK TO WORK!
BUT WHAT ABOUT THE NINJA KICKING BABY DOLLS?
THAT'S JUST IT! WE DID SOME TEST MARKETING AND THEY'RE NOW THE HOTTEST TOY OF THE SEASON!
20

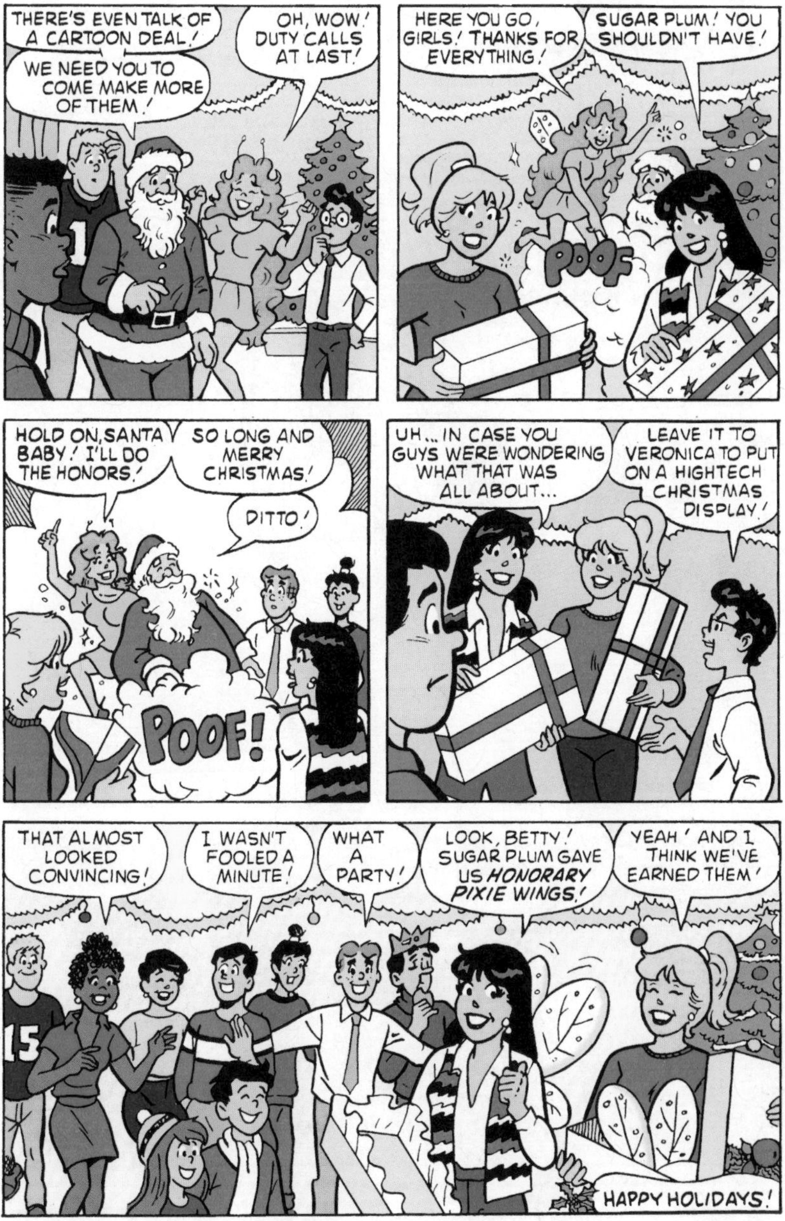
THERE'S EVEN TALK OF A CARTOON DEAL!
WE NEED YOU TO COME MAKE MORE OF THEM!
OH, WOW! DUTY CALLS AT LAST!
HERE YOU GO, GIRLS! THANKS FOR EVERYTHING!
SUGAR PLUM! YOU SHOULDN'T HAVE!
POOF
HOLD ON, SANTA BABY! I'LL DO THE HONORS!
SO LONG AND MERRY CHRISTMAS!
DITTO!
POOF!
UH... IN CASE YOU GUYS WERE WONDERING WHAT THAT WAS ALL ABOUT...
LEAVE IT TO VERONICA TO PUT ON A HIGHTECH CHRISTMAS DISPLAY!
THAT ALMOST LOOKED CONVINCING!
I WASN'T FOOLED A MINUTE!
WHAT A PARTY!
LOOK, BETTY! SUGAR PLUM GAVE US *HONORARY PIXIE WINGS*!
YEAH! AND I THINK WE'VE EARNED THEM!
HAPPY HOLIDAYS!

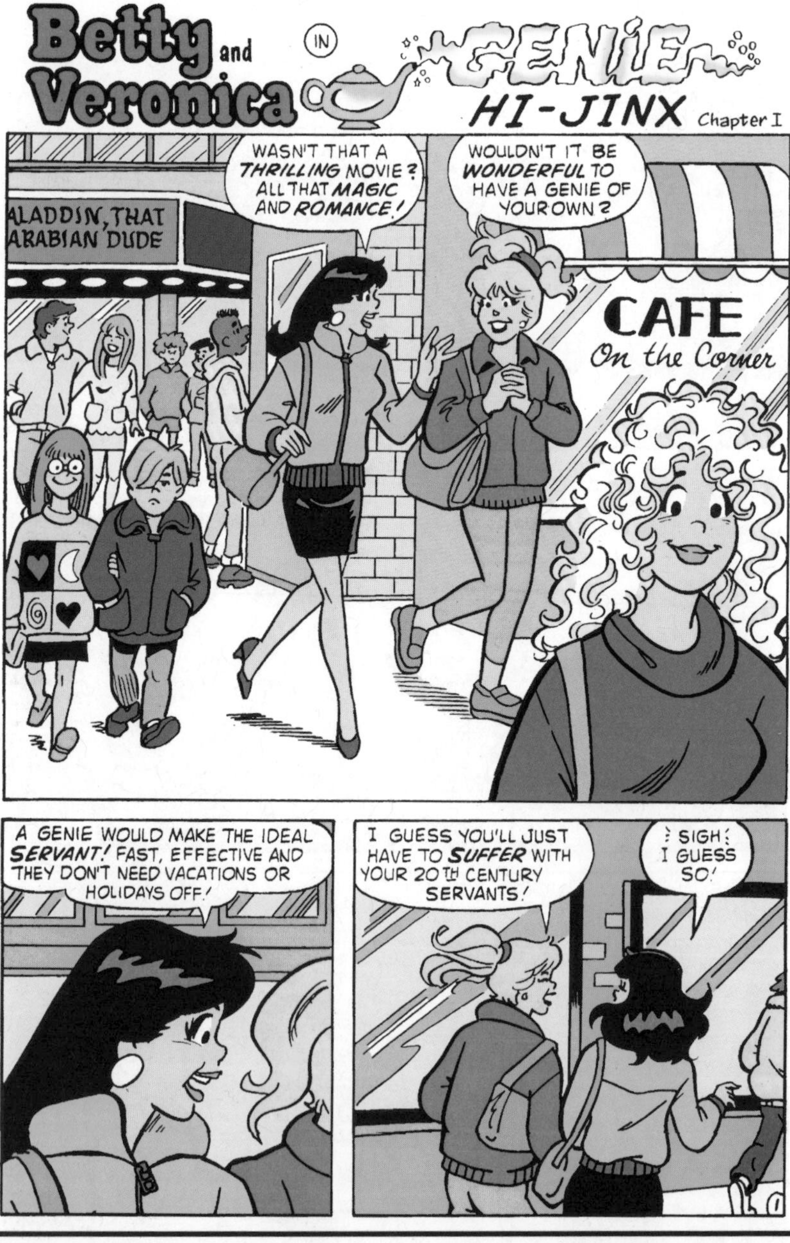
Betty and Veronica
IN
GENIE HI-JINX
Chapter I
ALADDIN, THAT ARABIAN DUDE
WASN'T THAT A THRILLING MOVIE? ALL THAT MAGIC AND ROMANCE!
WOULDN'T IT BE WONDERFUL TO HAVE A GENIE OF YOUR OWN?
CAFE On the Corner
A GENIE WOULD MAKE THE IDEAL SERVANT! FAST, EFFECTIVE AND THEY DON'T NEED VACATIONS OR HOLIDAYS OFF!
I GUESS YOU'LL JUST HAVE TO SUFFER WITH YOUR 20TH CENTURY SERVANTS!
SIGH! I GUESS SO!
1

Story: Dan Parent & Bill Golliher Pencils: Dan DeCarlo & Dan Parent
Inks: Henry Scarpelli Letters: Bill Yoshida Colors: Barry Grossman

Originally printed in BETTY & VERONICA SPECTACULAR #3, May 1993

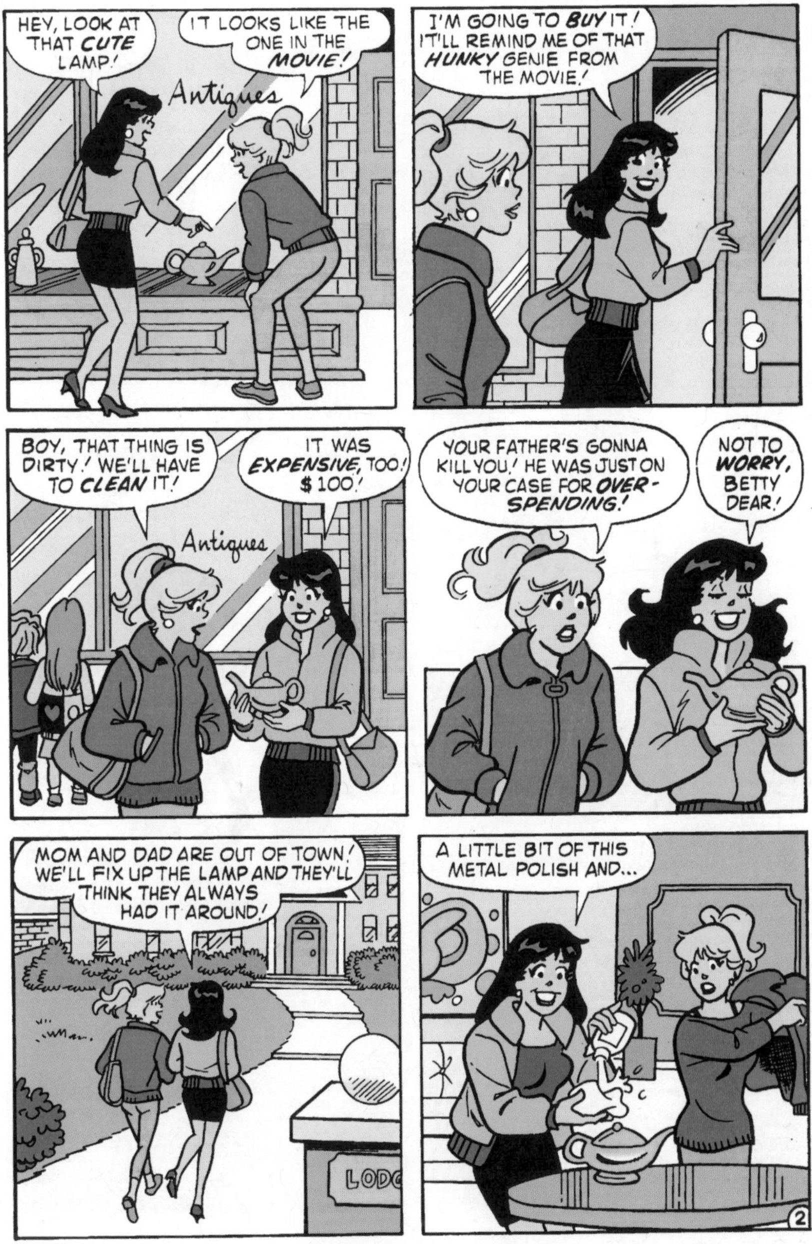
HEY, LOOK AT THAT CUTE LAMP!
IT LOOKS LIKE THE ONE IN THE MOVIE!
Antiques
I'M GOING TO BUY IT! IT'LL REMIND ME OF THAT HUNKY GENIE FROM THE MOVIE!
BOY, THAT THING IS DIRTY! WE'LL HAVE TO CLEAN IT!
IT WAS EXPENSIVE, TOO! $100!
Antiques
YOUR FATHER'S GONNA KILL YOU! HE WAS JUST ON YOUR CASE FOR OVER-SPENDING!
NOT TO WORRY, BETTY DEAR!
MOM AND DAD ARE OUT OF TOWN! WE'LL FIX UP THE LAMP AND THEY'LL THINK THEY ALWAYS HAD IT AROUND!
LODG
A LITTLE BIT OF THIS METAL POLISH AND...
2

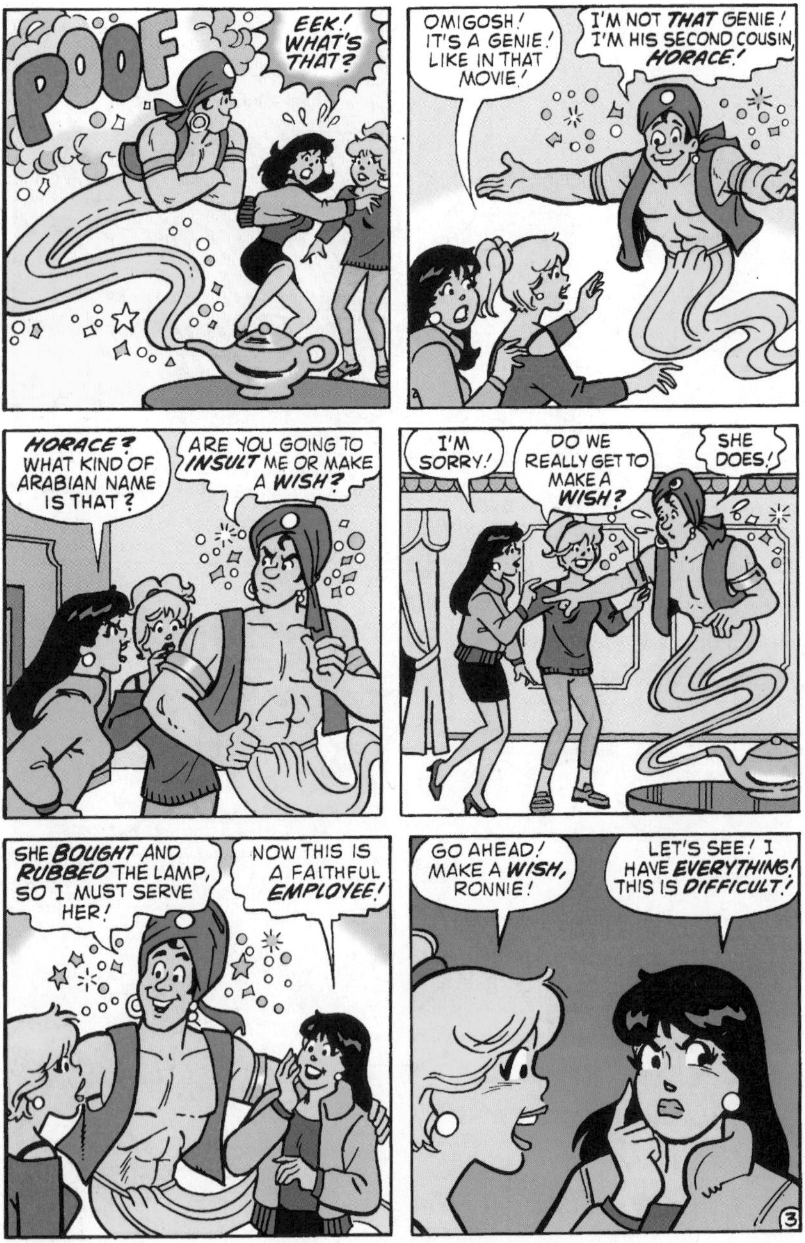
POOF
EEK! WHAT'S THAT?
OMIGOSH! IT'S A GENIE! LIKE IN THAT MOVIE!
I'M NOT THAT GENIE! I'M HIS SECOND COUSIN, HORACE!
HORACE? WHAT KIND OF ARABIAN NAME IS THAT?
ARE YOU GOING TO INSULT ME OR MAKE A WISH?
I'M SORRY!
DO WE REALLY GET TO MAKE A WISH?
SHE DOES!
SHE BOUGHT AND RUBBED THE LAMP, SO I MUST SERVE HER!
NOW THIS IS A FAITHFUL EMPLOYEE!
GO AHEAD! MAKE A WISH, RONNIE!
LET'S SEE! I HAVE EVERYTHING! THIS IS DIFFICULT!
3

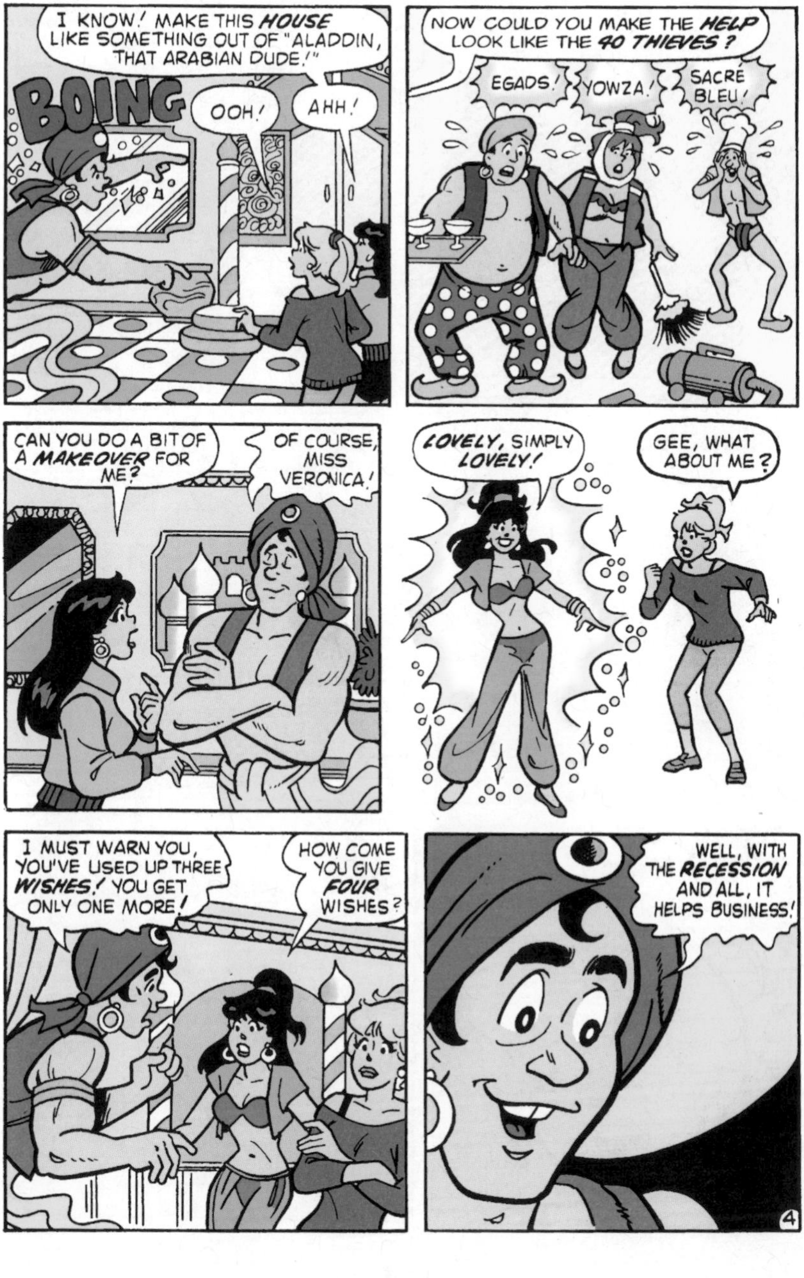
I KNOW! MAKE THIS HOUSE LIKE SOMETHING OUT OF "ALADDIN, THAT ARABIAN DUDE!"
BOING
OOH!
AHH!
NOW COULD YOU MAKE THE HELP LOOK LIKE THE 40 THIEVES?
EGADS!
YOWZA!
SACRÉ BLEU!
CAN YOU DO A BIT OF A MAKEOVER FOR ME?
OF COURSE, MISS VERONICA!
LOVELY, SIMPLY LOVELY!
GEE, WHAT ABOUT ME?
I MUST WARN YOU, YOU'VE USED UP THREE WISHES! YOU GET ONLY ONE MORE!
HOW COME YOU GIVE FOUR WISHES?
WELL, WITH THE RECESSION AND ALL, IT HELPS BUSINESS!
4

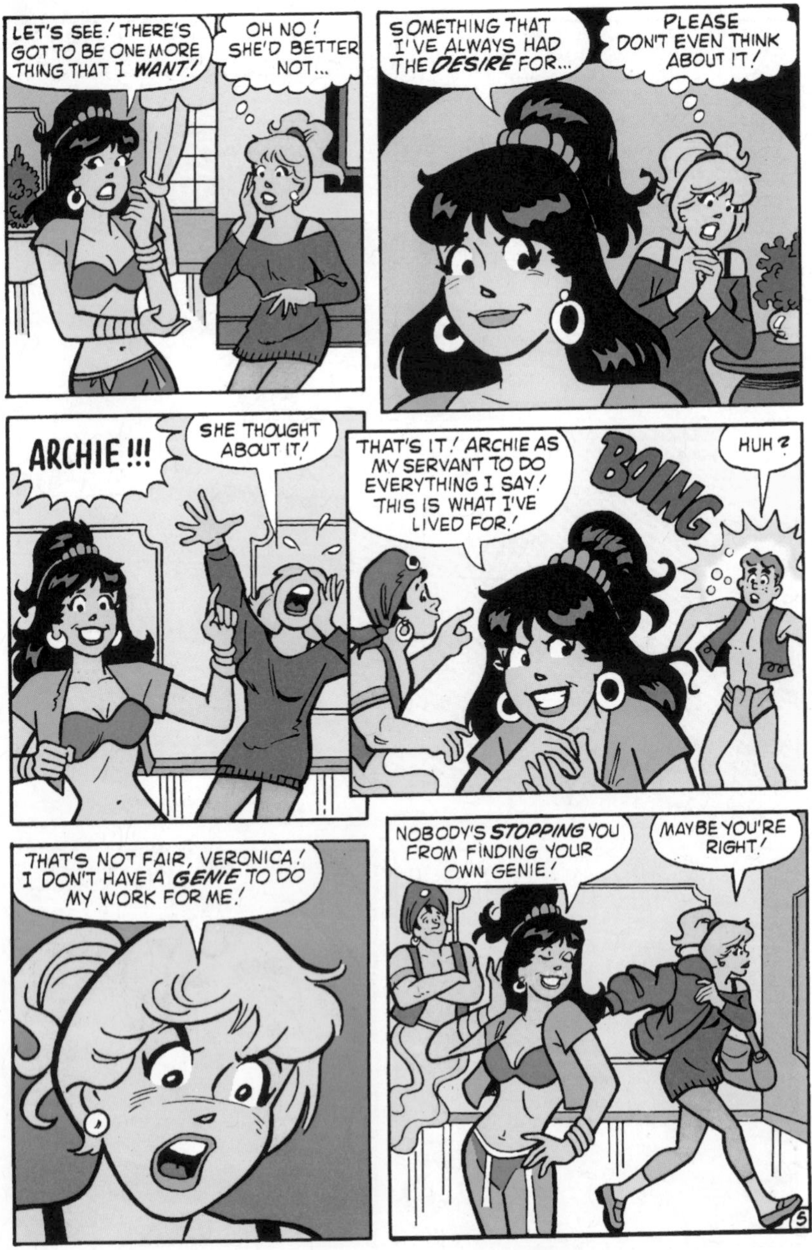
LET'S SEE! THERE'S GOT TO BE ONE MORE THING THAT I WANT!
OH NO! SHE'D BETTER NOT...
SOMETHING THAT I'VE ALWAYS HAD THE DESIRE FOR...
PLEASE DON'T EVEN THINK ABOUT IT!
ARCHIE!!!
SHE THOUGHT ABOUT IT!
THAT'S IT! ARCHIE AS MY SERVANT TO DO EVERYTHING I SAY! THIS IS WHAT I'VE LIVED FOR!
BOING
HUH?
THAT'S NOT FAIR, VERONICA! I DON'T HAVE A GENIE TO DO MY WORK FOR ME!
NOBODY'S STOPPING YOU FROM FINDING YOUR OWN GENIE!
MAYBE YOU'RE RIGHT!
5

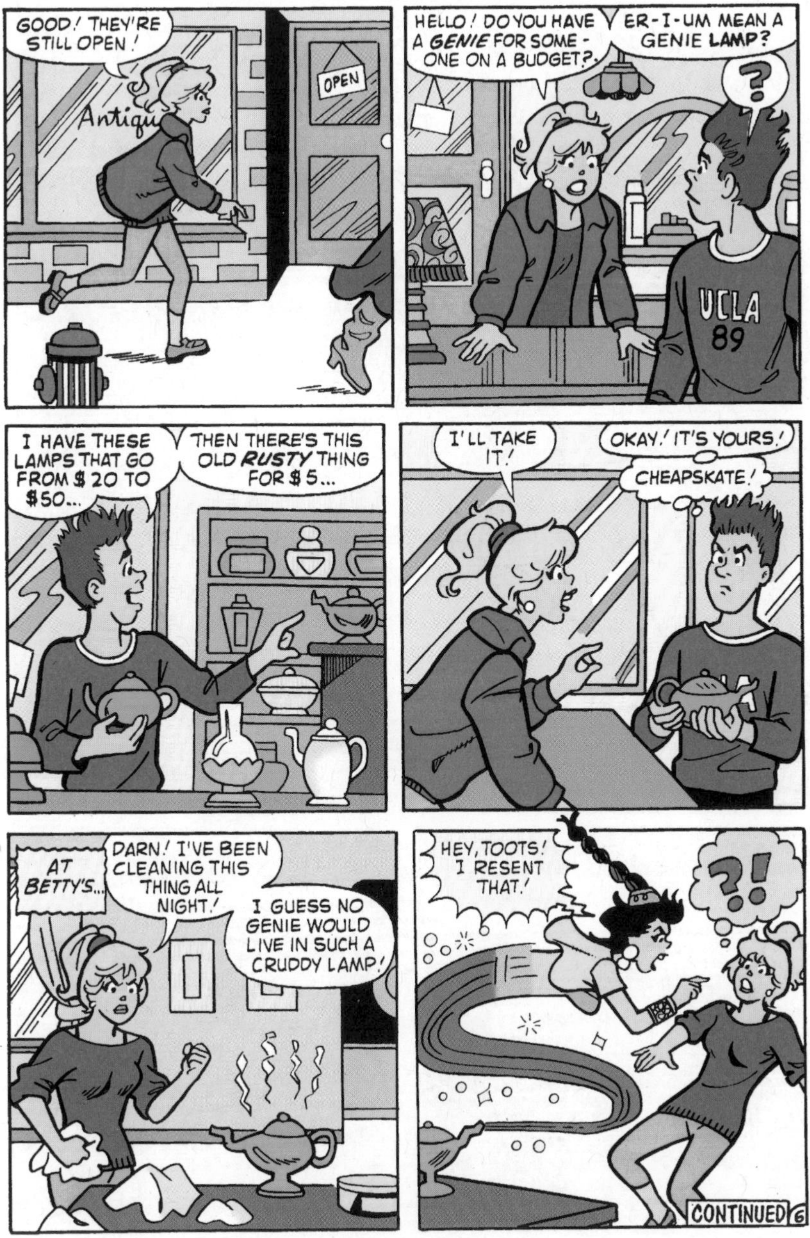
GOOD! THEY'RE STILL OPEN!
Antiqu
OPEN
HELLO! DO YOU HAVE A GENIE FOR SOME-ONE ON A BUDGET?
ER-I-UM MEAN A GENIE LAMP?
?
UCLA 89
I HAVE THESE LAMPS THAT GO FROM $ 20 TO $50...
THEN THERE'S THIS OLD RUSTY THING FOR $ 5...
I'LL TAKE IT!
OKAY! IT'S YOURS!
CHEAPSKATE!
AT BETTY'S...
DARN! I'VE BEEN CLEANING THIS THING ALL NIGHT!
I GUESS NO GENIE WOULD LIVE IN SUCH A CRUDDY LAMP!
HEY, TOOTS! I RESENT THAT!
?!
CONTINUED 6

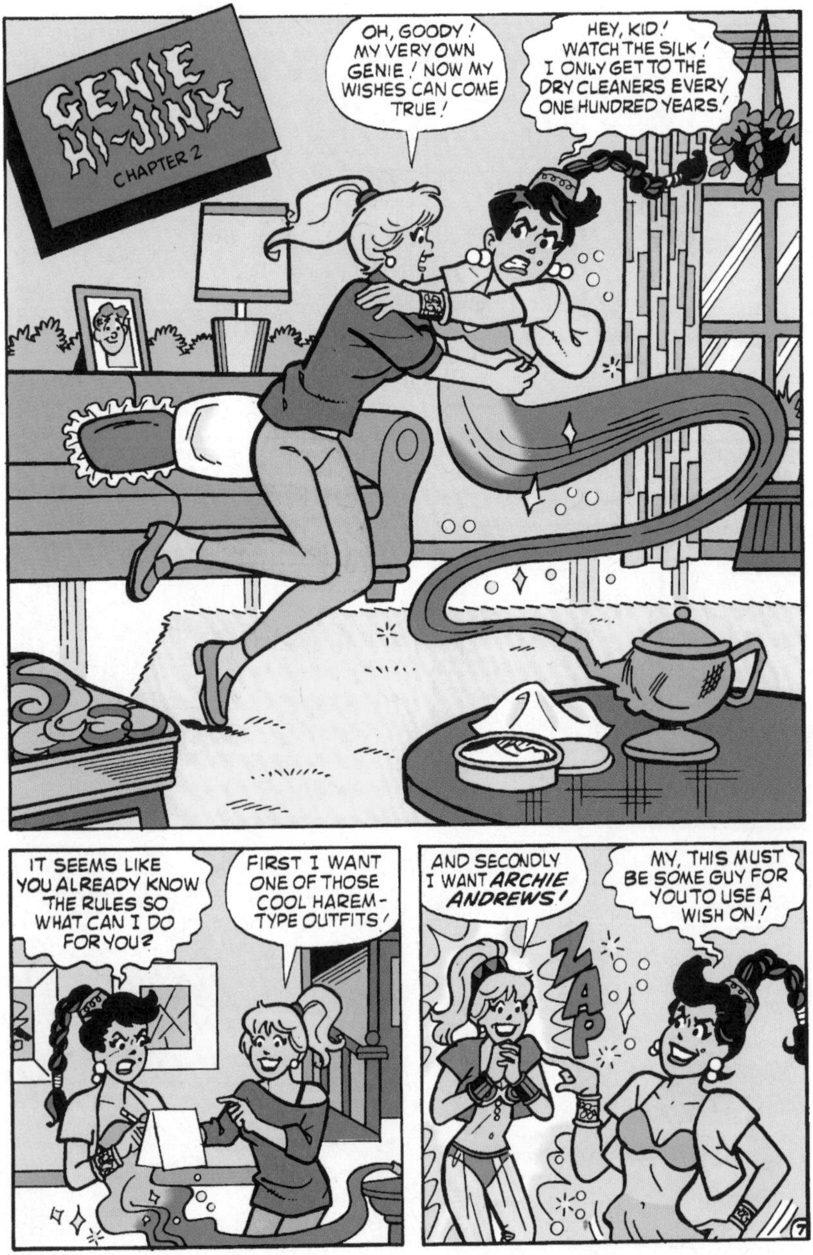
GENIE HI-JINX
CHAPTER 2
OH, GOODY! MY VERY OWN GENIE! NOW MY WISHES CAN COME TRUE!
HEY, KID! WATCH THE SILK! I ONLY GET TO THE DRY CLEANERS EVERY ONE HUNDRED YEARS!
IT SEEMS LIKE YOU ALREADY KNOW THE RULES SO WHAT CAN I DO FOR YOU?
FIRST I WANT ONE OF THOSE COOL HAREM-TYPE OUTFITS!
AND SECONDLY I WANT ARCHIE ANDREWS!
ZAP
MY, THIS MUST BE SOME GUY FOR YOU TO USE A WISH ON!
7

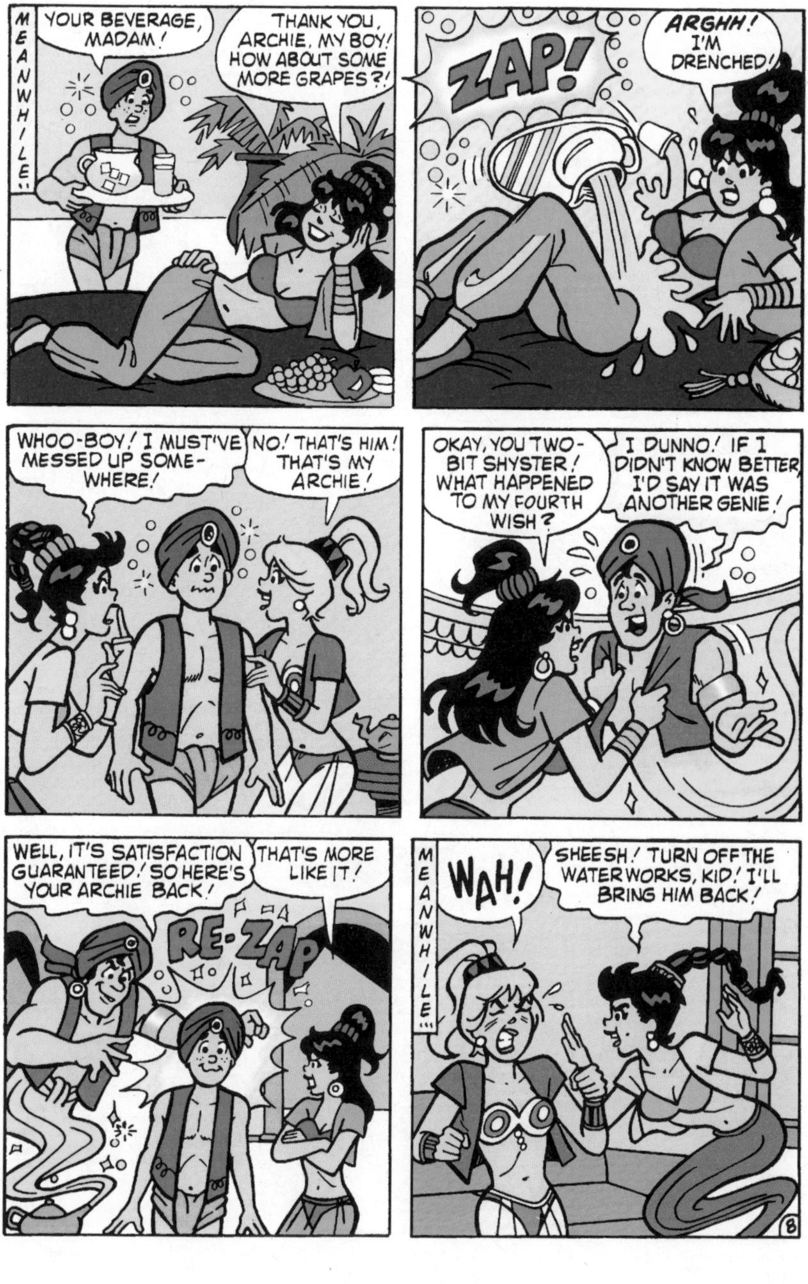
MEANWHILE...
YOUR BEVERAGE, MADAM!
THANK YOU, ARCHIE, MY BOY! HOW ABOUT SOME MORE GRAPES?!
ZAP!
ARGHH! I'M DRENCHED!
WHOO-BOY! I MUST'VE MESSED UP SOME-WHERE!
NO! THAT'S HIM! THAT'S MY ARCHIE!
OKAY, YOU TWO-BIT SHYSTER! WHAT HAPPENED TO MY FOURTH WISH?
I DUNNO! IF I DIDN'T KNOW BETTER, I'D SAY IT WAS ANOTHER GENIE!
WELL, IT'S SATISFACTION GUARANTEED! SO HERE'S YOUR ARCHIE BACK!
THAT'S MORE LIKE IT!
RE-ZAP
MEANWHILE...
WAH!
SHEESH! TURN OFF THE WATERWORKS, KID! I'LL BRING HIM BACK!
8

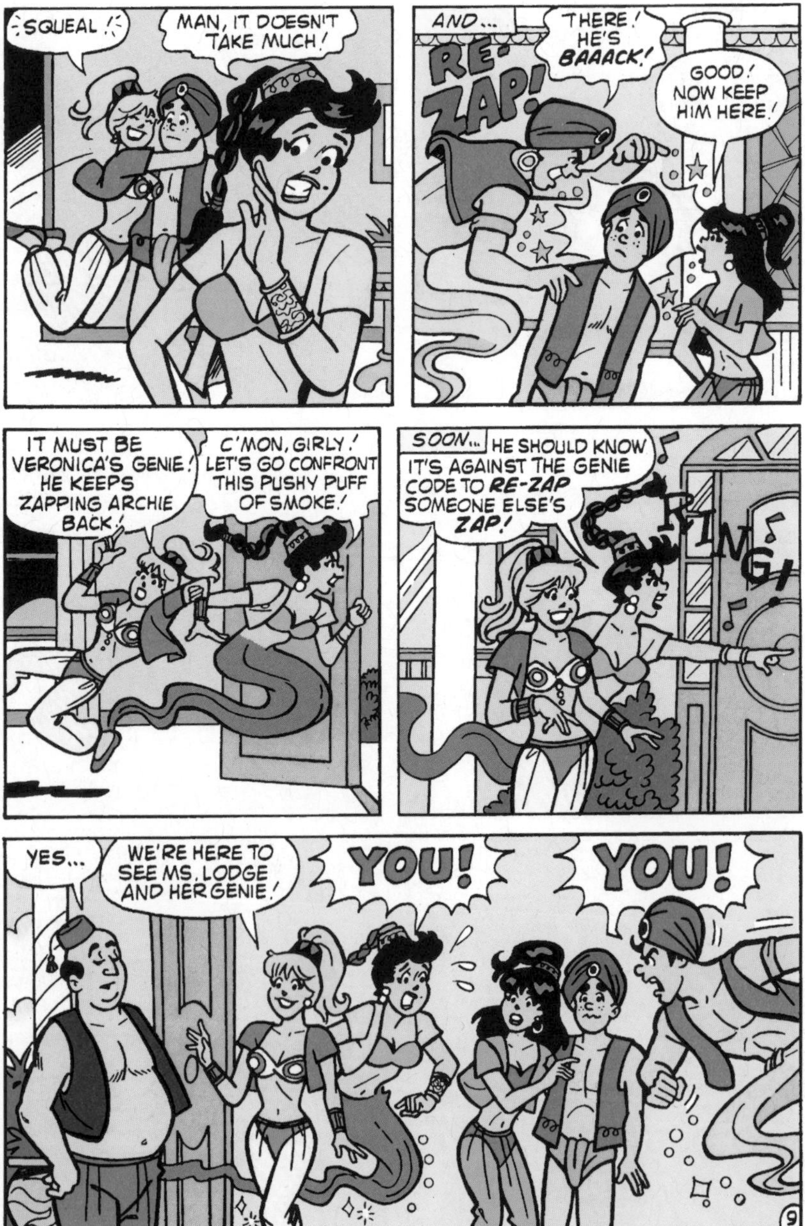
SQUEAL!
MAN, IT DOESN'T TAKE MUCH!
AND...
RE-ZAP!
THERE! HE'S BAAACK!
GOOD! NOW KEEP HIM HERE!
IT MUST BE VERONICA'S GENIE! HE KEEPS ZAPPING ARCHIE BACK!
C'MON, GIRLY! LET'S GO CONFRONT THIS PUSHY PUFF OF SMOKE!
SOON...
HE SHOULD KNOW IT'S AGAINST THE GENIE CODE TO RE-ZAP SOMEONE ELSE'S ZAP!
RING!
YES...
WE'RE HERE TO SEE MS. LODGE AND HER GENIE!
YOU!
YOU!
9

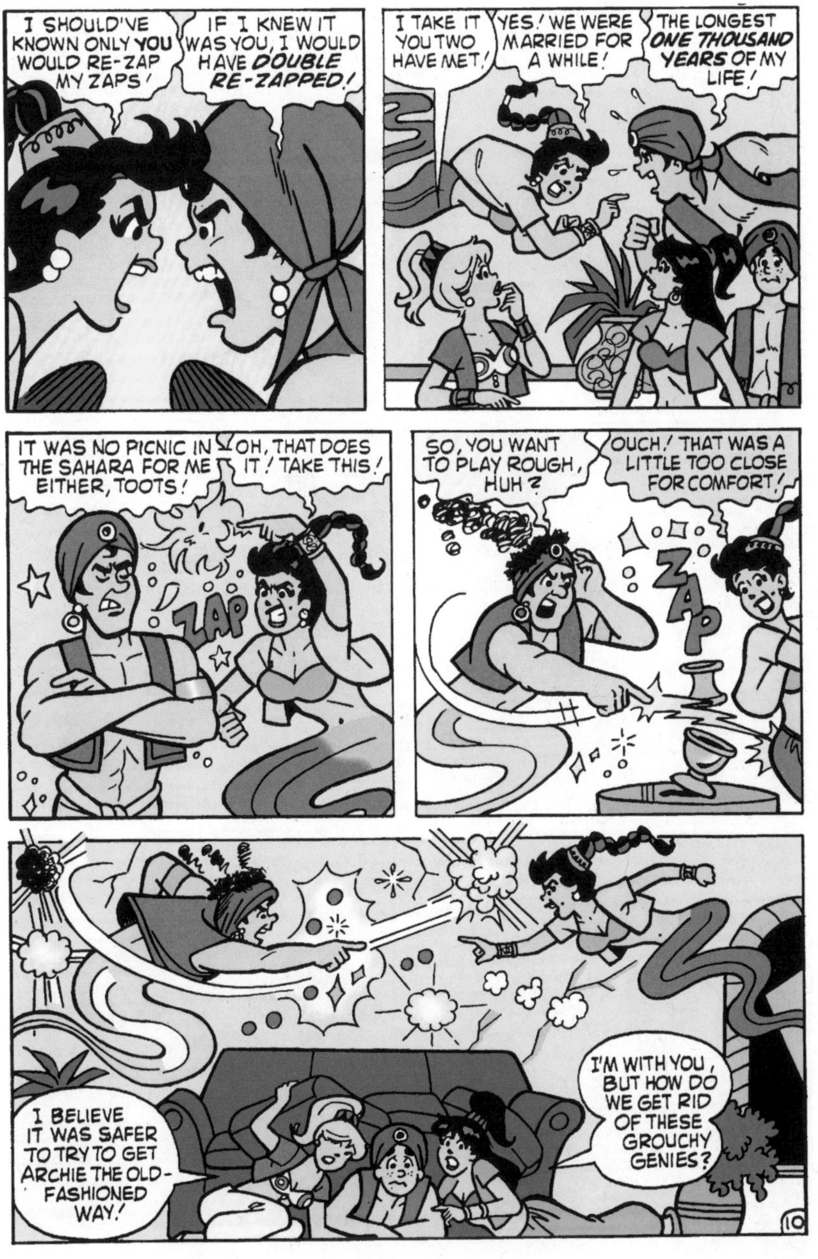
I SHOULD'VE KNOWN ONLY **YOU** WOULD RE-ZAP MY ZAPS!
IF I KNEW IT WAS YOU, I WOULD HAVE ***DOUBLE RE-ZAPPED!***
I TAKE IT YOU TWO HAVE MET!
YES! WE WERE MARRIED FOR A WHILE!
THE LONGEST ***ONE THOUSAND YEARS*** OF MY LIFE!
IT WAS NO PICNIC IN THE SAHARA FOR ME EITHER, TOOTS!
OH, THAT DOES IT! TAKE THIS!
ZAP
SO, YOU WANT TO PLAY ROUGH, HUH?
OUCH! THAT WAS A LITTLE TOO CLOSE FOR COMFORT!
ZAP
I BELIEVE IT WAS SAFER TO TRY TO GET ARCHIE THE OLD-FASHIONED WAY!
I'M WITH YOU, BUT HOW DO WE GET RID OF THESE GROUCHY GENIES?
10

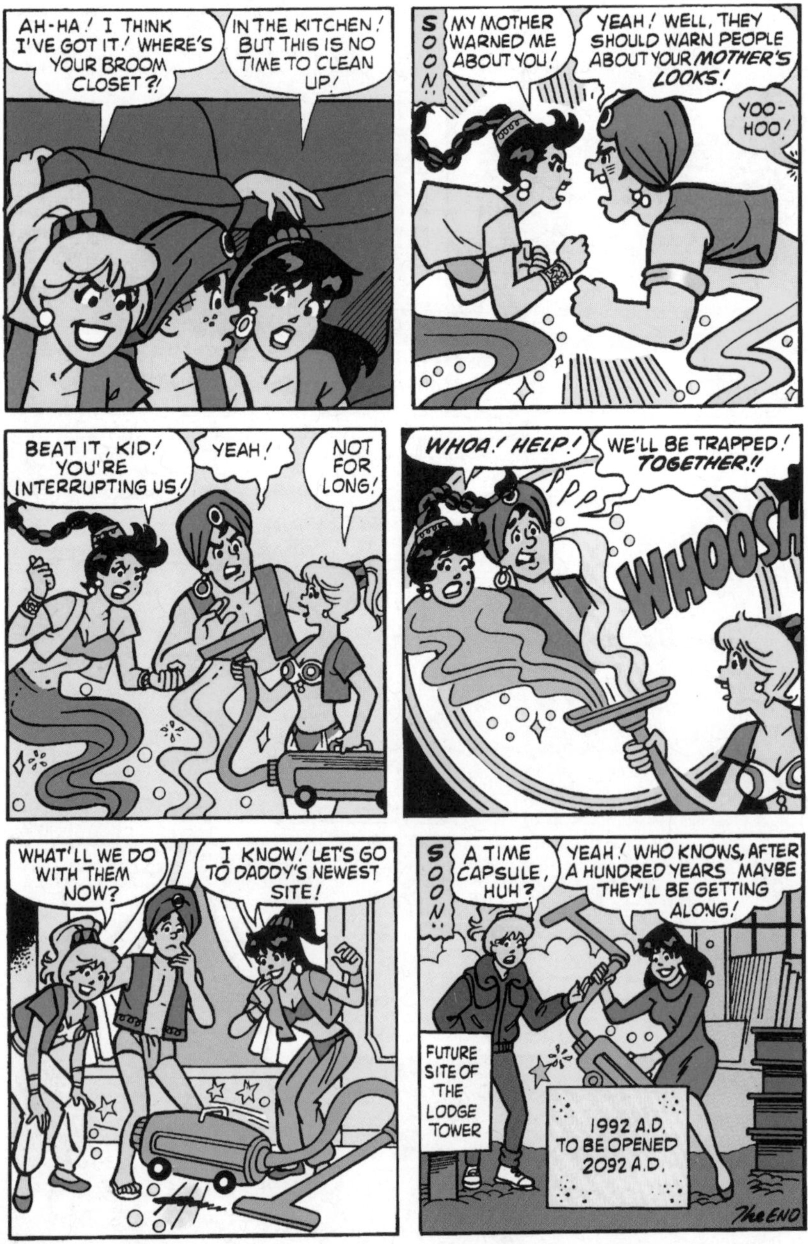
AH-HA! I THINK I'VE GOT IT! WHERE'S YOUR BROOM CLOSET?!
IN THE KITCHEN! BUT THIS IS NO TIME TO CLEAN UP!
SOON..
MY MOTHER WARNED ME ABOUT YOU!
YEAH! WELL, THEY SHOULD WARN PEOPLE ABOUT YOUR MOTHER'S LOOKS!
YOO-HOO!
BEAT IT, KID! YOU'RE INTERRUPTING US!
YEAH!
NOT FOR LONG!
WHOA! HELP!
WE'LL BE TRAPPED! TOGETHER!!
WHOOSH
WHAT'LL WE DO WITH THEM NOW?
I KNOW! LET'S GO TO DADDY'S NEWEST SITE!
SOON..
A TIME CAPSULE, HUH?
YEAH! WHO KNOWS, AFTER A HUNDRED YEARS MAYBE THEY'LL BE GETTING ALONG!
FUTURE SITE OF THE LODGE TOWER
1992 A.D. TO BE OPENED 2092 A.D.
The END

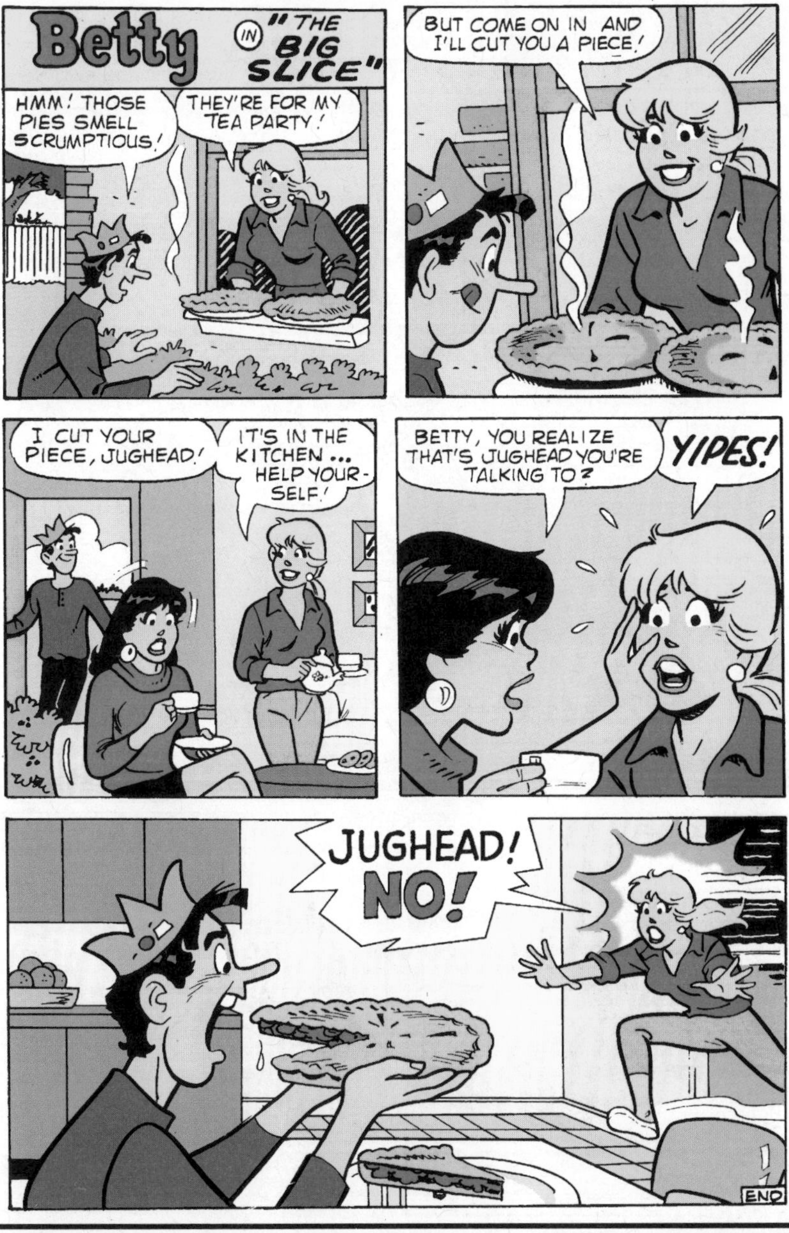
Betty IN "THE BIG SLICE"
HMM! THOSE PIES SMELL SCRUMPTIOUS!
THEY'RE FOR MY TEA PARTY!
BUT COME ON IN AND I'LL CUT YOU A PIECE!
I CUT YOUR PIECE, JUGHEAD!
IT'S IN THE KITCHEN ... HELP YOURSELF!
BETTY, YOU REALIZE THAT'S JUGHEAD YOU'RE TALKING TO?
YIPES!
JUGHEAD! NO!
END

Story: Dan Parent & Bill Golliher Pencils: Dan DeCarlo & Dan Parent
Inks: Henry Scarpelli Letters: Bill Yoshida Colors: Barry Grossman

Originally printed in BETTY & VERONICA SPECTACULAR #3, May 1993

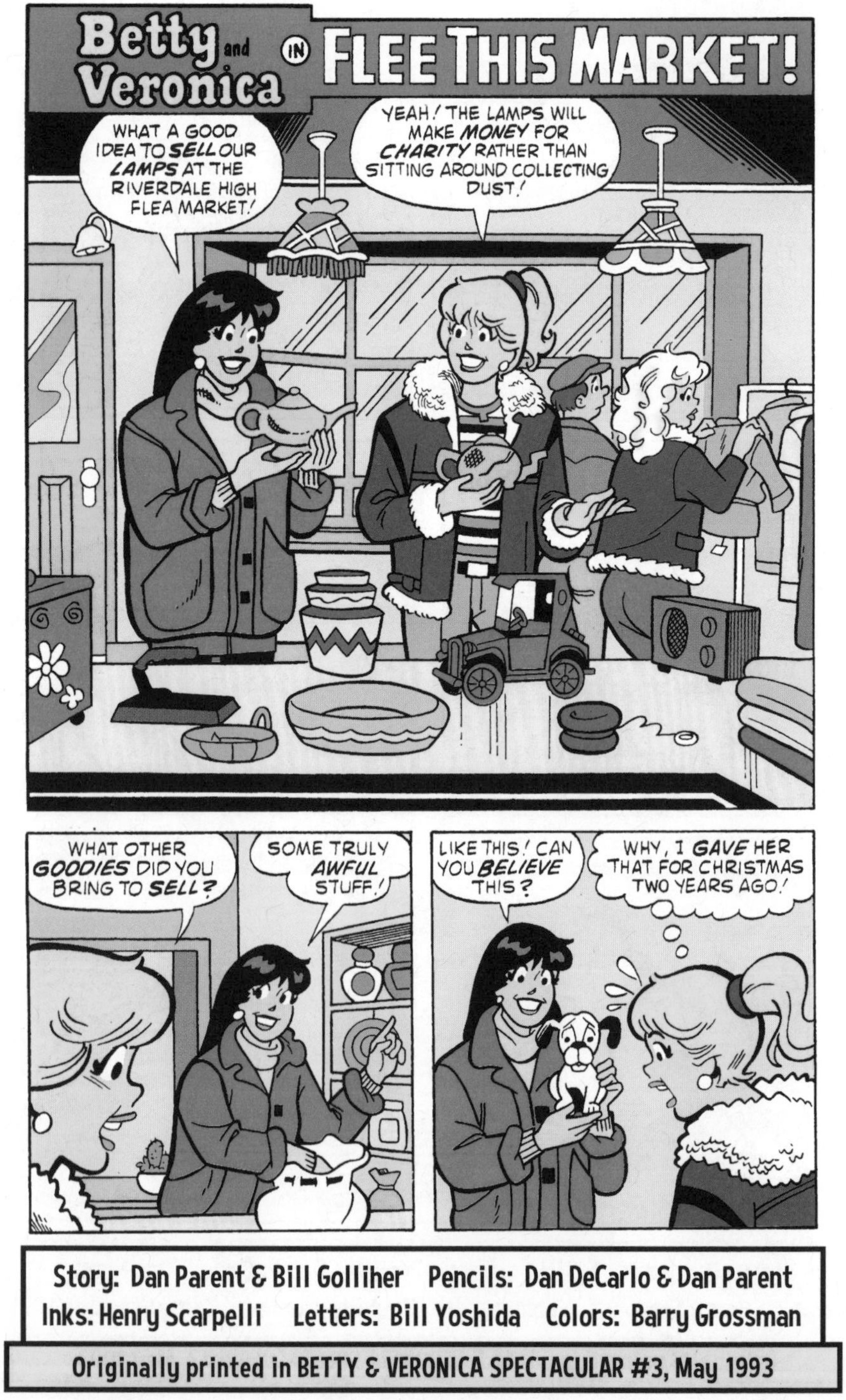
Betty and Veronica
IN
FLEE THIS MARKET!
WHAT A GOOD IDEA TO SELL OUR LAMPS AT THE RIVERDALE HIGH FLEA MARKET!
YEAH! THE LAMPS WILL MAKE MONEY FOR CHARITY RATHER THAN SITTING AROUND COLLECTING DUST!
WHAT OTHER GOODIES DID YOU BRING TO SELL?
SOME TRULY AWFUL STUFF!
LIKE THIS! CAN YOU BELIEVE THIS?
WHY, I GAVE HER THAT FOR CHRISTMAS TWO YEARS AGO!

Story: Dan Parent & Bill Golliher Pencils: Dan DeCarlo & Dan Parent
Inks: Henry Scarpelli Letters: Bill Yoshida Colors: Barry Grossman

Originally printed in BETTY & VERONICA SPECTACULAR #3, May 1993

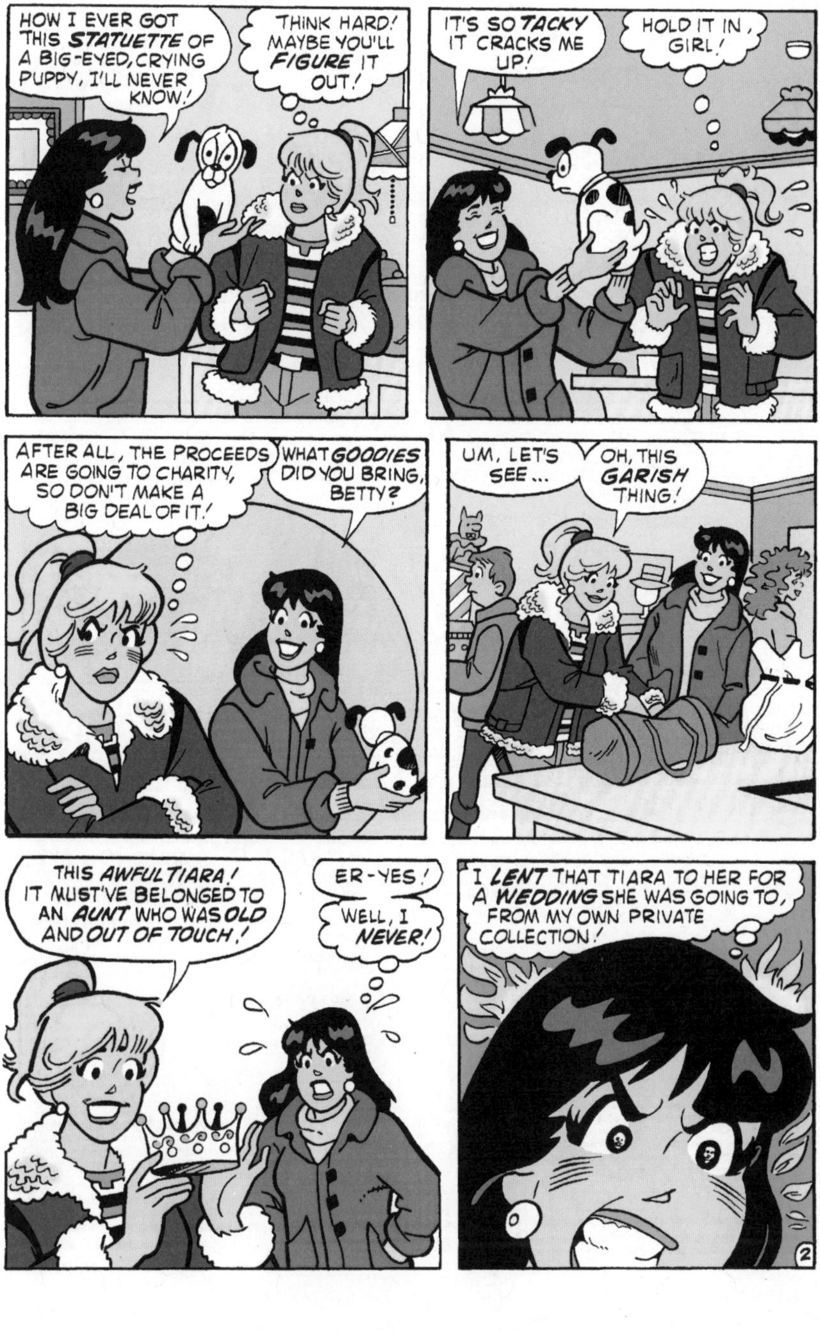
HOW I EVER GOT THIS STATUETTE OF A BIG-EYED, CRYING PUPPY, I'LL NEVER KNOW!
THINK HARD! MAYBE YOU'LL FIGURE IT OUT!
IT'S SO TACKY IT CRACKS ME UP!
HOLD IT IN, GIRL!
AFTER ALL, THE PROCEEDS ARE GOING TO CHARITY, SO DON'T MAKE A BIG DEAL OF IT!
WHAT GOODIES DID YOU BRING, BETTY?
UM, LET'S SEE ...
OH, THIS GARISH THING!
THIS AWFUL TIARA! IT MUST'VE BELONGED TO AN AUNT WHO WAS OLD AND OUT OF TOUCH!
ER-YES!
WELL, I NEVER!
I LENT THAT TIARA TO HER FOR A WEDDING SHE WAS GOING TO, FROM MY OWN PRIVATE COLLECTION!
2

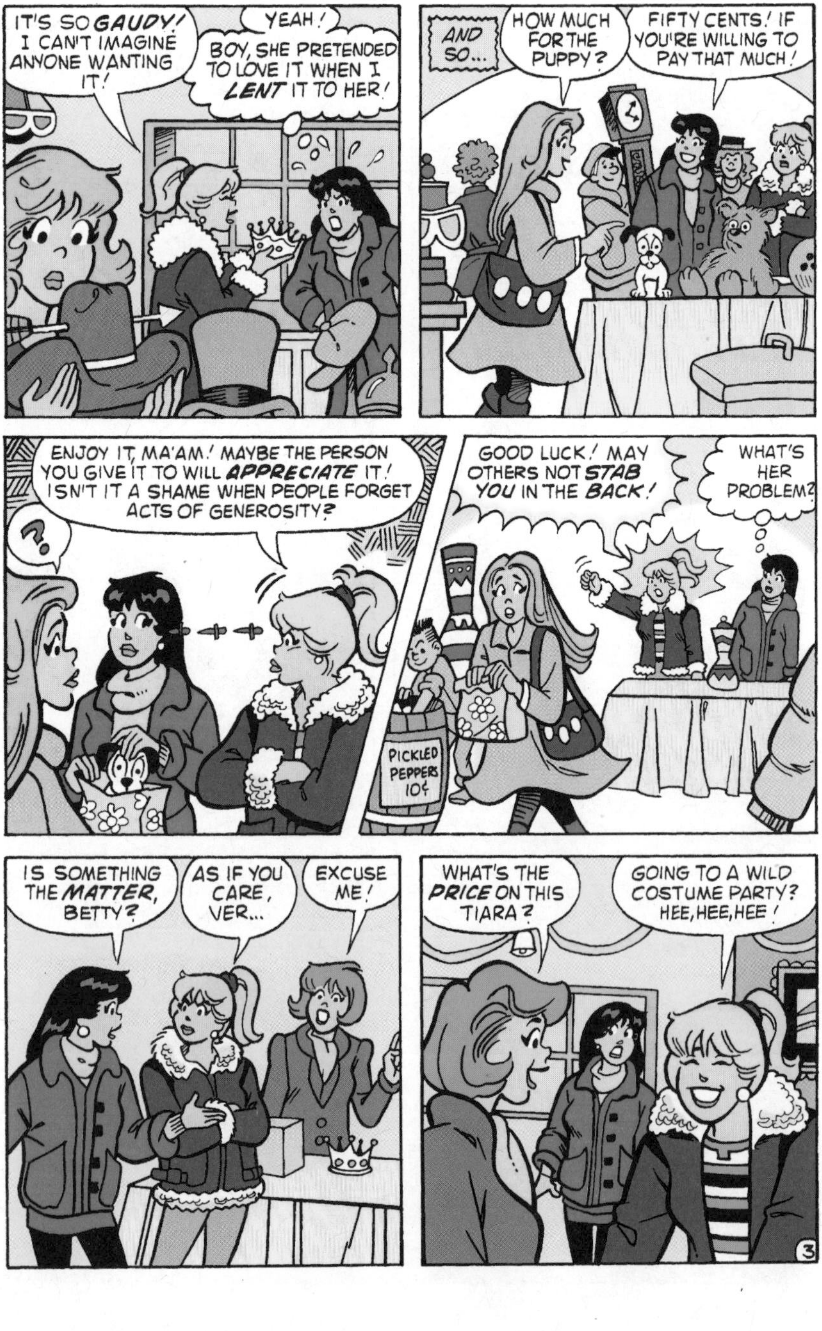

IT'S SO GAUDY! I CAN'T IMAGINE ANYONE WANTING IT!
YEAH!
BOY, SHE PRETENDED TO LOVE IT WHEN I LENT IT TO HER!
AND SO...
HOW MUCH FOR THE PUPPY?
FIFTY CENTS! IF YOU'RE WILLING TO PAY THAT MUCH!
ENJOY IT, MA'AM! MAYBE THE PERSON YOU GIVE IT TO WILL APPRECIATE IT! ISN'T IT A SHAME WHEN PEOPLE FORGET ACTS OF GENEROSITY?
?
GOOD LUCK! MAY OTHERS NOT STAB YOU IN THE BACK!
WHAT'S HER PROBLEM?
PICKLED PEPPERS 10¢
IS SOMETHING THE MATTER, BETTY?
AS IF YOU CARE, VER...
EXCUSE ME!
WHAT'S THE PRICE ON THIS TIARA?
GOING TO A WILD COSTUME PARTY? HEE, HEE, HEE!
3

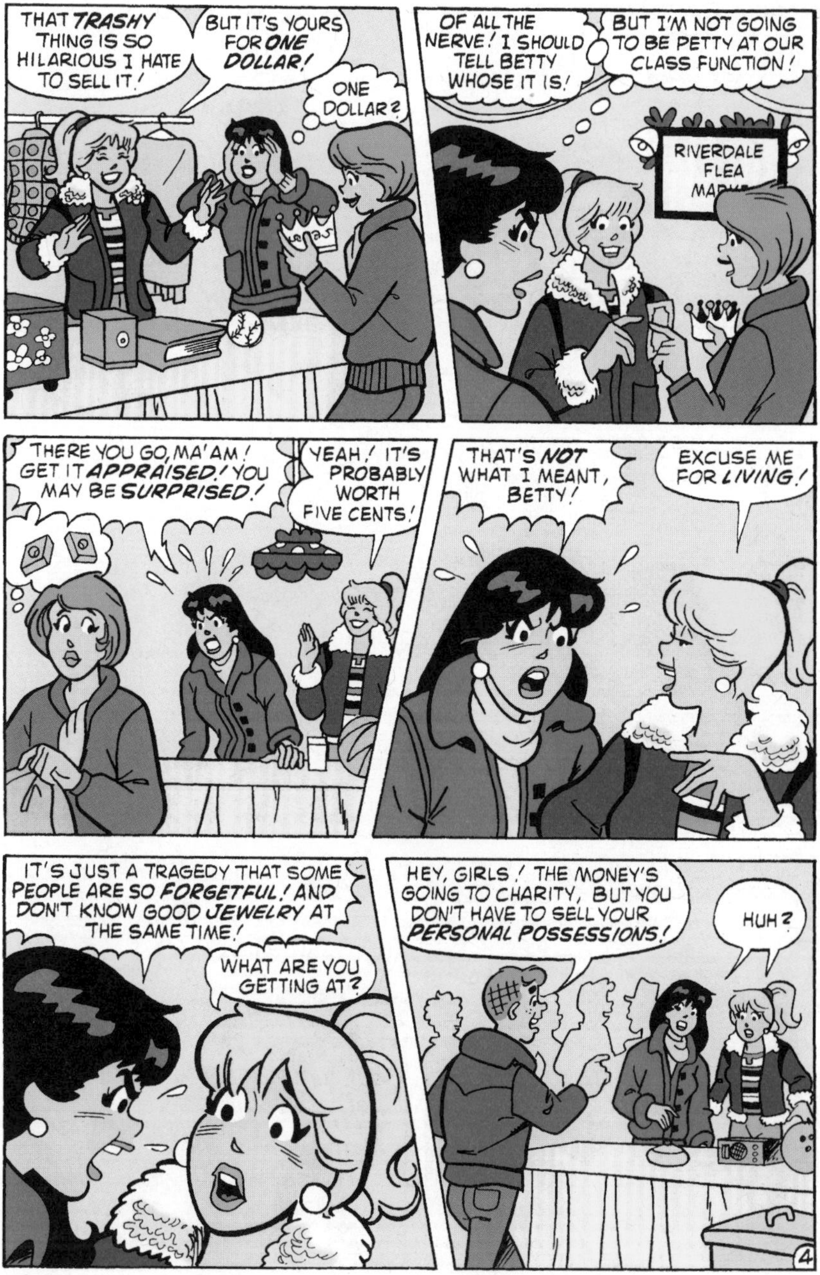
THAT TRASHY THING IS SO HILARIOUS I HATE TO SELL IT!
BUT IT'S YOURS FOR ONE DOLLAR!
ONE DOLLAR?
OF ALL THE NERVE! I SHOULD TELL BETTY WHOSE IT IS!
BUT I'M NOT GOING TO BE PETTY AT OUR CLASS FUNCTION!
RIVERDALE FLEA
THERE YOU GO, MA'AM! GET IT APPRAISED! YOU MAY BE SURPRISED!
YEAH! IT'S PROBABLY WORTH FIVE CENTS!
THAT'S NOT WHAT I MEANT, BETTY!
EXCUSE ME FOR LIVING!
IT'S JUST A TRAGEDY THAT SOME PEOPLE ARE SO FORGETFUL! AND DON'T KNOW GOOD JEWELRY AT THE SAME TIME!
WHAT ARE YOU GETTING AT?
HEY, GIRLS! THE MONEY'S GOING TO CHARITY, BUT YOU DON'T HAVE TO SELL YOUR PERSONAL POSSESSIONS!
HUH?
4

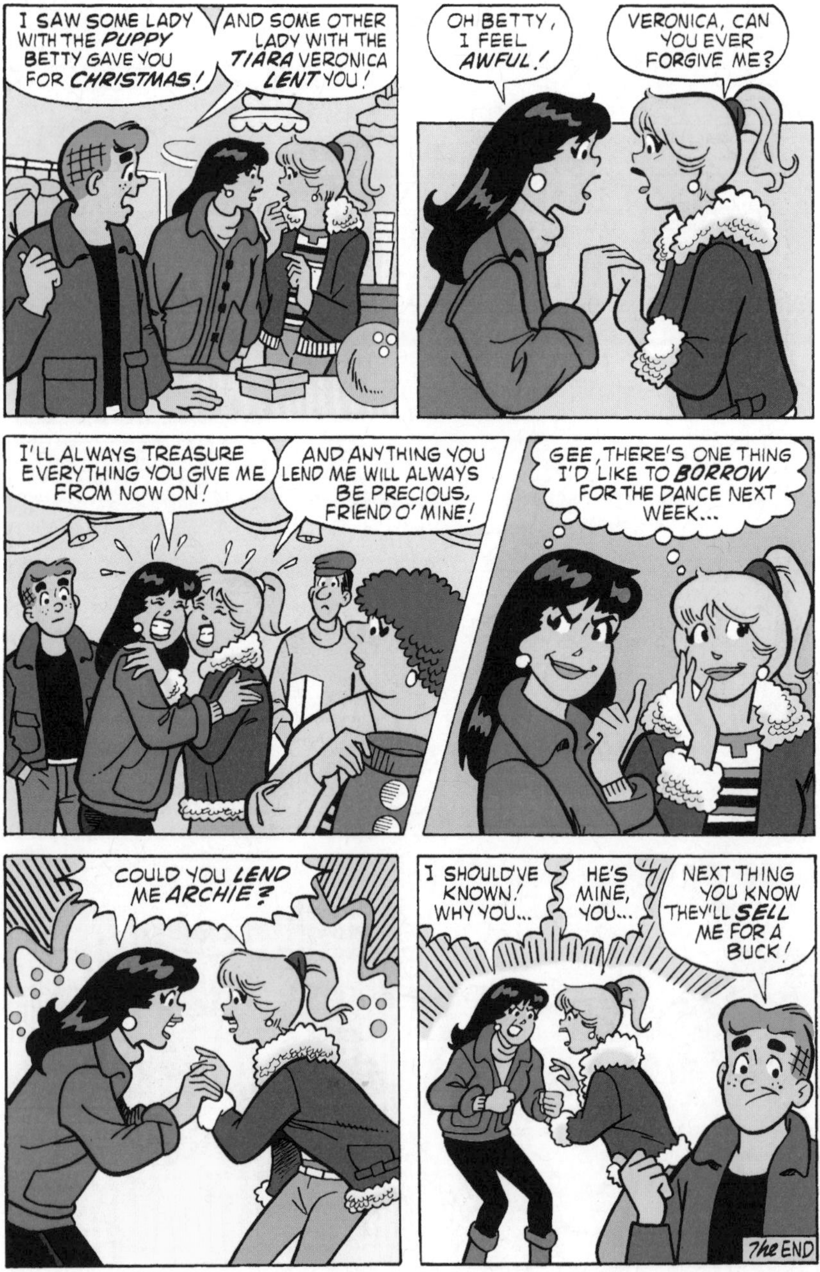

I SAW SOME LADY WITH THE PUPPY BETTY GAVE YOU FOR CHRISTMAS!
AND SOME OTHER LADY WITH THE TIARA VERONICA LENT YOU!
OH BETTY, I FEEL AWFUL!
VERONICA, CAN YOU EVER FORGIVE ME?
I'LL ALWAYS TREASURE EVERYTHING YOU GIVE ME FROM NOW ON!
AND ANYTHING YOU LEND ME WILL ALWAYS BE PRECIOUS, FRIEND O' MINE!
GEE, THERE'S ONE THING I'D LIKE TO BORROW FOR THE DANCE NEXT WEEK...
COULD YOU LEND ME ARCHIE?
I SHOULD'VE KNOWN! WHY YOU...
HE'S MINE, YOU...
NEXT THING YOU KNOW THEY'LL SELL ME FOR A BUCK!
The END

Betty and Veronica in "CLOTHES" MINDED!

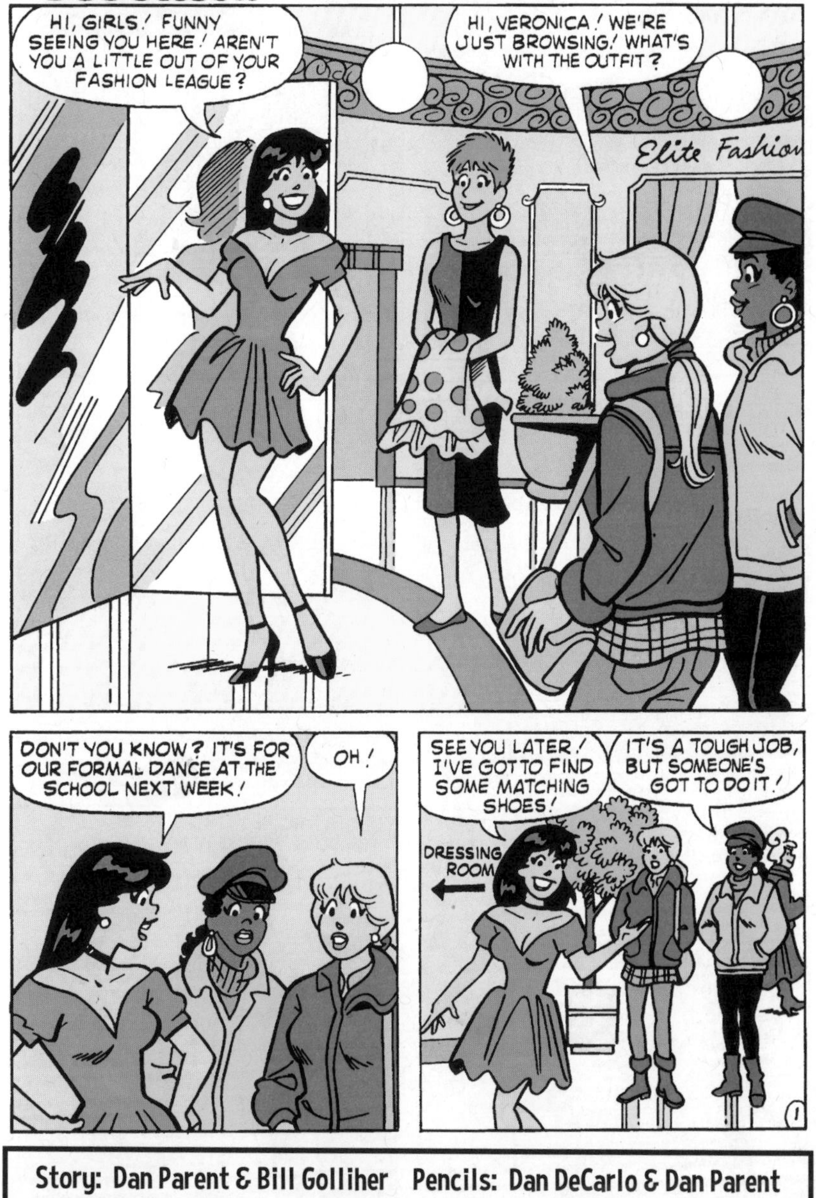
HI, GIRLS! FUNNY SEEING YOU HERE! AREN'T YOU A LITTLE OUT OF YOUR FASHION LEAGUE?
HI, VERONICA! WE'RE JUST BROWSING! WHAT'S WITH THE OUTFIT?
Elite Fashion
DON'T YOU KNOW? IT'S FOR OUR FORMAL DANCE AT THE SCHOOL NEXT WEEK!
OH!
SEE YOU LATER! I'VE GOT TO FIND SOME MATCHING SHOES!
IT'S A TOUGH JOB, BUT SOMEONE'S GOT TO DO IT!
DRESSING ROOM
1

Story: Dan Parent & Bill Golliher Pencils: Dan DeCarlo & Dan Parent
Inks: Henry Scarpelli Letters: Bill Yoshida Colors: Barry Grossman

Originally printed in BETTY & VERONICA SPECTACULAR #3, May 1993

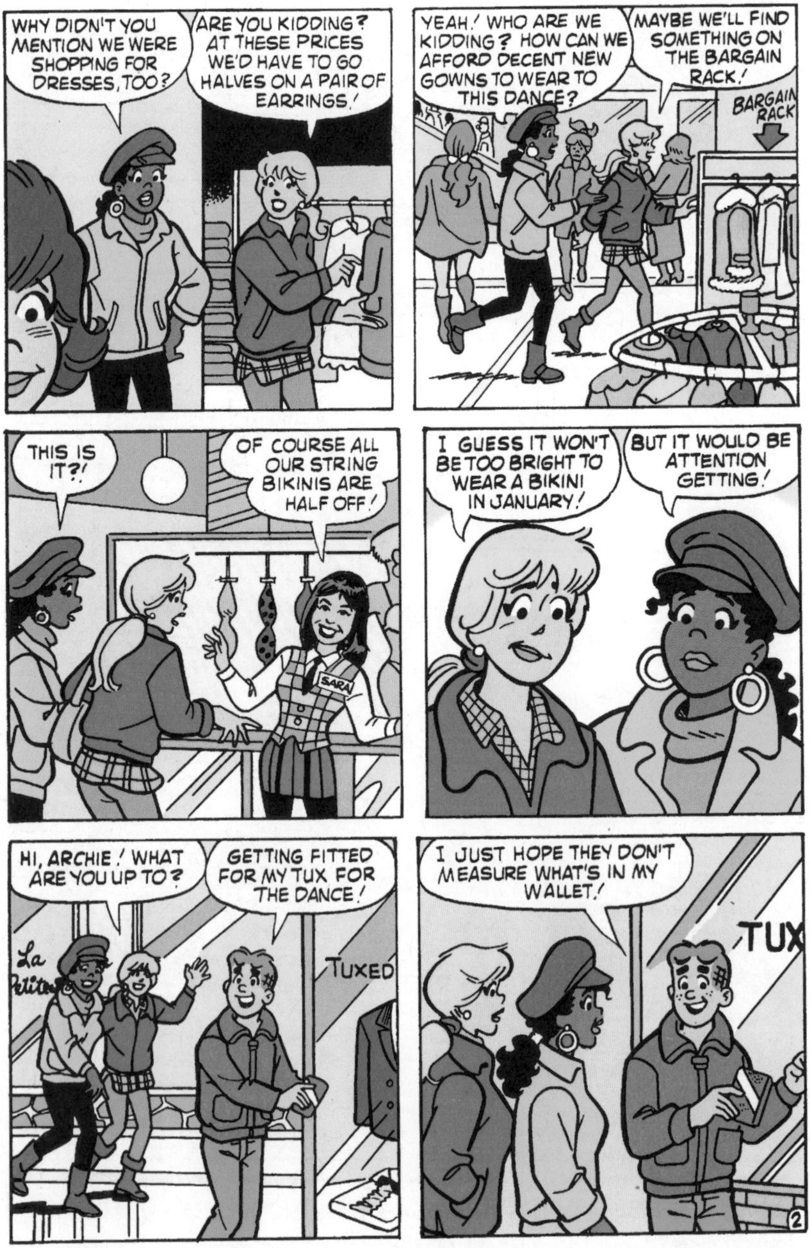
WHY DIDN'T YOU MENTION WE WERE SHOPPING FOR DRESSES, TOO?
ARE YOU KIDDING? AT THESE PRICES WE'D HAVE TO GO HALVES ON A PAIR OF EARRINGS!
YEAH! WHO ARE WE KIDDING? HOW CAN WE AFFORD DECENT NEW GOWNS TO WEAR TO THIS DANCE?
MAYBE WE'LL FIND SOMETHING ON THE BARGAIN RACK!
BARGAIN RACK
THIS IS IT?!
OF COURSE ALL OUR STRING BIKINIS ARE HALF OFF!
SARA
I GUESS IT WON'T BE TOO BRIGHT TO WEAR A BIKINI IN JANUARY!
BUT IT WOULD BE ATTENTION GETTING!
HI, ARCHIE! WHAT ARE YOU UP TO?
GETTING FITTED FOR MY TUX FOR THE DANCE!
La Petite
TUXED
I JUST HOPE THEY DON'T MEASURE WHAT'S IN MY WALLET!
TUX
2

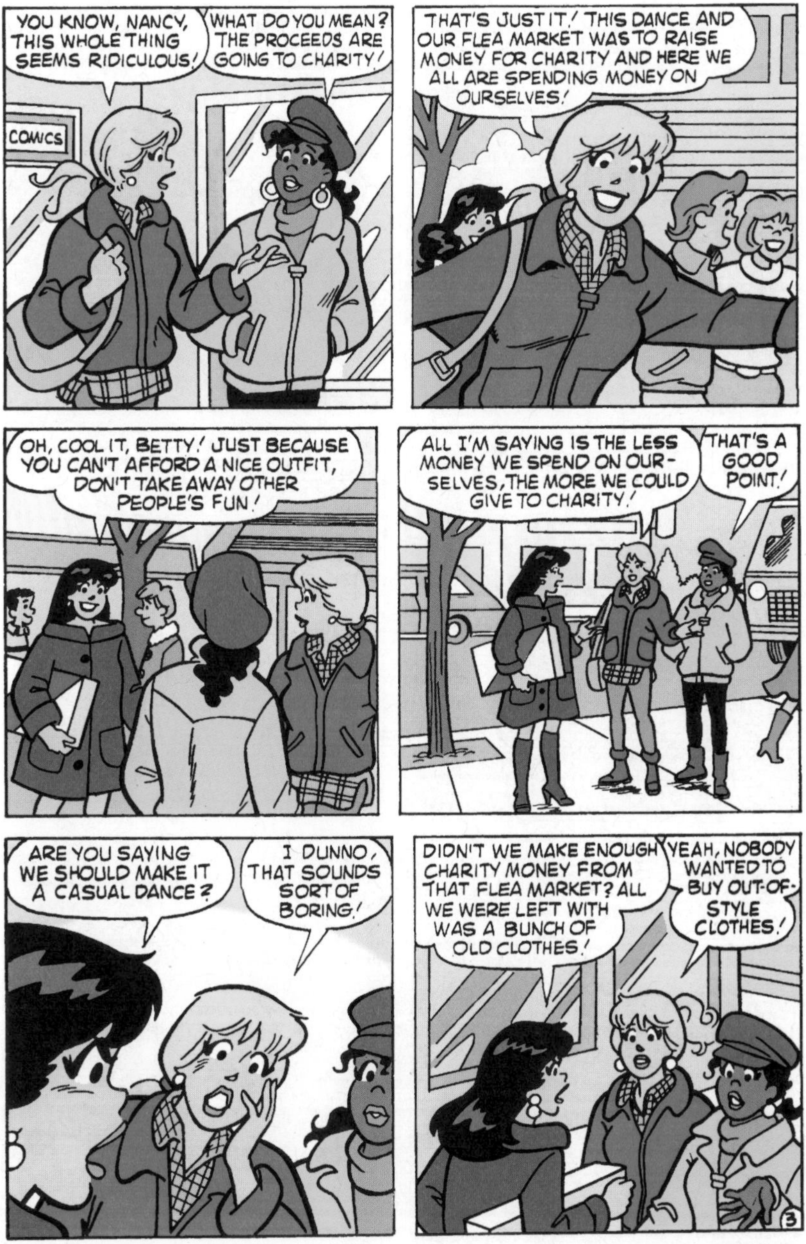
YOU KNOW, NANCY, THIS WHOLE THING SEEMS RIDICULOUS!
WHAT DO YOU MEAN? THE PROCEEDS ARE GOING TO CHARITY!
COMICS
THAT'S JUST IT! THIS DANCE AND OUR FLEA MARKET WAS TO RAISE MONEY FOR CHARITY AND HERE WE ALL ARE SPENDING MONEY ON OURSELVES!
OH, COOL IT, BETTY! JUST BECAUSE YOU CAN'T AFFORD A NICE OUTFIT, DON'T TAKE AWAY OTHER PEOPLE'S FUN!
ALL I'M SAYING IS THE LESS MONEY WE SPEND ON OUR-SELVES, THE MORE WE COULD GIVE TO CHARITY!
THAT'S A GOOD POINT!
ARE YOU SAYING WE SHOULD MAKE IT A CASUAL DANCE?
I DUNNO, THAT SOUNDS SORT OF BORING!
DIDN'T WE MAKE ENOUGH CHARITY MONEY FROM THAT FLEA MARKET? ALL WE WERE LEFT WITH WAS A BUNCH OF OLD CLOTHES!
YEAH, NOBODY WANTED TO BUY OUT-OF-STYLE CLOTHES!
3

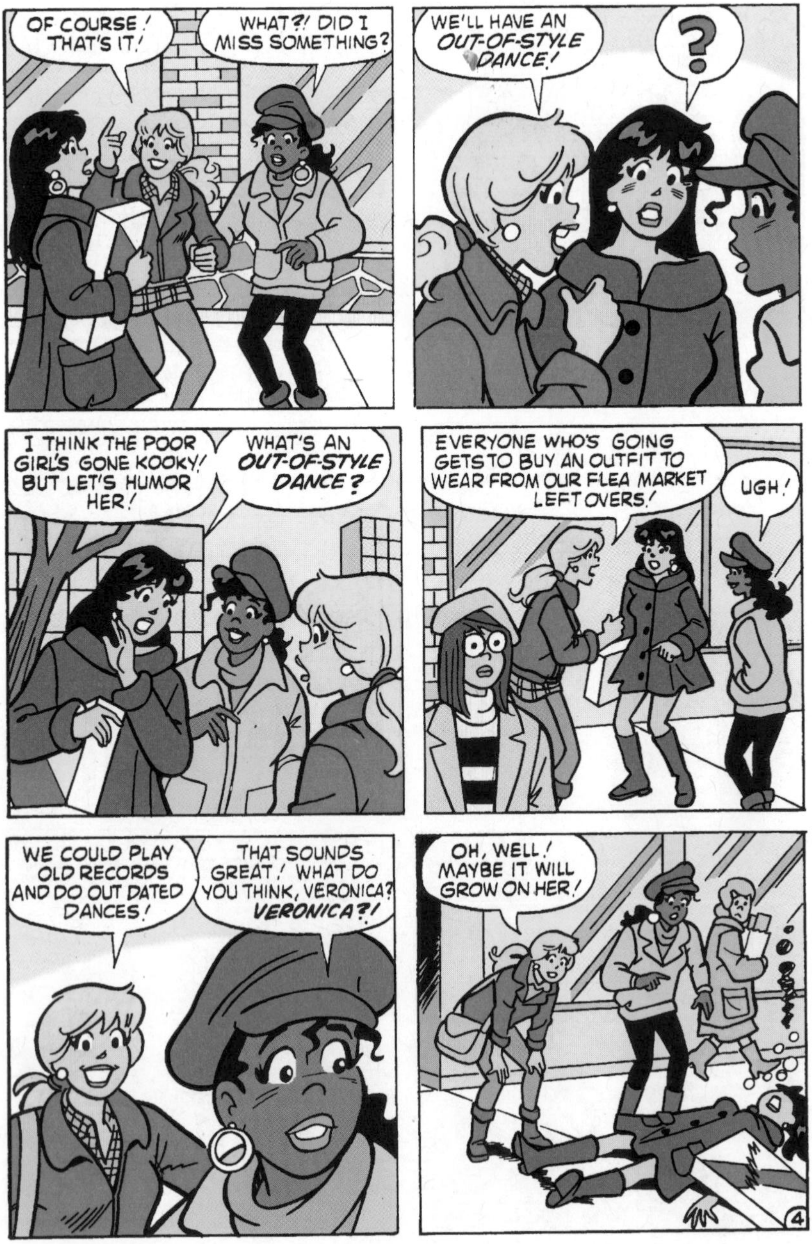

OF COURSE! THAT'S IT!
WHAT?! DID I MISS SOMETHING?
WE'LL HAVE AN OUT-OF-STYLE DANCE!
?
I THINK THE POOR GIRL'S GONE KOOKY! BUT LET'S HUMOR HER!
WHAT'S AN OUT-OF-STYLE DANCE?
EVERYONE WHO'S GOING GETS TO BUY AN OUTFIT TO WEAR FROM OUR FLEA MARKET LEFT OVERS!
UGH!
WE COULD PLAY OLD RECORDS AND DO OUT DATED DANCES!
THAT SOUNDS GREAT! WHAT DO YOU THINK, VERONICA? VERONICA?!
OH, WELL! MAYBE IT WILL GROW ON HER!
4

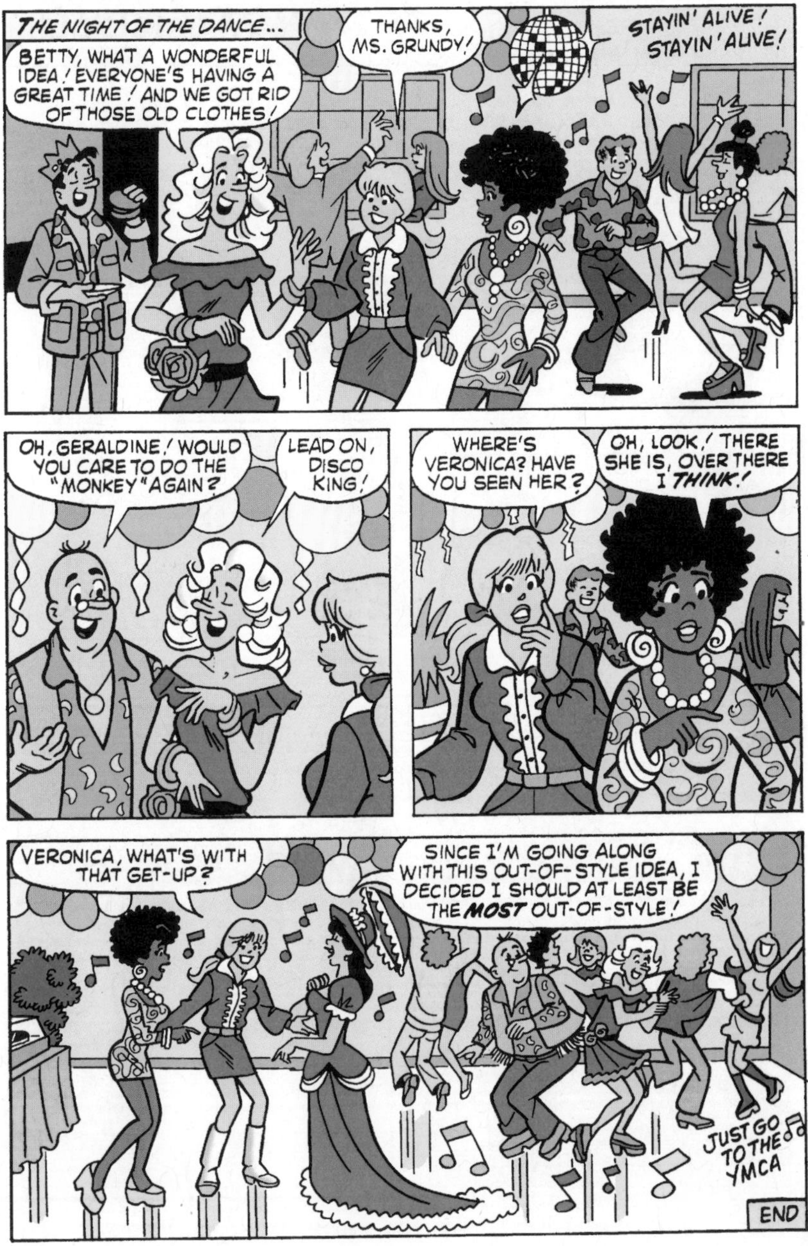
THE NIGHT OF THE DANCE...
BETTY, WHAT A WONDERFUL IDEA! EVERYONE'S HAVING A GREAT TIME! AND WE GOT RID OF THOSE OLD CLOTHES!
THANKS, MS. GRUNDY!
STAYIN' ALIVE! STAYIN' ALIVE!
OH, GERALDINE! WOULD YOU CARE TO DO THE "MONKEY" AGAIN?
LEAD ON, DISCO KING!
WHERE'S VERONICA? HAVE YOU SEEN HER?
OH, LOOK! THERE SHE IS, OVER THERE I THINK!
VERONICA, WHAT'S WITH THAT GET-UP?
SINCE I'M GOING ALONG WITH THIS OUT-OF-STYLE IDEA, I DECIDED I SHOULD AT LEAST BE THE MOST OUT-OF-STYLE!
JUST GO TO THE YMCA
END

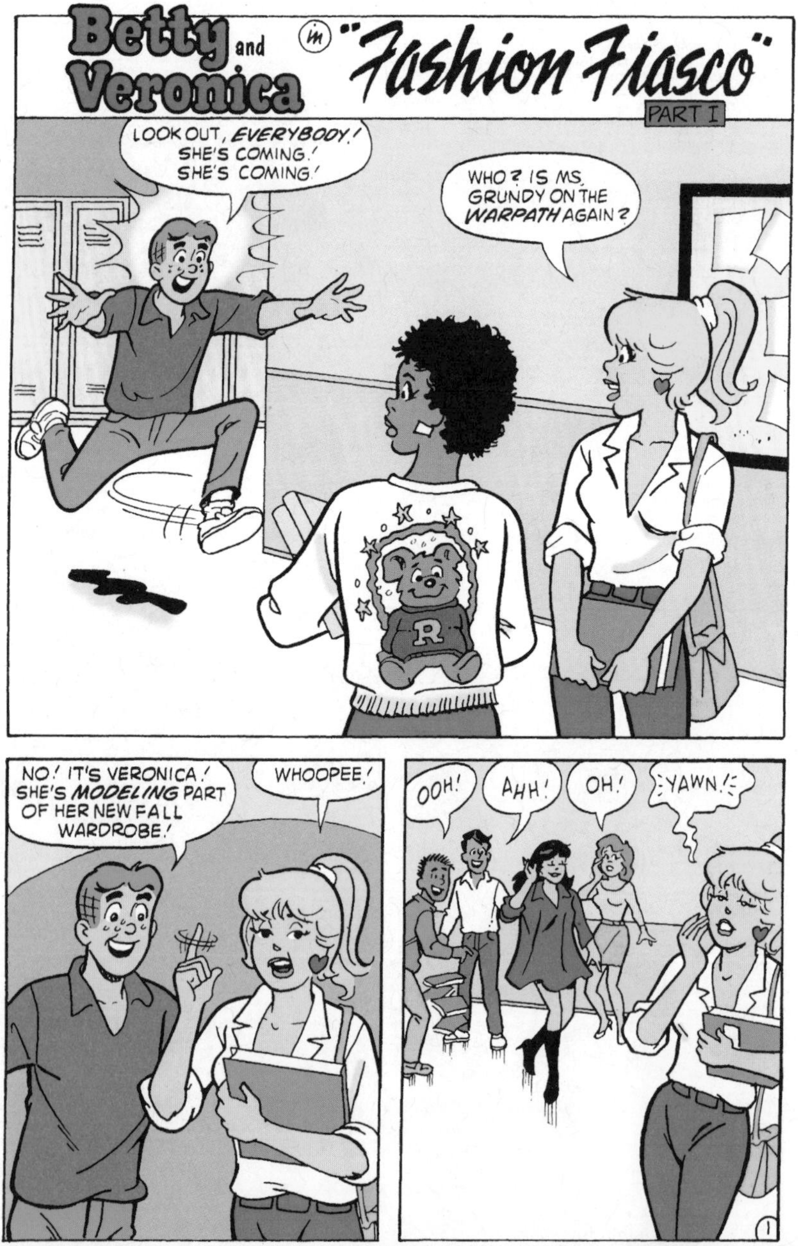
Betty and Veronica
in "Fashion Fiasco"
PART I
LOOK OUT, EVERYBODY! SHE'S COMING! SHE'S COMING!
WHO? IS MS. GRUNDY ON THE WARPATH AGAIN?
NO! IT'S VERONICA! SHE'S MODELING PART OF HER NEW FALL WARDROBE!
WHOOPEE!
OOH!
AHH!
OH!
YAWN!
1

Story: Dan Parent Pencils: Dan DeCarlo & Dan Parent
Inks: Alison Flood Letters: Bill Yoshida Colors: Barry Grossman

Originally printed in BETTY & VERONICA SPECTACULAR #4, July 1993

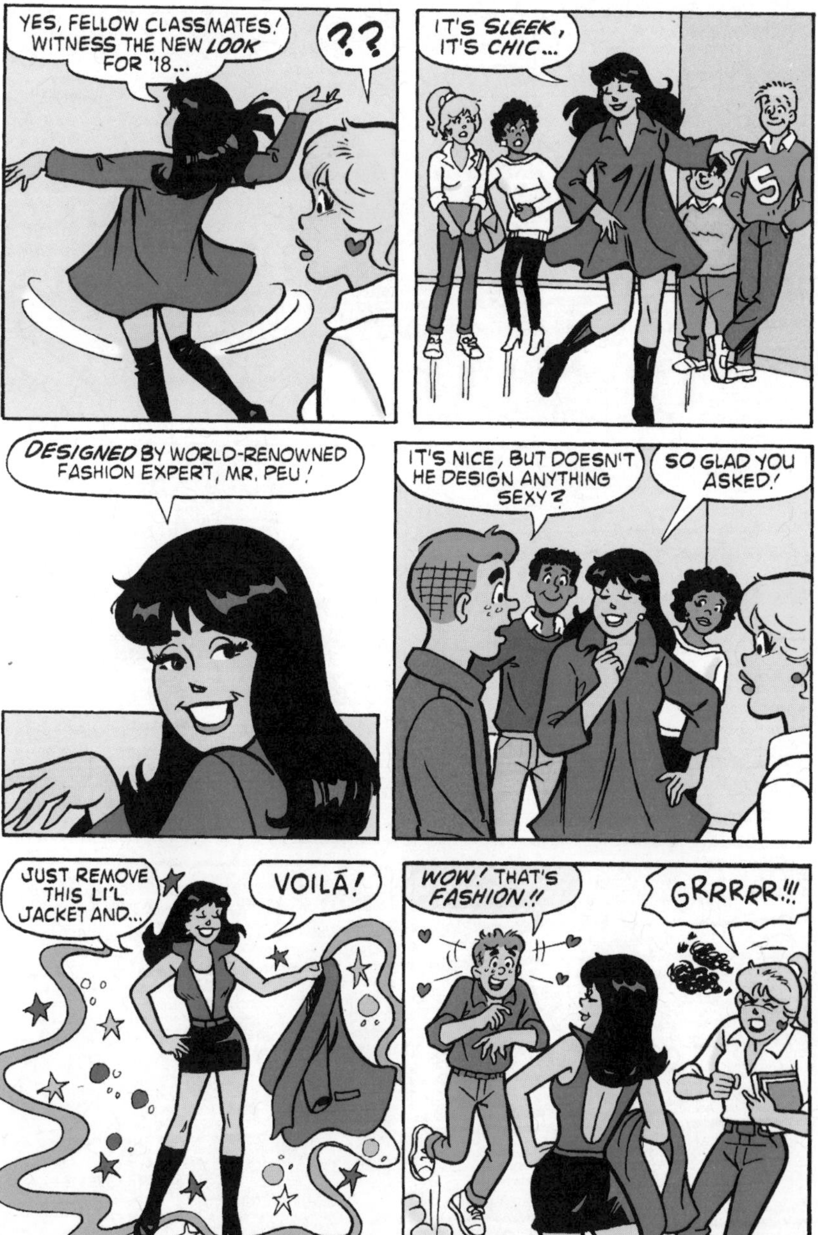
YES, FELLOW CLASSMATES! WITNESS THE NEW LOOK FOR '18...
??
IT'S SLEEK, IT'S CHIC...
DESIGNED BY WORLD-RENOWNED FASHION EXPERT, MR. PEU!
IT'S NICE, BUT DOESN'T HE DESIGN ANYTHING SEXY?
SO GLAD YOU ASKED!
JUST REMOVE THIS LI'L JACKET AND...
VOILÁ!
WOW! THAT'S FASHION!!
GRRRRR!!!
2

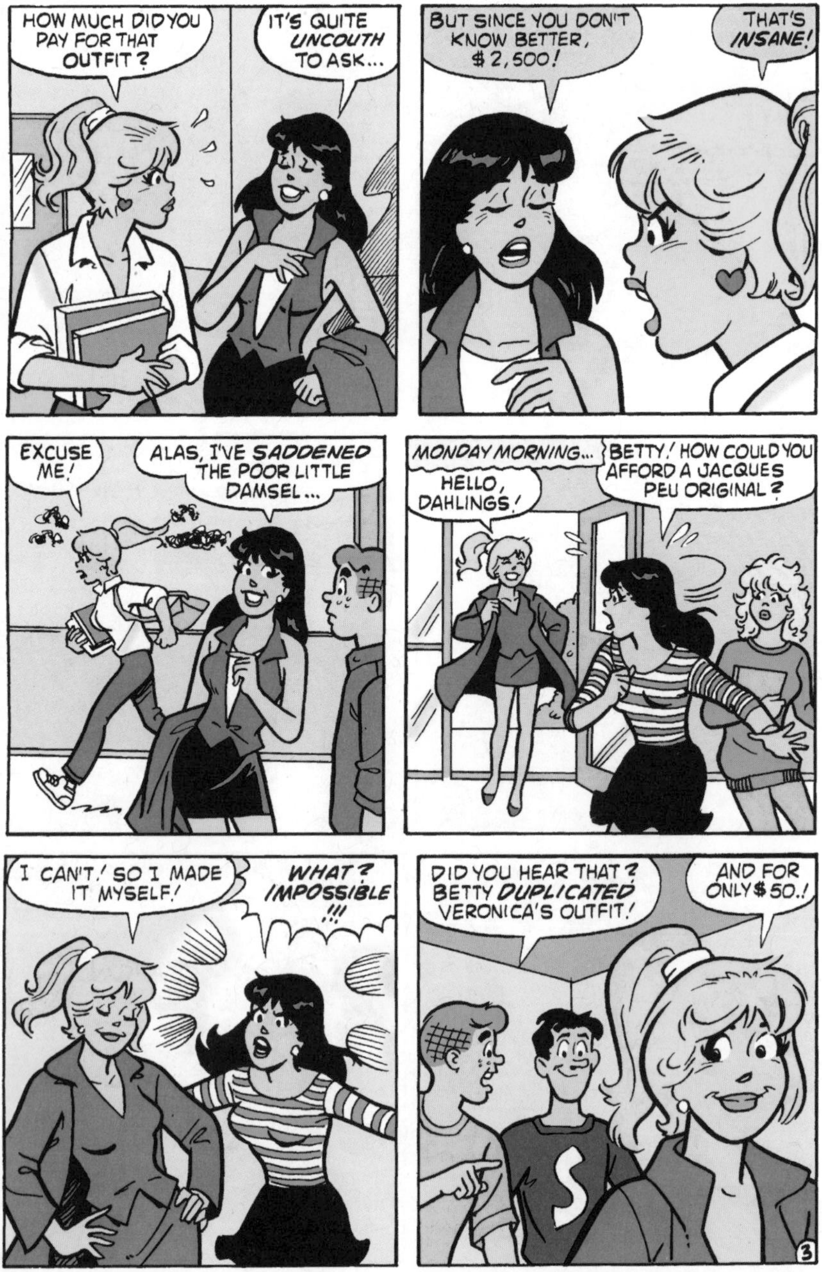
HOW MUCH DID YOU PAY FOR THAT OUTFIT?
IT'S QUITE UNCOUTH TO ASK...
BUT SINCE YOU DON'T KNOW BETTER, $2,500!
THAT'S INSANE!
EXCUSE ME!
ALAS, I'VE SADDENED THE POOR LITTLE DAMSEL...
MONDAY MORNING...
HELLO, DAHLINGS!
BETTY! HOW COULD YOU AFFORD A JACQUES PEU ORIGINAL?
I CAN'T! SO I MADE IT MYSELF!
WHAT? IMPOSSIBLE!!!
DID YOU HEAR THAT? BETTY DUPLICATED VERONICA'S OUTFIT!
AND FOR ONLY $50.!
3

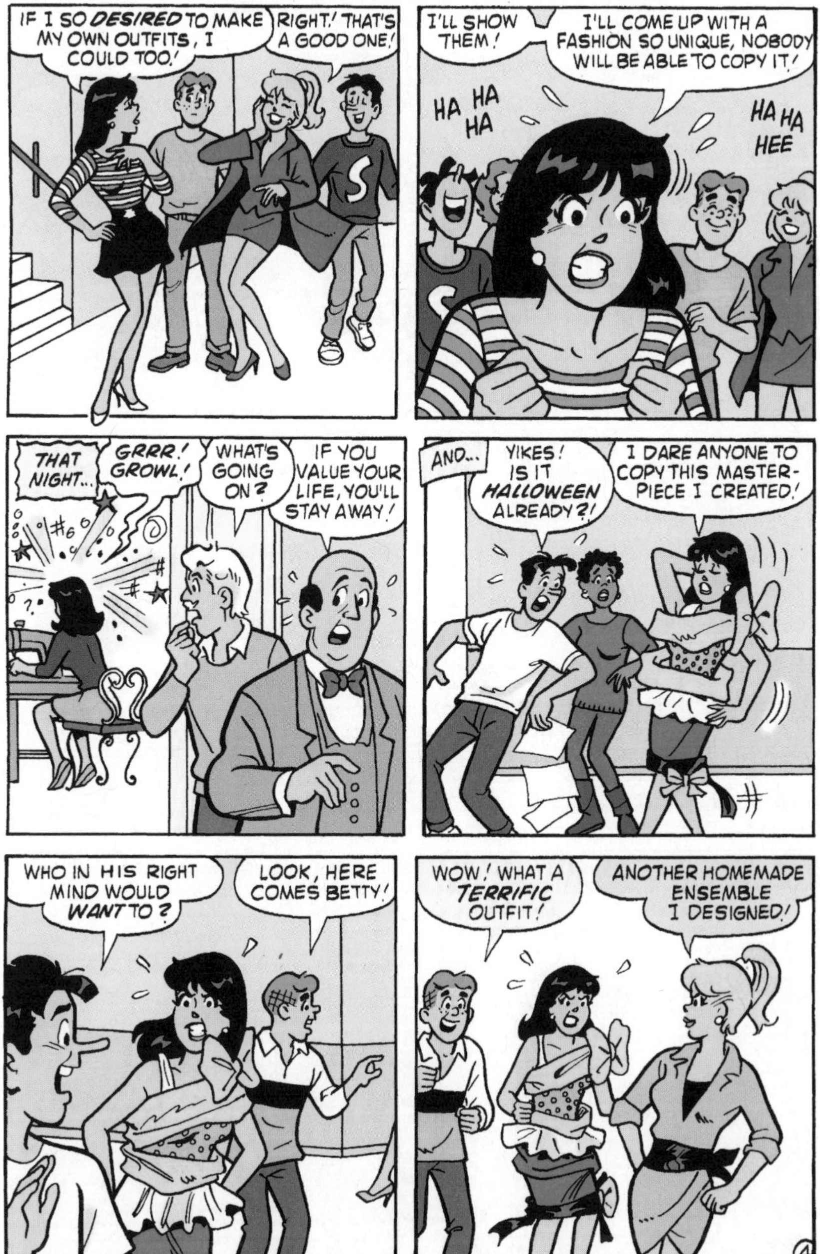
IF I SO DESIRED TO MAKE MY OWN OUTFITS, I COULD TOO!
RIGHT! THAT'S A GOOD ONE!
I'LL SHOW THEM!
I'LL COME UP WITH A FASHION SO UNIQUE, NOBODY WILL BE ABLE TO COPY IT!
HA HA HA
HA HA HEE
THAT NIGHT...
GRRR! GROWL!
WHAT'S GOING ON?
IF YOU VALUE YOUR LIFE, YOU'LL STAY AWAY!
AND...
YIKES! IS IT HALLOWEEN ALREADY?!
I DARE ANYONE TO COPY THIS MASTER-PIECE I CREATED!
WHO IN HIS RIGHT MIND WOULD WANT TO?
LOOK, HERE COMES BETTY!
WOW! WHAT A TERRIFIC OUTFIT!
ANOTHER HOMEMADE ENSEMBLE I DESIGNED!
4

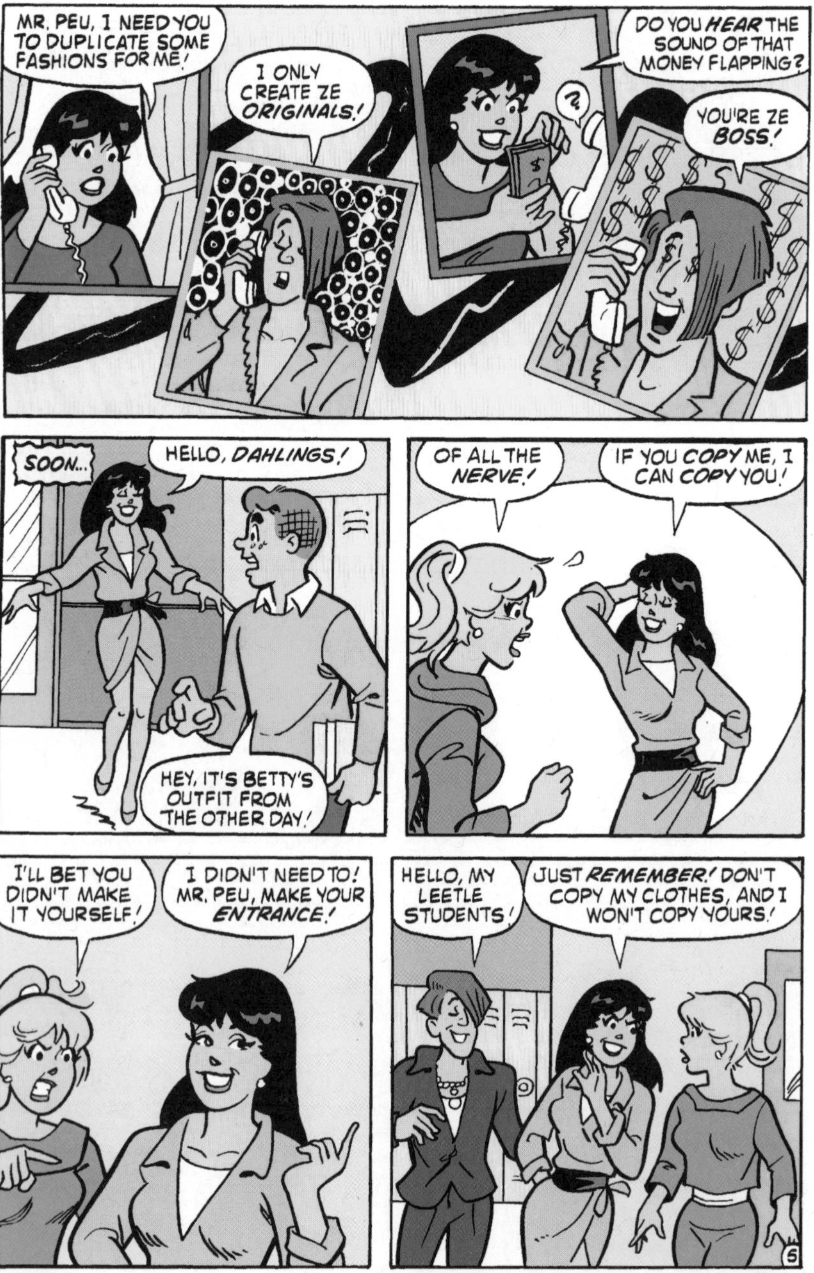
MR. PEU, I NEED YOU TO DUPLICATE SOME FASHIONS FOR ME!
I ONLY CREATE ZE ORIGINALS!
?
DO YOU HEAR THE SOUND OF THAT MONEY FLAPPING?
YOU'RE ZE BOSS!
SOON...
HELLO, DAHLINGS!
HEY, IT'S BETTY'S OUTFIT FROM THE OTHER DAY!
OF ALL THE NERVE!
IF YOU COPY ME, I CAN COPY YOU!
I'LL BET YOU DIDN'T MAKE IT YOURSELF!
I DIDN'T NEED TO! MR. PEU, MAKE YOUR ENTRANCE!
HELLO, MY LEETLE STUDENTS!
JUST REMEMBER! DON'T COPY MY CLOTHES, AND I WON'T COPY YOURS!
5

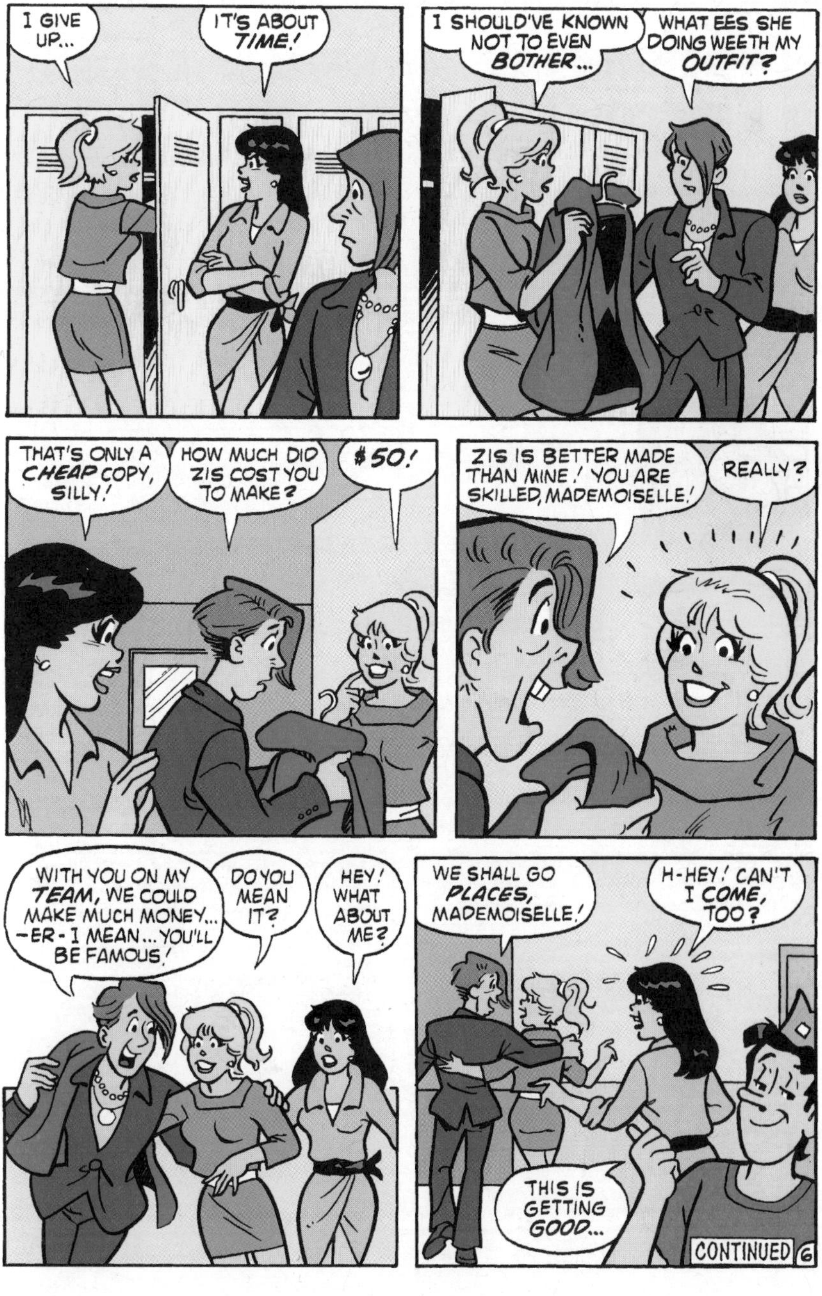
I GIVE UP...
IT'S ABOUT TIME!
I SHOULD'VE KNOWN NOT TO EVEN BOTHER...
WHAT EES SHE DOING WEETH MY OUTFIT?
THAT'S ONLY A CHEAP COPY, SILLY!
HOW MUCH DID ZIS COST YOU TO MAKE?
$50!
ZIS IS BETTER MADE THAN MINE! YOU ARE SKILLED, MADEMOISELLE!
REALLY?
WITH YOU ON MY TEAM, WE COULD MAKE MUCH MONEY... -ER- I MEAN... YOU'LL BE FAMOUS!
DO YOU MEAN IT?
HEY! WHAT ABOUT ME?
WE SHALL GO PLACES, MADEMOISELLE!
H-HEY! CAN'T I COME, TOO?
THIS IS GETTING GOOD...
CONTINUED 6

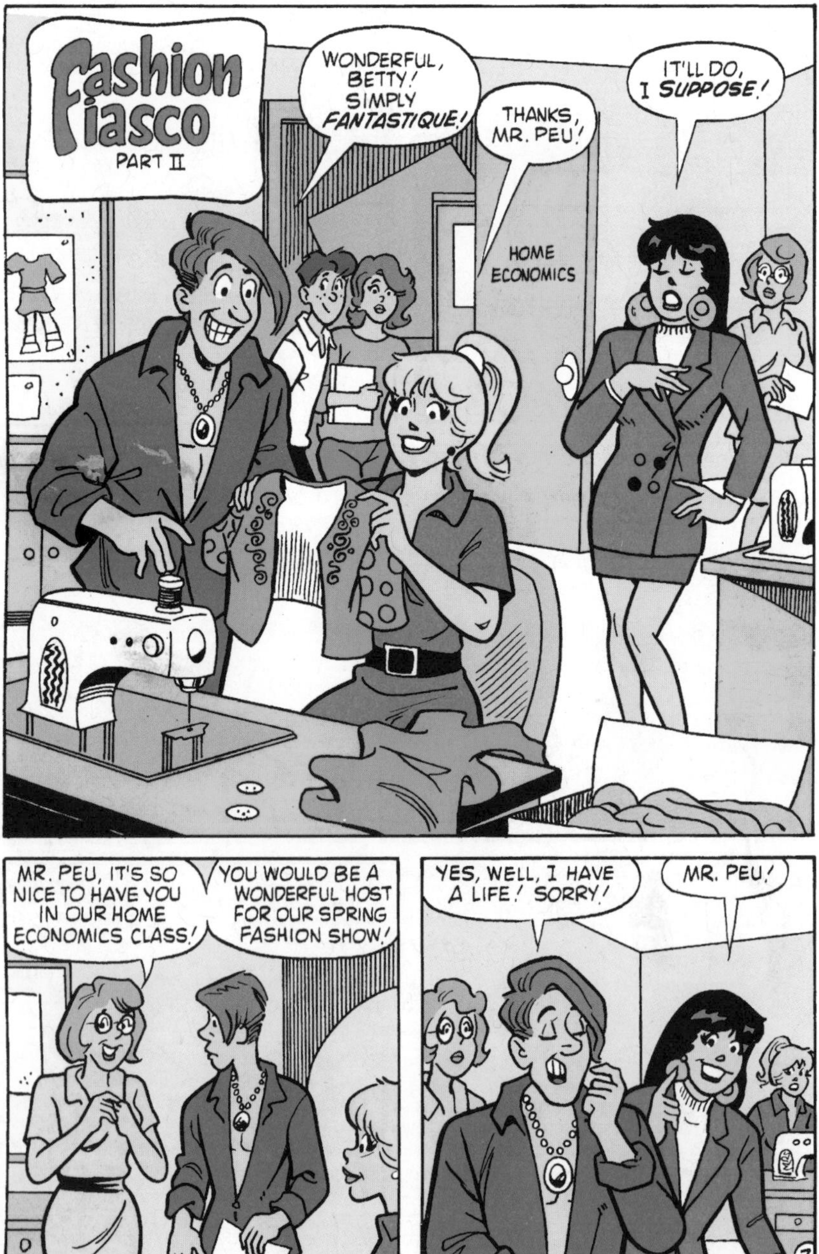
Fashion Fiasco
PART II
WONDERFUL, BETTY! SIMPLY FANTASTIQUE!
THANKS, MR. PEU!
IT'LL DO, I SUPPOSE!
HOME ECONOMICS
MR. PEU, IT'S SO NICE TO HAVE YOU IN OUR HOME ECONOMICS CLASS!
YOU WOULD BE A WONDERFUL HOST FOR OUR SPRING FASHION SHOW!
YES, WELL, I HAVE A LIFE! SORRY!
MR. PEU!
7

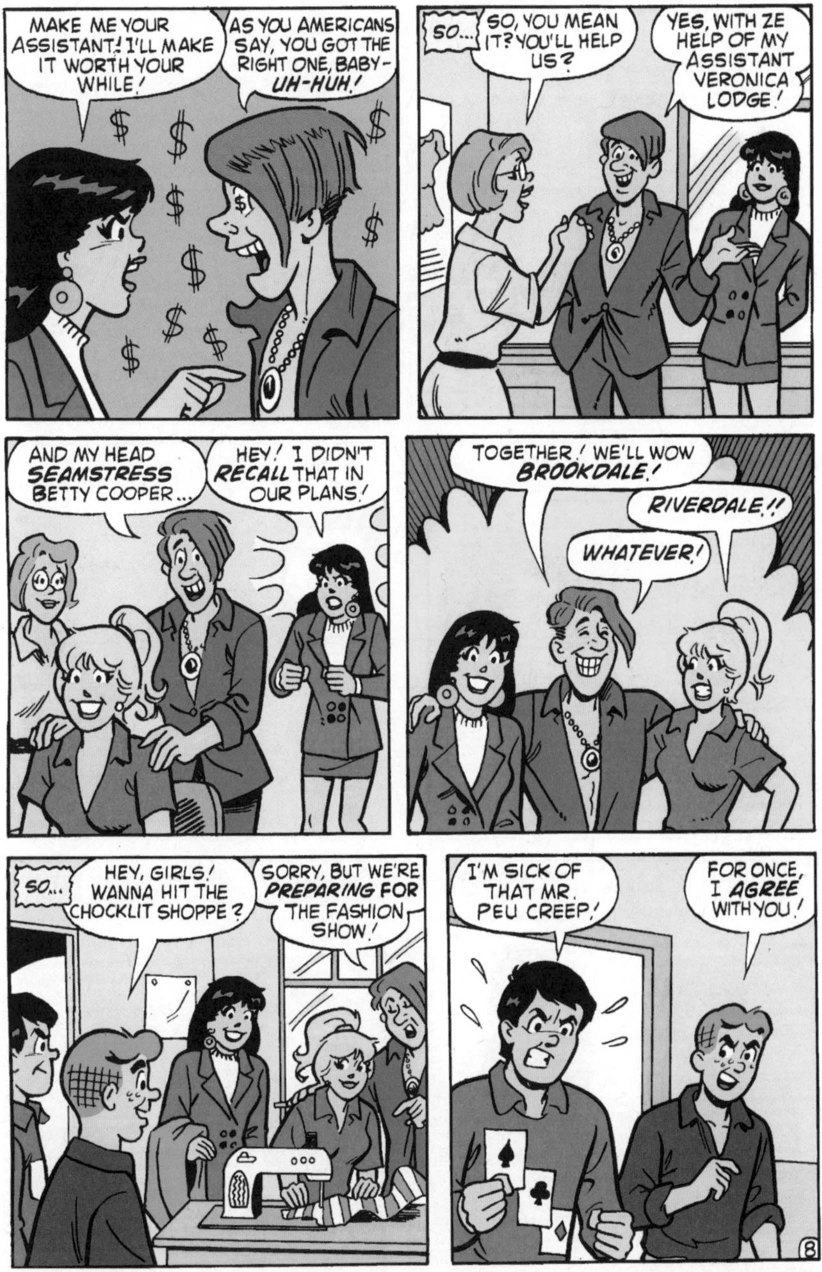
MAKE ME YOUR ASSISTANT! I'LL MAKE IT WORTH YOUR WHILE!
AS YOU AMERICANS SAY, YOU GOT THE RIGHT ONE, BABY- UH-HUH!
SO...
SO, YOU MEAN IT? YOU'LL HELP US?
YES, WITH ZE HELP OF MY ASSISTANT VERONICA LODGE!
AND MY HEAD SEAMSTRESS BETTY COOPER...
HEY! I DIDN'T RECALL THAT IN OUR PLANS!
TOGETHER! WE'LL WOW BROOKDALE!
RIVERDALE!!
WHATEVER!
SO...
HEY, GIRLS! WANNA HIT THE CHOCKLIT SHOPPE?
SORRY, BUT WE'RE PREPARING FOR THE FASHION SHOW!
I'M SICK OF THAT MR. PEU CREEP!
FOR ONCE, I AGREE WITH YOU!
8

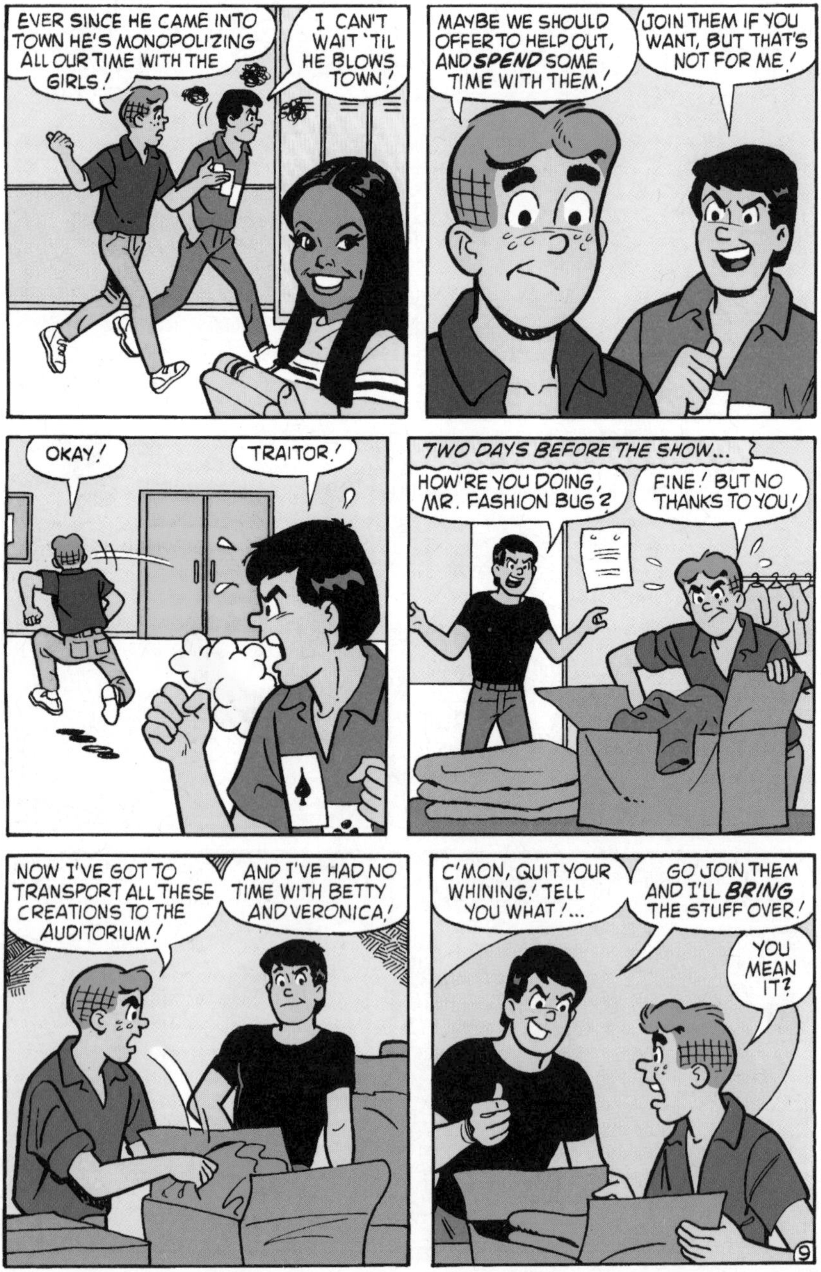
EVER SINCE HE CAME INTO TOWN HE'S MONOPOLIZING ALL OUR TIME WITH THE GIRLS!
I CAN'T WAIT 'TIL HE BLOWS TOWN!
MAYBE WE SHOULD OFFER TO HELP OUT, AND SPEND SOME TIME WITH THEM!
JOIN THEM IF YOU WANT, BUT THAT'S NOT FOR ME!
OKAY!
TRAITOR!
TWO DAYS BEFORE THE SHOW...
HOW'RE YOU DOING, MR. FASHION BUG?
FINE! BUT NO THANKS TO YOU!
NOW I'VE GOT TO TRANSPORT ALL THESE CREATIONS TO THE AUDITORIUM!
AND I'VE HAD NO TIME WITH BETTY AND VERONICA!
C'MON, QUIT YOUR WHINING! TELL YOU WHAT!...
GO JOIN THEM AND I'LL BRING THE STUFF OVER!
YOU MEAN IT?
9

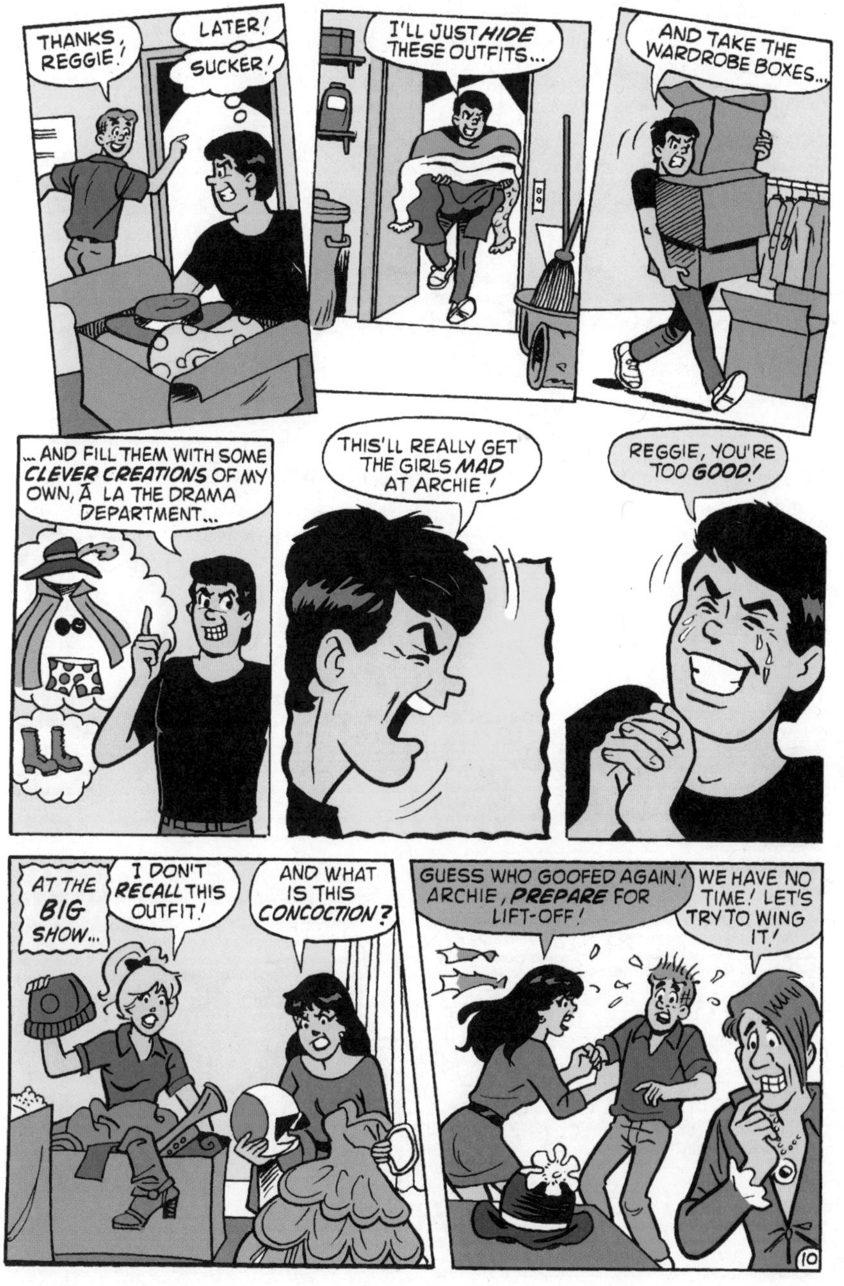
THANKS, REGGIE!
LATER!
SUCKER!
I'LL JUST HIDE THESE OUTFITS...
AND TAKE THE WARDROBE BOXES...
...AND FILL THEM WITH SOME CLEVER CREATIONS OF MY OWN, Ā LA THE DRAMA DEPARTMENT...
THIS'LL REALLY GET THE GIRLS MAD AT ARCHIE!
REGGIE, YOU'RE TOO GOOD!
AT THE BIG SHOW...
I DON'T RECALL THIS OUTFIT!
AND WHAT IS THIS CONCOCTION?
GUESS WHO GOOFED AGAIN! ARCHIE, PREPARE FOR LIFT-OFF!
WE HAVE NO TIME! LET'S TRY TO WING IT!
10

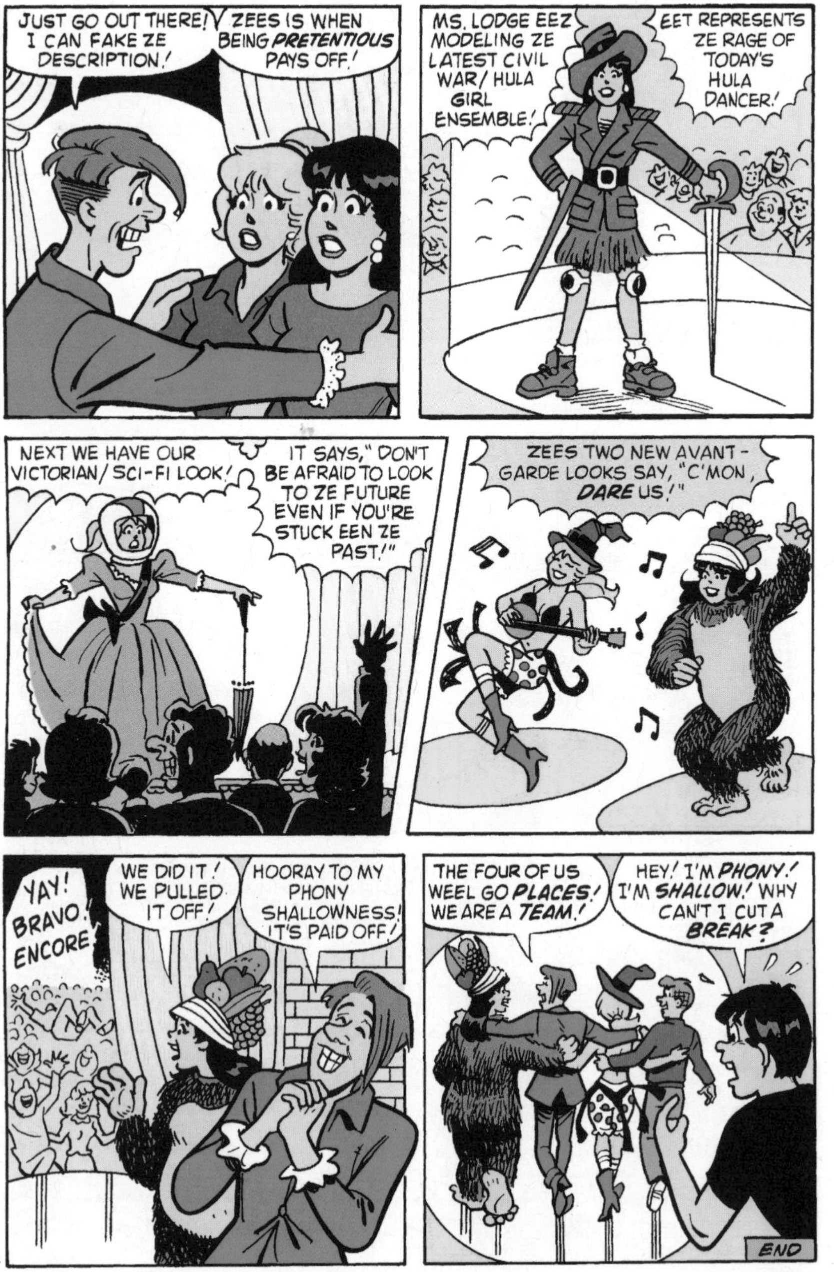
JUST GO OUT THERE! I CAN FAKE ZE DESCRIPTION!
ZEES IS WHEN BEING PRETENTIOUS PAYS OFF!
MS. LODGE EEZ MODELING ZE LATEST CIVIL WAR/ HULA GIRL ENSEMBLE!
EET REPRESENTS ZE RAGE OF TODAY'S HULA DANCER!
NEXT WE HAVE OUR VICTORIAN/ SCI-FI LOOK!
IT SAYS, "DON'T BE AFRAID TO LOOK TO ZE FUTURE EVEN IF YOU'RE STUCK EEN ZE PAST!"
ZEES TWO NEW AVANT-GARDE LOOKS SAY, "C'MON, DARE US!"
YAY! BRAVO! ENCORE!
WE DID IT! WE PULLED IT OFF!
HOORAY TO MY PHONY SHALLOWNESS! IT'S PAID OFF!
THE FOUR OF US WEEL GO PLACES! WE ARE A TEAM!
HEY! I'M PHONY! I'M SHALLOW! WHY CAN'T I CUT A BREAK?
END

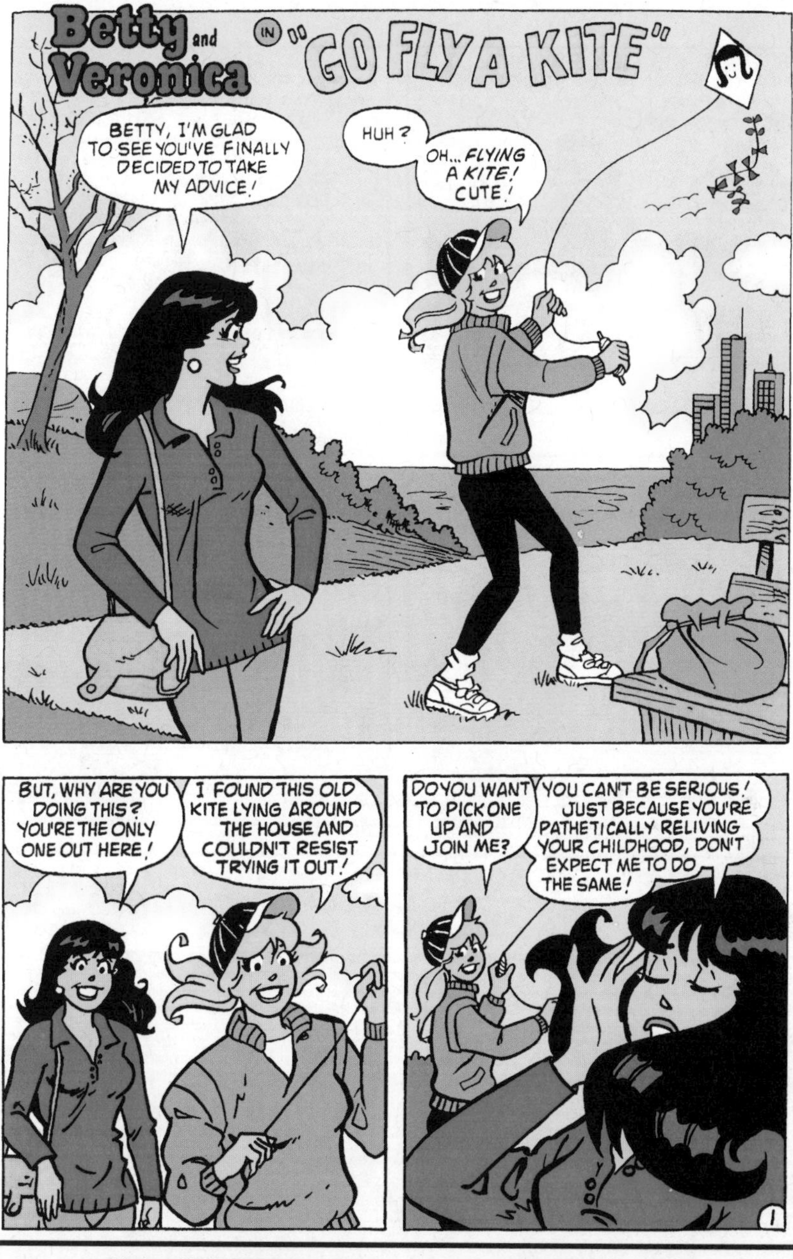
Betty and Veronica
IN "GO FLY A KITE"
BETTY, I'M GLAD TO SEE YOU'VE FINALLY DECIDED TO TAKE MY ADVICE!
HUH?
OH... FLYING A KITE! CUTE!
BUT, WHY ARE YOU DOING THIS? YOU'RE THE ONLY ONE OUT HERE!
I FOUND THIS OLD KITE LYING AROUND THE HOUSE AND COULDN'T RESIST TRYING IT OUT!
DO YOU WANT TO PICK ONE UP AND JOIN ME?
YOU CAN'T BE SERIOUS! JUST BECAUSE YOU'RE PATHETICALLY RELIVING YOUR CHILDHOOD, DON'T EXPECT ME TO DO THE SAME!
1

Story: Bill Golliher Pencils: Dan DeCarlo & Dan Parent
Inks: Alison Flood Letters: Bill Yoshida Colors: Barry Grossman

Originally printed in BETTY & VERONICA SPECTACULAR #4, July 1993

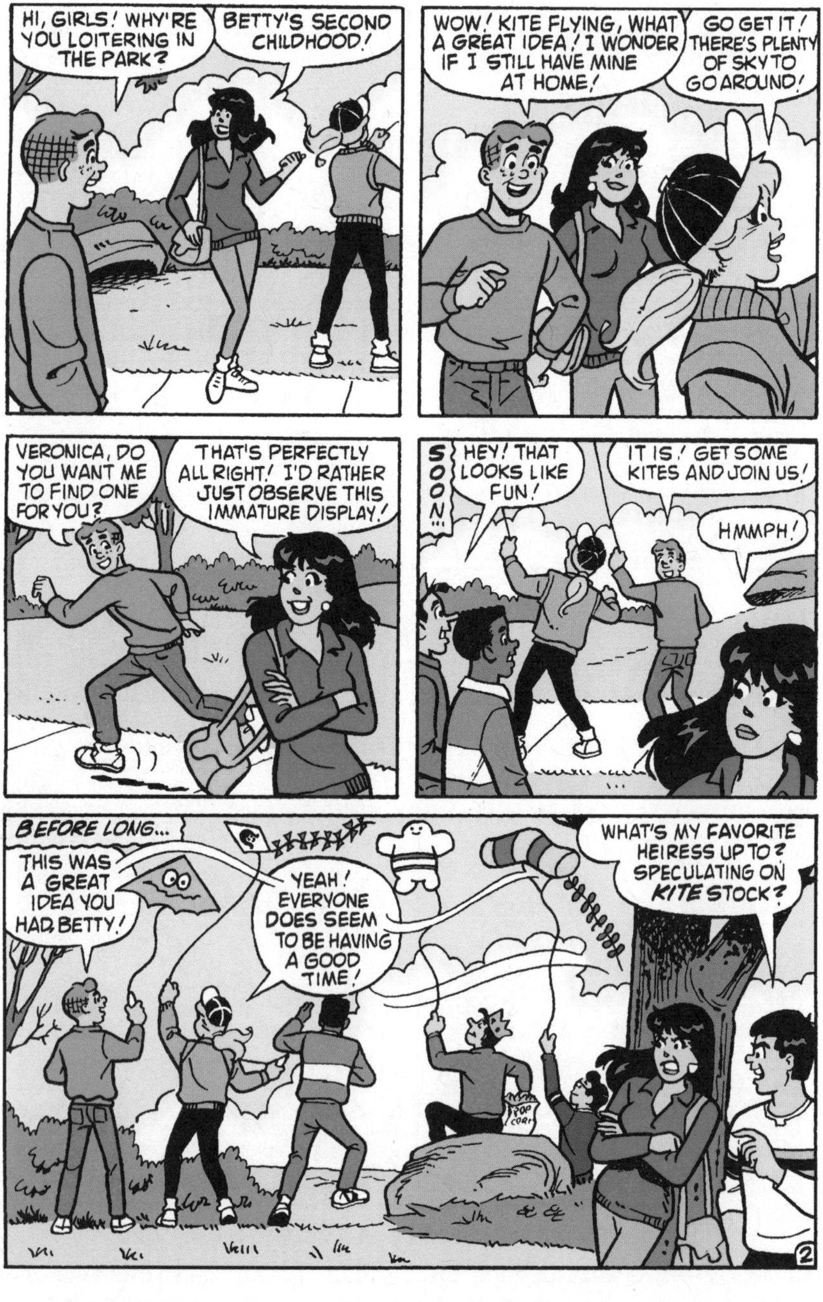

HI, GIRLS! WHY'RE YOU LOITERING IN THE PARK?
BETTY'S SECOND CHILDHOOD!
WOW! KITE FLYING, WHAT A GREAT IDEA! I WONDER IF I STILL HAVE MINE AT HOME!
GO GET IT! THERE'S PLENTY OF SKY TO GO AROUND!
VERONICA, DO YOU WANT ME TO FIND ONE FOR YOU?
THAT'S PERFECTLY ALL RIGHT! I'D RATHER JUST OBSERVE THIS IMMATURE DISPLAY!
SOON...
HEY! THAT LOOKS LIKE FUN!
IT IS! GET SOME KITES AND JOIN US!
HMMPH!
BEFORE LONG...
THIS WAS A GREAT IDEA YOU HAD, BETTY!
YEAH! EVERYONE DOES SEEM TO BE HAVING A GOOD TIME!
WHAT'S MY FAVORITE HEIRESS UP TO? SPECULATING ON KITE STOCK?
POP CORN
2

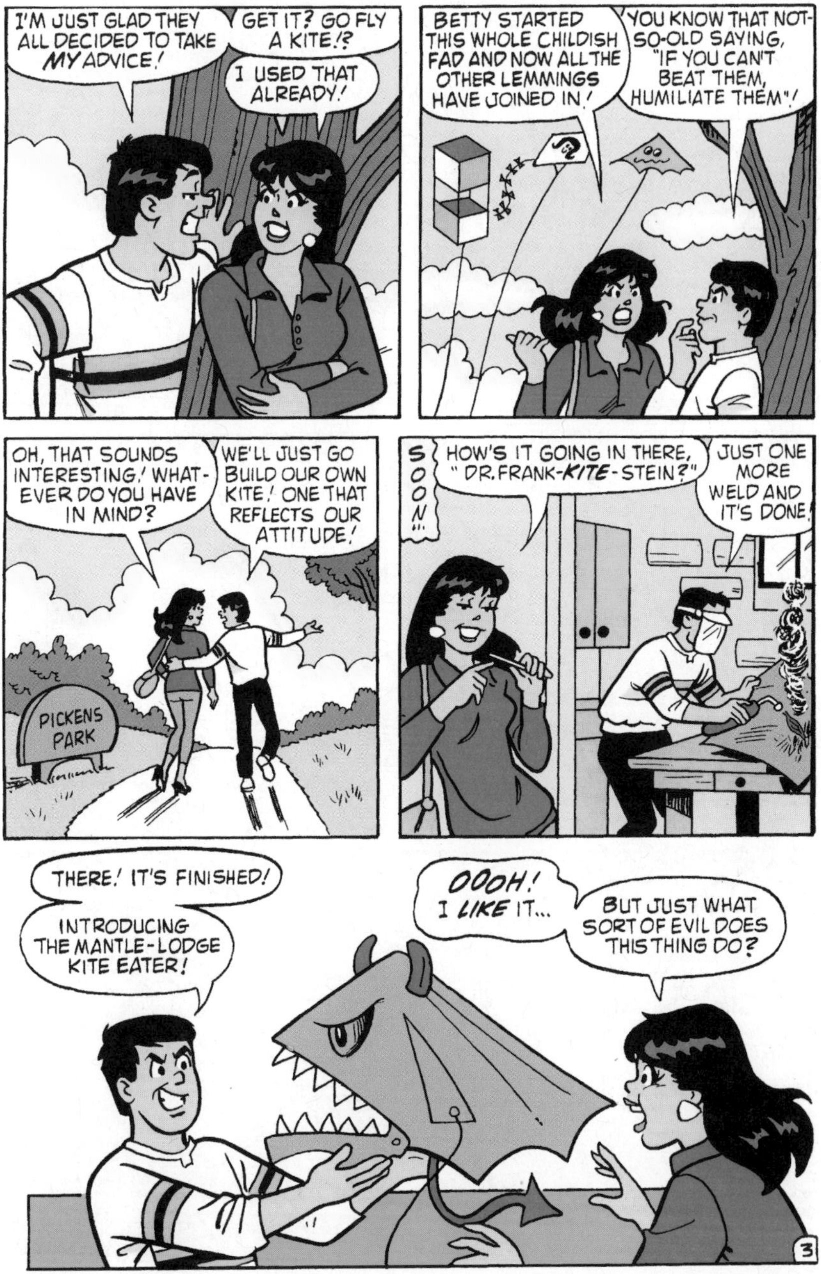
I'M JUST GLAD THEY ALL DECIDED TO TAKE MY ADVICE!
GET IT? GO FLY A KITE!?
I USED THAT ALREADY!
BETTY STARTED THIS WHOLE CHILDISH FAD AND NOW ALL THE OTHER LEMMINGS HAVE JOINED IN!
YOU KNOW THAT NOT-SO-OLD SAYING, "IF YOU CAN'T BEAT THEM, HUMILIATE THEM"!
OH, THAT SOUNDS INTERESTING! WHAT-EVER DO YOU HAVE IN MIND?
WE'LL JUST GO BUILD OUR OWN KITE! ONE THAT REFLECTS OUR ATTITUDE!
PICKENS PARK
SOON...
HOW'S IT GOING IN THERE, "DR. FRANK-KITE-STEIN?"
JUST ONE MORE WELD AND IT'S DONE!
THERE! IT'S FINISHED!
INTRODUCING THE MANTLE-LODGE KITE EATER!
OOOH! I LIKE IT...
BUT JUST WHAT SORT OF EVIL DOES THIS THING DO?
3

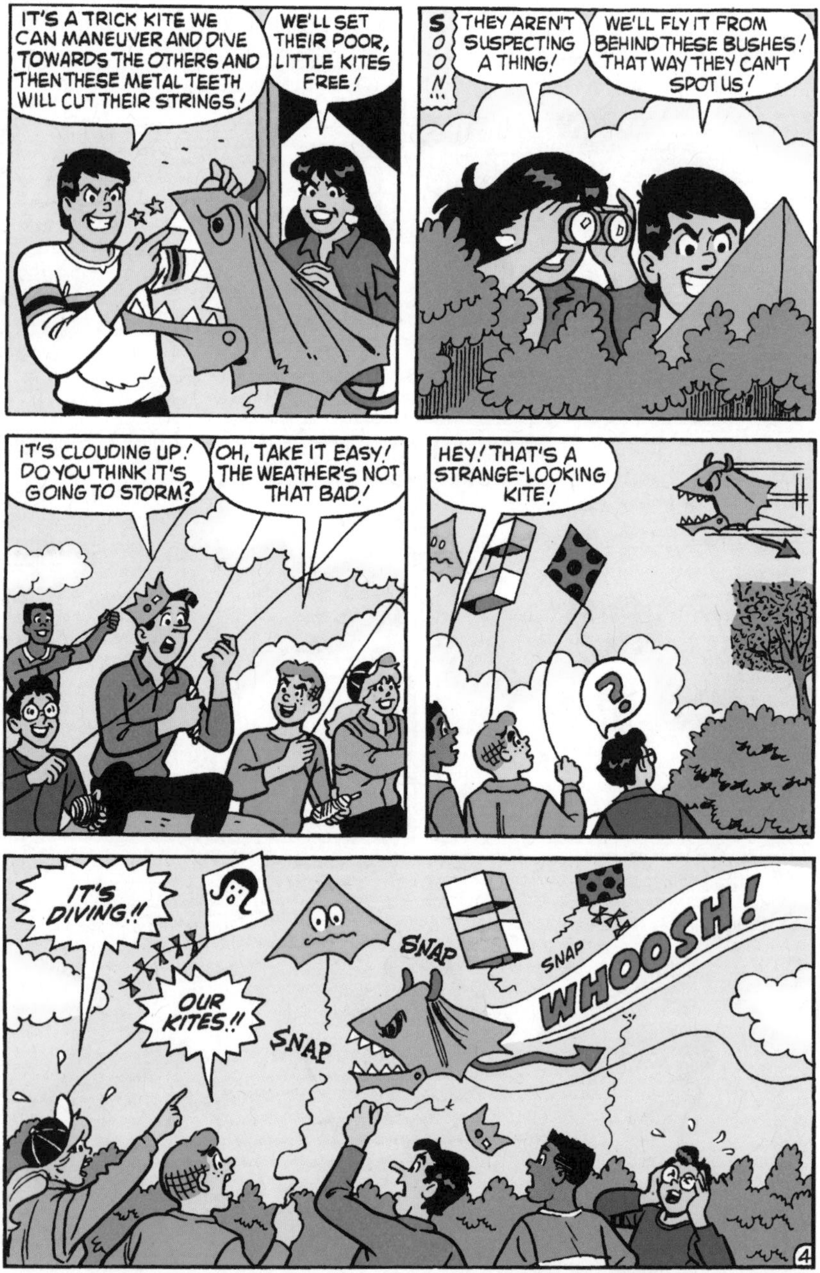
IT'S A TRICK KITE WE CAN MANEUVER AND DIVE TOWARDS THE OTHERS AND THEN THESE METAL TEETH WILL CUT THEIR STRINGS!
WE'LL SET THEIR POOR, LITTLE KITES FREE!
SOON...
THEY AREN'T SUSPECTING A THING!
WE'LL FLY IT FROM BEHIND THESE BUSHES! THAT WAY THEY CAN'T SPOT US!
IT'S CLOUDING UP! DO YOU THINK IT'S GOING TO STORM?
OH, TAKE IT EASY! THE WEATHER'S NOT THAT BAD!
HEY! THAT'S A STRANGE-LOOKING KITE!
?
IT'S DIVING!!
OUR KITES!!
SNAP
SNAP
SNAP
WHOOSH!
4

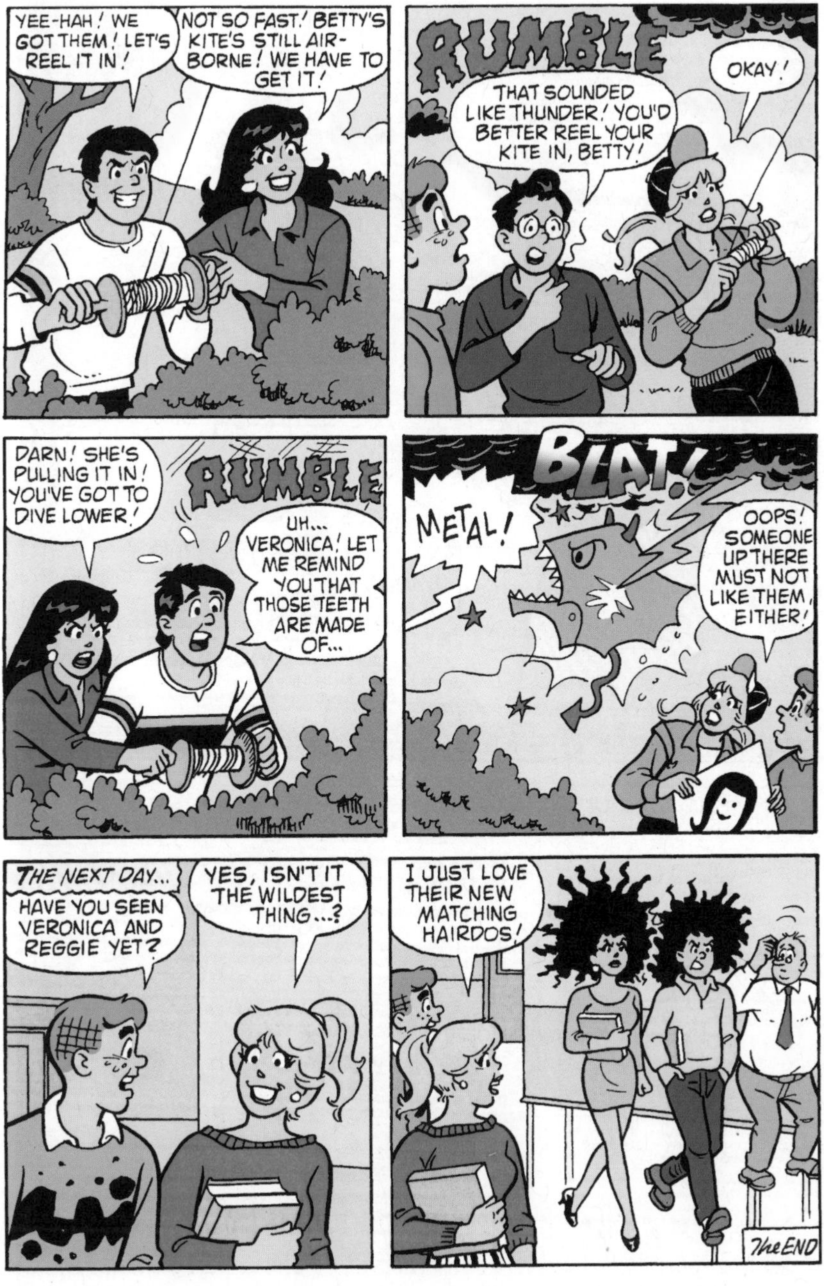
YEE-HAH! WE GOT THEM! LET'S REEL IT IN!
NOT SO FAST! BETTY'S KITE'S STILL AIR-BORNE! WE HAVE TO GET IT!
RUMBLE
THAT SOUNDED LIKE THUNDER! YOU'D BETTER REEL YOUR KITE IN, BETTY!
OKAY!
DARN! SHE'S PULLING IT IN! YOU'VE GOT TO DIVE LOWER!
RUMBLE
UH... VERONICA! LET ME REMIND YOU THAT THOSE TEETH ARE MADE OF...
BLAT!
METAL!
OOPS! SOMEONE UP THERE MUST NOT LIKE THEM, EITHER!
THE NEXT DAY...
HAVE YOU SEEN VERONICA AND REGGIE YET?
YES, ISN'T IT THE WILDEST THING...?
I JUST LOVE THEIR NEW MATCHING HAIRDOS!
The END

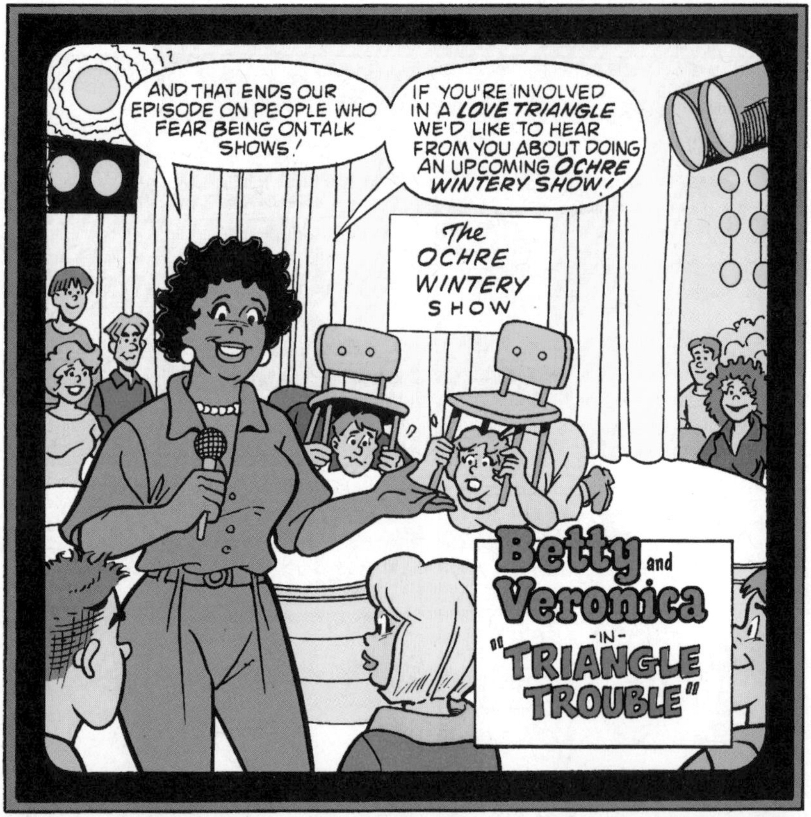
AND THAT ENDS OUR EPISODE ON PEOPLE WHO FEAR BEING ON TALK SHOWS!
IF YOU'RE INVOLVED IN A LOVE TRIANGLE WE'D LIKE TO HEAR FROM YOU ABOUT DOING AN UPCOMING OCHRE WINTERY SHOW!
The OCHRE WINTERY SHOW
Betty and Veronica -IN- "TRIANGLE TROUBLE"

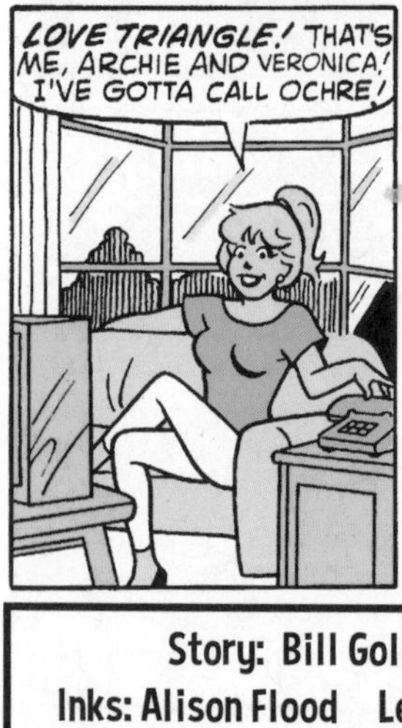
LOVE TRIANGLE! THAT'S ME, ARCHIE AND VERONICA! I'VE GOTTA CALL OCHRE!

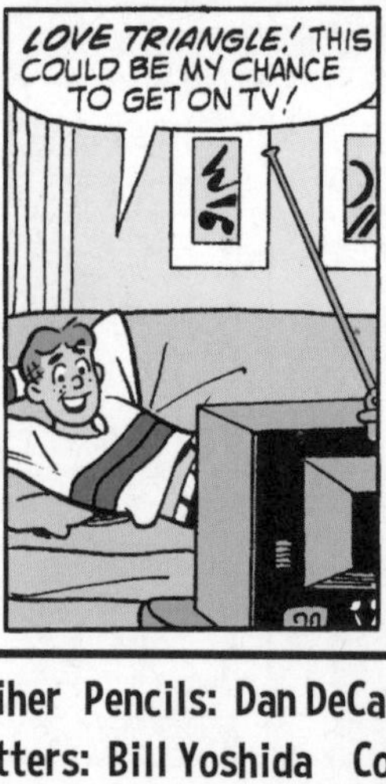
LOVE TRIANGLE! THIS COULD BE MY CHANCE TO GET ON TV!

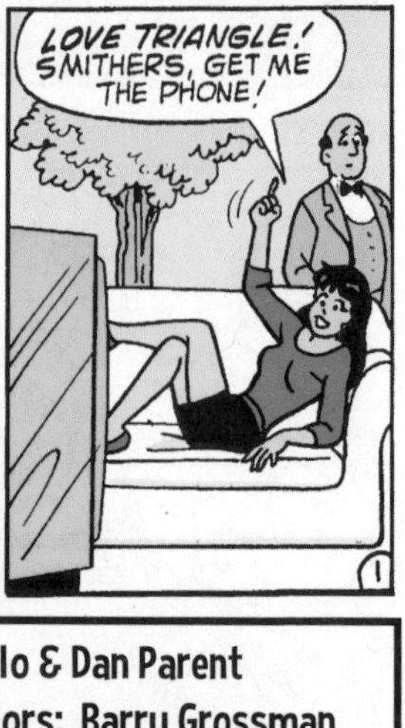
LOVE TRIANGLE! SMITHERS, GET ME THE PHONE!
1

Story: Bill Golliher Pencils: Dan DeCarlo & Dan Parent
Inks: Alison Flood Letters: Bill Yoshida Colors: Barry Grossman

Originally printed in BETTY & VERONICA SPECTACULAR #4, July 1993

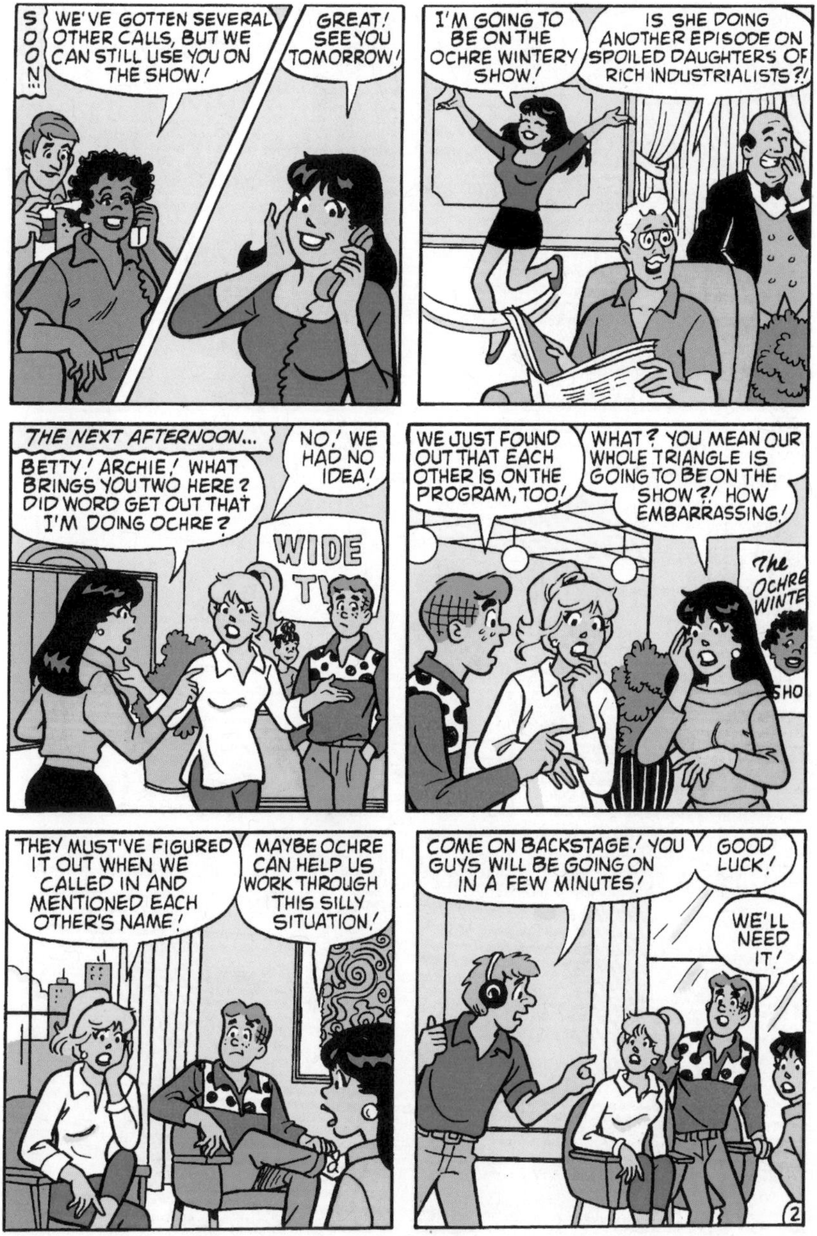
SOON!!!
WE'VE GOTTEN SEVERAL OTHER CALLS, BUT WE CAN STILL USE YOU ON THE SHOW!
GREAT! SEE YOU TOMORROW!
I'M GOING TO BE ON THE OCHRE WINTERY SHOW!
IS SHE DOING ANOTHER EPISODE ON SPOILED DAUGHTERS OF RICH INDUSTRIALISTS?!
THE NEXT AFTERNOON...
BETTY! ARCHIE! WHAT BRINGS YOU TWO HERE? DID WORD GET OUT THAT I'M DOING OCHRE?
NO! WE HAD NO IDEA!
WIDE TV
WE JUST FOUND OUT THAT EACH OTHER IS ON THE PROGRAM, TOO!
WHAT? YOU MEAN OUR WHOLE TRIANGLE IS GOING TO BE ON THE SHOW?! HOW EMBARRASSING!
The OCHRE WINTE
SHO
THEY MUST'VE FIGURED IT OUT WHEN WE CALLED IN AND MENTIONED EACH OTHER'S NAME!
MAYBE OCHRE CAN HELP US WORK THROUGH THIS SILLY SITUATION!
COME ON BACKSTAGE! YOU GUYS WILL BE GOING ON IN A FEW MINUTES!
GOOD LUCK!
WE'LL NEED IT!
2

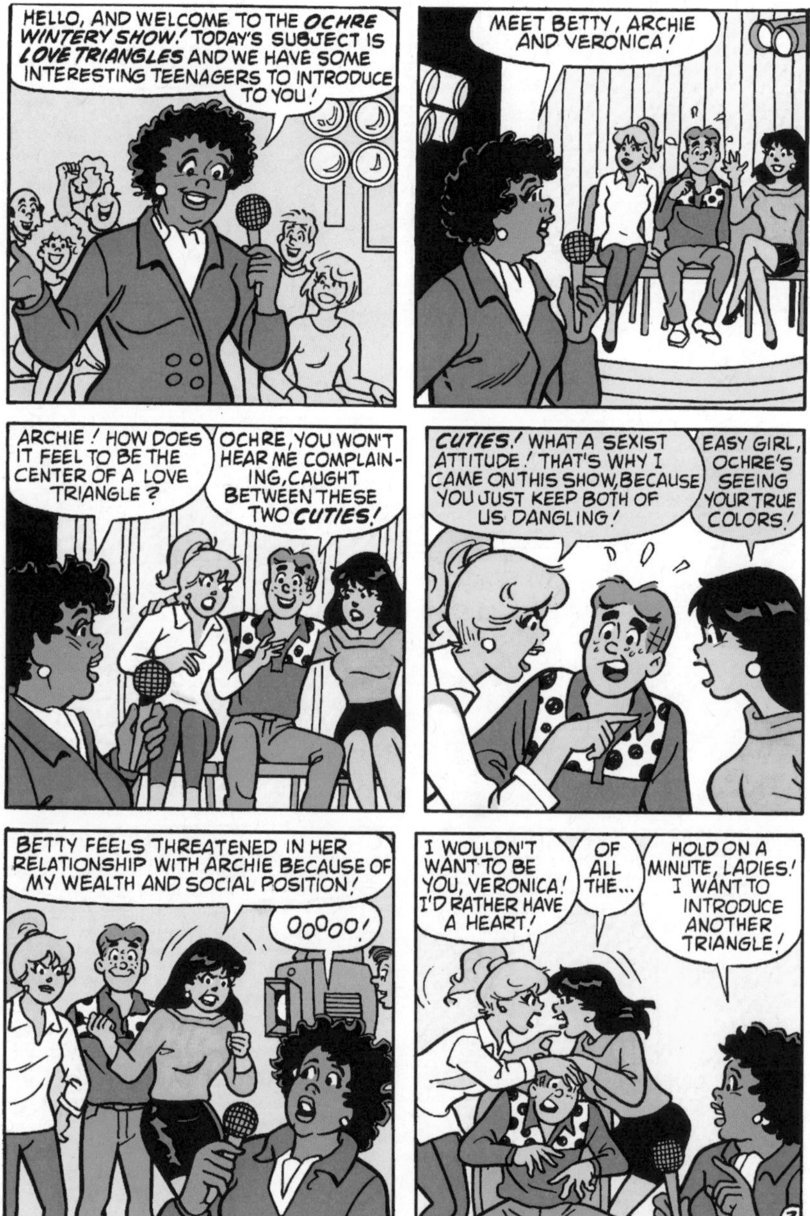
HELLO, AND WELCOME TO THE OCHRE WINTERY SHOW! TODAY'S SUBJECT IS LOVE TRIANGLES AND WE HAVE SOME INTERESTING TEENAGERS TO INTRODUCE TO YOU!
MEET BETTY, ARCHIE AND VERONICA!
ARCHIE! HOW DOES IT FEEL TO BE THE CENTER OF A LOVE TRIANGLE?
OCHRE, YOU WON'T HEAR ME COMPLAINING, CAUGHT BETWEEN THESE TWO CUTIES!
CUTIES! WHAT A SEXIST ATTITUDE! THAT'S WHY I CAME ON THIS SHOW, BECAUSE YOU JUST KEEP BOTH OF US DANGLING!
EASY GIRL, OCHRE'S SEEING YOUR TRUE COLORS!
BETTY FEELS THREATENED IN HER RELATIONSHIP WITH ARCHIE BECAUSE OF MY WEALTH AND SOCIAL POSITION!
OOOOO!
I WOULDN'T WANT TO BE YOU, VERONICA! I'D RATHER HAVE A HEART!
OF ALL THE...
HOLD ON A MINUTE, LADIES! I WANT TO INTRODUCE ANOTHER TRIANGLE!
3

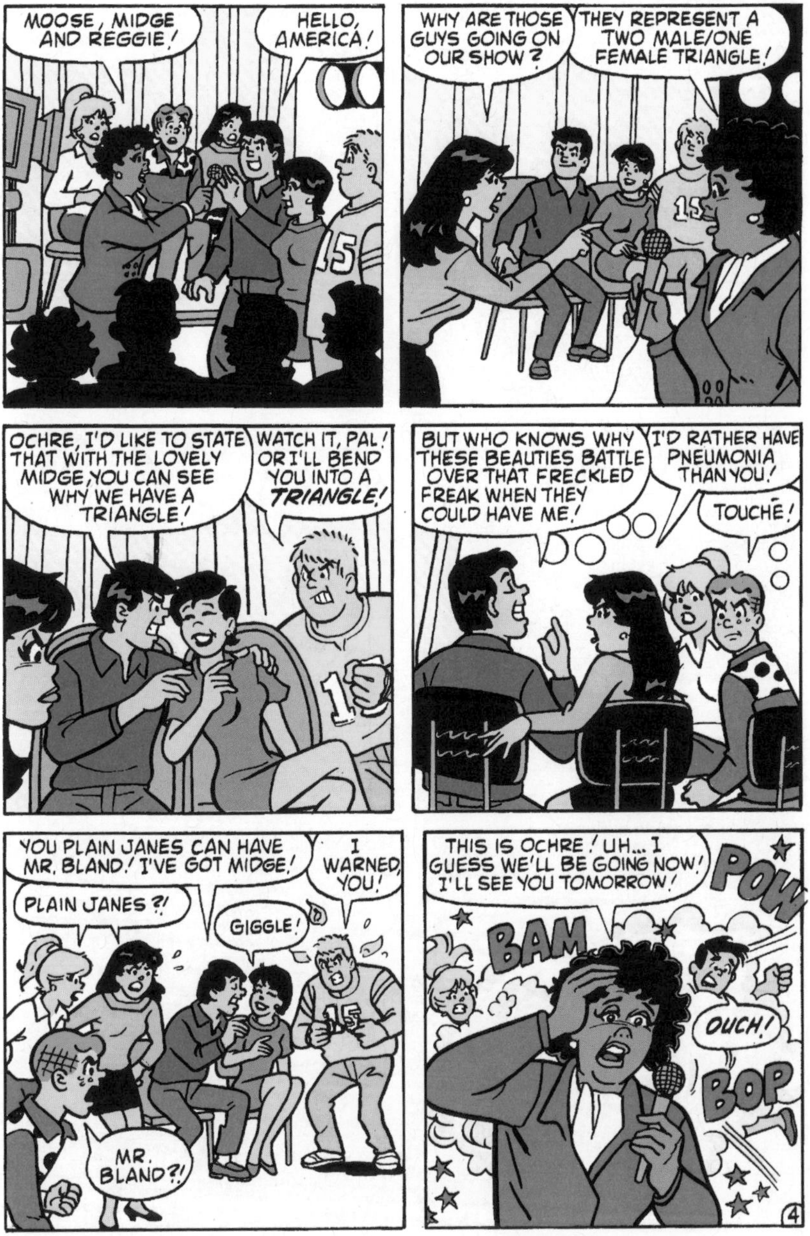
MOOSE, MIDGE AND REGGIE!
HELLO, AMERICA!
WHY ARE THOSE GUYS GOING ON OUR SHOW?
THEY REPRESENT A TWO MALE/ONE FEMALE TRIANGLE!
OCHRE, I'D LIKE TO STATE THAT WITH THE LOVELY MIDGE, YOU CAN SEE WHY WE HAVE A TRIANGLE!
WATCH IT, PAL! OR I'LL BEND YOU INTO A TRIANGLE!
BUT WHO KNOWS WHY THESE BEAUTIES BATTLE OVER THAT FRECKLED FREAK WHEN THEY COULD HAVE ME!
I'D RATHER HAVE PNEUMONIA THAN YOU!
TOUCHÉ!
YOU PLAIN JANES CAN HAVE MR. BLAND! I'VE GOT MIDGE!
I WARNED YOU!
PLAIN JANES?!
GIGGLE!
MR. BLAND?!
THIS IS OCHRE! UH... I GUESS WE'LL BE GOING NOW! I'LL SEE YOU TOMORROW!
POW
BAM
OUCH!
BOP
4

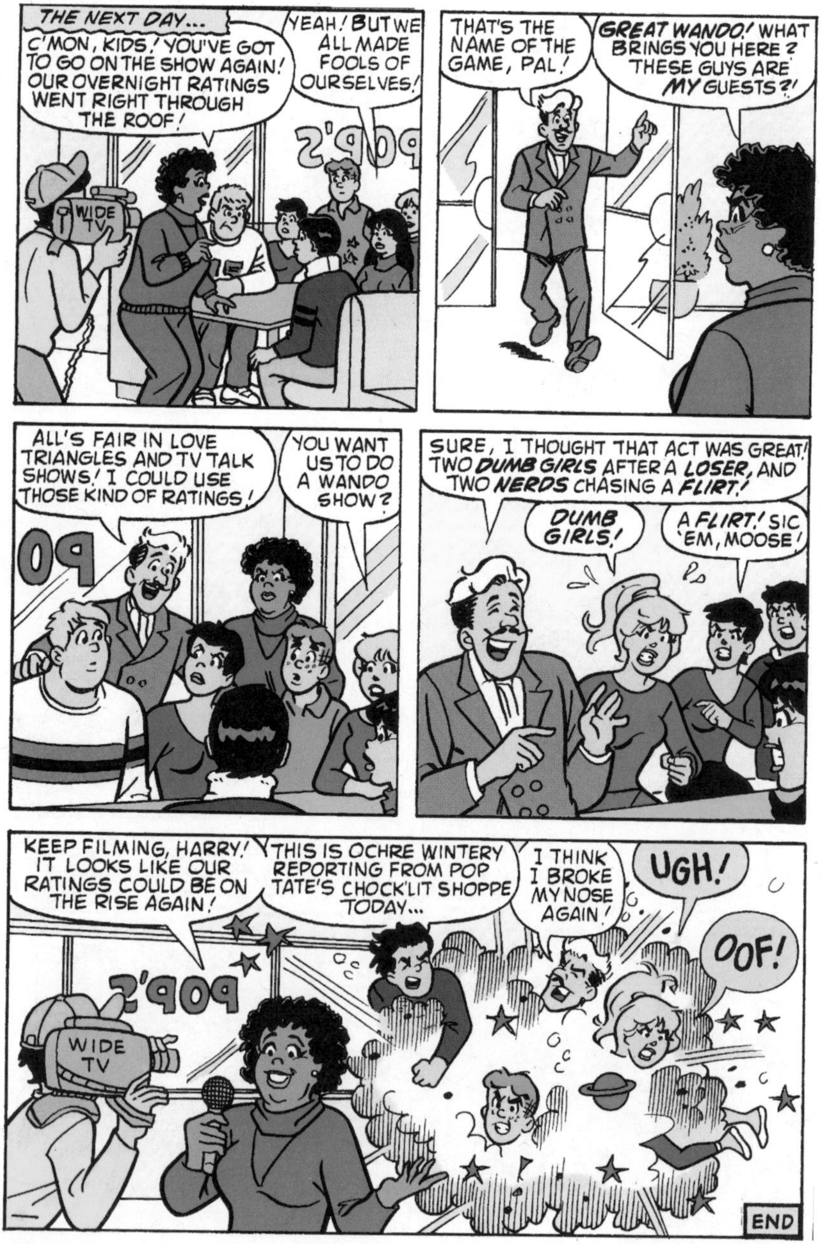
THE NEXT DAY...
C'MON, KIDS! YOU'VE GOT TO GO ON THE SHOW AGAIN! OUR OVERNIGHT RATINGS WENT RIGHT THROUGH THE ROOF!
YEAH! BUT WE ALL MADE FOOLS OF OURSELVES!
WIDE TV
POP'S
THAT'S THE NAME OF THE GAME, PAL!
GREAT WANDO! WHAT BRINGS YOU HERE? THESE GUYS ARE MY GUESTS?!
ALL'S FAIR IN LOVE TRIANGLES AND TV TALK SHOWS! I COULD USE THOSE KIND OF RATINGS!
YOU WANT US TO DO A WANDO SHOW?
PO
SURE, I THOUGHT THAT ACT WAS GREAT! TWO DUMB GIRLS AFTER A LOSER, AND TWO NERDS CHASING A FLIRT!
DUMB GIRLS!
A FLIRT! SIC 'EM, MOOSE!
KEEP FILMING, HARRY! IT LOOKS LIKE OUR RATINGS COULD BE ON THE RISE AGAIN!
THIS IS OCHRE WINTERY REPORTING FROM POP TATE'S CHOCK'LIT SHOPPE TODAY...
I THINK I BROKE MY NOSE AGAIN!
UGH!
OOF!
POP'S
WIDE TV
END

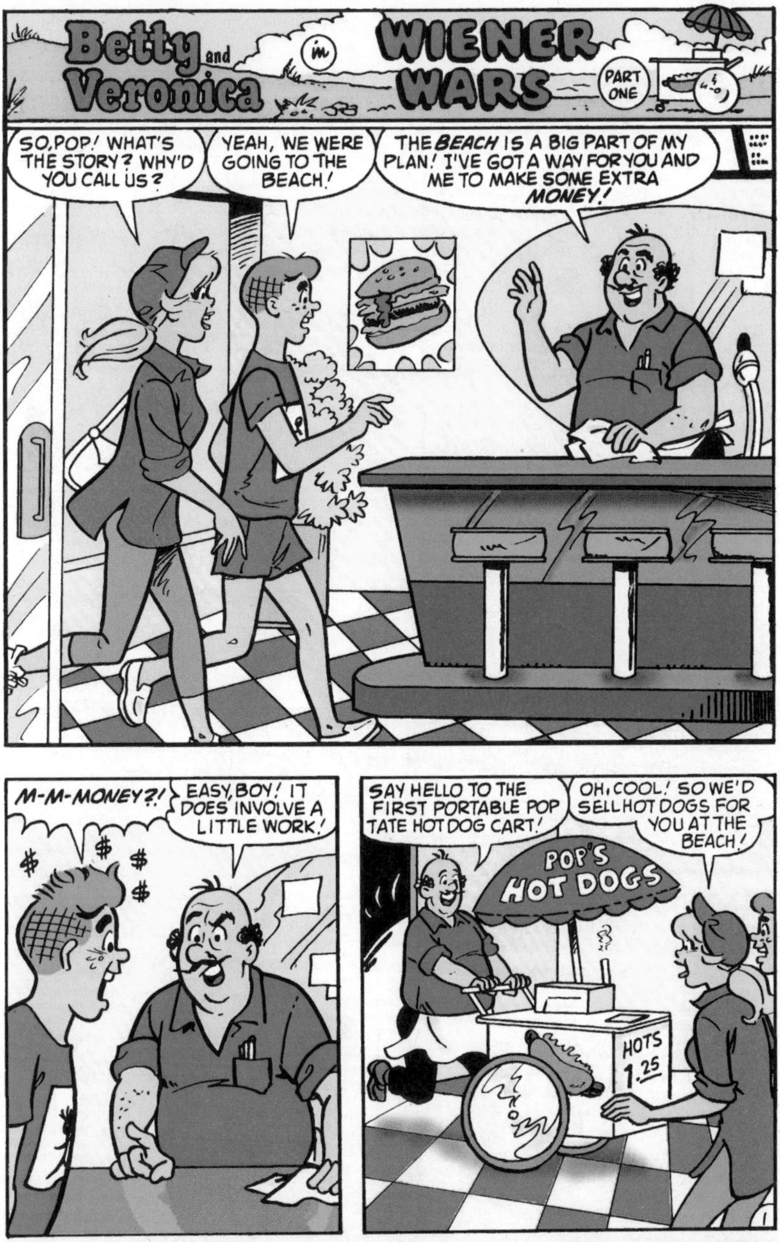
Betty and Veronica in WIENER WARS PART ONE
SO, POP! WHAT'S THE STORY? WHY'D YOU CALL US?
YEAH, WE WERE GOING TO THE BEACH!
THE BEACH IS A BIG PART OF MY PLAN! I'VE GOT A WAY FOR YOU AND ME TO MAKE SOME EXTRA MONEY!
M-M-MONEY?!
EASY, BOY! IT DOES INVOLVE A LITTLE WORK!
SAY HELLO TO THE FIRST PORTABLE POP TATE HOT DOG CART!
OH, COOL! SO WE'D SELL HOT DOGS FOR YOU AT THE BEACH!
POP'S HOT DOGS
HOTS 1.25
1

Story: Dan Parent & Bill Golliher Pencils: Dan DeCarlo & Dan Parent
Inks: Alison Flood Letters: Bill Yoshida Colors: Barry Grossman

Originally printed in BETTY & VERONICA SPECTACULAR #5, October 1993

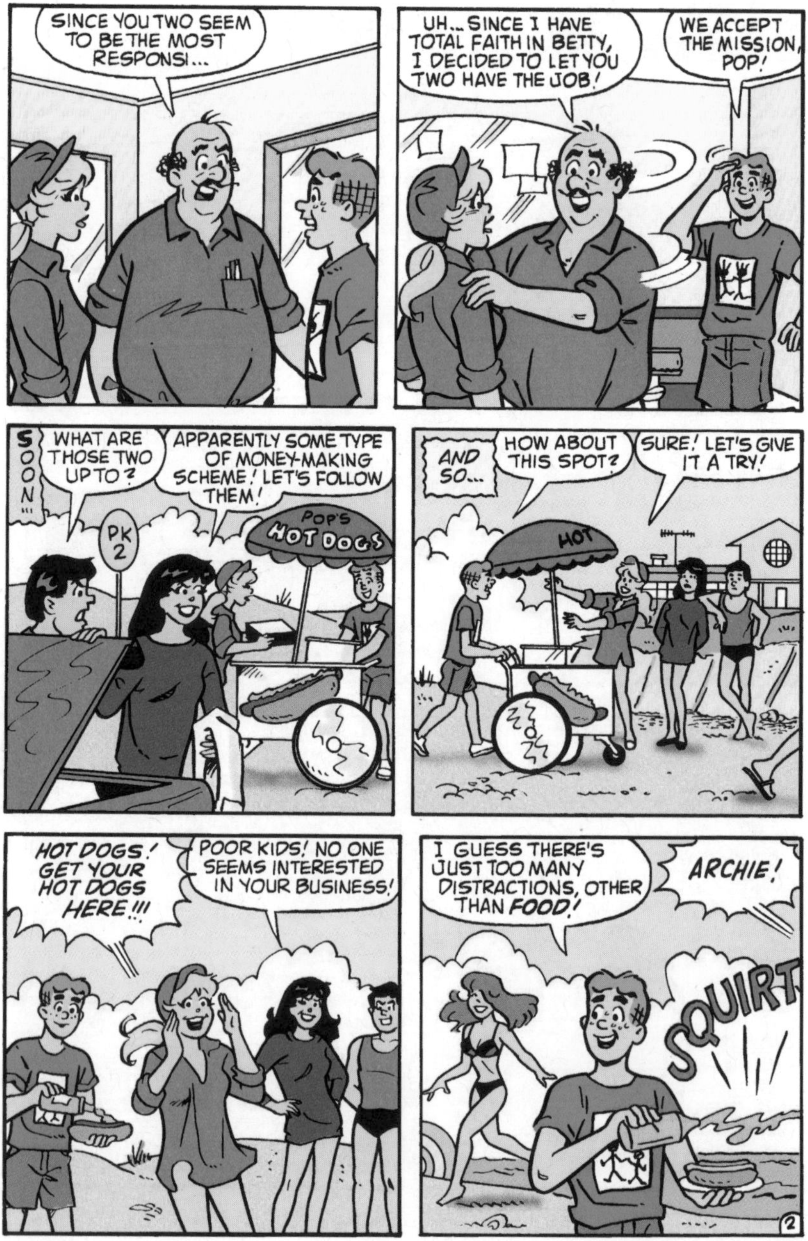
SINCE YOU TWO SEEM TO BE THE MOST RESPONSI...
UH... SINCE I HAVE TOTAL FAITH IN BETTY, I DECIDED TO LET YOU TWO HAVE THE JOB!
WE ACCEPT THE MISSION, POP!
SOON...
WHAT ARE THOSE TWO UP TO?
APPARENTLY SOME TYPE OF MONEY-MAKING SCHEME! LET'S FOLLOW THEM!
PK 2
POP'S HOT DOGS
HOT
AND SO...
HOW ABOUT THIS SPOT?
SURE! LET'S GIVE IT A TRY!
HOT
HOT DOGS! GET YOUR HOT DOGS HERE!!!
POOR KIDS! NO ONE SEEMS INTERESTED IN YOUR BUSINESS!
I GUESS THERE'S JUST TOO MANY DISTRACTIONS, OTHER THAN FOOD!
ARCHIE!
SQUIRT
2

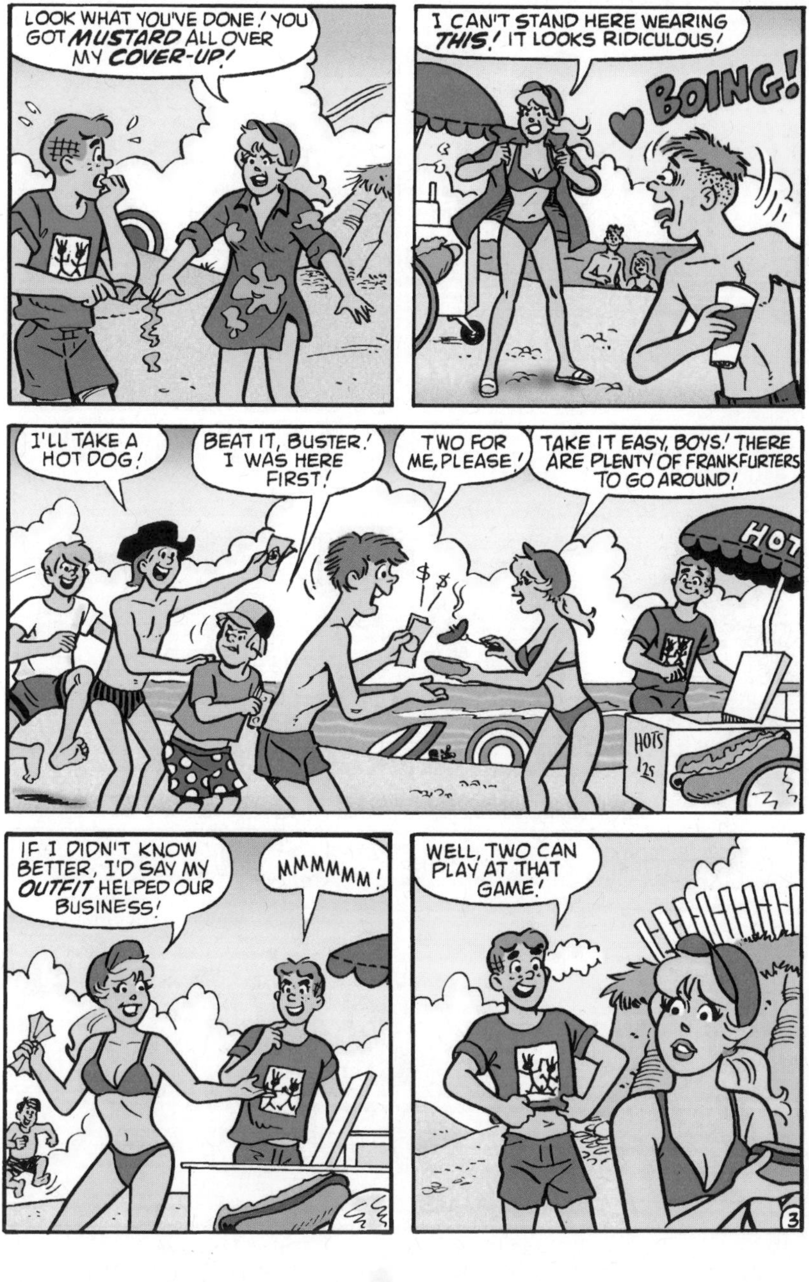
LOOK WHAT YOU'VE DONE! YOU GOT MUSTARD ALL OVER MY COVER-UP!
I CAN'T STAND HERE WEARING THIS! IT LOOKS RIDICULOUS!
BOING!
I'LL TAKE A HOT DOG!
BEAT IT, BUSTER! I WAS HERE FIRST!
TWO FOR ME, PLEASE!
TAKE IT EASY, BOYS! THERE ARE PLENTY OF FRANKFURTERS TO GO AROUND!
HOT
HOTS 1.25
IF I DIDN'T KNOW BETTER, I'D SAY MY OUTFIT HELPED OUR BUSINESS!
MMMMMM!
WELL, TWO CAN PLAY AT THAT GAME!
3

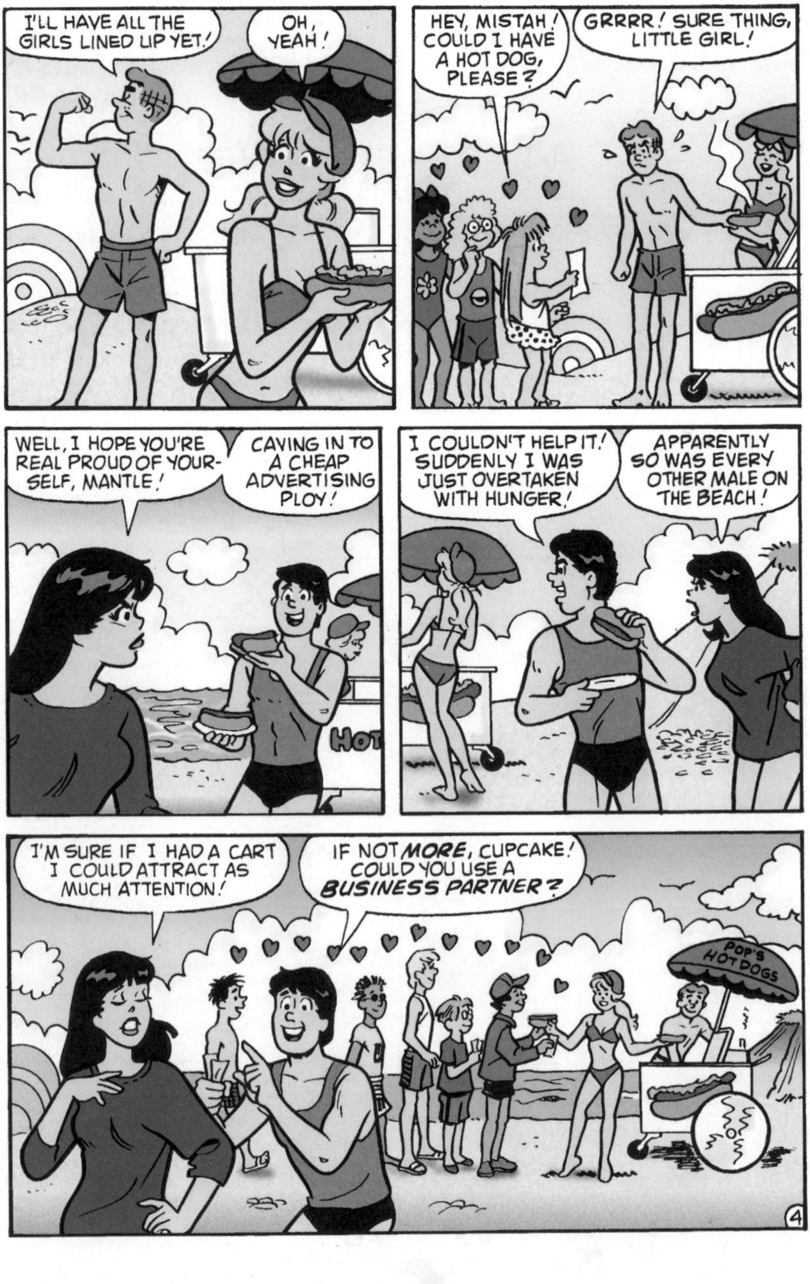
I'LL HAVE ALL THE GIRLS LINED UP YET!
OH, YEAH!
HEY, MISTAH! COULD I HAVE A HOT DOG, PLEASE?
GRRRR! SURE THING, LITTLE GIRL!
WELL, I HOPE YOU'RE REAL PROUD OF YOURSELF, MANTLE!
CAVING IN TO A CHEAP ADVERTISING PLOY!
HOT
I COULDN'T HELP IT! SUDDENLY I WAS JUST OVERTAKEN WITH HUNGER!
APPARENTLY SO WAS EVERY OTHER MALE ON THE BEACH!
I'M SURE IF I HAD A CART I COULD ATTRACT AS MUCH ATTENTION!
IF NOT MORE, CUPCAKE! COULD YOU USE A BUSINESS PARTNER?
POP'S HOT DOGS
4

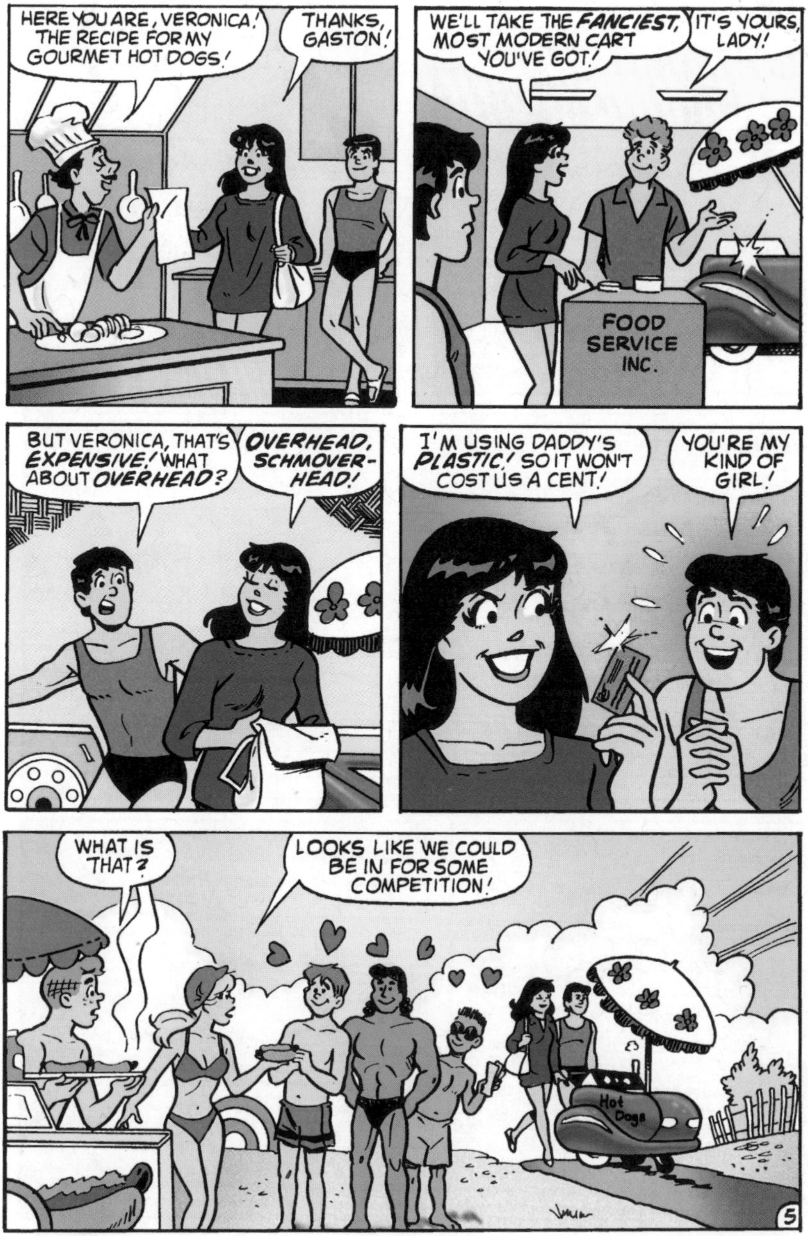
HERE YOU ARE, VERONICA! THE RECIPE FOR MY GOURMET HOT DOGS!
THANKS, GASTON!
WE'LL TAKE THE FANCIEST, MOST MODERN CART YOU'VE GOT!
IT'S YOURS, LADY!
FOOD SERVICE INC.
BUT VERONICA, THAT'S EXPENSIVE! WHAT ABOUT OVERHEAD?
OVERHEAD, SCHMOVER-HEAD!
I'M USING DADDY'S PLASTIC! SO IT WON'T COST US A CENT!
YOU'RE MY KIND OF GIRL!
WHAT IS THAT?
LOOKS LIKE WE COULD BE IN FOR SOME COMPETITION!
Hot Dogs
5

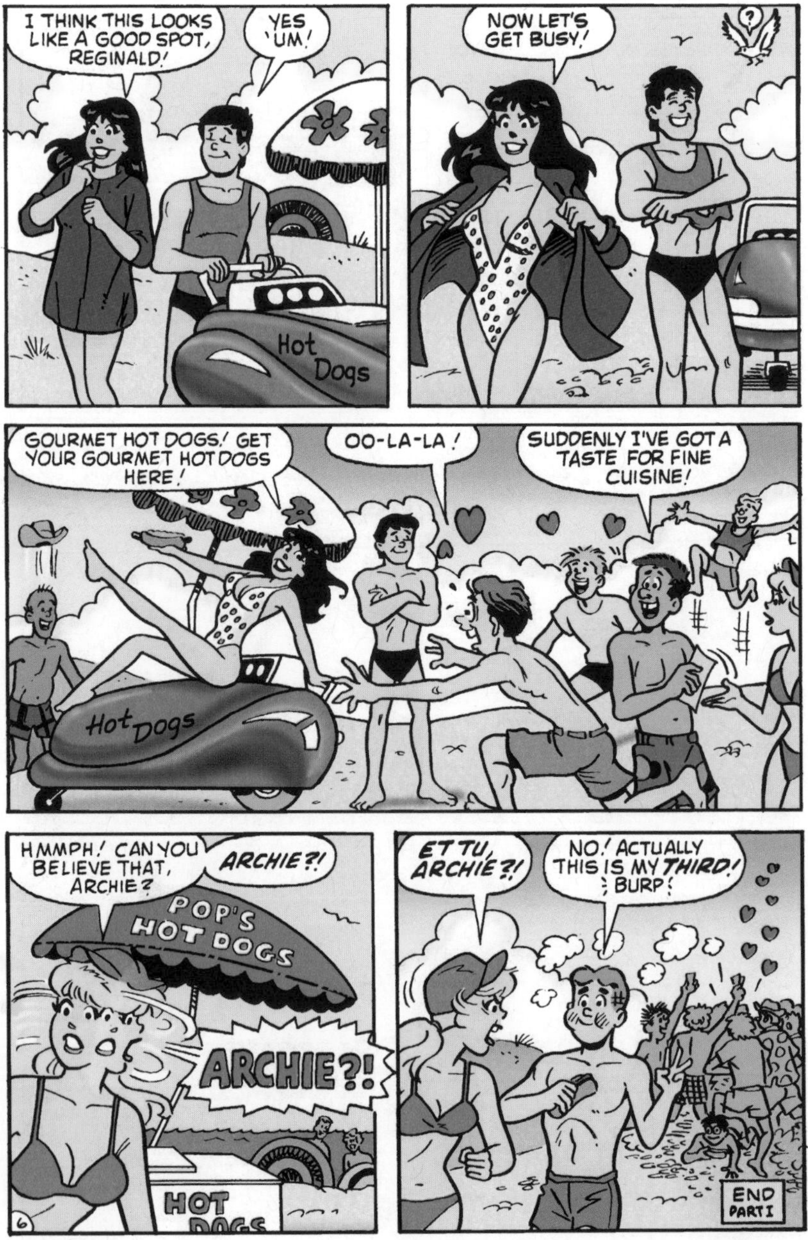
I THINK THIS LOOKS LIKE A GOOD SPOT, REGINALD!
YES 'UM!
Hot Dogs
NOW LET'S GET BUSY!
?
GOURMET HOT DOGS! GET YOUR GOURMET HOT DOGS HERE!
OO-LA-LA!
SUDDENLY I'VE GOT A TASTE FOR FINE CUISINE!
Hot Dogs
HMMPH! CAN YOU BELIEVE THAT, ARCHIE?
ARCHIE?!
POP'S HOT DOGS
ARCHIE?!
HOT DOGS
ET TU, ARCHIE?!
NO! ACTUALLY THIS IS MY THIRD! BURP!
END PART I

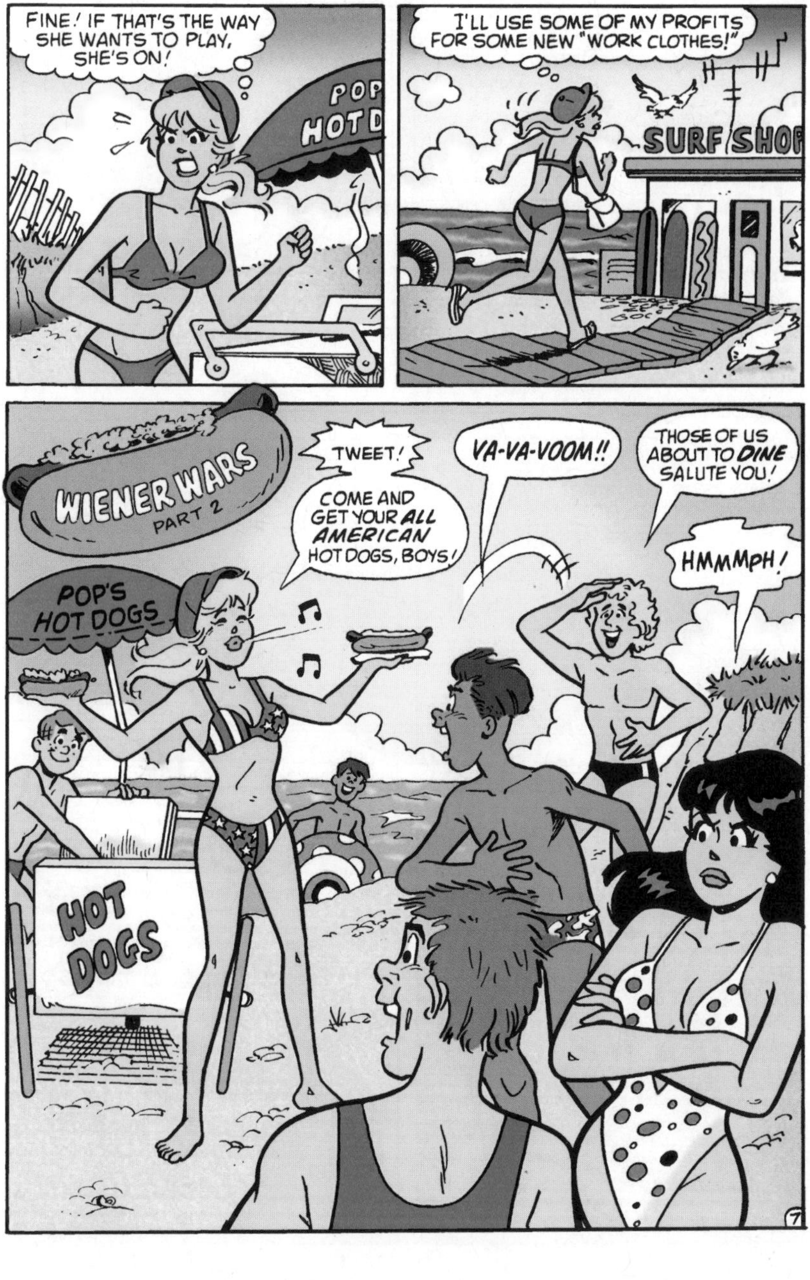
FINE! IF THAT'S THE WAY SHE WANTS TO PLAY, SHE'S ON!
POP'S HOT D
I'LL USE SOME OF MY PROFITS FOR SOME NEW "WORK CLOTHES!"
SURF SHOP
WIENER WARS PART 2
TWEET!
COME AND GET YOUR ALL AMERICAN HOT DOGS, BOYS!
VA-VA-VOOM!!
THOSE OF US ABOUT TO DINE SALUTE YOU!
HMMMPH!
POP'S HOT DOGS
HOT DOGS
7

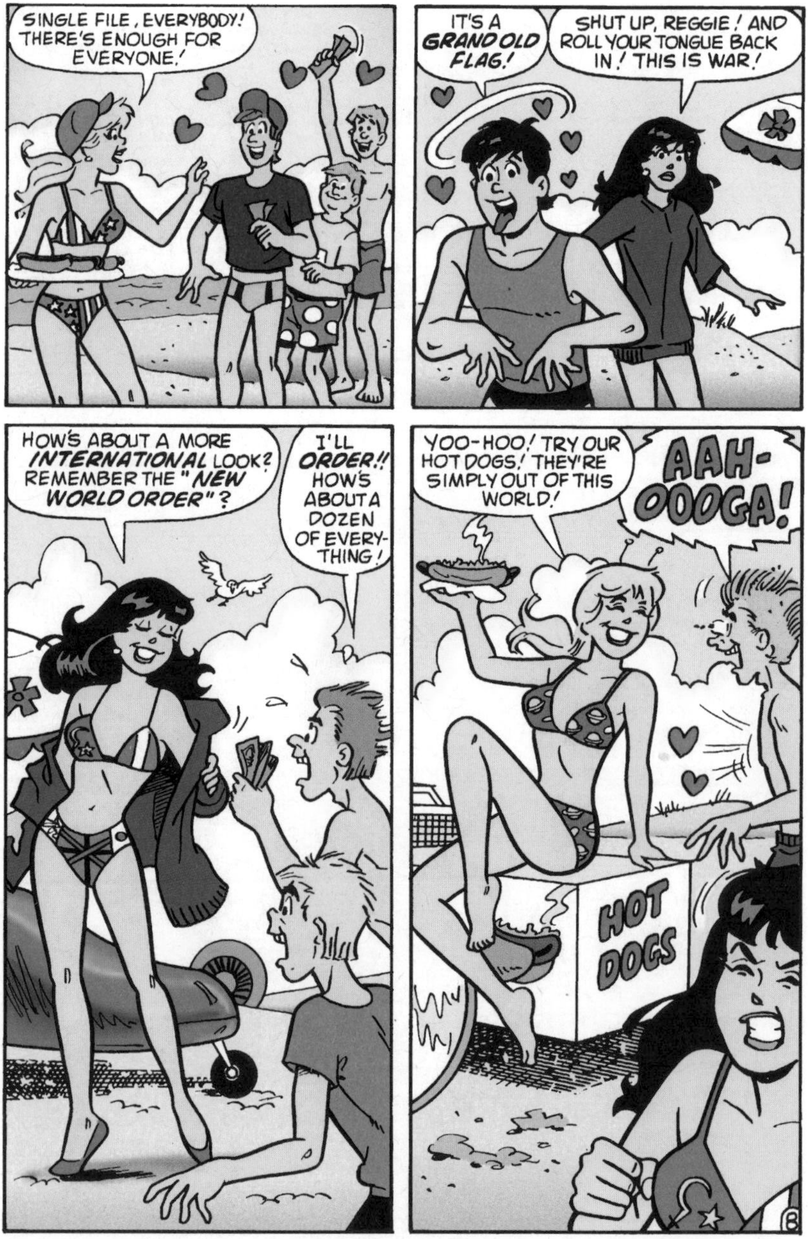
SINGLE FILE, EVERYBODY! THERE'S ENOUGH FOR EVERYONE!
IT'S A GRAND OLD FLAG!
SHUT UP, REGGIE! AND ROLL YOUR TONGUE BACK IN! THIS IS WAR!
HOW'S ABOUT A MORE INTERNATIONAL LOOK? REMEMBER THE "NEW WORLD ORDER"?
I'LL ORDER!! HOW'S ABOUT A DOZEN OF EVERY-THING!
YOO-HOO! TRY OUR HOT DOGS! THEY'RE SIMPLY OUT OF THIS WORLD!
AAH-OOOGA!
HOT DOGS
8

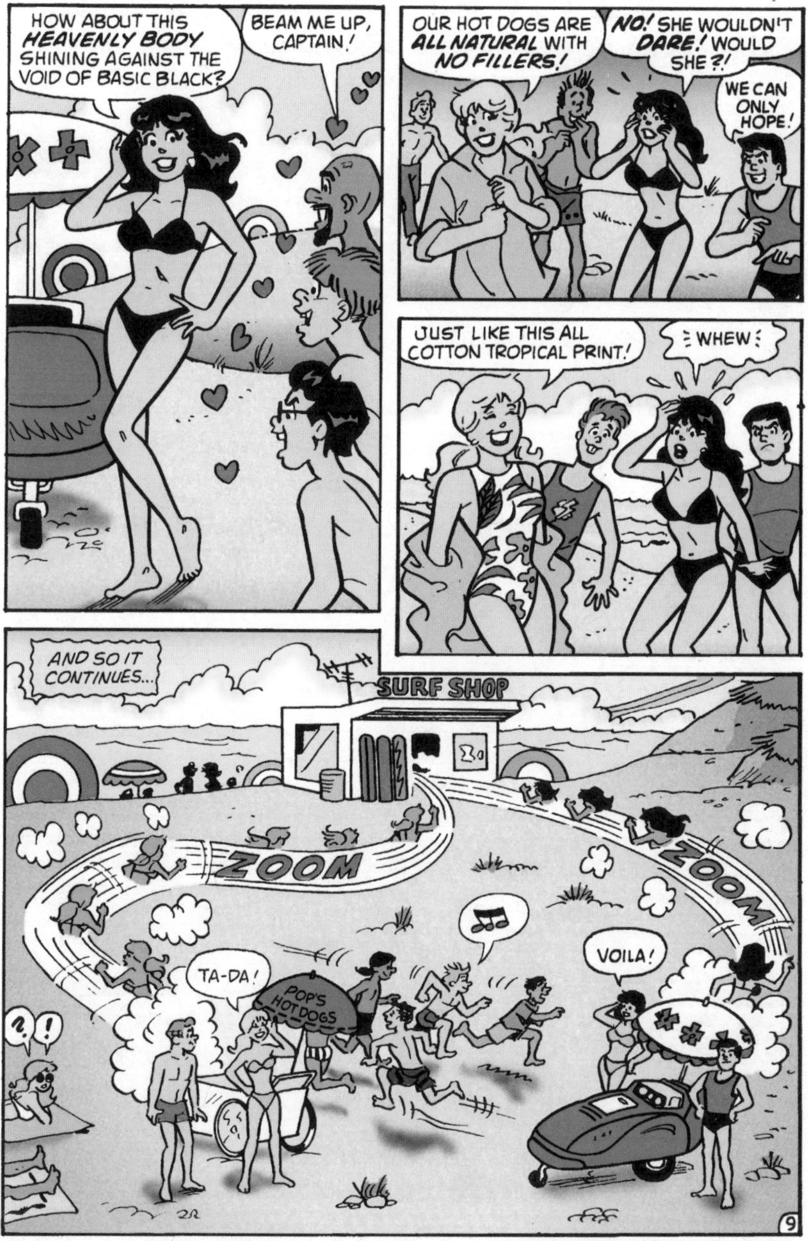
HOW ABOUT THIS HEAVENLY BODY SHINING AGAINST THE VOID OF BASIC BLACK?
BEAM ME UP, CAPTAIN!
OUR HOT DOGS ARE ALL NATURAL WITH NO FILLERS!
NO! SHE WOULDN'T DARE! WOULD SHE?!
WE CAN ONLY HOPE!
JUST LIKE THIS ALL COTTON TROPICAL PRINT!
WHEW
AND SO IT CONTINUES...
SURF SHOP
ZOOM
ZOOM
TA-DA!
POP'S HOT DOGS
VOILA!
?!
9

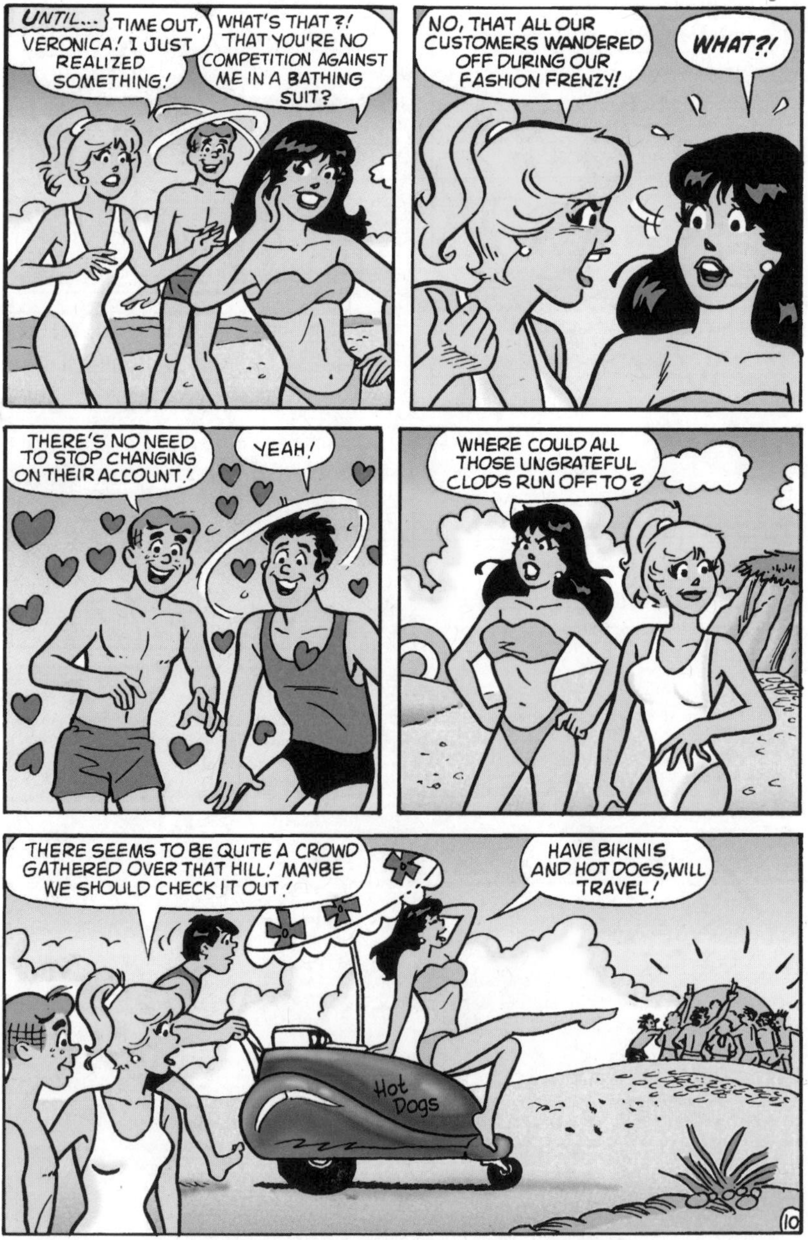
UNTIL...
TIME OUT, VERONICA! I JUST REALIZED SOMETHING!
WHAT'S THAT ?! THAT YOU'RE NO COMPETITION AGAINST ME IN A BATHING SUIT?
NO, THAT ALL OUR CUSTOMERS WANDERED OFF DURING OUR FASHION FRENZY!
WHAT?!
THERE'S NO NEED TO STOP CHANGING ON THEIR ACCOUNT!
YEAH!
WHERE COULD ALL THOSE UNGRATEFUL CLODS RUN OFF TO ?
THERE SEEMS TO BE QUITE A CROWD GATHERED OVER THAT HILL! MAYBE WE SHOULD CHECK IT OUT!
HAVE BIKINIS AND HOT DOGS, WILL TRAVEL!
Hot Dogs
10

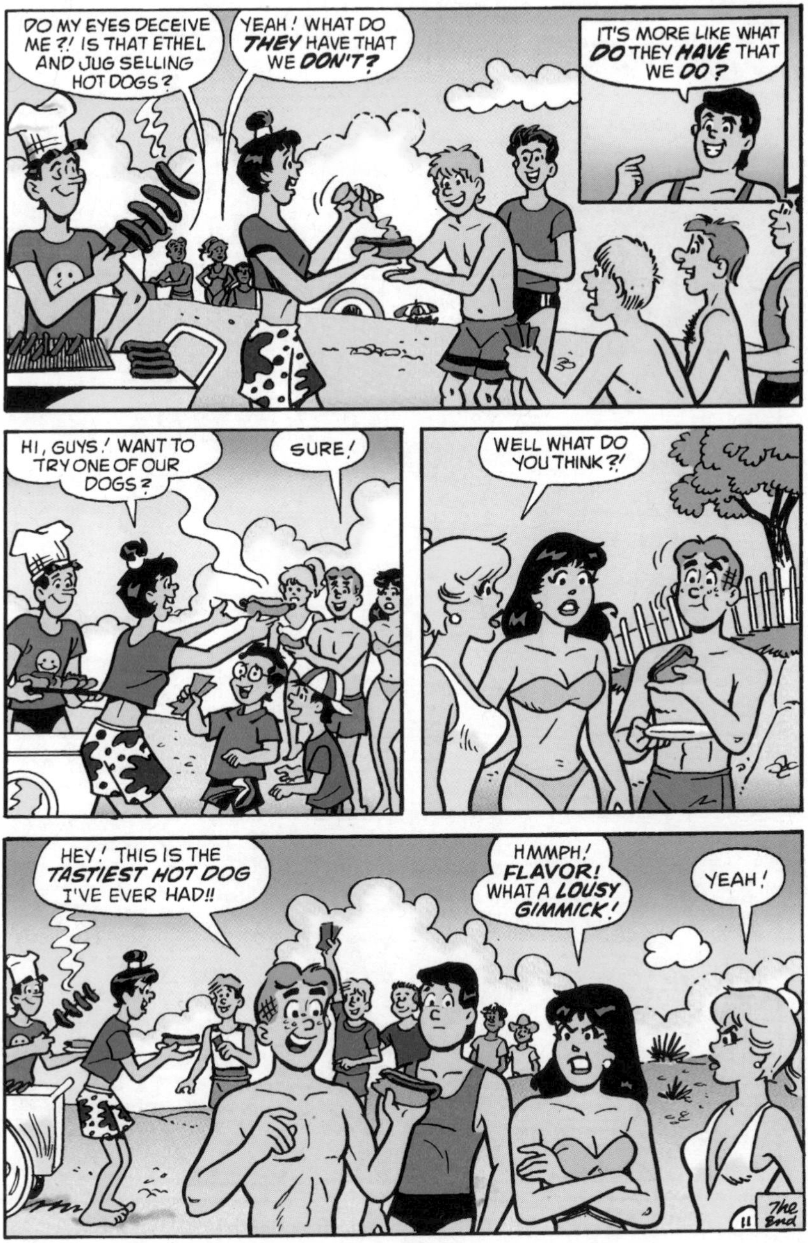
DO MY EYES DECEIVE ME ?! IS THAT ETHEL AND JUG SELLING HOT DOGS ?
YEAH ! WHAT DO THEY HAVE THAT WE DON'T ?
IT'S MORE LIKE WHAT DO THEY HAVE THAT WE DO ?
HI, GUYS ! WANT TO TRY ONE OF OUR DOGS ?
SURE !
WELL WHAT DO YOU THINK ?!
HEY ! THIS IS THE TASTIEST HOT DOG I'VE EVER HAD!!
HMMPH ! FLAVOR! WHAT A LOUSY GIMMICK !
YEAH !
11
The End

Betty and Veronica in Princess and the Pauper

Chapter One

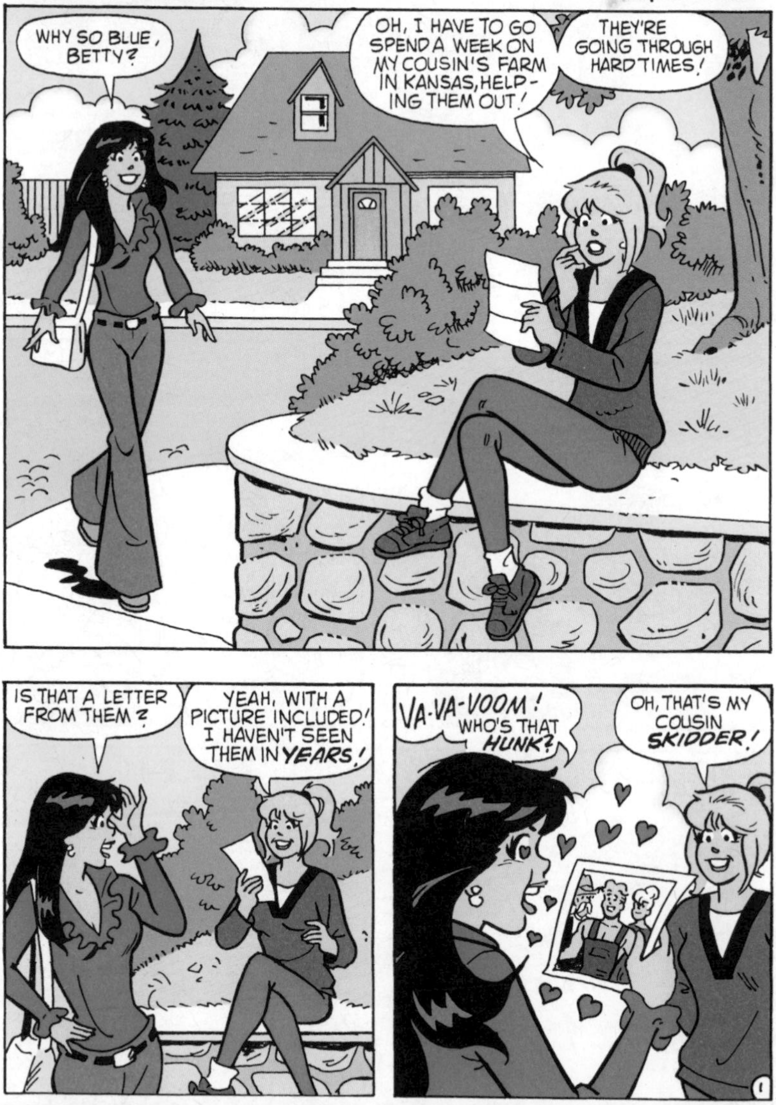
WHY SO BLUE, BETTY?
OH, I HAVE TO GO SPEND A WEEK ON MY COUSIN'S FARM IN KANSAS, HELPING THEM OUT!
THEY'RE GOING THROUGH HARD TIMES!
IS THAT A LETTER FROM THEM?
YEAH, WITH A PICTURE INCLUDED! I HAVEN'T SEEN THEM IN YEARS!
VA-VA-VOOM! WHO'S THAT HUNK?
OH, THAT'S MY COUSIN SKIDDER!
1

Story: Dan Parent & Bill Golliher Art: Dan DeCarlo & Dan Parent
Letters: Bill Yoshida Colors: Barry Grossman

Originally printed in BETTY & VERONICA SPECTACULAR #6, February 1994

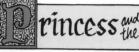

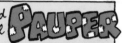

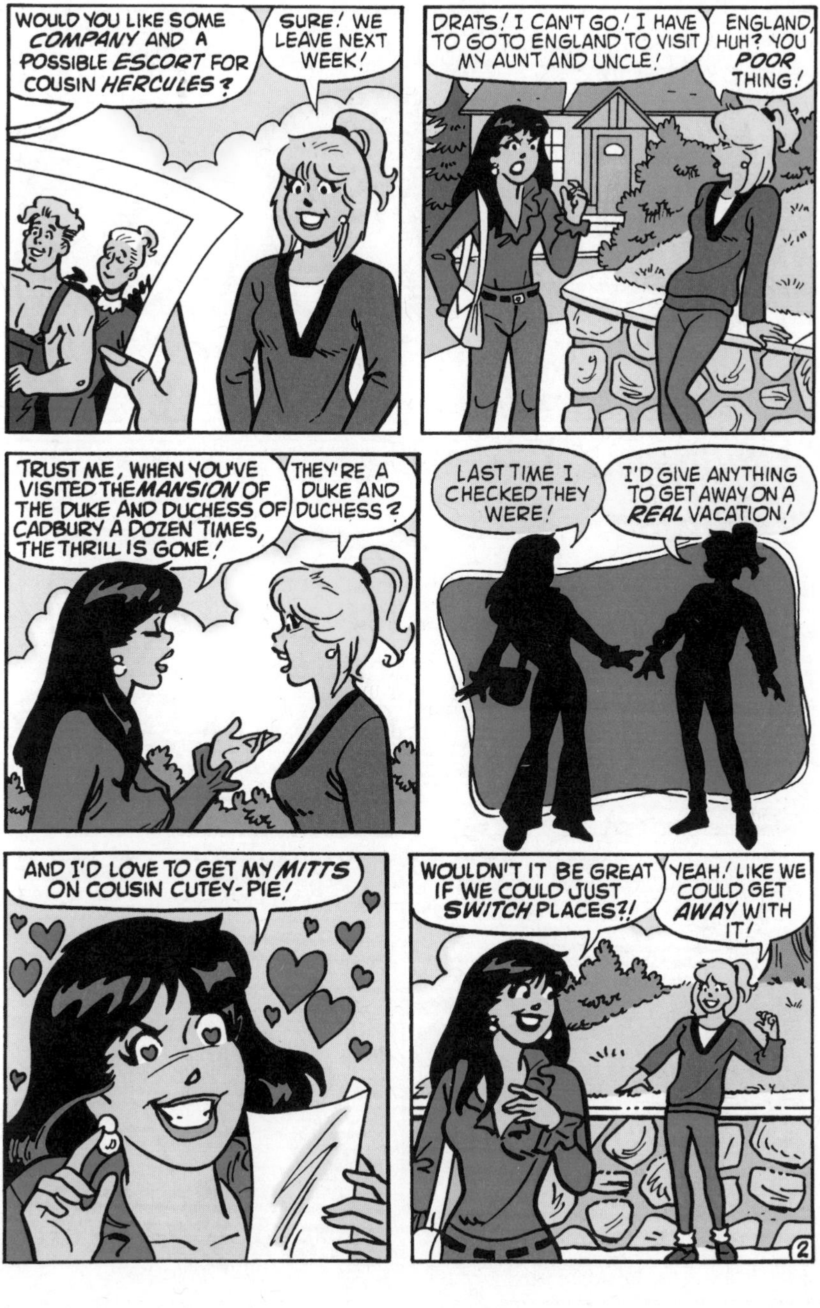
WOULD YOU LIKE SOME COMPANY AND A POSSIBLE ESCORT FOR COUSIN HERCULES?
SURE! WE LEAVE NEXT WEEK!
DRATS! I CAN'T GO! I HAVE TO GO TO ENGLAND TO VISIT MY AUNT AND UNCLE!
ENGLAND, HUH? YOU POOR THING!
TRUST ME, WHEN YOU'VE VISITED THE MANSION OF THE DUKE AND DUCHESS OF CADBURY A DOZEN TIMES, THE THRILL IS GONE!
THEY'RE A DUKE AND DUCHESS?
LAST TIME I CHECKED THEY WERE!
I'D GIVE ANYTHING TO GET AWAY ON A REAL VACATION!
AND I'D LOVE TO GET MY MITTS ON COUSIN CUTEY-PIE!
WOULDN'T IT BE GREAT IF WE COULD JUST SWITCH PLACES?!
YEAH! LIKE WE COULD GET AWAY WITH IT!
2

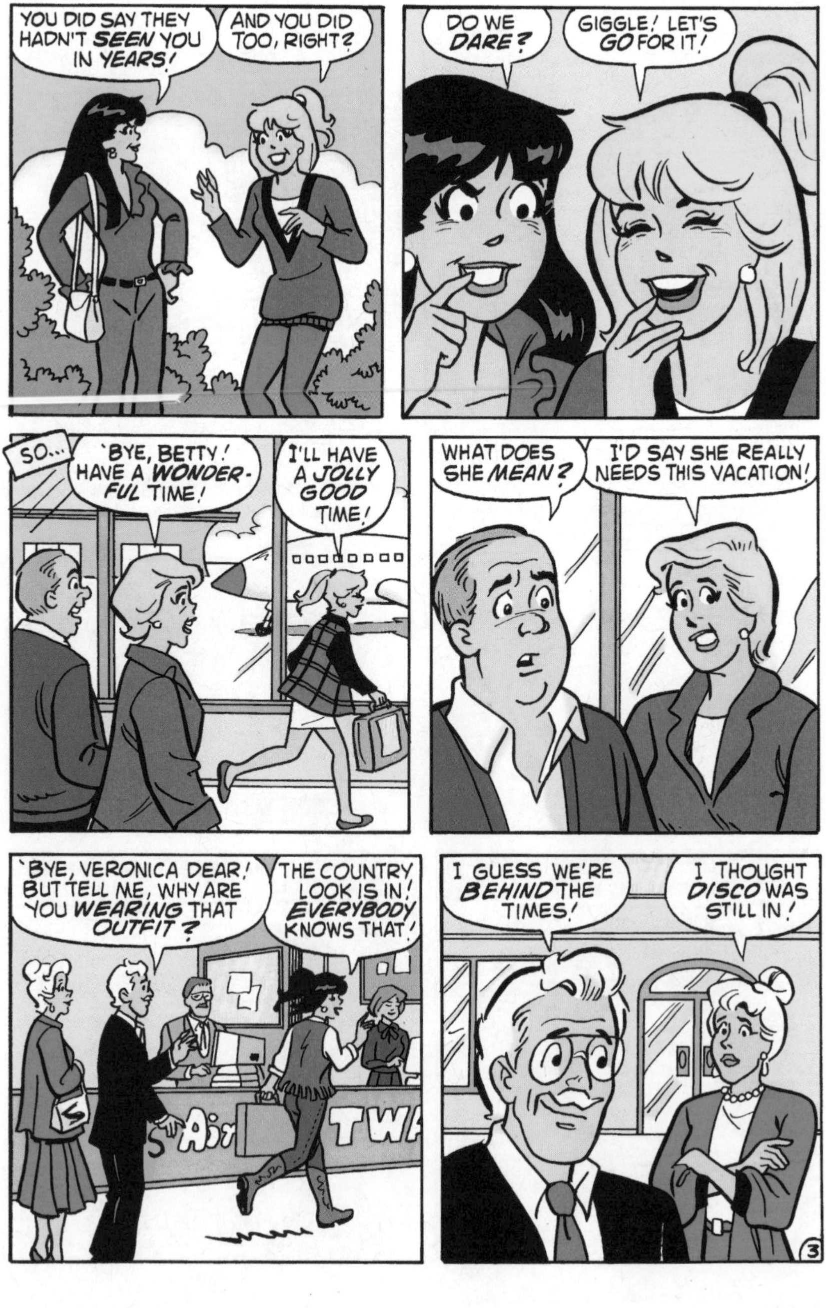
YOU DID SAY THEY HADN'T SEEN YOU IN YEARS!
AND YOU DID TOO, RIGHT?
DO WE DARE?
GIGGLE! LET'S GO FOR IT!
SO...
'BYE, BETTY! HAVE A WONDERFUL TIME!
I'LL HAVE A JOLLY GOOD TIME!
WHAT DOES SHE MEAN?
I'D SAY SHE REALLY NEEDS THIS VACATION!
'BYE, VERONICA DEAR! BUT TELL ME, WHY ARE YOU WEARING THAT OUTFIT?
THE COUNTRY LOOK IS IN! EVERYBODY KNOWS THAT!
TWA
I GUESS WE'RE BEHIND THE TIMES!
I THOUGHT DISCO WAS STILL IN!
3

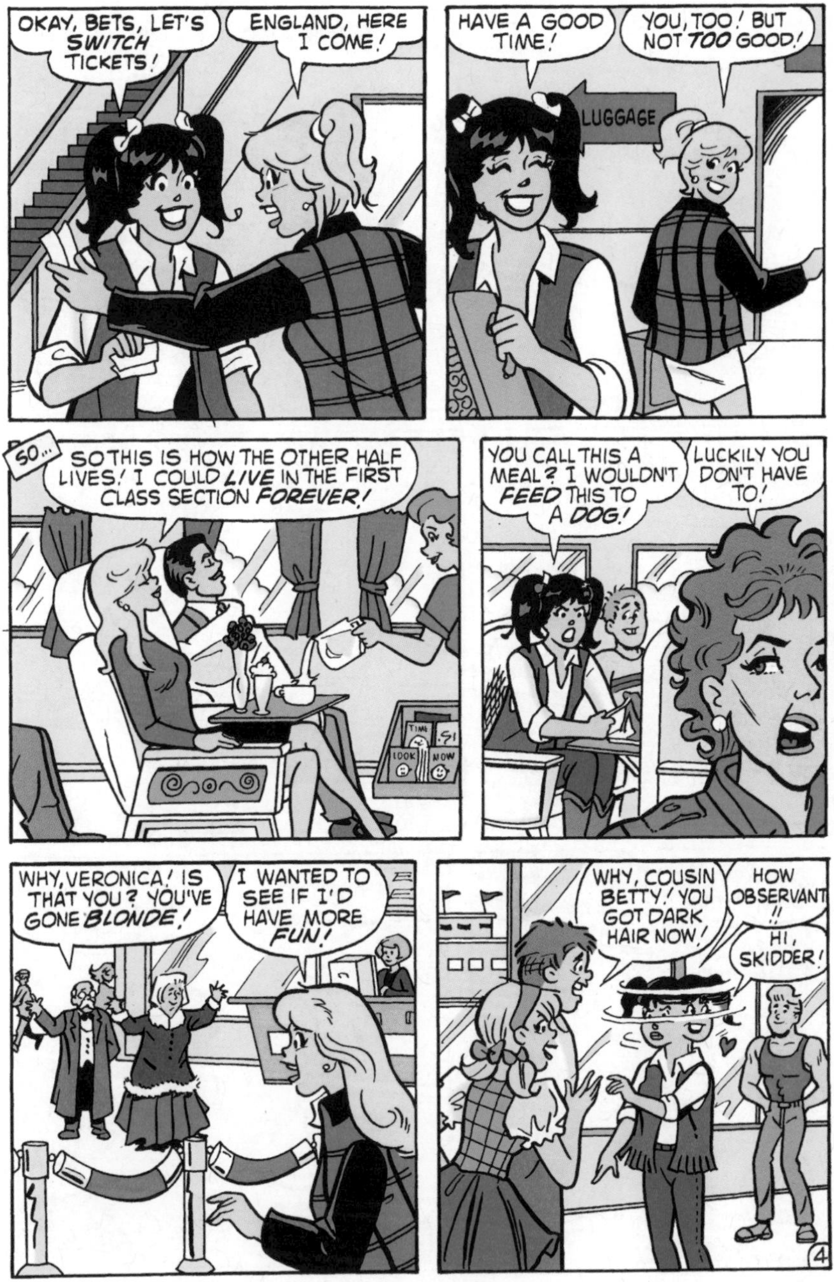
OKAY, BETS, LET'S SWITCH TICKETS!
ENGLAND, HERE I COME!
HAVE A GOOD TIME!
YOU, TOO! BUT NOT TOO GOOD!
LUGGAGE
SO...
SO THIS IS HOW THE OTHER HALF LIVES! I COULD LIVE IN THE FIRST CLASS SECTION FOREVER!
TIME
LOOK
NOW
YOU CALL THIS A MEAL? I WOULDN'T FEED THIS TO A DOG!
LUCKILY YOU DON'T HAVE TO!
WHY, VERONICA! IS THAT YOU? YOU'VE GONE BLONDE!
I WANTED TO SEE IF I'D HAVE MORE FUN!
WHY, COUSIN BETTY! YOU GOT DARK HAIR NOW!
HOW OBSERVANT!!
HI, SKIDDER!
4

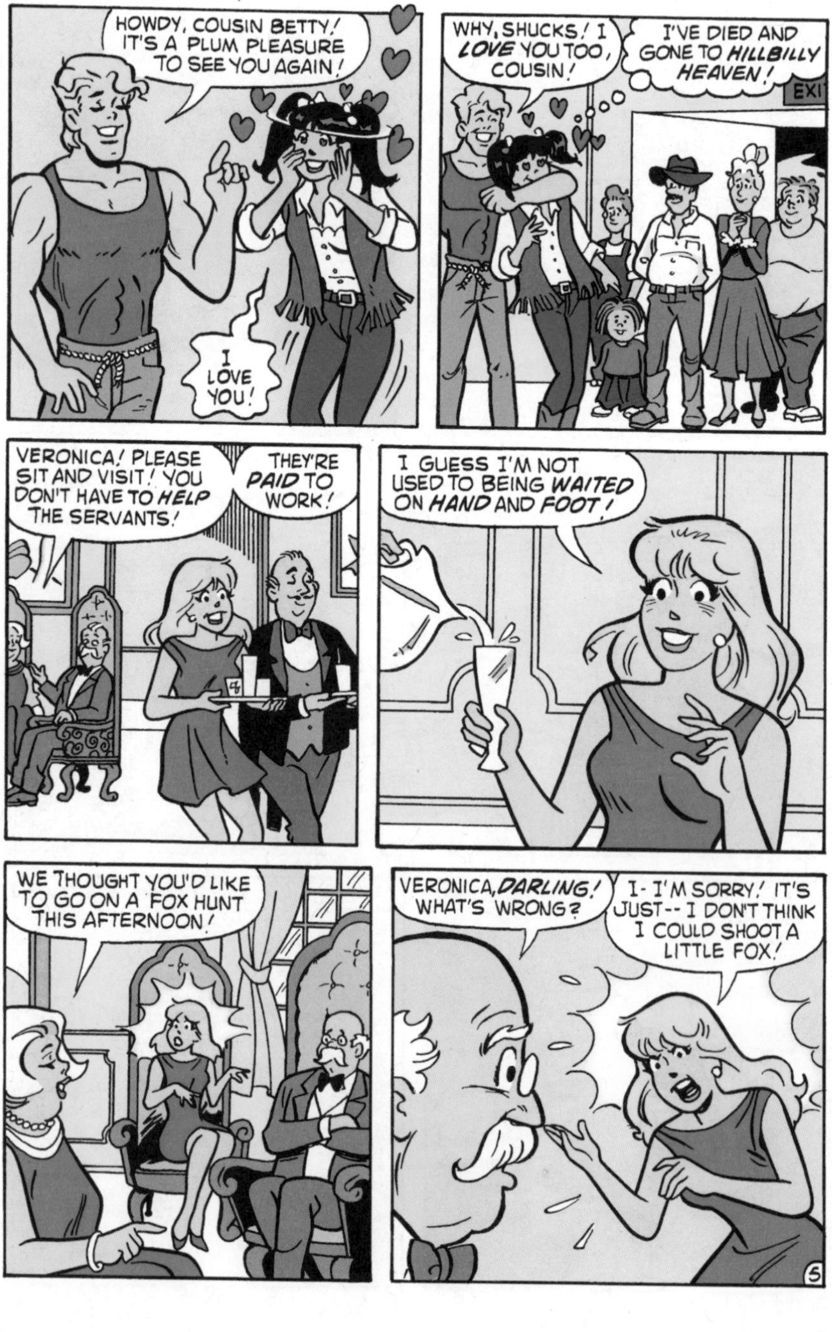
HOWDY, COUSIN BETTY! IT'S A PLUM PLEASURE TO SEE YOU AGAIN!
I LOVE YOU!
WHY, SHUCKS! I LOVE YOU TOO, COUSIN!
I'VE DIED AND GONE TO HILLBILLY HEAVEN!
EXI
VERONICA! PLEASE SIT AND VISIT! YOU DON'T HAVE TO HELP THE SERVANTS!
THEY'RE PAID TO WORK!
I GUESS I'M NOT USED TO BEING WAITED ON HAND AND FOOT!
WE THOUGHT YOU'D LIKE TO GO ON A FOX HUNT THIS AFTERNOON!
VERONICA, DARLING! WHAT'S WRONG?
I- I'M SORRY! IT'S JUST-- I DON'T THINK I COULD SHOOT A LITTLE FOX!
5

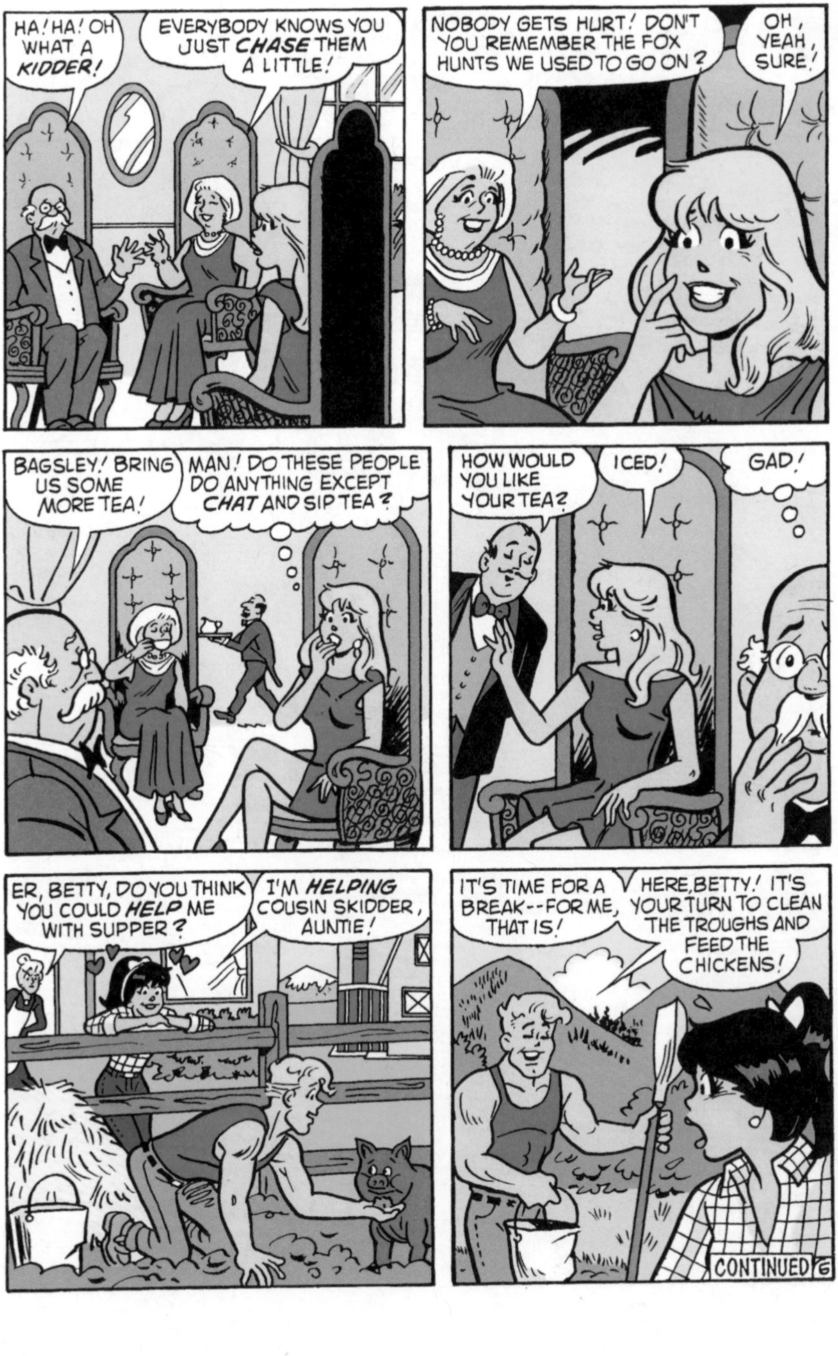
HA! HA! OH WHAT A KIDDER!
EVERYBODY KNOWS YOU JUST CHASE THEM A LITTLE!
NOBODY GETS HURT! DON'T YOU REMEMBER THE FOX HUNTS WE USED TO GO ON?
OH, YEAH, SURE!
BAGSLEY! BRING US SOME MORE TEA!
MAN! DO THESE PEOPLE DO ANYTHING EXCEPT CHAT AND SIP TEA?
HOW WOULD YOU LIKE YOUR TEA?
ICED!
GAD!
ER, BETTY, DO YOU THINK YOU COULD HELP ME WITH SUPPER?
I'M HELPING COUSIN SKIDDER, AUNTIE!
IT'S TIME FOR A BREAK--FOR ME, THAT IS!
HERE, BETTY! IT'S YOUR TURN TO CLEAN THE TROUGHS AND FEED THE CHICKENS!
CONTINUED 6

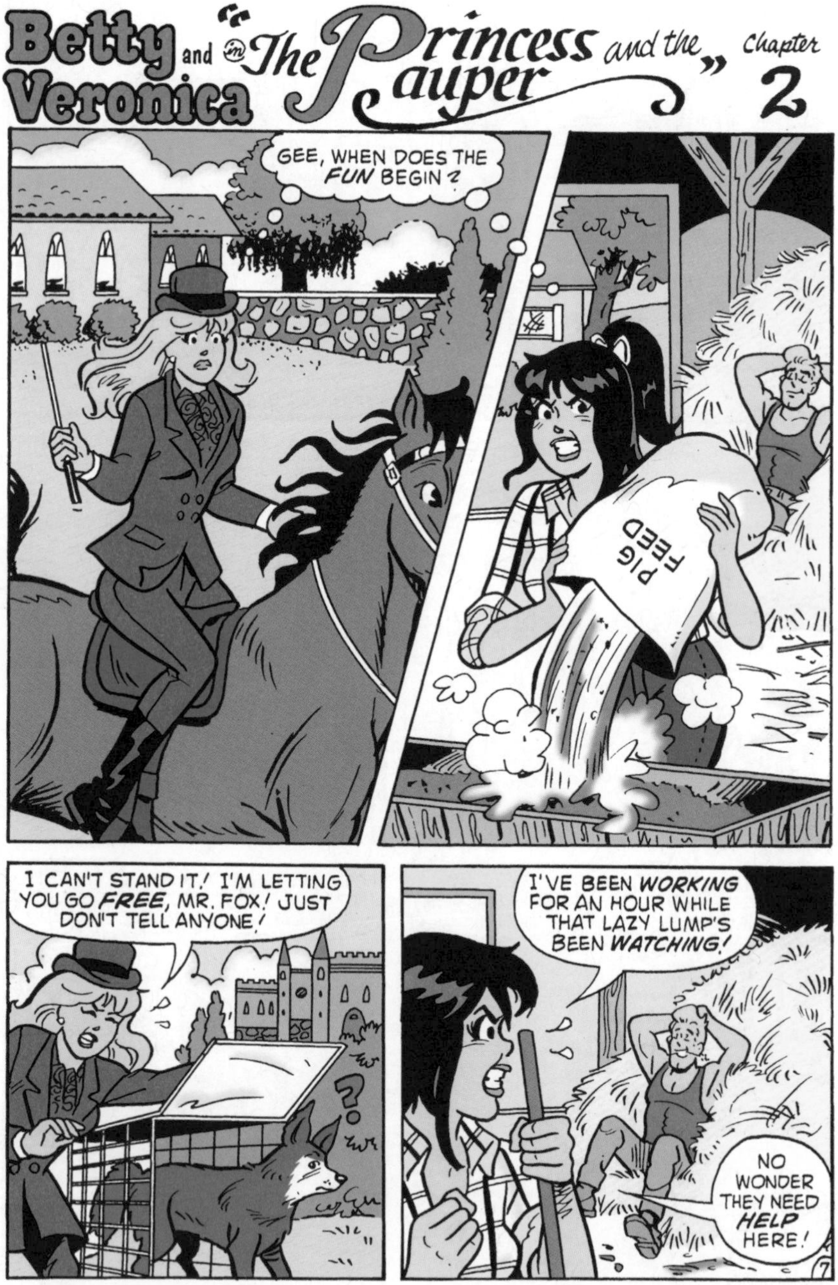
Betty and Veronica in "The Princess and the Pauper" Chapter 2
GEE, WHEN DOES THE FUN BEGIN?
PIG FEED
I CAN'T STAND IT! I'M LETTING YOU GO FREE, MR. FOX! JUST DON'T TELL ANYONE!
I'VE BEEN WORKING FOR AN HOUR WHILE THAT LAZY LUMP'S BEEN WATCHING!
NO WONDER THEY NEED HELP HERE!
7

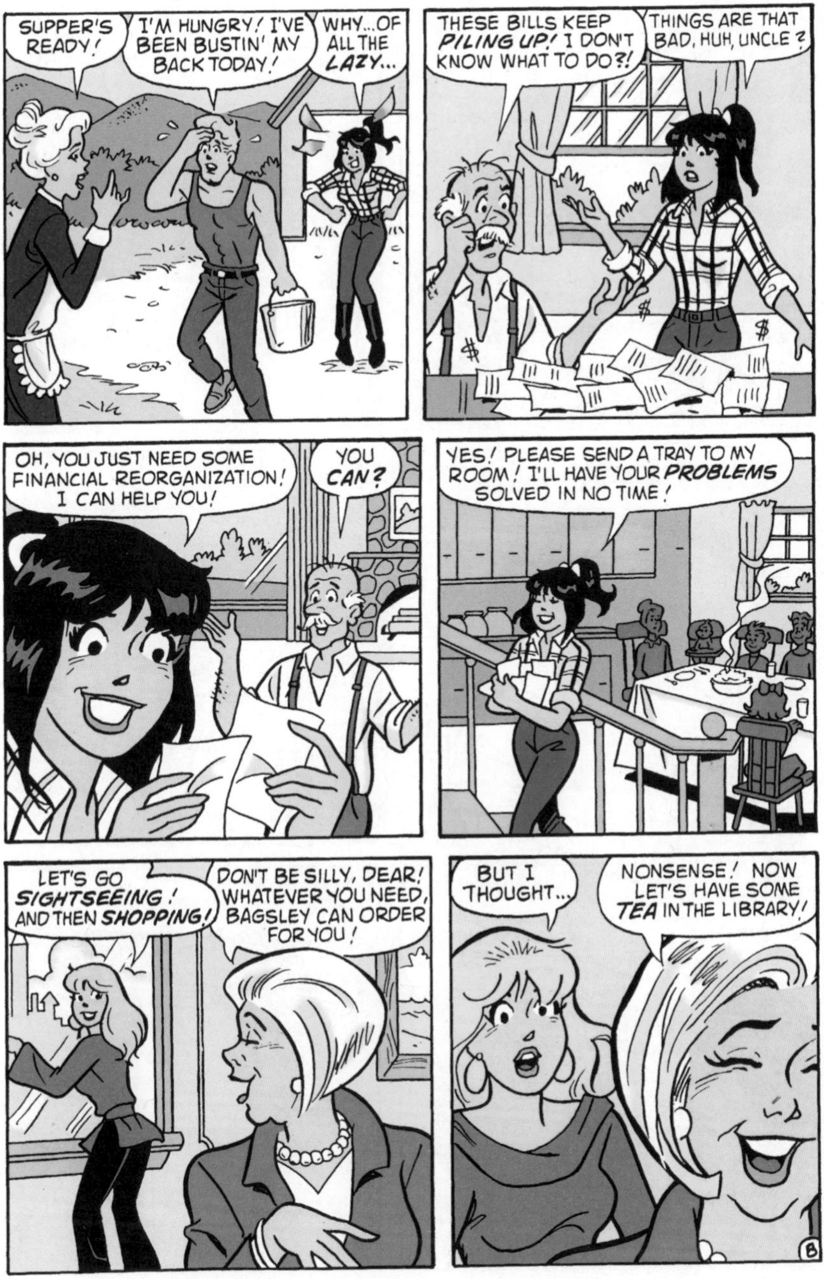
SUPPER'S READY!
I'M HUNGRY! I'VE BEEN BUSTIN' MY BACK TODAY!
WHY...OF ALL THE LAZY...
THESE BILLS KEEP PILING UP! I DON'T KNOW WHAT TO DO?!
THINGS ARE THAT BAD, HUH, UNCLE?
OH, YOU JUST NEED SOME FINANCIAL REORGANIZATION! I CAN HELP YOU!
YOU CAN?
YES! PLEASE SEND A TRAY TO MY ROOM! I'LL HAVE YOUR PROBLEMS SOLVED IN NO TIME!
LET'S GO SIGHTSEEING! AND THEN SHOPPING!
DON'T BE SILLY, DEAR! WHATEVER YOU NEED, BAGSLEY CAN ORDER FOR YOU!
BUT I THOUGHT...
NONSENSE! NOW LET'S HAVE SOME TEA IN THE LIBRARY!
8

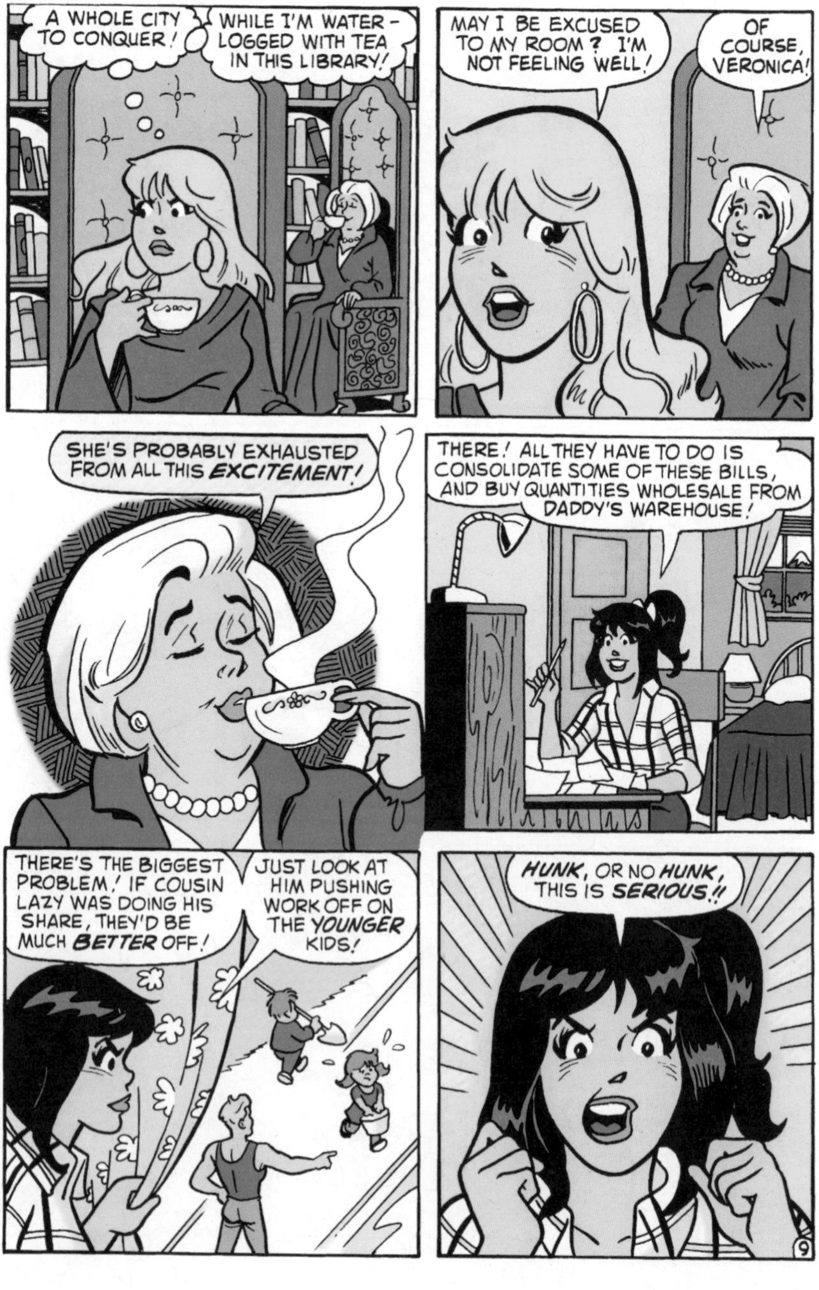
A WHOLE CITY TO CONQUER!
WHILE I'M WATER-LOGGED WITH TEA IN THIS LIBRARY!
MAY I BE EXCUSED TO MY ROOM? I'M NOT FEELING WELL!
OF COURSE, VERONICA!
SHE'S PROBABLY EXHAUSTED FROM ALL THIS EXCITEMENT!
THERE! ALL THEY HAVE TO DO IS CONSOLIDATE SOME OF THESE BILLS, AND BUY QUANTITIES WHOLESALE FROM DADDY'S WAREHOUSE!
THERE'S THE BIGGEST PROBLEM! IF COUSIN LAZY WAS DOING HIS SHARE, THEY'D BE MUCH BETTER OFF!
JUST LOOK AT HIM PUSHING WORK OFF ON THE YOUNGER KIDS!
HUNK, OR NO HUNK, THIS IS SERIOUS!!
9

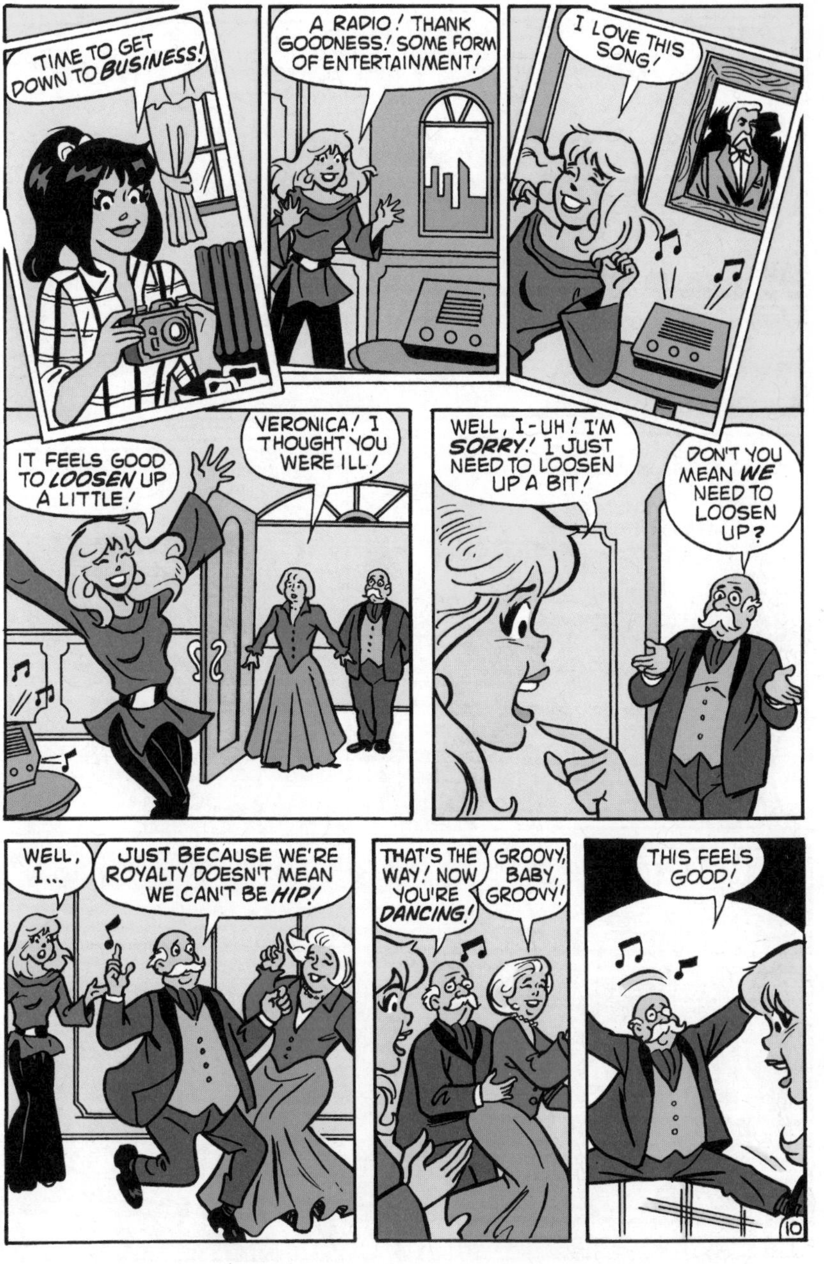
TIME TO GET DOWN TO BUSINESS!
A RADIO! THANK GOODNESS! SOME FORM OF ENTERTAINMENT!
I LOVE THIS SONG!
IT FEELS GOOD TO LOOSEN UP A LITTLE!
VERONICA! I THOUGHT YOU WERE ILL!
WELL, I-UH! I'M SORRY! I JUST NEED TO LOOSEN UP A BIT!
DON'T YOU MEAN WE NEED TO LOOSEN UP?
WELL, I...
JUST BECAUSE WE'RE ROYALTY DOESN'T MEAN WE CAN'T BE HIP!
THAT'S THE WAY! NOW YOU'RE DANCING!
GROOVY, BABY, GROOVY!
THIS FEELS GOOD!
10

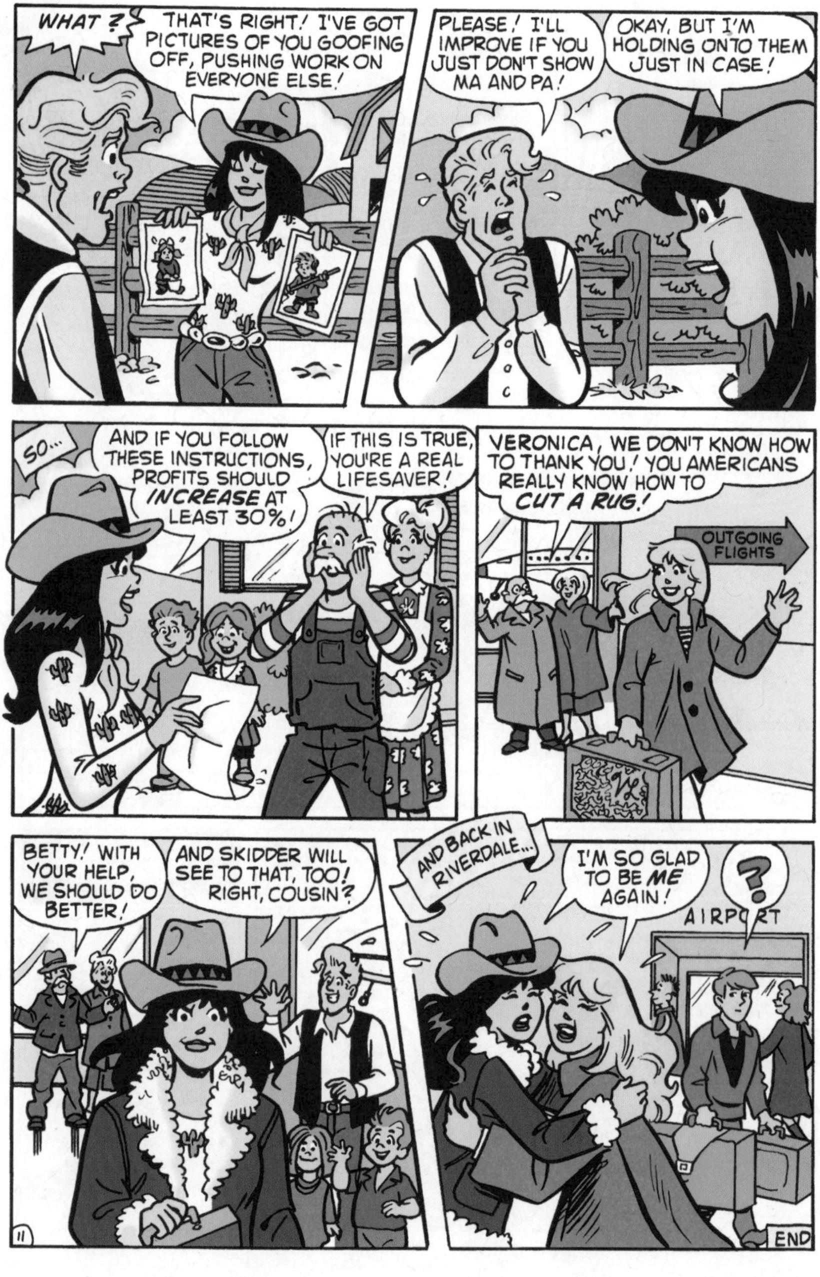
WHAT ?
THAT'S RIGHT! I'VE GOT PICTURES OF YOU GOOFING OFF, PUSHING WORK ON EVERYONE ELSE!
PLEASE! I'LL IMPROVE IF YOU JUST DON'T SHOW MA AND PA!
OKAY, BUT I'M HOLDING ONTO THEM JUST IN CASE!
SO...
AND IF YOU FOLLOW THESE INSTRUCTIONS, PROFITS SHOULD INCREASE AT LEAST 30%!
IF THIS IS TRUE, YOU'RE A REAL LIFESAVER!
VERONICA, WE DON'T KNOW HOW TO THANK YOU! YOU AMERICANS REALLY KNOW HOW TO CUT A RUG!
OUTGOING FLIGHTS
BETTY! WITH YOUR HELP, WE SHOULD DO BETTER!
AND SKIDDER WILL SEE TO THAT, TOO! RIGHT, COUSIN?
11
AND BACK IN RIVERDALE...
I'M SO GLAD TO BE ME AGAIN!
?
AIRPORT
END

Betty and Veronica in Chances are....

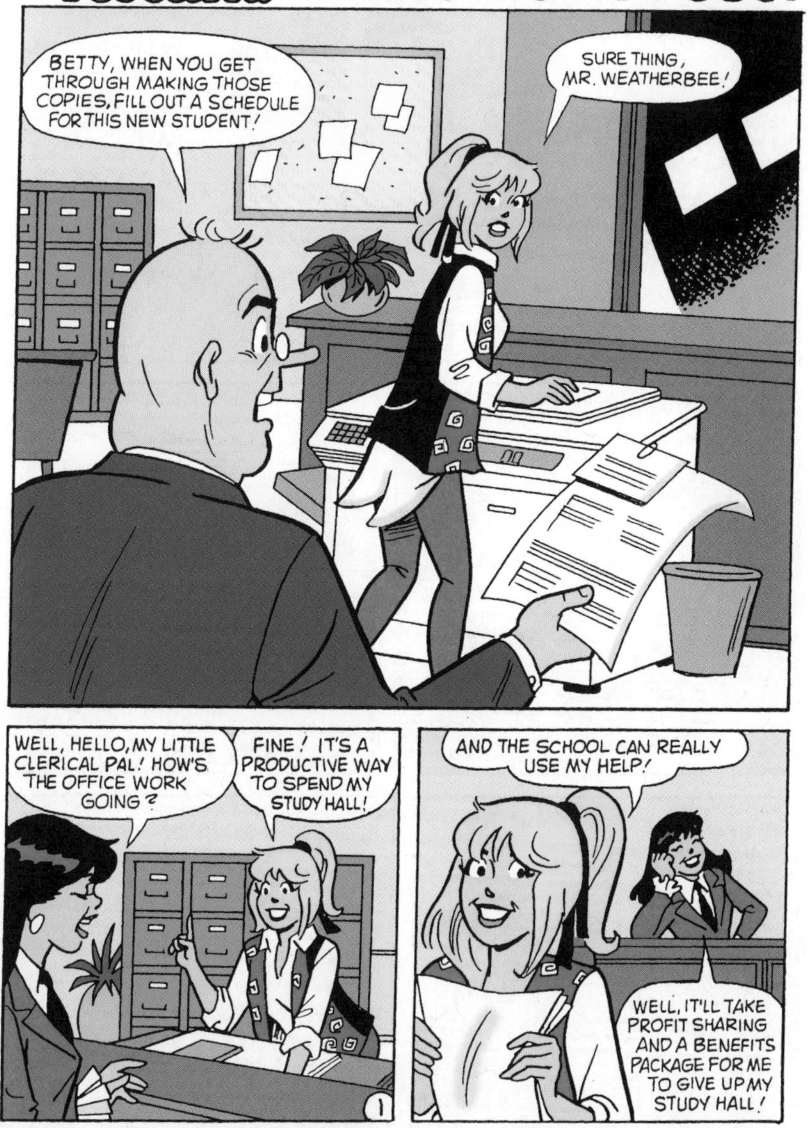
BETTY, WHEN YOU GET THROUGH MAKING THOSE COPIES, FILL OUT A SCHEDULE FOR THIS NEW STUDENT!
SURE THING, MR. WEATHERBEE!
WELL, HELLO, MY LITTLE CLERICAL PAL! HOW'S THE OFFICE WORK GOING?
FINE! IT'S A PRODUCTIVE WAY TO SPEND MY STUDY HALL!
AND THE SCHOOL CAN REALLY USE MY HELP!
WELL, IT'LL TAKE PROFIT SHARING AND A BENEFITS PACKAGE FOR ME TO GIVE UP MY STUDY HALL!

Story: Dan Parent & Bill Golliher **Art:** Dan DeCarlo & Dan Parent
Letters: Bill Yoshida **Colors:** Barry Grossman

Originally printed in BETTY & VERONICA SPECTACULAR #6, February 1994

I ALMOST FORGOT! MR. WEATHERBEE WANTED ME TO FILL OUT A SCHEDULE FOR A NEW STUDENT!
OH, A NEW INMATE!
WHO'S THE UNLUCKY VICTIM ?!
LET'S SEE HERE! ONE CHANCE REVOIR! A FRENCH FOREIGN EXCHANGE STUDENT!
OUI! TELL ME MORE!
HE EXCELS IN SOCCER, VOLLEYBALL AND TENNIS! HE'S ALSO QUITE A MUSICIAN!
HMMM! SOUNDS LIKE MY KIND OF GUY!
YEAH! MINE, TOO!
I GUESS I'LL JUST HAVE TO SCHEDULE HIM INTO ALL MY CLASSES!
WHAT?!
WELL, I GUESS IT IS ONE OF THE PERKS OF MY JOB!
AS A FRIEND I DEMAND YOU ALLOW ME EQUAL TIME!
2

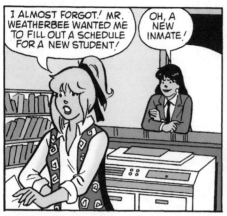

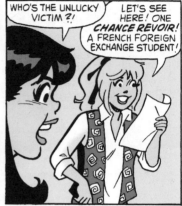

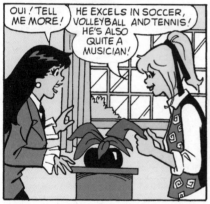

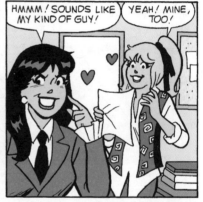

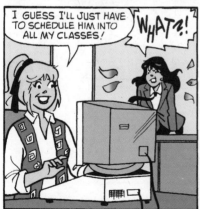

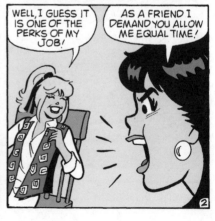

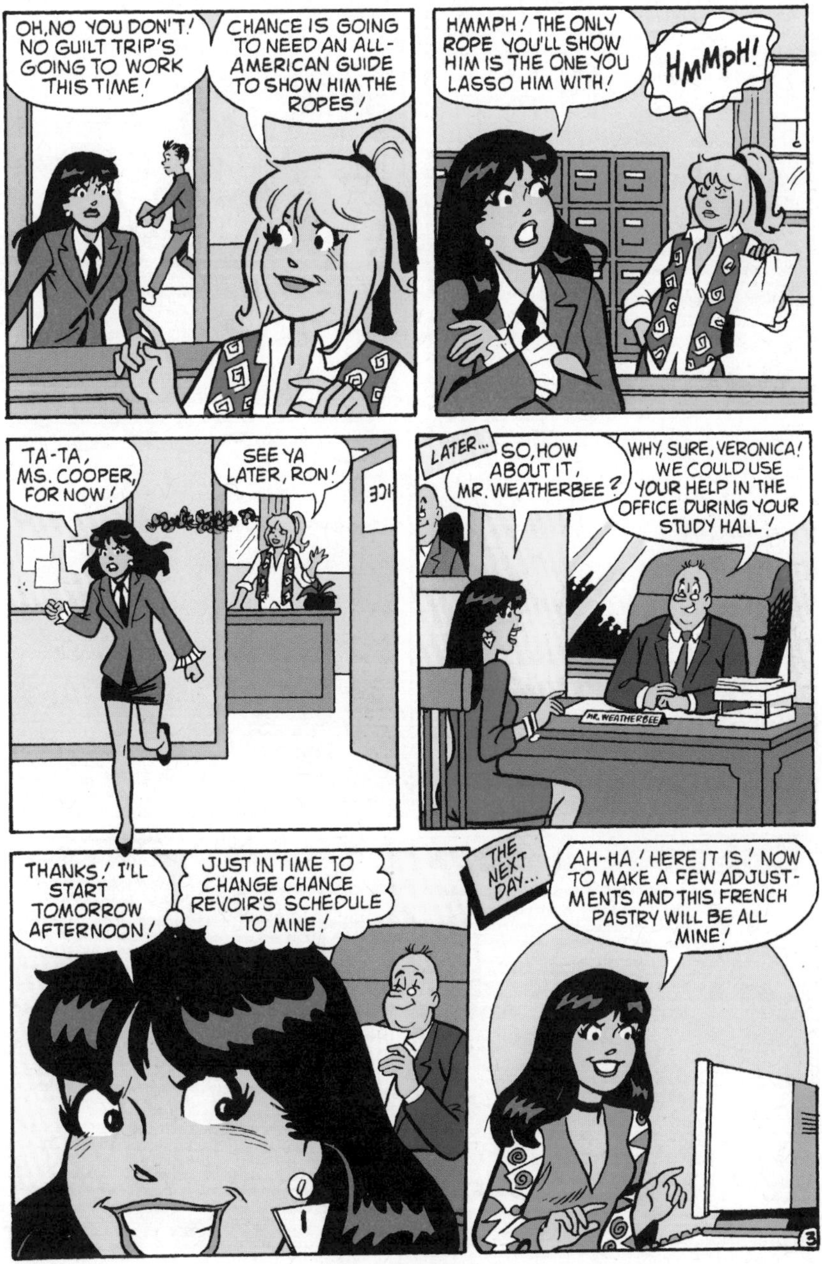
OH, NO YOU DON'T! NO GUILT TRIP'S GOING TO WORK THIS TIME!
CHANCE IS GOING TO NEED AN ALL-AMERICAN GUIDE TO SHOW HIM THE ROPES!
HMMPH! THE ONLY ROPE YOU'LL SHOW HIM IS THE ONE YOU LASSO HIM WITH!
HMMPH!
TA-TA, MS. COOPER, FOR NOW!
SEE YA LATER, RON!
LATER...
SO, HOW ABOUT IT, MR. WEATHERBEE?
WHY, SURE, VERONICA! WE COULD USE YOUR HELP IN THE OFFICE DURING YOUR STUDY HALL!
MR. WEATHERBEE
THANKS! I'LL START TOMORROW AFTERNOON!
JUST IN TIME TO CHANGE CHANCE REVOIR'S SCHEDULE TO MINE!
THE NEXT DAY...
AH-HA! HERE IT IS! NOW TO MAKE A FEW ADJUSTMENTS AND THIS FRENCH PASTRY WILL BE ALL MINE!
3

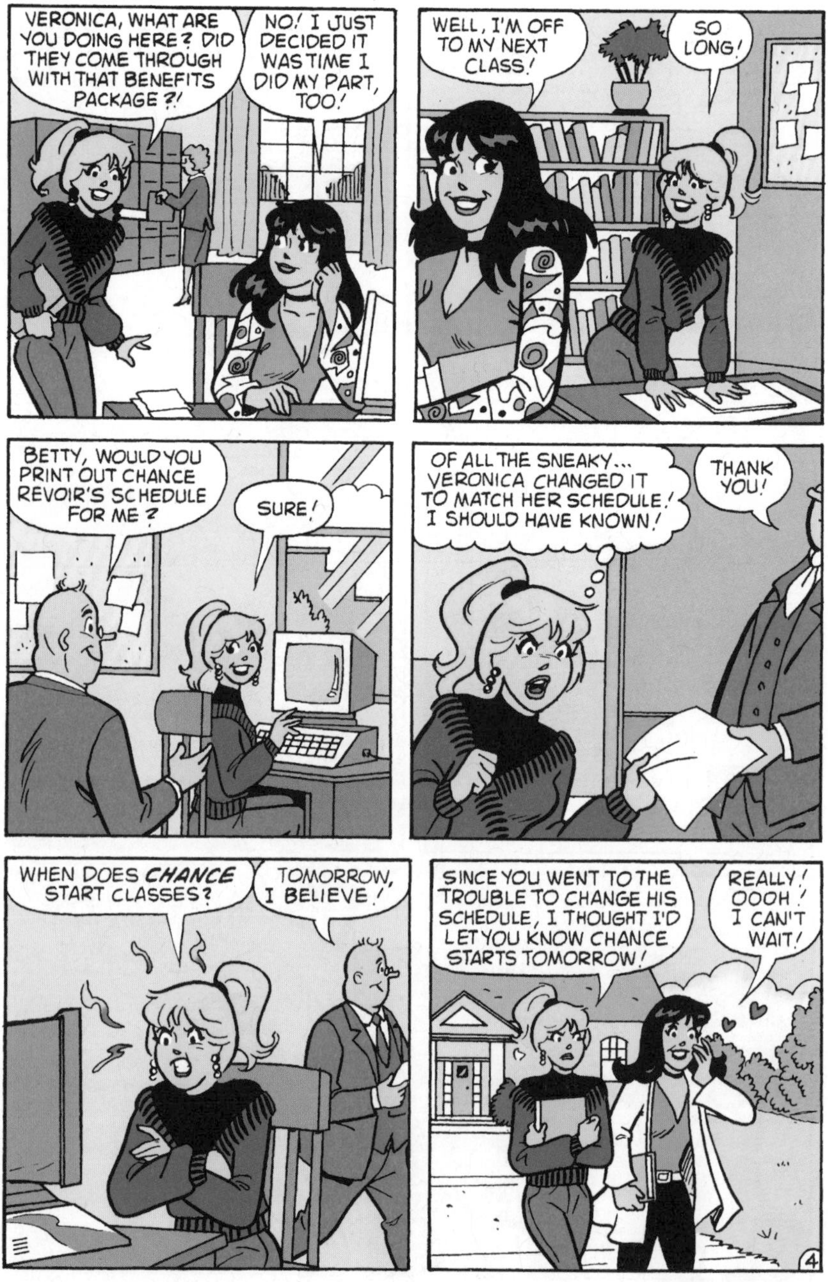
VERONICA, WHAT ARE YOU DOING HERE? DID THEY COME THROUGH WITH THAT BENEFITS PACKAGE?!
NO! I JUST DECIDED IT WAS TIME I DID MY PART, TOO!
WELL, I'M OFF TO MY NEXT CLASS!
SO LONG!
BETTY, WOULD YOU PRINT OUT CHANCE REVOIR'S SCHEDULE FOR ME?
SURE!
OF ALL THE SNEAKY... VERONICA CHANGED IT TO MATCH HER SCHEDULE! I SHOULD HAVE KNOWN!
THANK YOU!
WHEN DOES CHANCE START CLASSES?
TOMORROW, I BELIEVE!
SINCE YOU WENT TO THE TROUBLE TO CHANGE HIS SCHEDULE, I THOUGHT I'D LET YOU KNOW CHANCE STARTS TOMORROW!
REALLY! OOOH! I CAN'T WAIT!
4

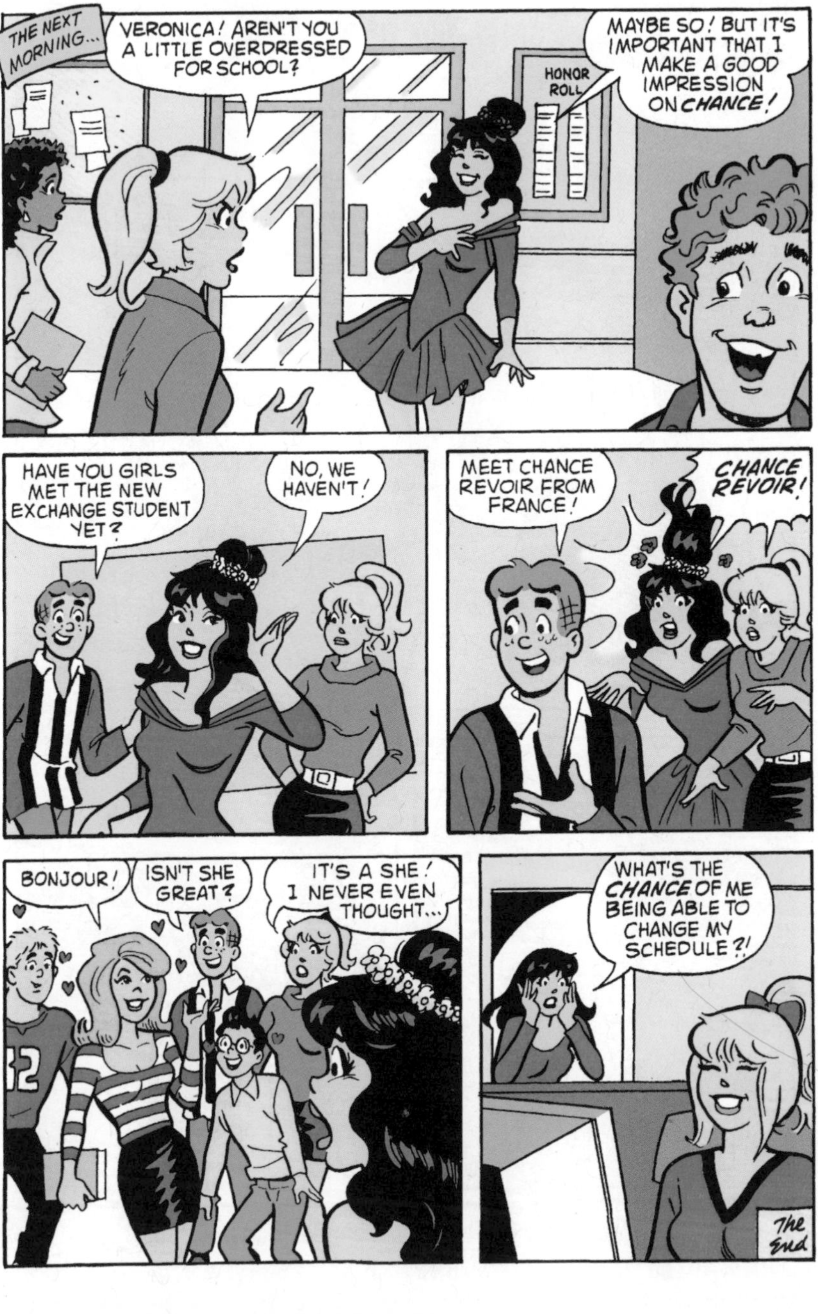
THE NEXT MORNING...
VERONICA! AREN'T YOU A LITTLE OVERDRESSED FOR SCHOOL?
HONOR ROLL
MAYBE SO! BUT IT'S IMPORTANT THAT I MAKE A GOOD IMPRESSION ON CHANCE!
HAVE YOU GIRLS MET THE NEW EXCHANGE STUDENT YET?
NO, WE HAVEN'T!
MEET CHANCE REVOIR FROM FRANCE!
CHANCE REVOIR!
BONJOUR!
ISN'T SHE GREAT?
IT'S A SHE! I NEVER EVEN THOUGHT...
WHAT'S THE CHANCE OF ME BEING ABLE TO CHANGE MY SCHEDULE?!
The End

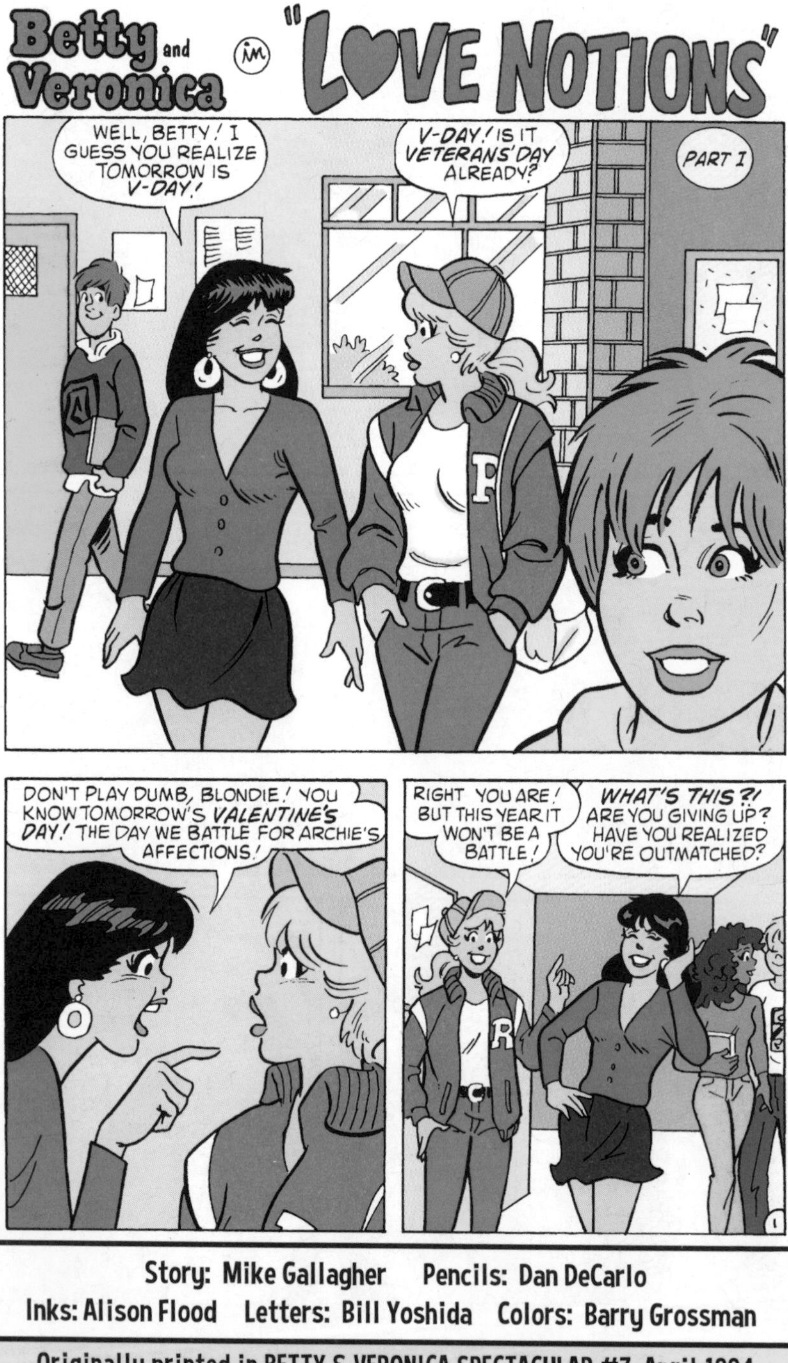
Betty and Veronica in "LOVE NOTIONS"
WELL, BETTY! I GUESS YOU REALIZE TOMORROW IS V-DAY!
V-DAY! IS IT VETERANS' DAY ALREADY?
PART I
DON'T PLAY DUMB, BLONDIE! YOU KNOW TOMORROW'S VALENTINE'S DAY! THE DAY WE BATTLE FOR ARCHIE'S AFFECTIONS!
RIGHT YOU ARE! BUT THIS YEAR IT WON'T BE A BATTLE!
WHAT'S THIS?! ARE YOU GIVING UP? HAVE YOU REALIZED YOU'RE OUTMATCHED?

Story: Mike Gallagher Pencils: Dan DeCarlo

Inks: Alison Flood Letters: Bill Yoshida Colors: Barry Grossman

Originally printed in BETTY & VERONICA SPECTACULAR #7, April 1994

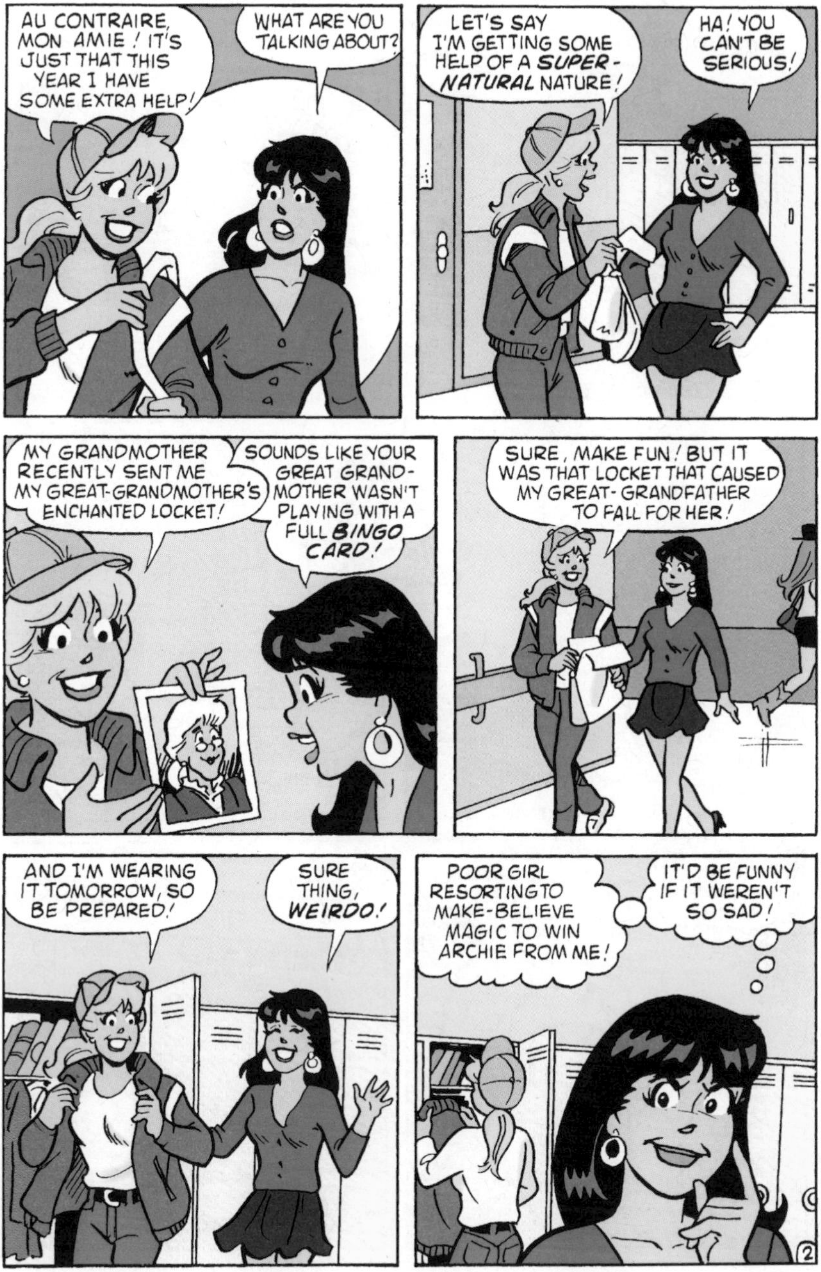
AU CONTRAIRE, MON AMIE! IT'S JUST THAT THIS YEAR I HAVE SOME EXTRA HELP!
WHAT ARE YOU TALKING ABOUT?
LET'S SAY I'M GETTING SOME HELP OF A SUPER-NATURAL NATURE!
HA! YOU CAN'T BE SERIOUS!
MY GRANDMOTHER RECENTLY SENT ME MY GREAT-GRANDMOTHER'S ENCHANTED LOCKET!
SOUNDS LIKE YOUR GREAT GRAND-MOTHER WASN'T PLAYING WITH A FULL BINGO CARD!
SURE, MAKE FUN! BUT IT WAS THAT LOCKET THAT CAUSED MY GREAT-GRANDFATHER TO FALL FOR HER!
AND I'M WEARING IT TOMORROW, SO BE PREPARED!
SURE THING, WEIRDO!
POOR GIRL RESORTING TO MAKE-BELIEVE MAGIC TO WIN ARCHIE FROM ME!
IT'D BE FUNNY IF IT WEREN'T SO SAD!
2

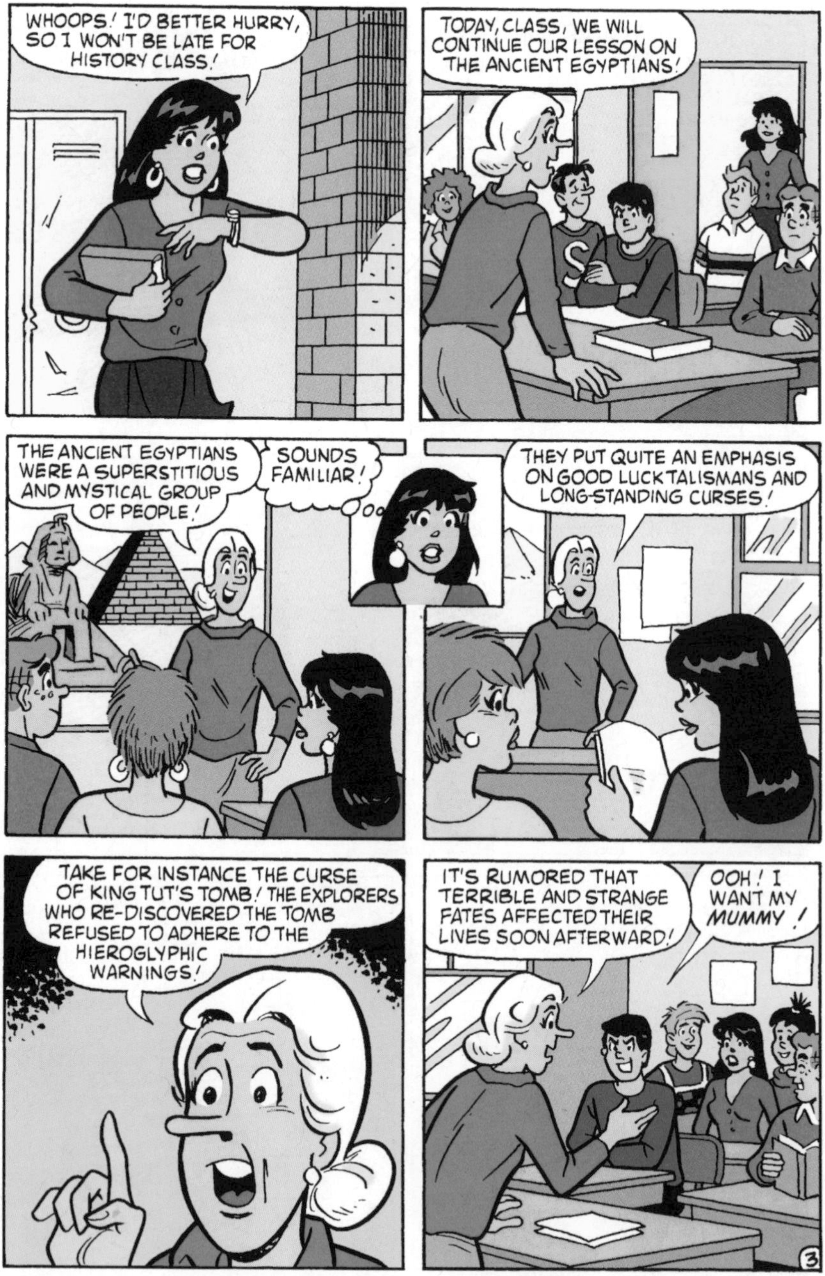
WHOOPS! I'D BETTER HURRY, SO I WON'T BE LATE FOR HISTORY CLASS!
TODAY, CLASS, WE WILL CONTINUE OUR LESSON ON THE ANCIENT EGYPTIANS!
THE ANCIENT EGYPTIANS WERE A SUPERSTITIOUS AND MYSTICAL GROUP OF PEOPLE!
SOUNDS FAMILIAR!
THEY PUT QUITE AN EMPHASIS ON GOOD LUCK TALISMANS AND LONG-STANDING CURSES!
TAKE FOR INSTANCE THE CURSE OF KING TUT'S TOMB! THE EXPLORERS WHO RE-DISCOVERED THE TOMB REFUSED TO ADHERE TO THE HIEROGLYPHIC WARNINGS!
IT'S RUMORED THAT TERRIBLE AND STRANGE FATES AFFECTED THEIR LIVES SOON AFTERWARD!
OOH! I WANT MY *MUMMY*!
3

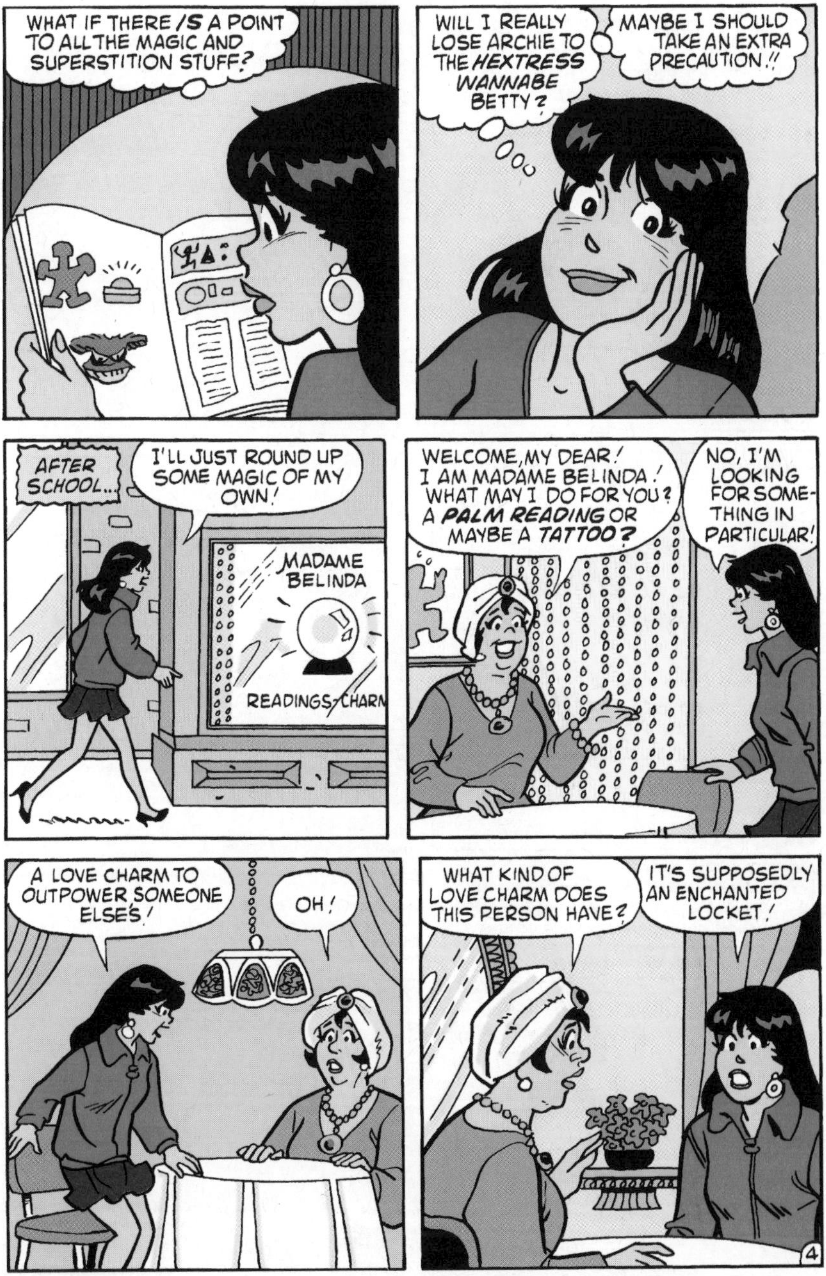
WHAT IF THERE *IS* A POINT TO ALL THE MAGIC AND SUPERSTITION STUFF?
WILL I REALLY LOSE ARCHIE TO THE *HEXTRESS WANNABE* BETTY?
MAYBE I SHOULD TAKE AN EXTRA PRECAUTION!!
AFTER SCHOOL...
I'LL JUST ROUND UP SOME MAGIC OF MY OWN!
MADAME BELINDA
READINGS/CHARM
WELCOME, MY DEAR! I AM MADAME BELINDA! WHAT MAY I DO FOR YOU? A *PALM READING* OR MAYBE A *TATTOO?*
NO, I'M LOOKING FOR SOMETHING IN PARTICULAR!
A LOVE CHARM TO OUTPOWER SOMEONE ELSE'S!
OH!
WHAT KIND OF LOVE CHARM DOES THIS PERSON HAVE?
IT'S SUPPOSEDLY AN ENCHANTED LOCKET!
4

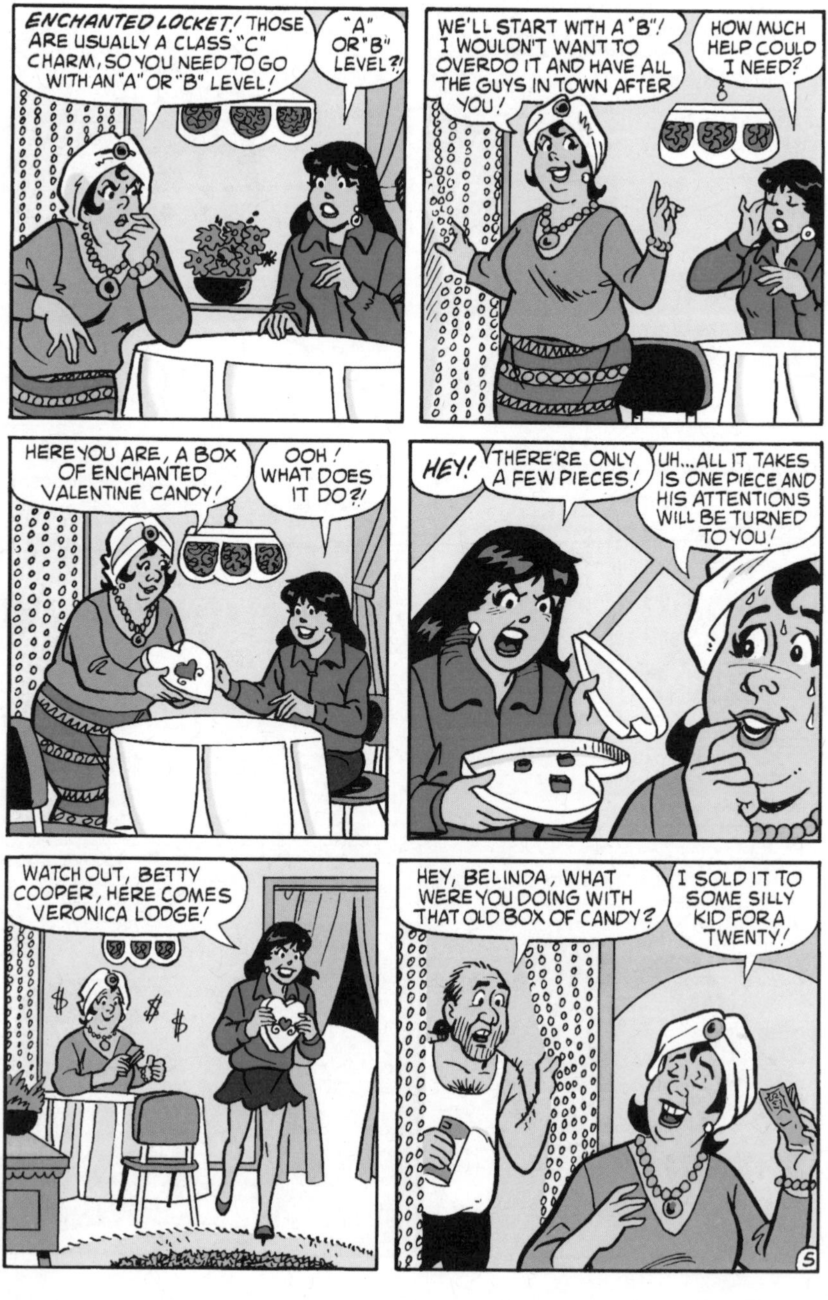
ENCHANTED LOCKET! THOSE ARE USUALLY A CLASS "C" CHARM, SO YOU NEED TO GO WITH AN "A" OR "B" LEVEL!
"A" OR "B" LEVEL?!
WE'LL START WITH A "B"! I WOULDN'T WANT TO OVERDO IT AND HAVE ALL THE GUYS IN TOWN AFTER YOU!
HOW MUCH HELP COULD I NEED?
HERE YOU ARE, A BOX OF ENCHANTED VALENTINE CANDY!
OOH! WHAT DOES IT DO?!
HEY!
THERE'RE ONLY A FEW PIECES!
UH... ALL IT TAKES IS ONE PIECE AND HIS ATTENTIONS WILL BE TURNED TO YOU!
WATCH OUT, BETTY COOPER, HERE COMES VERONICA LODGE!
HEY, BELINDA, WHAT WERE YOU DOING WITH THAT OLD BOX OF CANDY?
I SOLD IT TO SOME SILLY KID FOR A TWENTY!
5

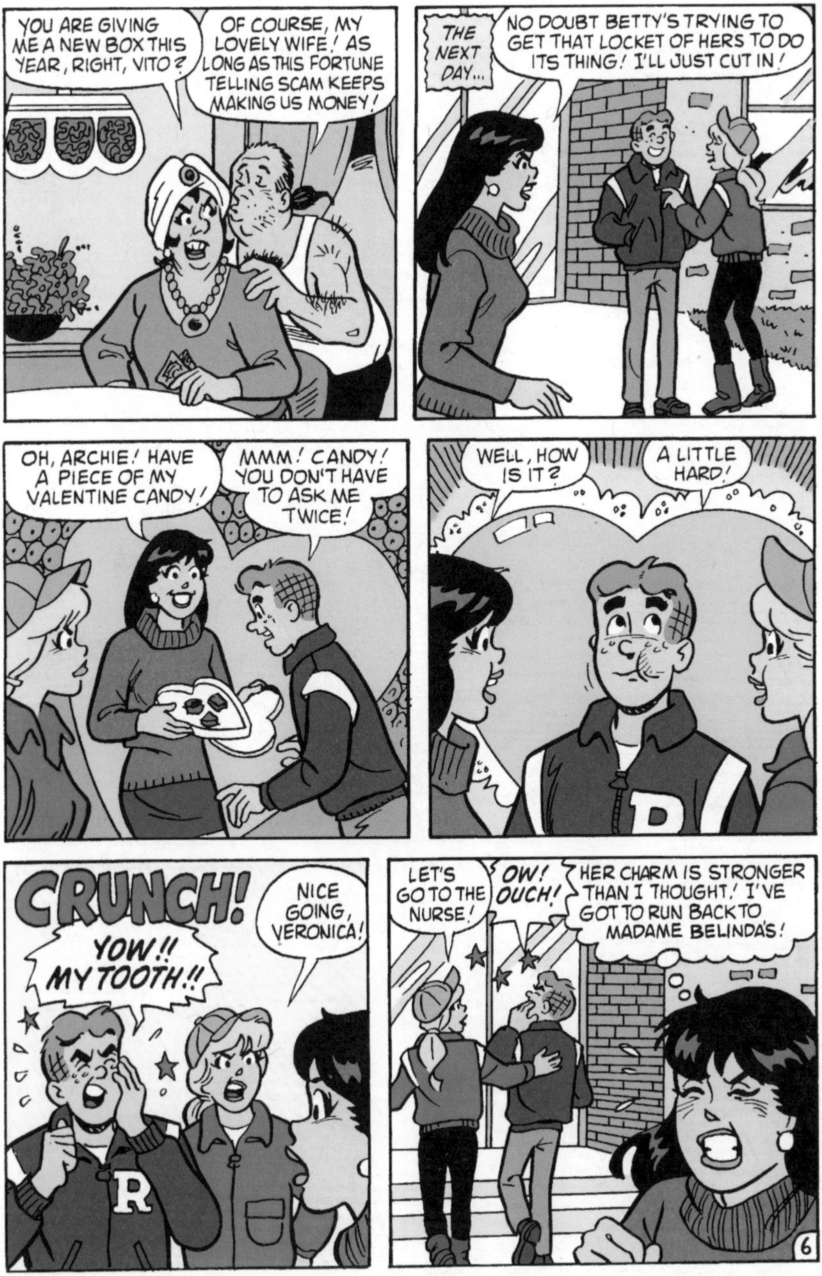
YOU ARE GIVING ME A NEW BOX THIS YEAR, RIGHT, VITO?
OF COURSE, MY LOVELY WIFE! AS LONG AS THIS FORTUNE TELLING SCAM KEEPS MAKING US MONEY!
THE NEXT DAY...
NO DOUBT BETTY'S TRYING TO GET THAT LOCKET OF HERS TO DO ITS THING! I'LL JUST CUT IN!
OH, ARCHIE! HAVE A PIECE OF MY VALENTINE CANDY!
MMM! CANDY! YOU DON'T HAVE TO ASK ME TWICE!
WELL, HOW IS IT?
A LITTLE HARD!
CRUNCH!
YOW!! MY TOOTH!!
NICE GOING, VERONICA!
LET'S GO TO THE NURSE!
OW! OUCH!
HER CHARM IS STRONGER THAN I THOUGHT! I'VE GOT TO RUN BACK TO MADAME BELINDA'S!
6

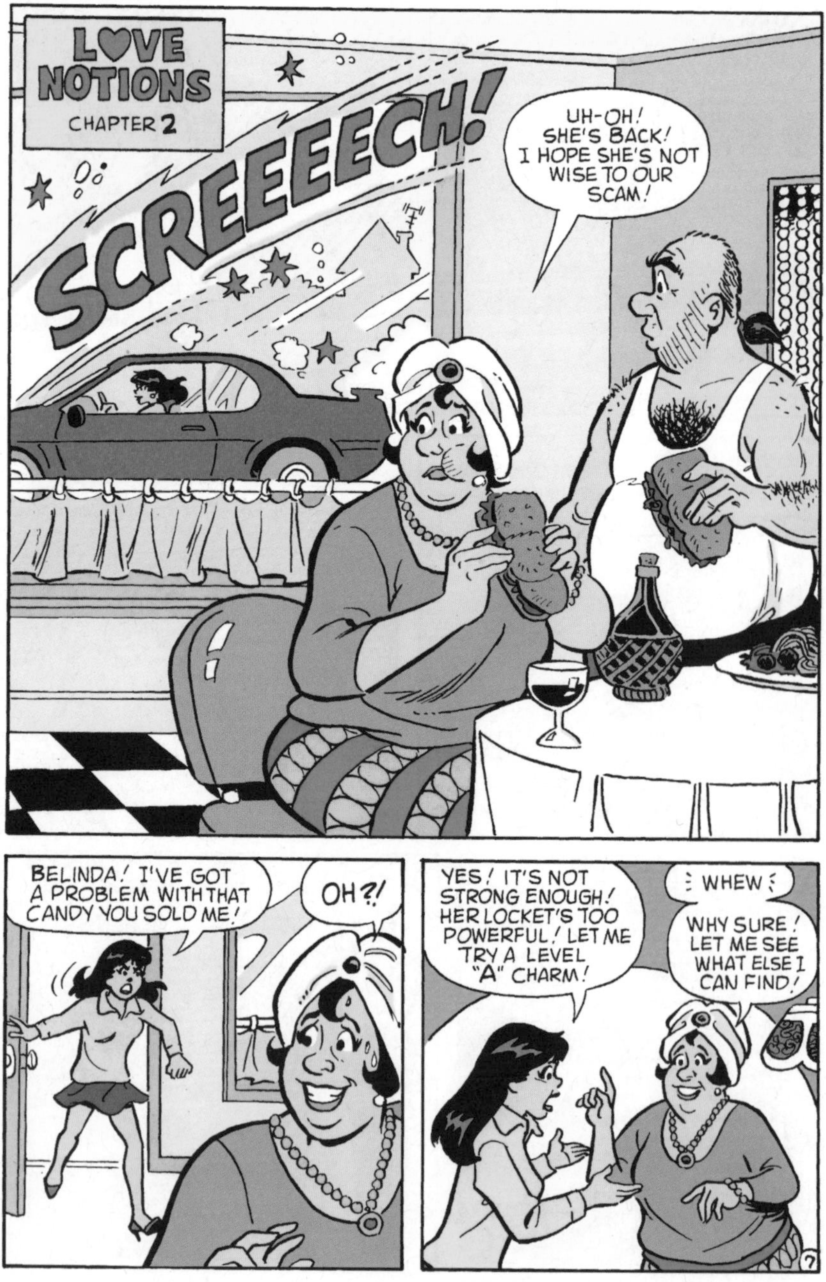
LOVE NOTIONS
CHAPTER 2
SCREEEECH!
UH-OH! SHE'S BACK! I HOPE SHE'S NOT WISE TO OUR SCAM!
BELINDA! I'VE GOT A PROBLEM WITH THAT CANDY YOU SOLD ME!
OH?!
YES! IT'S NOT STRONG ENOUGH! HER LOCKET'S TOO POWERFUL! LET ME TRY A LEVEL "A" CHARM!
WHEW
WHY SURE! LET ME SEE WHAT ELSE I CAN FIND!
7

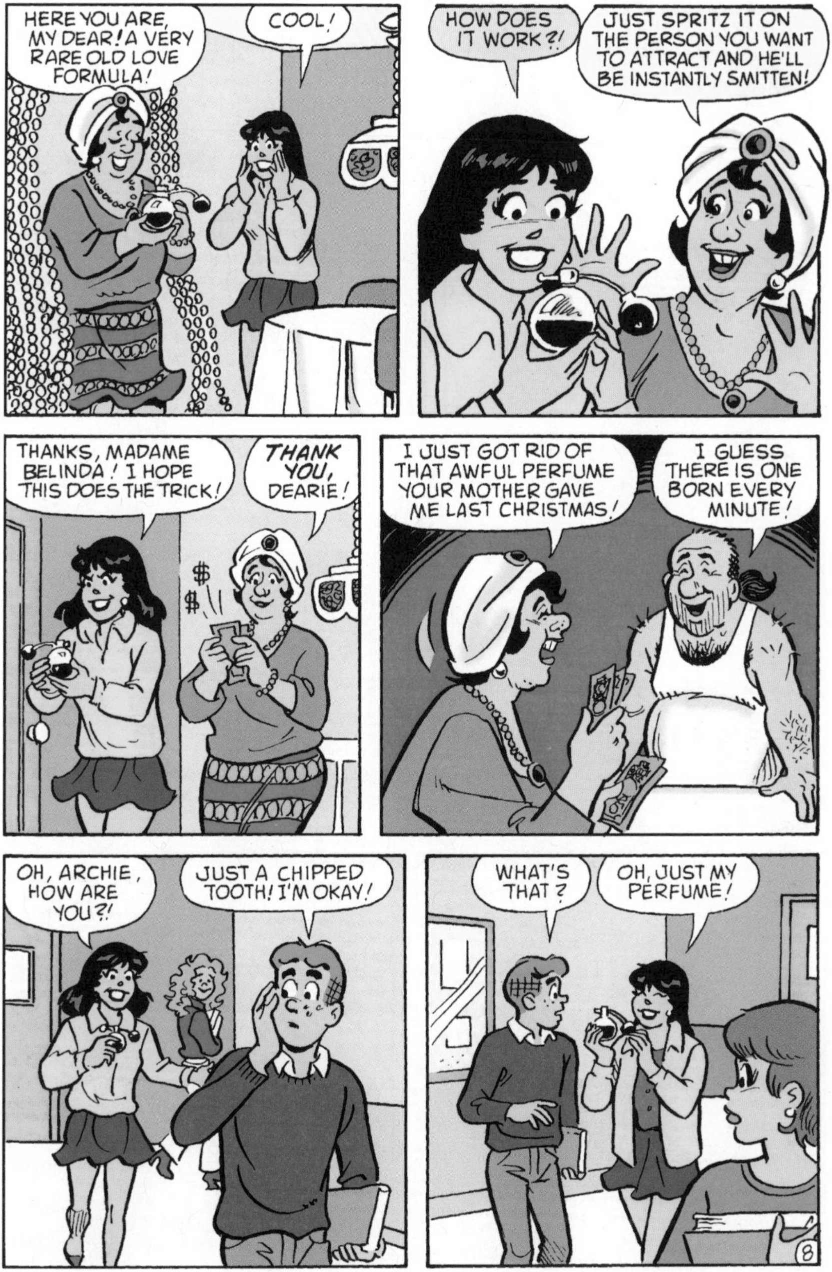
HERE YOU ARE, MY DEAR! A VERY RARE OLD LOVE FORMULA!
COOL!
HOW DOES IT WORK?!
JUST SPRITZ IT ON THE PERSON YOU WANT TO ATTRACT AND HE'LL BE INSTANTLY SMITTEN!
THANKS, MADAME BELINDA! I HOPE THIS DOES THE TRICK!
THANK YOU, DEARIE!
$
$
I JUST GOT RID OF THAT AWFUL PERFUME YOUR MOTHER GAVE ME LAST CHRISTMAS!
I GUESS THERE IS ONE BORN EVERY MINUTE!
OH, ARCHIE, HOW ARE YOU?!
JUST A CHIPPED TOOTH! I'M OKAY!
WHAT'S THAT?
OH, JUST MY PERFUME!
8

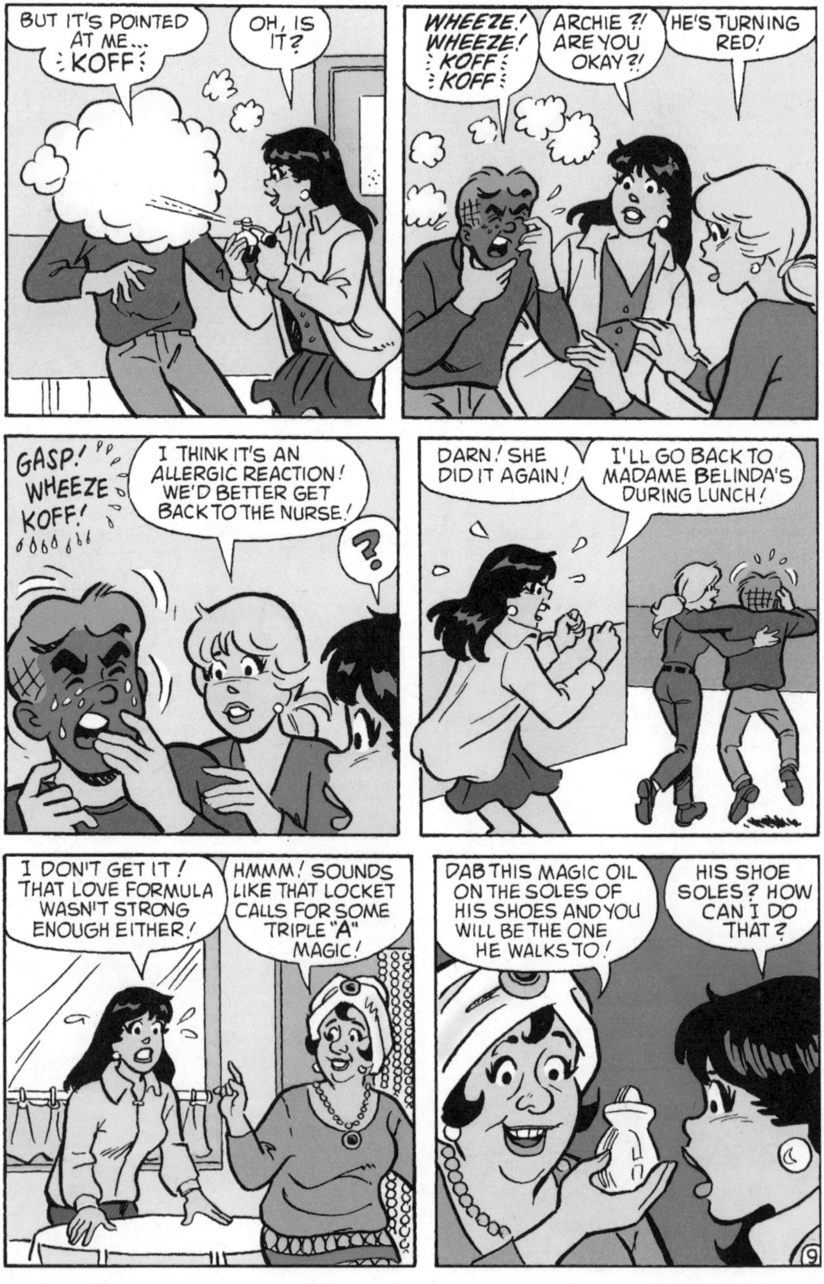
BUT IT'S POINTED AT ME... KOFF
OH, IS IT?
WHEEZE! WHEEZE! KOFF KOFF
ARCHIE ?! ARE YOU OKAY ?!
HE'S TURNING RED!
GASP! WHEEZE KOFF!
I THINK IT'S AN ALLERGIC REACTION! WE'D BETTER GET BACK TO THE NURSE!
?
DARN! SHE DID IT AGAIN!
I'LL GO BACK TO MADAME BELINDA'S DURING LUNCH!
I DON'T GET IT! THAT LOVE FORMULA WASN'T STRONG ENOUGH EITHER!
HMMM! SOUNDS LIKE THAT LOCKET CALLS FOR SOME TRIPLE "A" MAGIC!
DAB THIS MAGIC OIL ON THE SOLES OF HIS SHOES AND YOU WILL BE THE ONE HE WALKS TO!
HIS SHOE SOLES? HOW CAN I DO THAT?
9

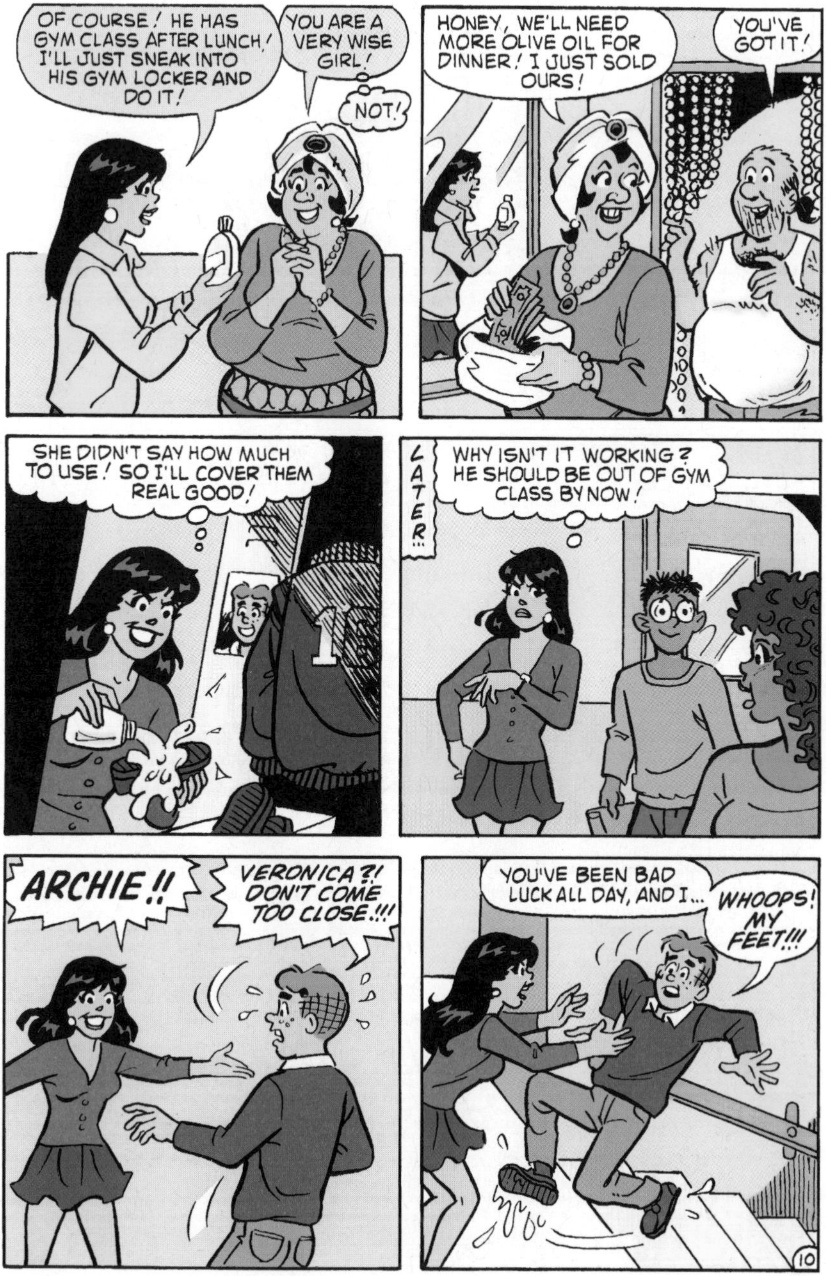
OF COURSE! HE HAS GYM CLASS AFTER LUNCH! I'LL JUST SNEAK INTO HIS GYM LOCKER AND DO IT!
YOU ARE A VERY WISE GIRL!
NOT!
HONEY, WE'LL NEED MORE OLIVE OIL FOR DINNER! I JUST SOLD OURS!
YOU'VE GOT IT!
SHE DIDN'T SAY HOW MUCH TO USE! SO I'LL COVER THEM REAL GOOD!
LATER...
WHY ISN'T IT WORKING? HE SHOULD BE OUT OF GYM CLASS BY NOW!
ARCHIE!!
VERONICA?! DON'T COME TOO CLOSE!!!
YOU'VE BEEN BAD LUCK ALL DAY, AND I...
WHOOPS! MY FEET!!!
10

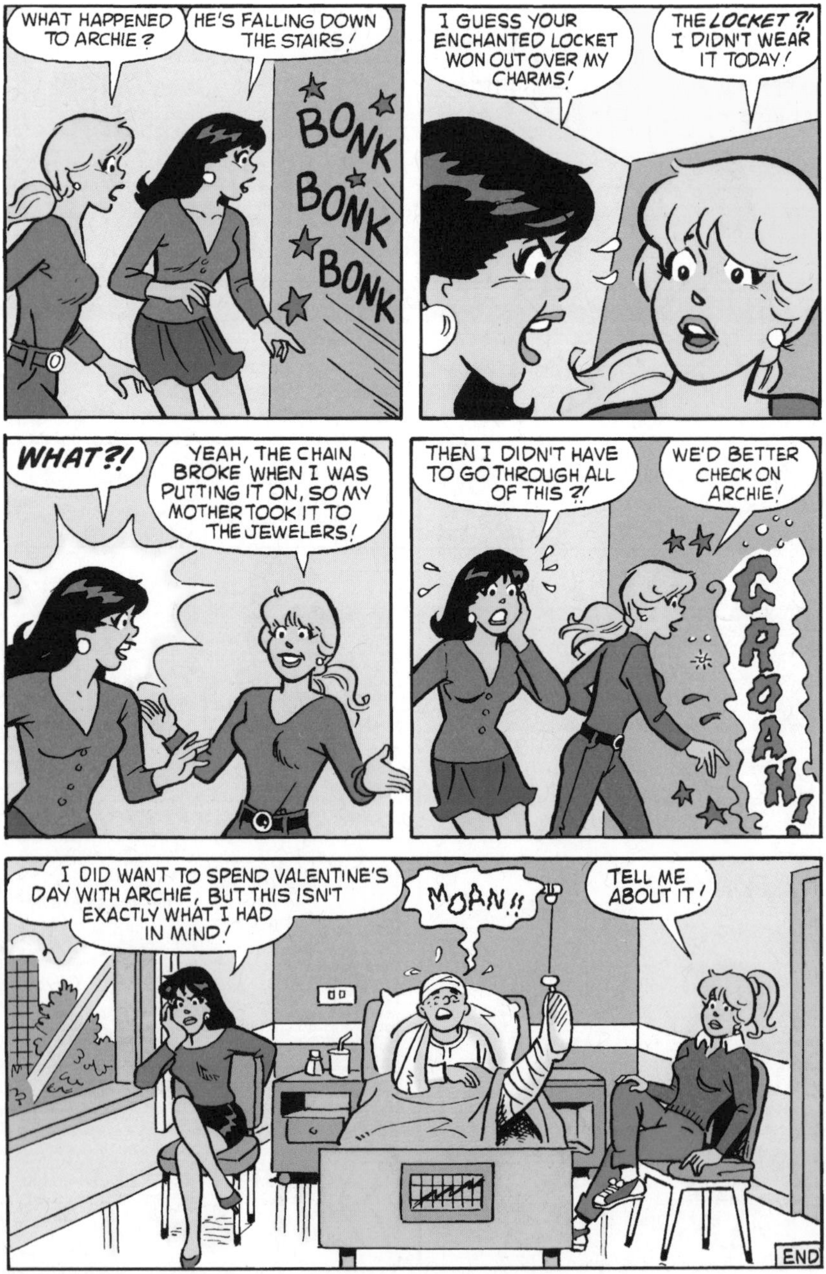
WHAT HAPPENED TO ARCHIE?
HE'S FALLING DOWN THE STAIRS!
BONK
BONK
BONK
I GUESS YOUR ENCHANTED LOCKET WON OUT OVER MY CHARMS!
THE *LOCKET*?! I DIDN'T WEAR IT TODAY!
WHAT?!
YEAH, THE CHAIN BROKE WHEN I WAS PUTTING IT ON, SO MY MOTHER TOOK IT TO THE JEWELERS!
THEN I DIDN'T HAVE TO GO THROUGH ALL OF THIS?!
WE'D BETTER CHECK ON ARCHIE!
GROAN!
I DID WANT TO SPEND VALENTINE'S DAY WITH ARCHIE, BUT THIS ISN'T EXACTLY WHAT I HAD IN MIND!
MOAN!!
TELL ME ABOUT IT!
END

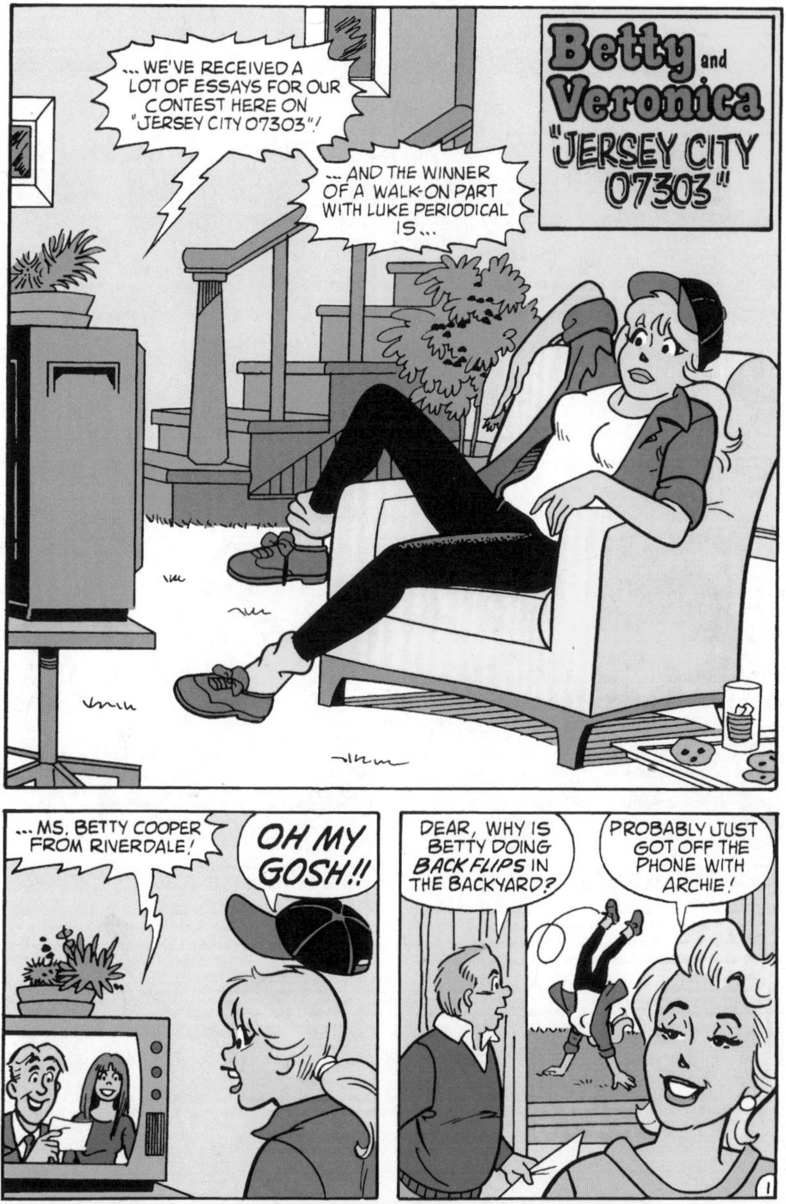
Betty and Veronica
"JERSEY CITY 07303"
... WE'VE RECEIVED A LOT OF ESSAYS FOR OUR CONTEST HERE ON "JERSEY CITY 07303"!
... AND THE WINNER OF A WALK-ON PART WITH LUKE PERIODICAL IS...
... MS. BETTY COOPER FROM RIVERDALE!
OH MY GOSH!!
DEAR, WHY IS BETTY DOING BACK FLIPS IN THE BACKYARD?
PROBABLY JUST GOT OFF THE PHONE WITH ARCHIE!

Story: Dan Parent Pencils: Dan DeCarlo
Inks: Alison Flood Letters: Bill Yoshida Colors: Barry Grossman

Originally printed in BETTY & VERONICA SPECTACULAR #7, April 1994

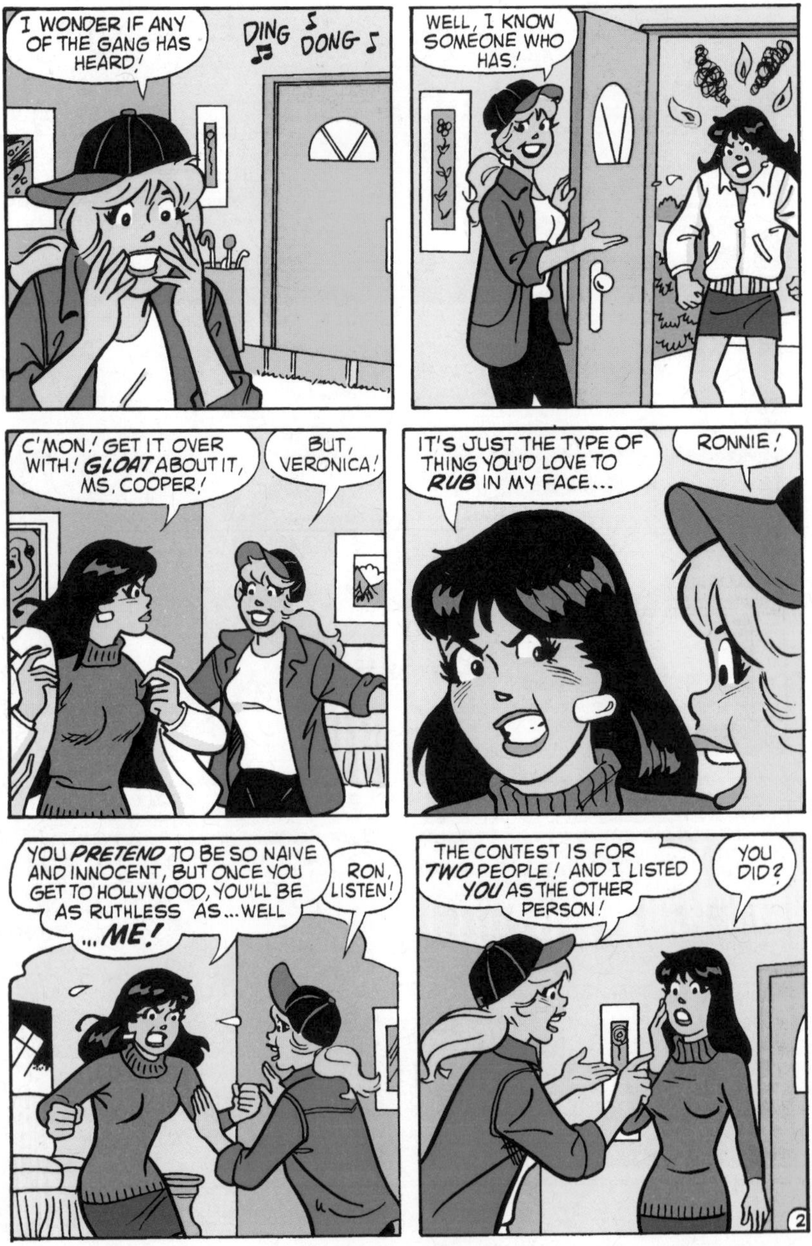
I WONDER IF ANY OF THE GANG HAS HEARD!
DING DONG
WELL, I KNOW SOMEONE WHO HAS!
C'MON! GET IT OVER WITH! GLOAT ABOUT IT, MS. COOPER!
BUT, VERONICA!
IT'S JUST THE TYPE OF THING YOU'D LOVE TO RUB IN MY FACE...
RONNIE!
YOU PRETEND TO BE SO NAIVE AND INNOCENT, BUT ONCE YOU GET TO HOLLYWOOD, YOU'LL BE AS RUTHLESS AS... WELL ...ME!
RON, LISTEN!
THE CONTEST IS FOR TWO PEOPLE! AND I LISTED YOU AS THE OTHER PERSON!
YOU DID?
2

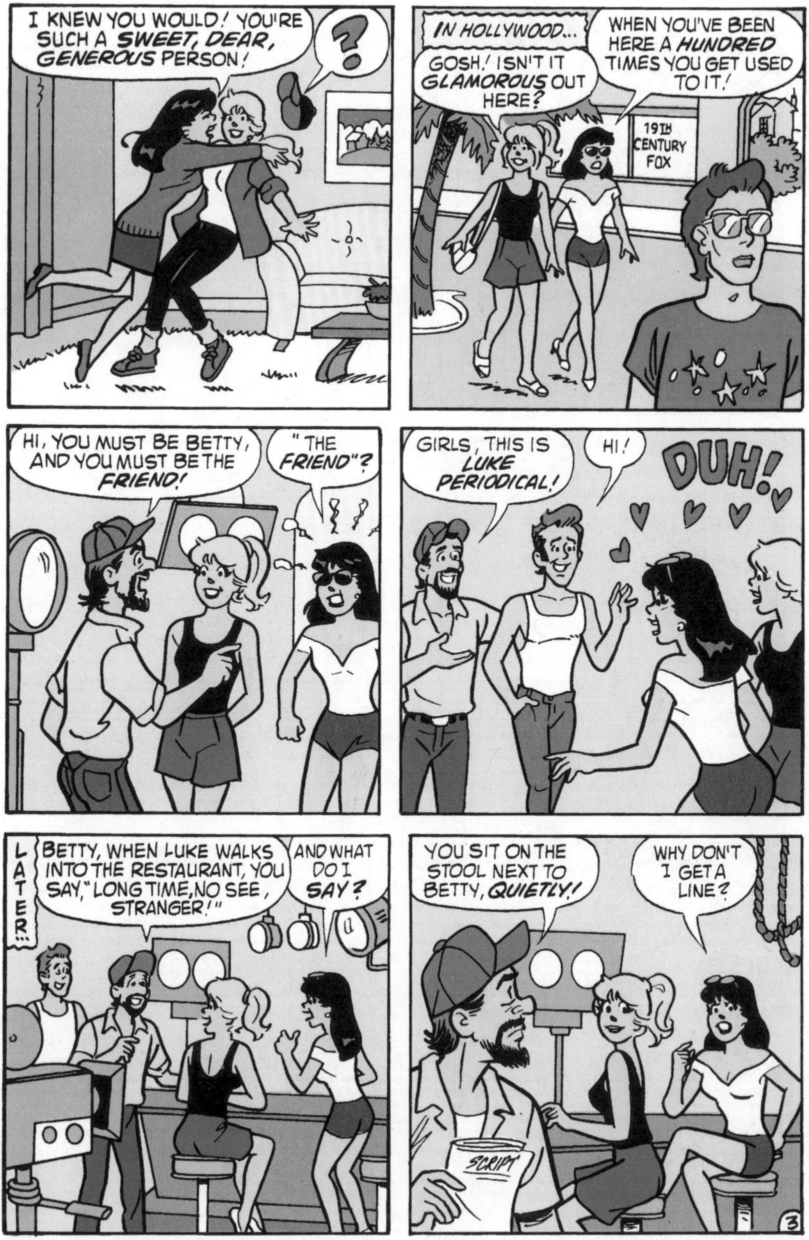
I KNEW YOU WOULD! YOU'RE SUCH A SWEET, DEAR, GENEROUS PERSON!
?
IN HOLLYWOOD...
GOSH! ISN'T IT GLAMOROUS OUT HERE?
WHEN YOU'VE BEEN HERE A HUNDRED TIMES YOU GET USED TO IT!
19TH CENTURY FOX
HI, YOU MUST BE BETTY, AND YOU MUST BE THE FRIEND!
"THE FRIEND"?
GIRLS, THIS IS LUKE PERIODICAL!
HI!
DUH!
LATER...
BETTY, WHEN LUKE WALKS INTO THE RESTAURANT, YOU SAY, "LONG TIME, NO SEE, STRANGER!"
AND WHAT DO I SAY?
YOU SIT ON THE STOOL NEXT TO BETTY, QUIETLY!
WHY DON'T I GET A LINE?
SCRIPT
3

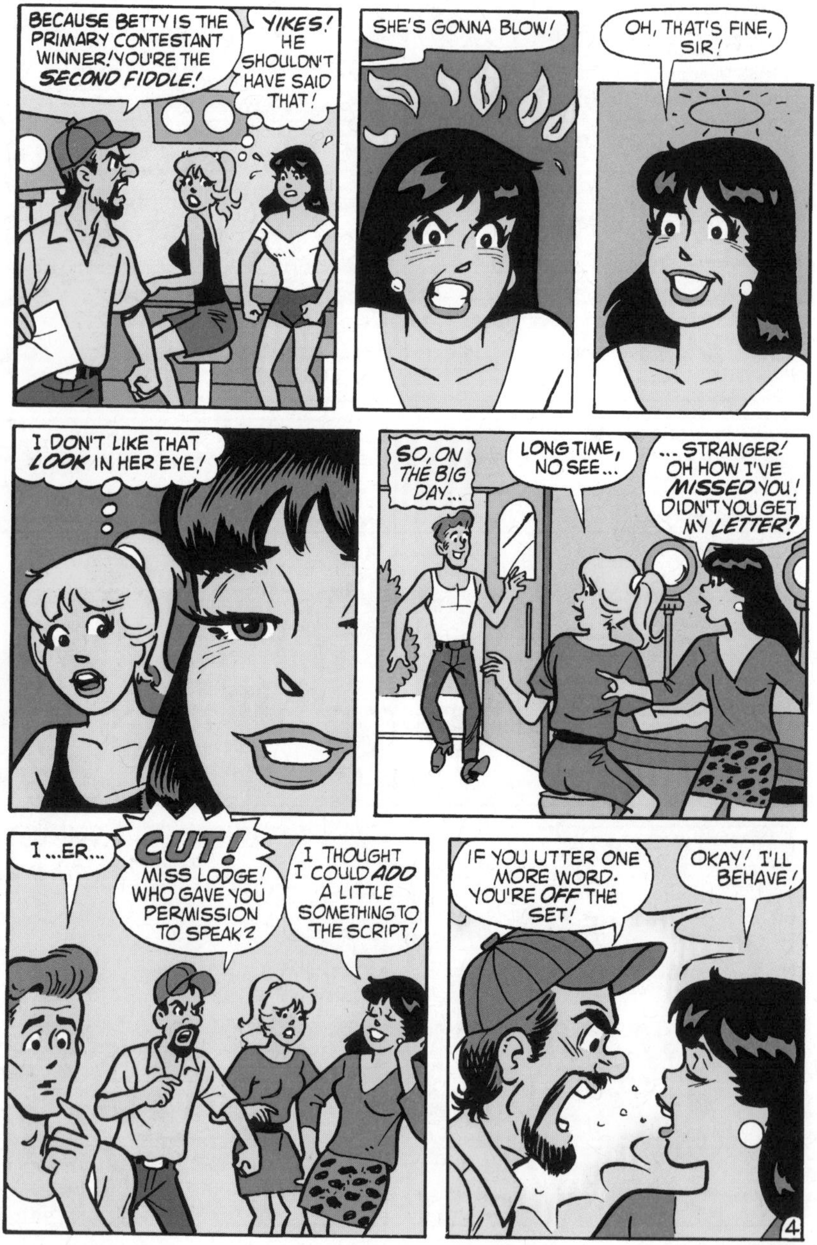
BECAUSE BETTY IS THE PRIMARY CONTESTANT WINNER! YOU'RE THE SECOND FIDDLE!
YIKES! HE SHOULDN'T HAVE SAID THAT!
SHE'S GONNA BLOW!
OH, THAT'S FINE, SIR!
I DON'T LIKE THAT LOOK IN HER EYE!
SO, ON THE BIG DAY...
LONG TIME, NO SEE...
... STRANGER! OH HOW I'VE MISSED YOU! DIDN'T YOU GET MY LETTER?
I ...ER...
CUT!
MISS LODGE! WHO GAVE YOU PERMISSION TO SPEAK?
I THOUGHT I COULD ADD A LITTLE SOMETHING TO THE SCRIPT!
IF YOU UTTER ONE MORE WORD. YOU'RE OFF THE SET!
OKAY! I'LL BEHAVE!
4

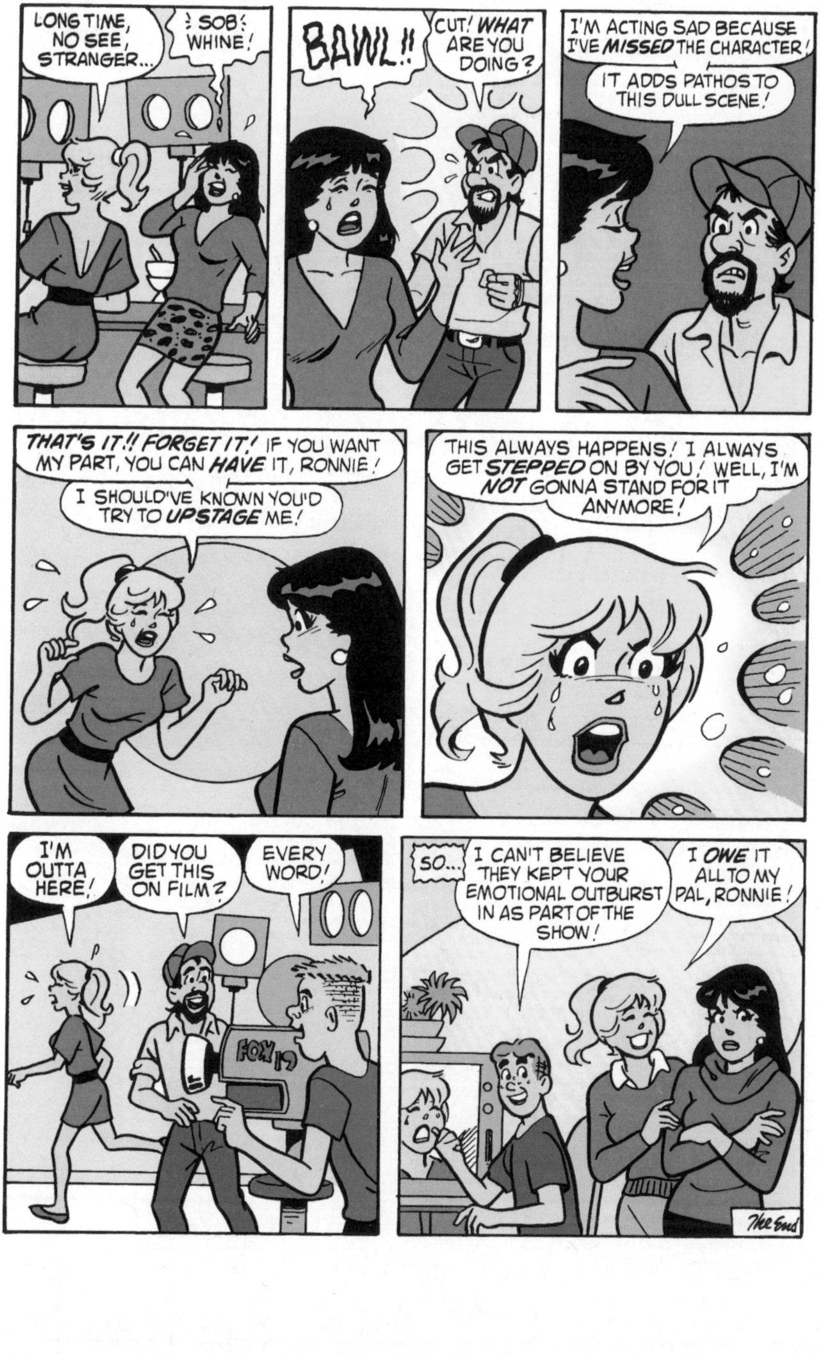
LONG TIME, NO SEE, STRANGER...
SOB WHINE!
BAWL!!
CUT! WHAT ARE YOU DOING?
I'M ACTING SAD BECAUSE I'VE MISSED THE CHARACTER!
IT ADDS PATHOS TO THIS DULL SCENE!
THAT'S IT!! FORGET IT! IF YOU WANT MY PART, YOU CAN HAVE IT, RONNIE!
I SHOULD'VE KNOWN YOU'D TRY TO UPSTAGE ME!
THIS ALWAYS HAPPENS! I ALWAYS GET STEPPED ON BY YOU! WELL, I'M NOT GONNA STAND FOR IT ANYMORE!
I'M OUTTA HERE!
DID YOU GET THIS ON FILM?
EVERY WORD!
FOX 19
SO...
I CAN'T BELIEVE THEY KEPT YOUR EMOTIONAL OUTBURST IN AS PART OF THE SHOW!
I OWE IT ALL TO MY PAL, RONNIE!
The End

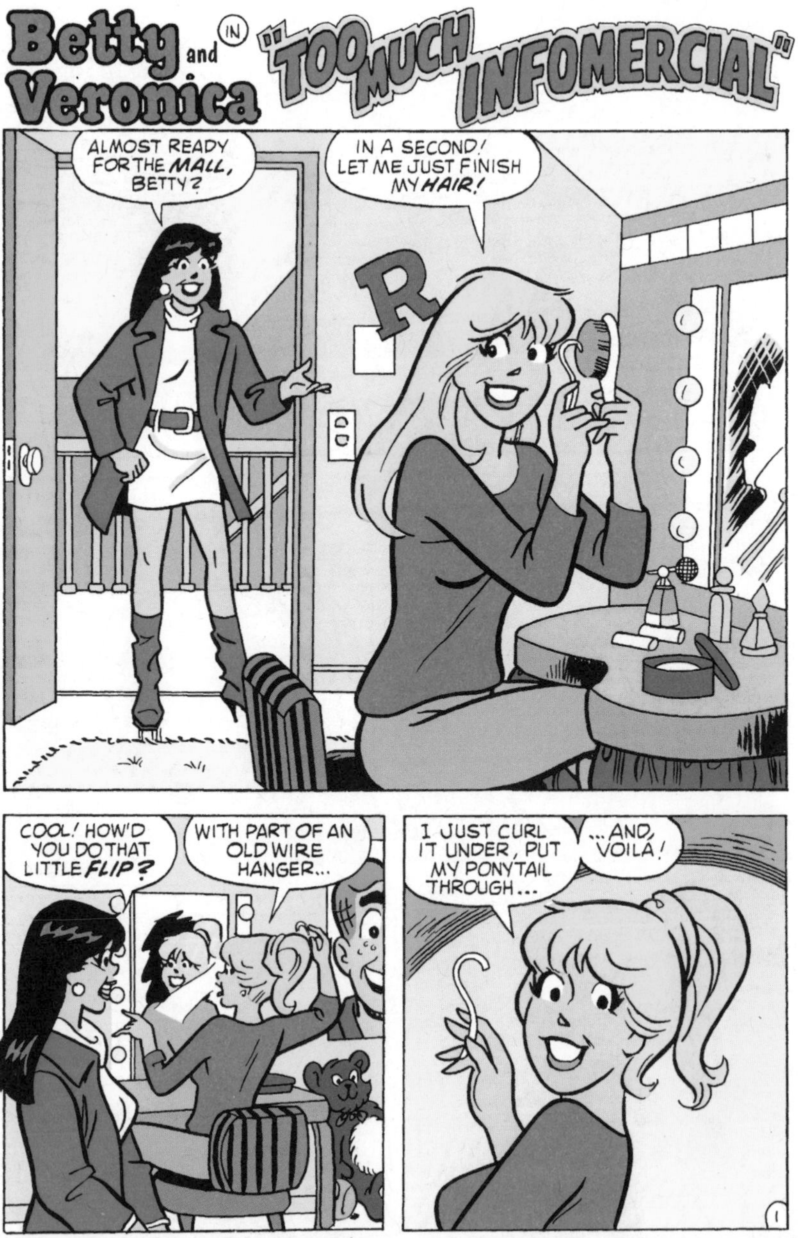
Betty and Veronica
IN
"TOO MUCH INFOMERCIAL"
ALMOST READY FOR THE MALL, BETTY?
IN A SECOND! LET ME JUST FINISH MY HAIR!
R
COOL! HOW'D YOU DO THAT LITTLE FLIP?
WITH PART OF AN OLD WIRE HANGER...
I JUST CURL IT UNDER, PUT MY PONYTAIL THROUGH...
...AND, VOILÀ!
1

Story: Dan Parent Pencils: Dan DeCarlo
Inks: Alison Flood Letters: Bill Yoshida Colors: Barry Grossman

Originally printed in BETTY & VERONICA SPECTACULAR #7, April 1994

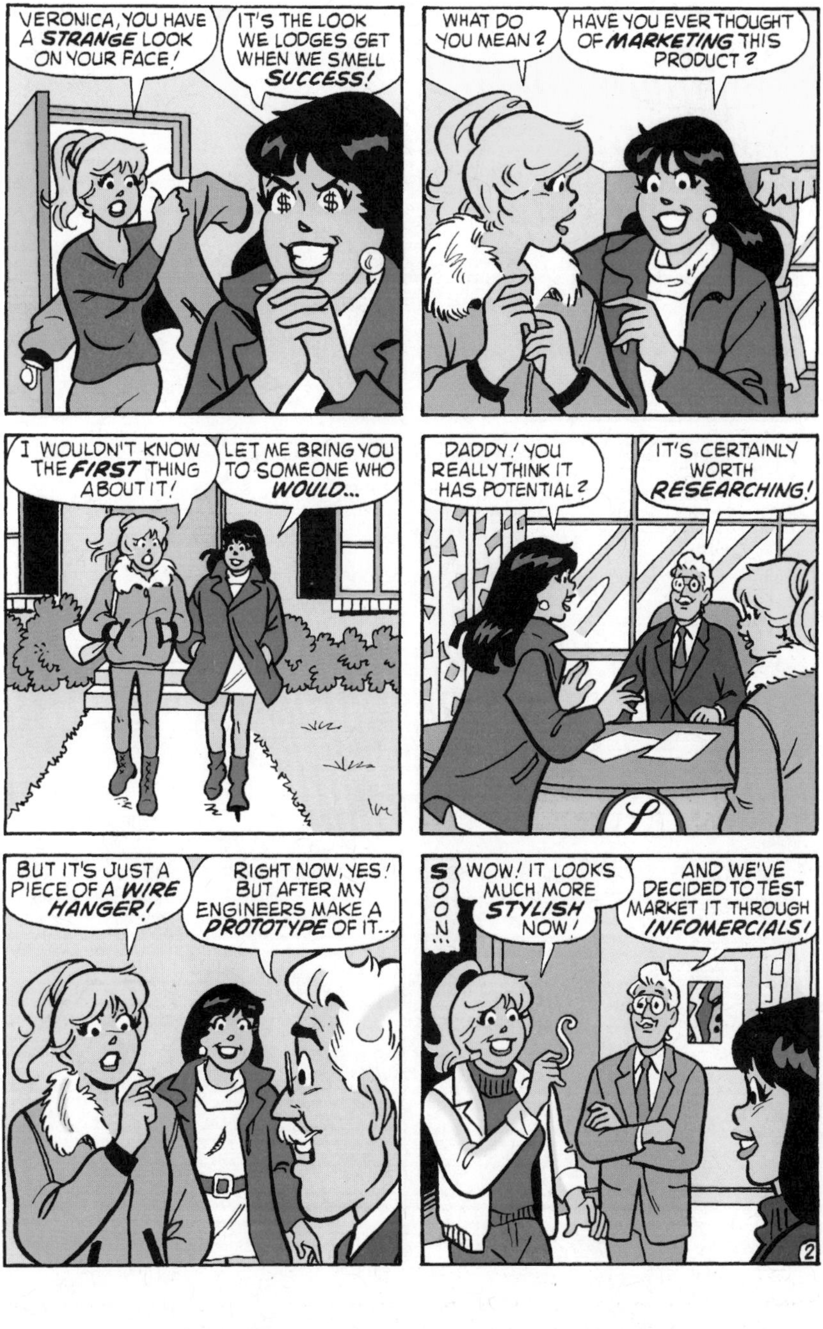
VERONICA, YOU HAVE A STRANGE LOOK ON YOUR FACE!
IT'S THE LOOK WE LODGES GET WHEN WE SMELL SUCCESS!
WHAT DO YOU MEAN?
HAVE YOU EVER THOUGHT OF MARKETING THIS PRODUCT?
I WOULDN'T KNOW THE FIRST THING ABOUT IT!
LET ME BRING YOU TO SOMEONE WHO WOULD...
DADDY! YOU REALLY THINK IT HAS POTENTIAL?
IT'S CERTAINLY WORTH RESEARCHING!
BUT IT'S JUST A PIECE OF A WIRE HANGER!
RIGHT NOW, YES! BUT AFTER MY ENGINEERS MAKE A PROTOTYPE OF IT...
SOON...
WOW! IT LOOKS MUCH MORE STYLISH NOW!
AND WE'VE DECIDED TO TEST MARKET IT THROUGH INFOMERCIALS!
2

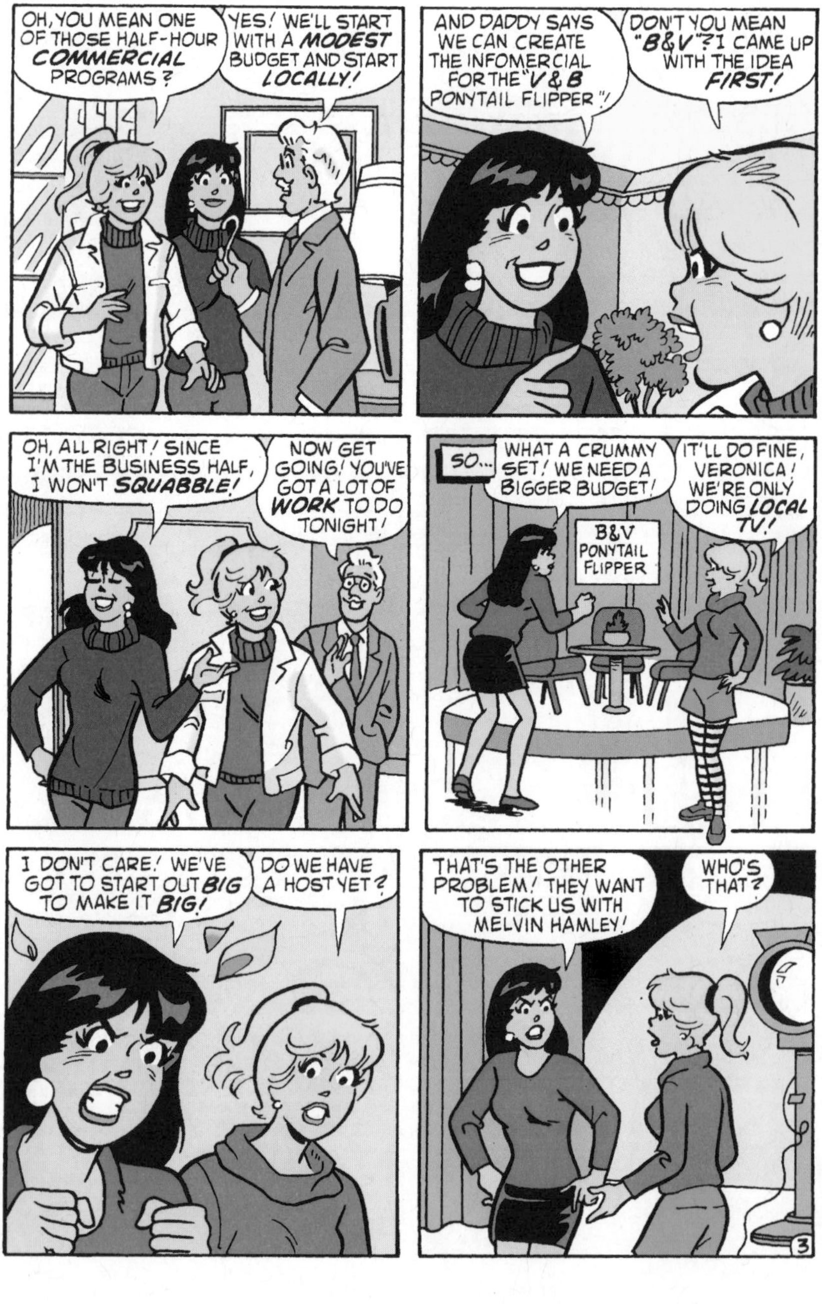
OH, YOU MEAN ONE OF THOSE HALF-HOUR COMMERCIAL PROGRAMS?
YES! WE'LL START WITH A MODEST BUDGET AND START LOCALLY!
AND DADDY SAYS WE CAN CREATE THE INFOMERCIAL FOR THE "V & B PONYTAIL FLIPPER"!
DON'T YOU MEAN "B&V"? I CAME UP WITH THE IDEA FIRST!
OH, ALL RIGHT! SINCE I'M THE BUSINESS HALF, I WON'T SQUABBLE!
NOW GET GOING! YOU'VE GOT A LOT OF WORK TO DO TONIGHT!
SO...
WHAT A CRUMMY SET! WE NEED A BIGGER BUDGET!
B&V PONYTAIL FLIPPER
IT'LL DO FINE, VERONICA! WE'RE ONLY DOING LOCAL TV!
I DON'T CARE! WE'VE GOT TO START OUT BIG TO MAKE IT BIG!
DO WE HAVE A HOST YET?
THAT'S THE OTHER PROBLEM! THEY WANT TO STICK US WITH MELVIN HAMLEY!
WHO'S THAT?
3

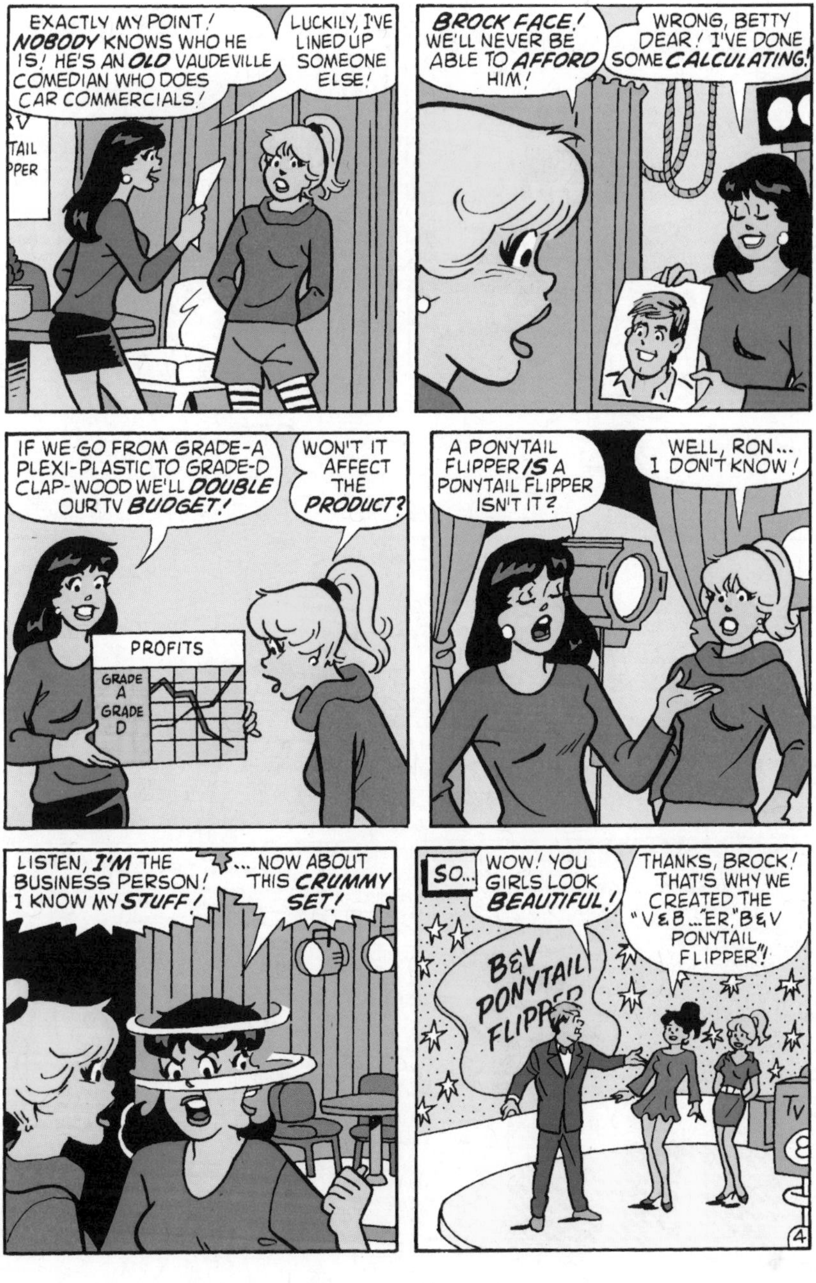
EXACTLY MY POINT! NOBODY KNOWS WHO HE IS! HE'S AN OLD VAUDEVILLE COMEDIAN WHO DOES CAR COMMERCIALS!
LUCKILY, I'VE LINED UP SOMEONE ELSE!
BROCK FACE! WE'LL NEVER BE ABLE TO AFFORD HIM!
WRONG, BETTY DEAR! I'VE DONE SOME CALCULATING!
IF WE GO FROM GRADE-A PLEXI-PLASTIC TO GRADE-D CLAP-WOOD WE'LL DOUBLE OUR TV BUDGET!
WON'T IT AFFECT THE PRODUCT?
PROFITS
GRADE A
GRADE D
A PONYTAIL FLIPPER IS A PONYTAIL FLIPPER ISN'T IT?
WELL, RON... I DON'T KNOW!
LISTEN, I'M THE BUSINESS PERSON! I KNOW MY STUFF!
... NOW ABOUT THIS CRUMMY SET!
SO...
WOW! YOU GIRLS LOOK BEAUTIFUL!
THANKS, BROCK! THAT'S WHY WE CREATED THE "V&B..."ER," B&V PONYTAIL FLIPPER"!
B&V PONYTAIL FLIPPER
TV
8
4

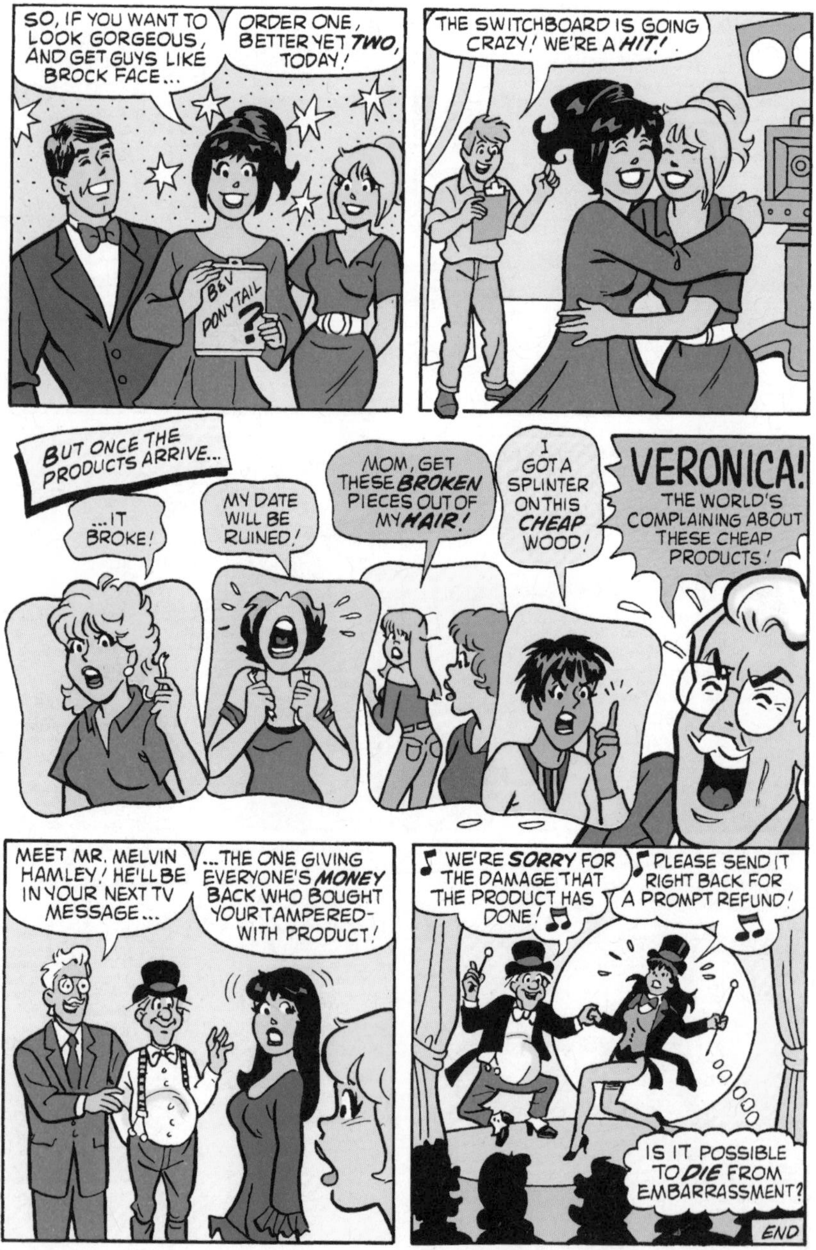
SO, IF YOU WANT TO LOOK GORGEOUS, AND GET GUYS LIKE BROCK FACE...
ORDER ONE, BETTER YET TWO, TODAY!
B&V PONYTAIL
THE SWITCHBOARD IS GOING CRAZY! WE'RE A HIT!
BUT ONCE THE PRODUCTS ARRIVE...
...IT BROKE!
MY DATE WILL BE RUINED!
MOM, GET THESE BROKEN PIECES OUT OF MY HAIR!
I GOT A SPLINTER ON THIS CHEAP WOOD!
VERONICA! THE WORLD'S COMPLAINING ABOUT THESE CHEAP PRODUCTS!
MEET MR. MELVIN HAMLEY! HE'LL BE IN YOUR NEXT TV MESSAGE...
...THE ONE GIVING EVERYONE'S MONEY BACK WHO BOUGHT YOUR TAMPERED-WITH PRODUCT!
WE'RE SORRY FOR THE DAMAGE THAT THE PRODUCT HAS DONE!
PLEASE SEND IT RIGHT BACK FOR A PROMPT REFUND!
IS IT POSSIBLE TO DIE FROM EMBARRASSMENT?
END

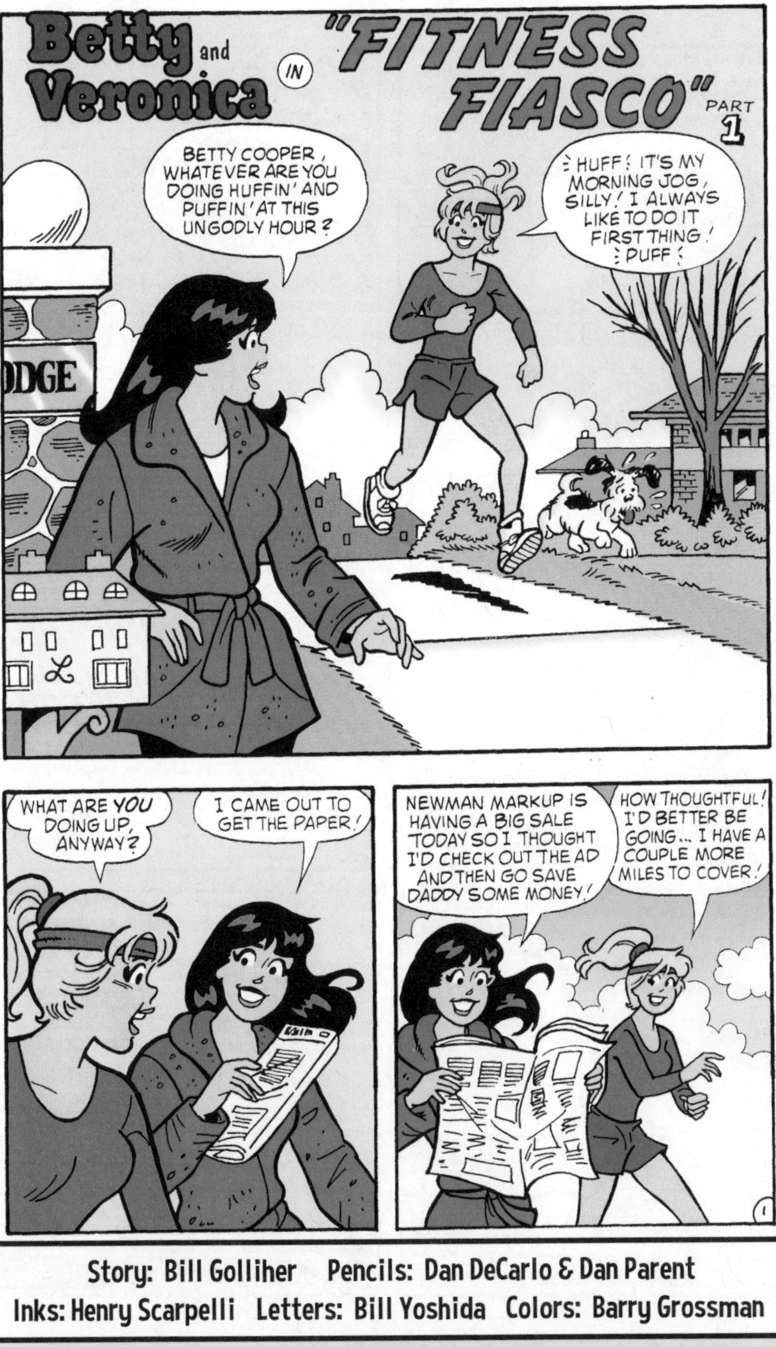
Betty and Veronica IN "FITNESS FIASCO" PART 1
BETTY COOPER, WHATEVER ARE YOU DOING HUFFIN' AND PUFFIN' AT THIS UNGODLY HOUR?
:HUFF: IT'S MY MORNING JOG, SILLY! I ALWAYS LIKE TO DO IT FIRST THING! :PUFF:
ODGE
WHAT ARE YOU DOING UP, ANYWAY?
I CAME OUT TO GET THE PAPER!
NEWMAN MARKUP IS HAVING A BIG SALE TODAY SO I THOUGHT I'D CHECK OUT THE AD AND THEN GO SAVE DADDY SOME MONEY!
HOW THOUGHTFUL! I'D BETTER BE GOING... I HAVE A COUPLE MORE MILES TO COVER!
1

Story: Bill Golliher Pencils: Dan DeCarlo & Dan Parent
Inks: Henry Scarpelli Letters: Bill Yoshida Colors: Barry Grossman

Originally printed in BETTY & VERONICA SPECTACULAR #8, May 1994

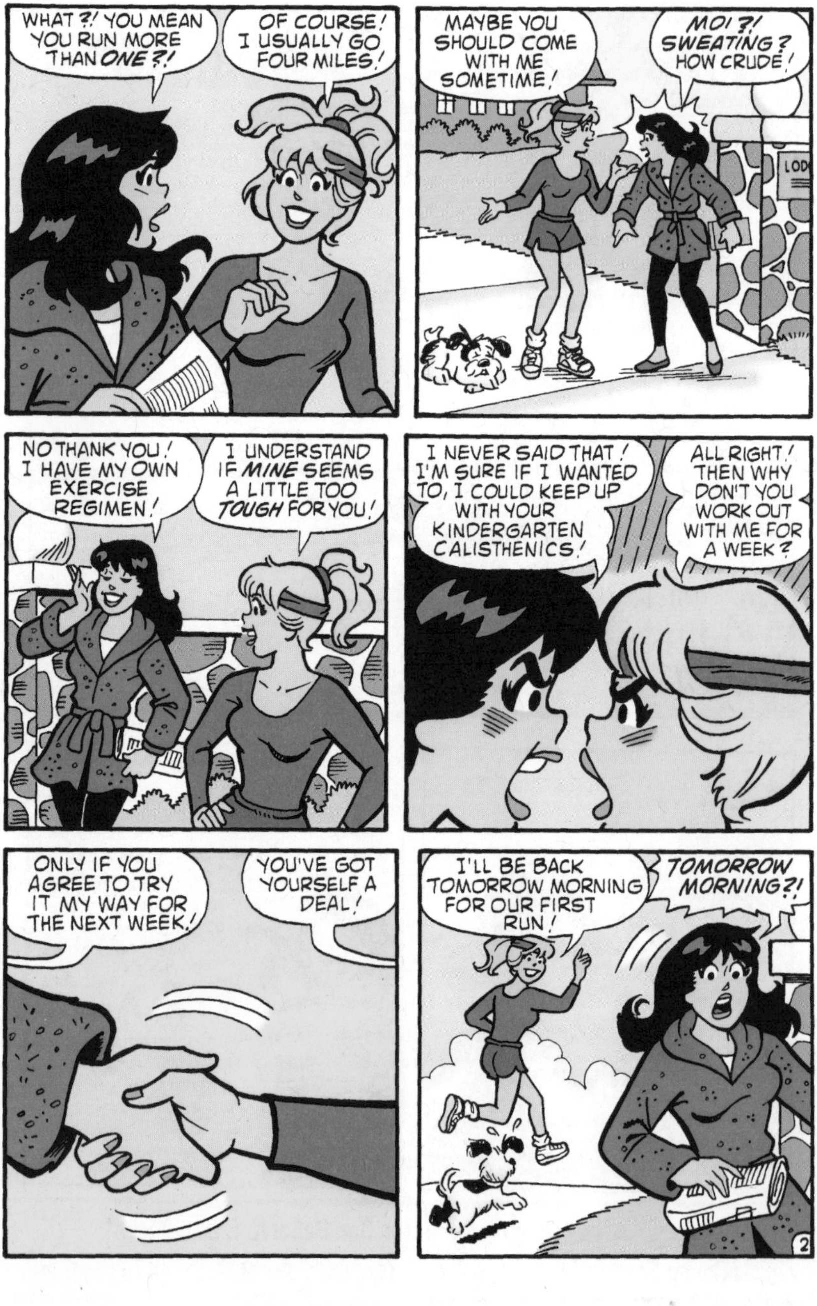
WHAT ?! YOU MEAN YOU RUN MORE THAN ONE ?!
OF COURSE! I USUALLY GO FOUR MILES!
MAYBE YOU SHOULD COME WITH ME SOMETIME!
MOI ?! SWEATING? HOW CRUDE!
NO THANK YOU! I HAVE MY OWN EXERCISE REGIMEN!
I UNDERSTAND IF MINE SEEMS A LITTLE TOO TOUGH FOR YOU!
I NEVER SAID THAT! I'M SURE IF I WANTED TO, I COULD KEEP UP WITH YOUR KINDERGARTEN CALISTHENICS!
ALL RIGHT! THEN WHY DON'T YOU WORK OUT WITH ME FOR A WEEK?
ONLY IF YOU AGREE TO TRY IT MY WAY FOR THE NEXT WEEK!
YOU'VE GOT YOURSELF A DEAL!
I'LL BE BACK TOMORROW MORNING FOR OUR FIRST RUN!
TOMORROW MORNING?!
2

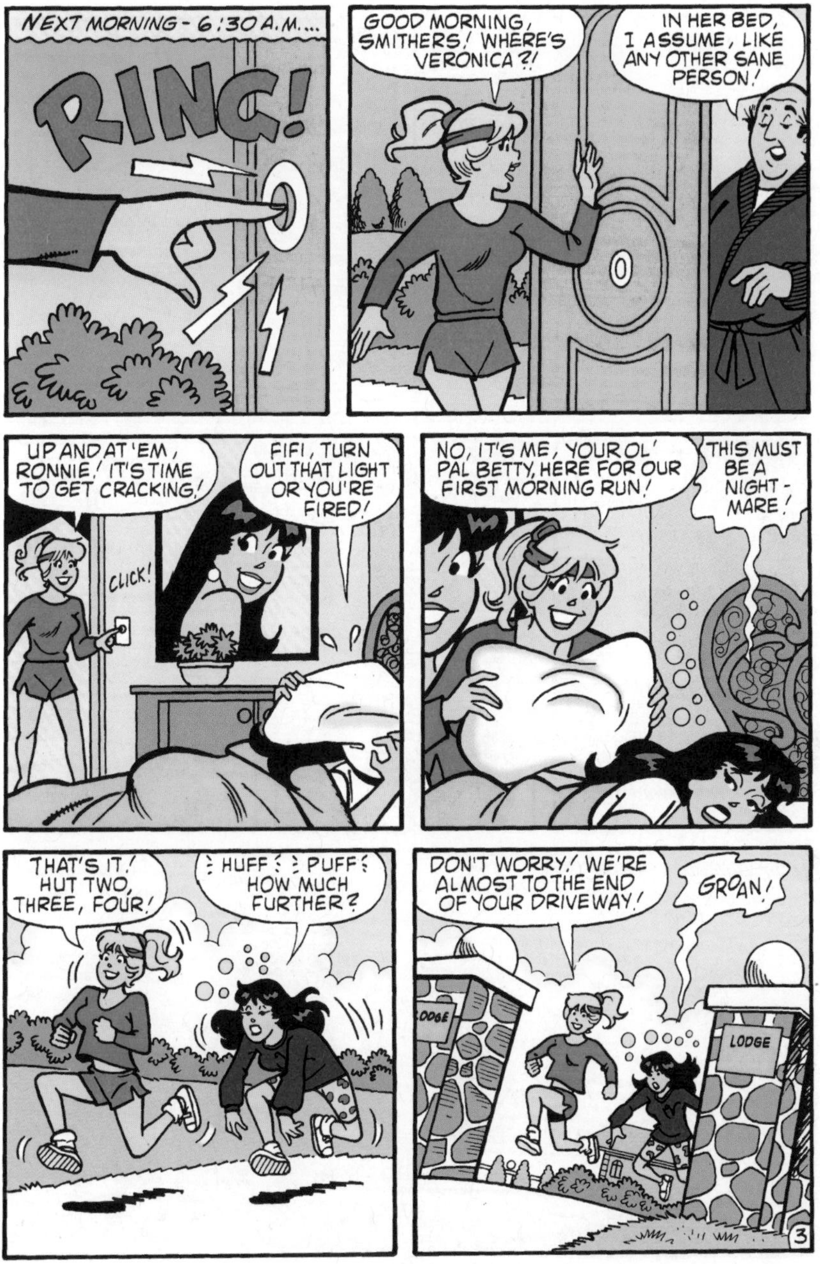
NEXT MORNING - 6:30 A.M....
RING!
GOOD MORNING, SMITHERS! WHERE'S VERONICA ?!
IN HER BED, I ASSUME, LIKE ANY OTHER SANE PERSON!
UP AND AT 'EM, RONNIE! IT'S TIME TO GET CRACKING!
CLICK!
FIFI, TURN OUT THAT LIGHT OR YOU'RE FIRED!
NO, IT'S ME, YOUR OL' PAL BETTY, HERE FOR OUR FIRST MORNING RUN!
THIS MUST BE A NIGHT-MARE!
THAT'S IT! HUT TWO, THREE, FOUR!
HUFF PUFF HOW MUCH FURTHER?
DON'T WORRY! WE'RE ALMOST TO THE END OF YOUR DRIVEWAY!
GROAN!
LODGE
LODGE
3

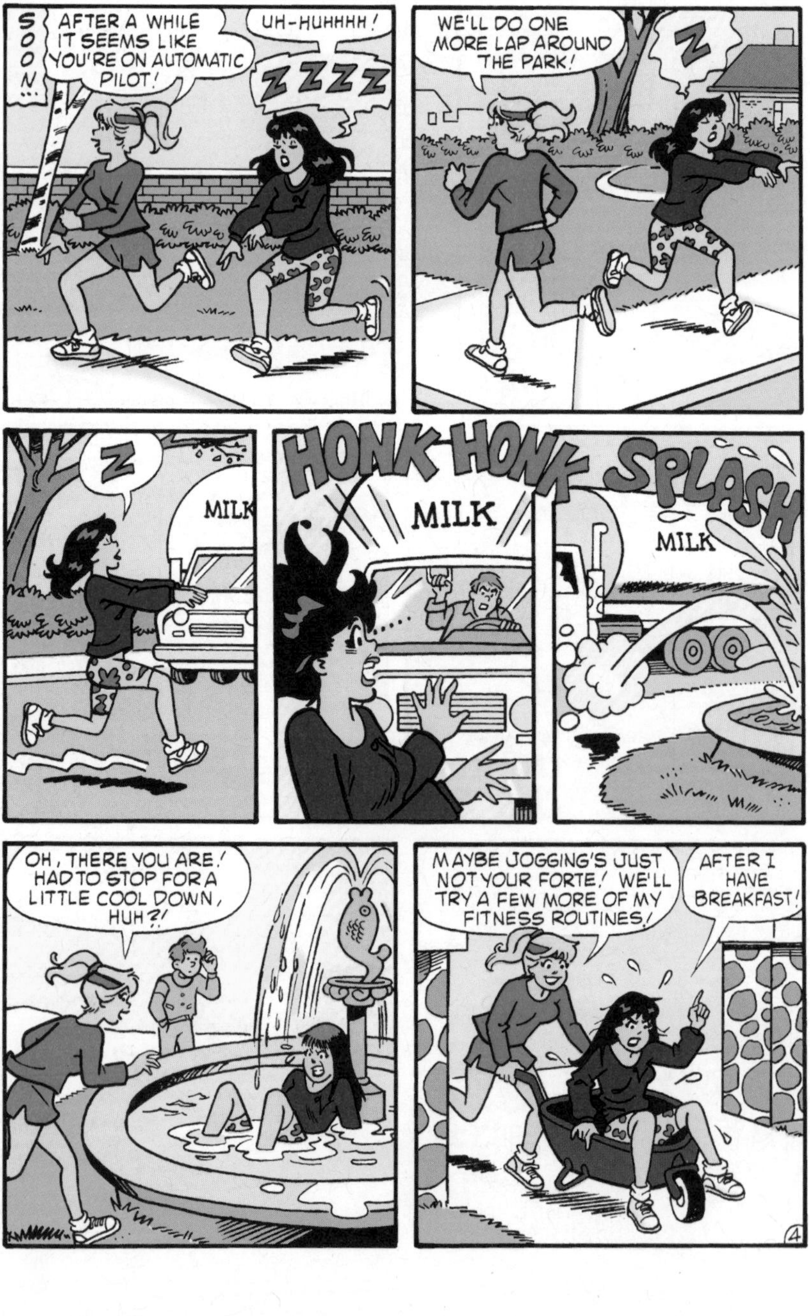
SOON...
AFTER A WHILE IT SEEMS LIKE YOU'RE ON AUTOMATIC PILOT!
UH-HUHHHH!
ZZZZ
WE'LL DO ONE MORE LAP AROUND THE PARK!
Z
Z
MILK
HONK HONK
MILK
SPLASH
MILK
OH, THERE YOU ARE! HAD TO STOP FOR A LITTLE COOL DOWN, HUH?!
MAYBE JOGGING'S JUST NOT YOUR FORTE! WE'LL TRY A FEW MORE OF MY FITNESS ROUTINES!
AFTER I HAVE BREAKFAST!
4

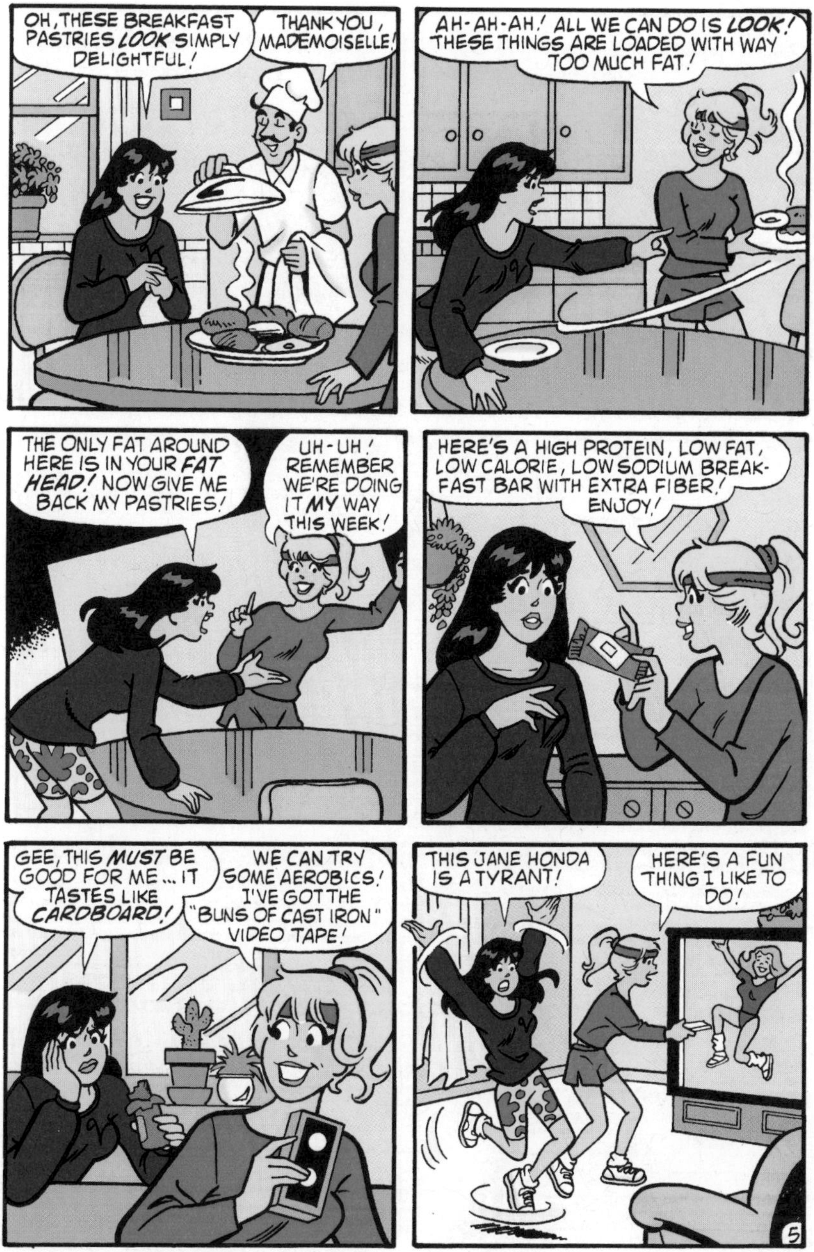
OH, THESE BREAKFAST PASTRIES LOOK SIMPLY DELIGHTFUL!
THANK YOU, MADEMOISELLE!
AH-AH-AH! ALL WE CAN DO IS LOOK! THESE THINGS ARE LOADED WITH WAY TOO MUCH FAT!
THE ONLY FAT AROUND HERE IS IN YOUR FAT HEAD! NOW GIVE ME BACK MY PASTRIES!
UH-UH! REMEMBER WE'RE DOING IT MY WAY THIS WEEK!
HERE'S A HIGH PROTEIN, LOW FAT, LOW CALORIE, LOW SODIUM BREAK-FAST BAR WITH EXTRA FIBER! ENJOY!
GEE, THIS MUST BE GOOD FOR ME... IT TASTES LIKE CARDBOARD!
WE CAN TRY SOME AEROBICS! I'VE GOT THE "BUNS OF CAST IRON" VIDEO TAPE!
THIS JANE HONDA IS A TYRANT!
HERE'S A FUN THING I LIKE TO DO!
5

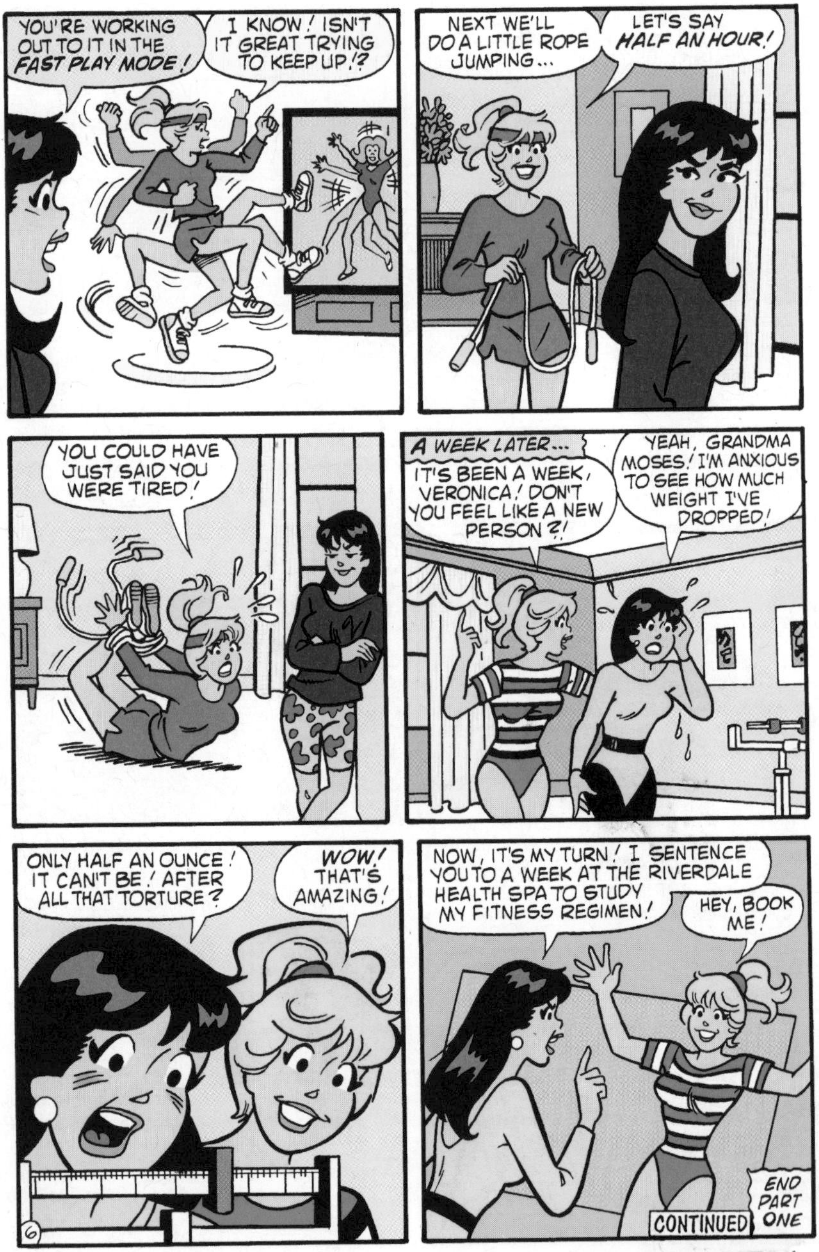
YOU'RE WORKING OUT TO IT IN THE FAST PLAY MODE!
I KNOW! ISN'T IT GREAT TRYING TO KEEP UP!?
NEXT WE'LL DO A LITTLE ROPE JUMPING...
LET'S SAY HALF AN HOUR!
YOU COULD HAVE JUST SAID YOU WERE TIRED!
A WEEK LATER...
IT'S BEEN A WEEK, VERONICA! DON'T YOU FEEL LIKE A NEW PERSON?!
YEAH, GRANDMA MOSES! I'M ANXIOUS TO SEE HOW MUCH WEIGHT I'VE DROPPED!
ONLY HALF AN OUNCE! IT CAN'T BE! AFTER ALL THAT TORTURE?
WOW! THAT'S AMAZING!
6
NOW, IT'S MY TURN! I SENTENCE YOU TO A WEEK AT THE RIVERDALE HEALTH SPA TO STUDY MY FITNESS REGIMEN!
HEY, BOOK ME!
CONTINUED
END PART ONE

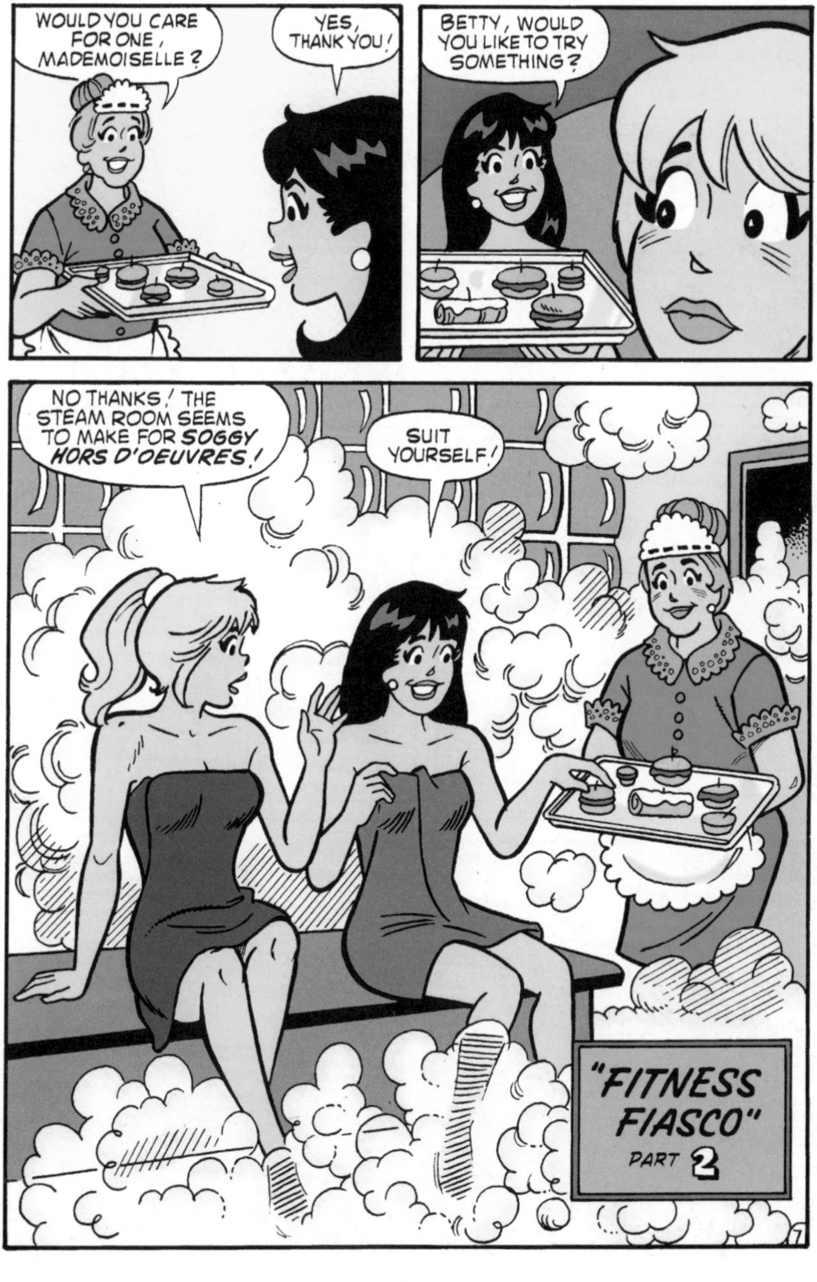
WOULD YOU CARE FOR ONE, MADEMOISELLE?
YES, THANK YOU!
BETTY, WOULD YOU LIKE TO TRY SOMETHING?
NO THANKS! THE STEAM ROOM SEEMS TO MAKE FOR SOGGY HORS D'OEUVRES!
SUIT YOURSELF!
"FITNESS FIASCO"
PART 2
7

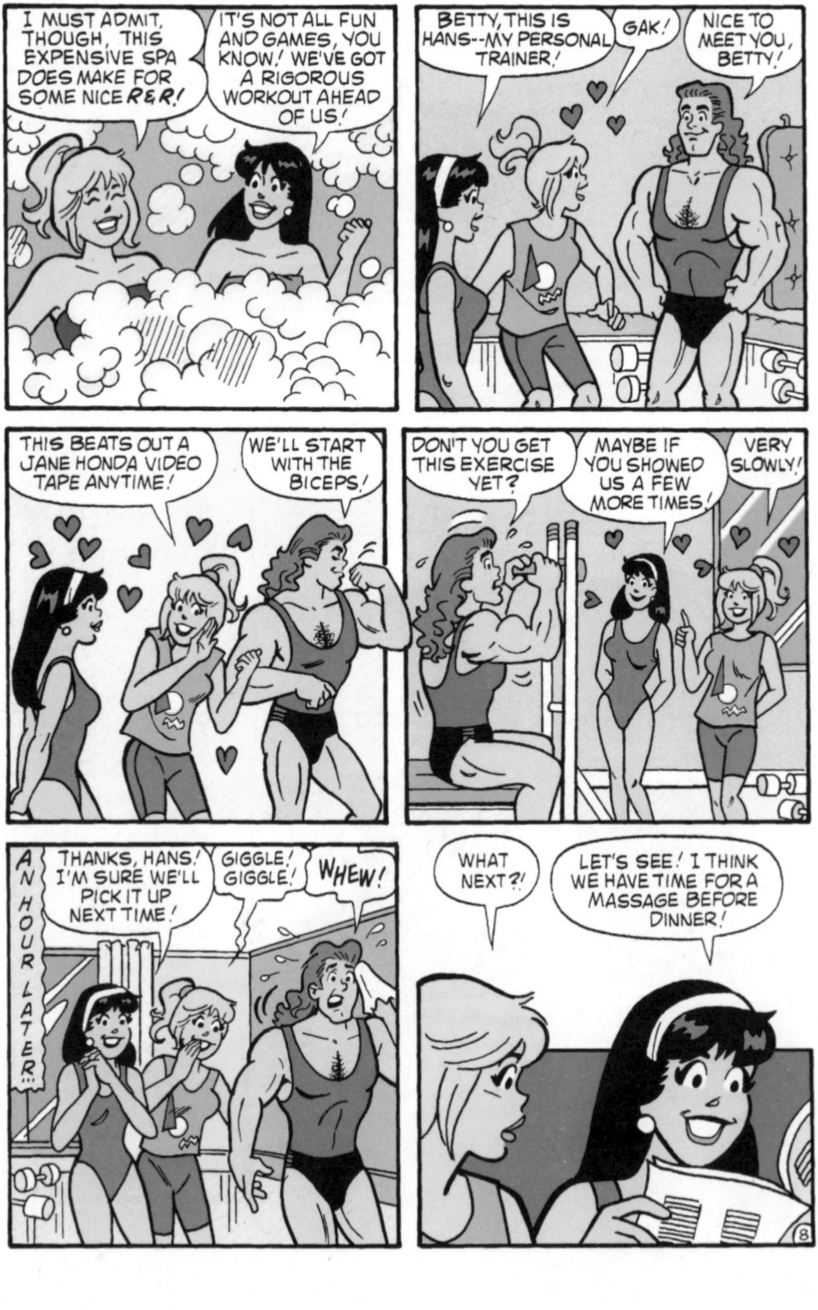
I MUST ADMIT, THOUGH, THIS EXPENSIVE SPA DOES MAKE FOR SOME NICE R&R!
IT'S NOT ALL FUN AND GAMES, YOU KNOW! WE'VE GOT A RIGOROUS WORKOUT AHEAD OF US!
BETTY, THIS IS HANS--MY PERSONAL TRAINER!
GAK!
NICE TO MEET YOU, BETTY!
THIS BEATS OUT A JANE HONDA VIDEO TAPE ANYTIME!
WE'LL START WITH THE BICEPS!
DON'T YOU GET THIS EXERCISE YET?
MAYBE IF YOU SHOWED US A FEW MORE TIMES!
VERY SLOWLY!
AN HOUR LATER...
THANKS, HANS! I'M SURE WE'LL PICK IT UP NEXT TIME!
GIGGLE! GIGGLE!
WHEW!
WHAT NEXT?!
LET'S SEE! I THINK WE HAVE TIME FOR A MASSAGE BEFORE DINNER!
8

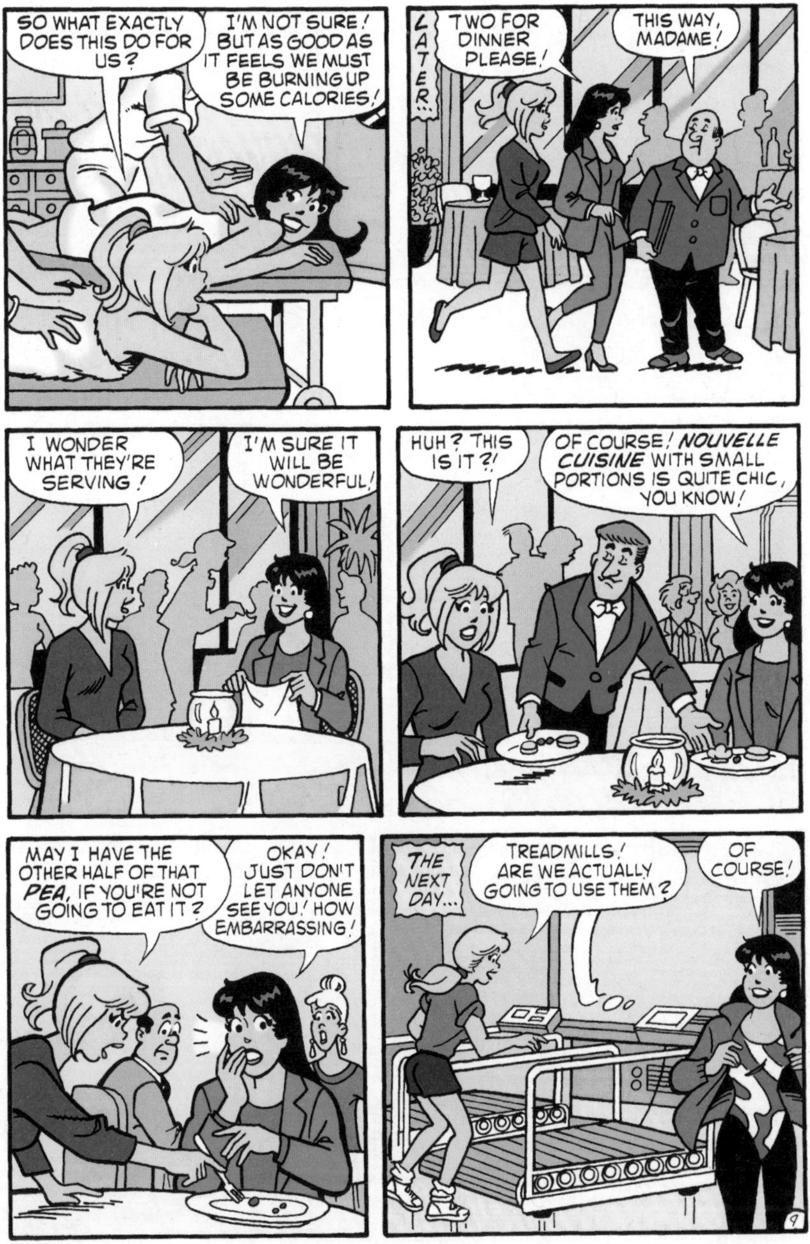
SO WHAT EXACTLY DOES THIS DO FOR US?
I'M NOT SURE! BUT AS GOOD AS IT FEELS WE MUST BE BURNING UP SOME CALORIES!
LATER...
TWO FOR DINNER PLEASE!
THIS WAY, MADAME!
I WONDER WHAT THEY'RE SERVING!
I'M SURE IT WILL BE WONDERFUL!
HUH? THIS IS IT?!
OF COURSE! NOUVELLE CUISINE WITH SMALL PORTIONS IS QUITE CHIC, YOU KNOW!
MAY I HAVE THE OTHER HALF OF THAT PEA, IF YOU'RE NOT GOING TO EAT IT?
OKAY! JUST DON'T LET ANYONE SEE YOU! HOW EMBARRASSING!
THE NEXT DAY...
TREADMILLS! ARE WE ACTUALLY GOING TO USE THEM?
OF COURSE!
9

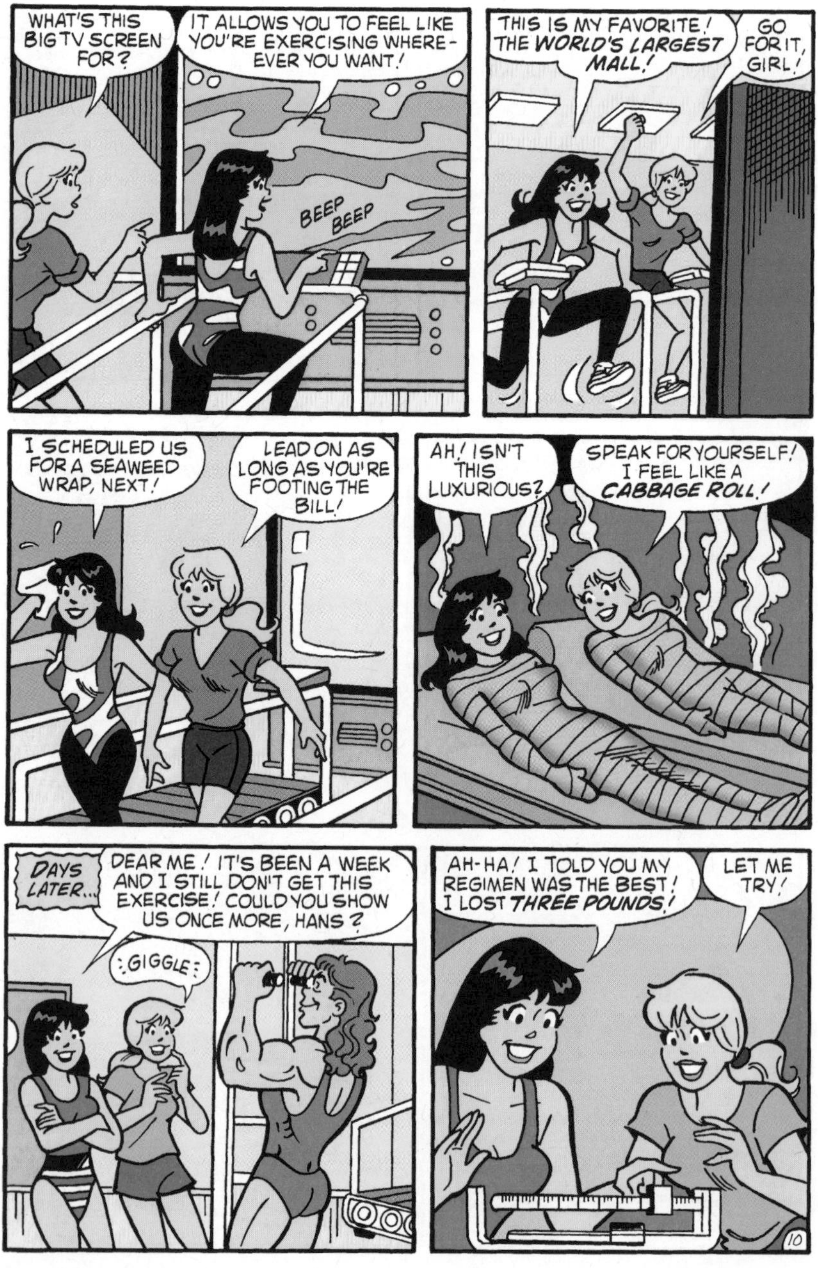
WHAT'S THIS BIG TV SCREEN FOR?
IT ALLOWS YOU TO FEEL LIKE YOU'RE EXERCISING WHERE-EVER YOU WANT!
BEEP BEEP
THIS IS MY FAVORITE! THE WORLD'S LARGEST MALL!
GO FOR IT, GIRL!
I SCHEDULED US FOR A SEAWEED WRAP, NEXT!
LEAD ON AS LONG AS YOU'RE FOOTING THE BILL!
AH! ISN'T THIS LUXURIOUS?
SPEAK FOR YOURSELF! I FEEL LIKE A CABBAGE ROLL!
DAYS LATER...
DEAR ME! IT'S BEEN A WEEK AND I STILL DON'T GET THIS EXERCISE! COULD YOU SHOW US ONCE MORE, HANS?
GIGGLE
AH-HA! I TOLD YOU MY REGIMEN WAS THE BEST! I LOST THREE POUNDS!
LET ME TRY!
10

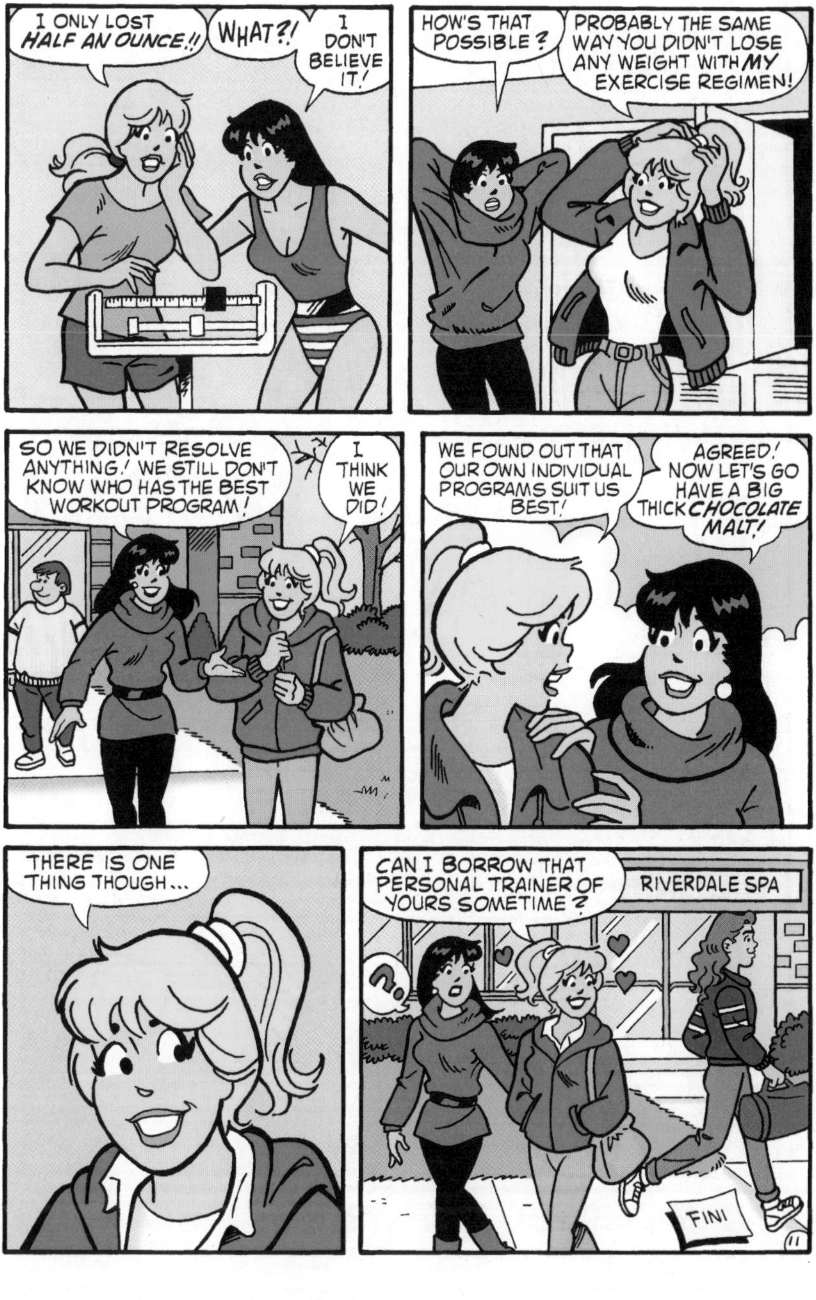
I ONLY LOST HALF AN OUNCE!!
WHAT?!
I DON'T BELIEVE IT!
HOW'S THAT POSSIBLE?
PROBABLY THE SAME WAY YOU DIDN'T LOSE ANY WEIGHT WITH MY EXERCISE REGIMEN!
SO WE DIDN'T RESOLVE ANYTHING! WE STILL DON'T KNOW WHO HAS THE BEST WORKOUT PROGRAM!
I THINK WE DID!
WE FOUND OUT THAT OUR OWN INDIVIDUAL PROGRAMS SUIT US BEST!
AGREED! NOW LET'S GO HAVE A BIG THICK CHOCOLATE MALT!
THERE IS ONE THING THOUGH...
CAN I BORROW THAT PERSONAL TRAINER OF YOURS SOMETIME?
RIVERDALE SPA
?
FINI
11

Betty and Veronica in "MOODY & SNOOTY"

THAT'S SO *COOL*, BETTY! IT'S THE '70s!

?

I'VE GOT TO GET ONE OF THOSE, TOO!

WHAT'S THE BIG *HUBBUB* ABOUT?

MY *MOOD RING!* IT CHANGES *COLORS* TO REFLECT YOUR MOOD!

SEE! IT'S *LIGHT BLUE!* THAT MEANS *HAPPY* AND *PEACEFUL!*

Story: Dan Parent   Pencils: Dan DeCarlo & Dan Parent
Inks: Henry Scarpelli   Letters: Bill Yoshida   Colors: Barry Grossman

Originally printed in BETTY & VERONICA SPECTACULAR #8, May 1994

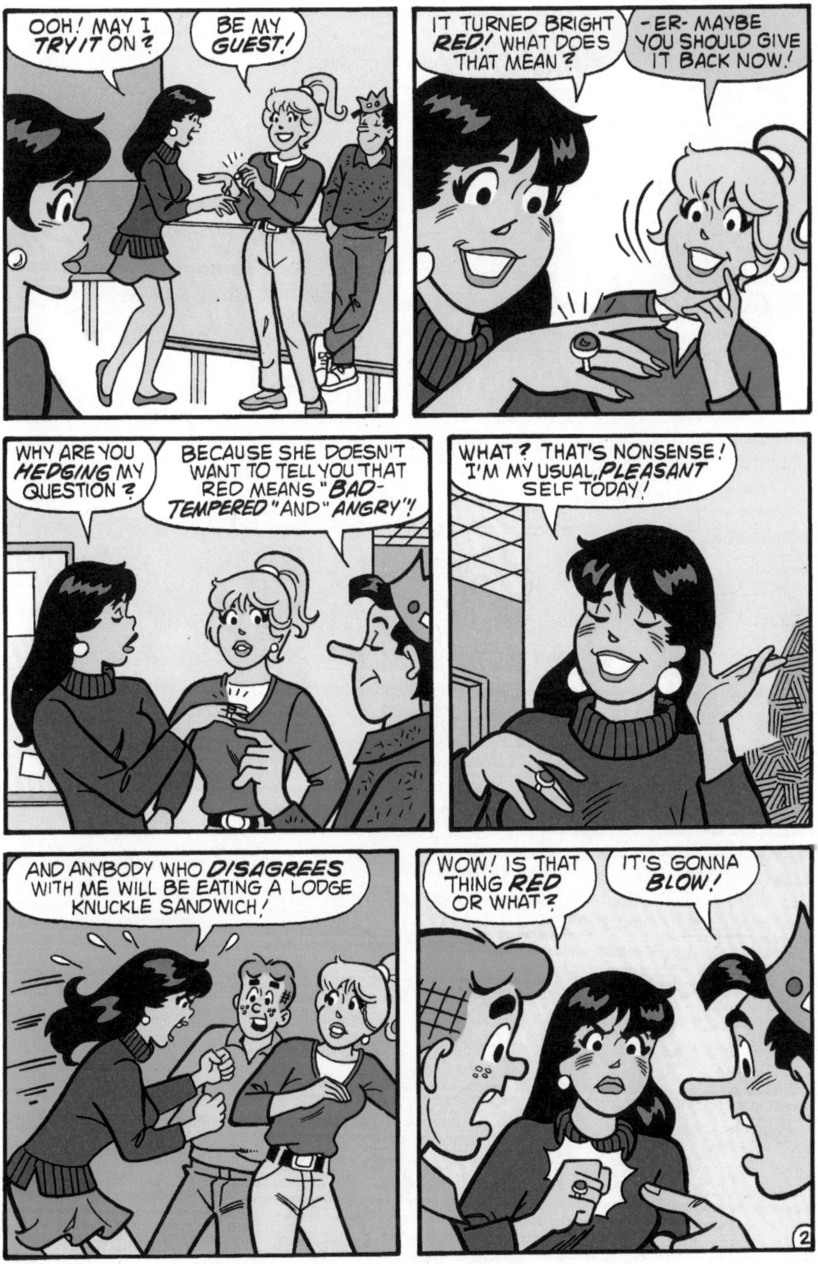
OOH! MAY I TRY IT ON?
BE MY GUEST!
IT TURNED BRIGHT RED! WHAT DOES THAT MEAN?
-ER- MAYBE YOU SHOULD GIVE IT BACK NOW!
WHY ARE YOU HEDGING MY QUESTION?
BECAUSE SHE DOESN'T WANT TO TELL YOU THAT RED MEANS "BAD-TEMPERED" AND "ANGRY"!
WHAT? THAT'S NONSENSE! I'M MY USUAL, PLEASANT SELF TODAY!
AND ANYBODY WHO DISAGREES WITH ME WILL BE EATING A LODGE KNUCKLE SANDWICH!
WOW! IS THAT THING RED OR WHAT?
IT'S GONNA BLOW!
2

MAY I TRY IT ON ?
BE MY GUEST! IT'S A WORTHLESS PIECE OF JUNK, ANYWAY!
OH, IT'S YELLOW! WHAT DOES THAT MEAN ?
CALM AND CONCERNED, YET PLEASANT!
WE'VE GOT TO GET SOME OF THESE!
I'M NOT GOING TO BE LEFT OUT! I'LL GET ONE, TOO!
AND I'LL DO THINGS THAT MAKE ME SO HAPPY MY RING WILL BE OH-SO-BLUE!
THE NEXT DAY!
MINE'S GREEN! I'M WORRIED!
MINES YELLOW-BLUE... I'M SERIOUS BUT A BIT DELIRIOUS, TOO!
DID YOU GET A RING, TOO, RONNIE ?
I SURE DID!
3

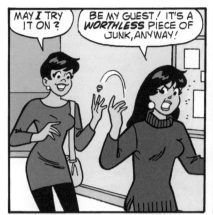

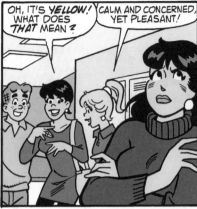

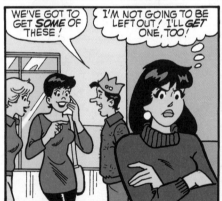

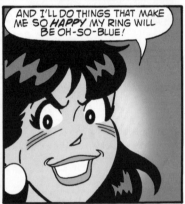

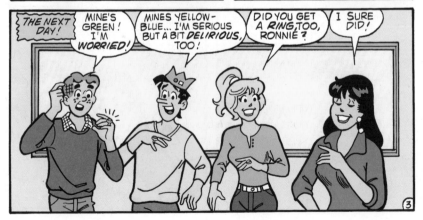

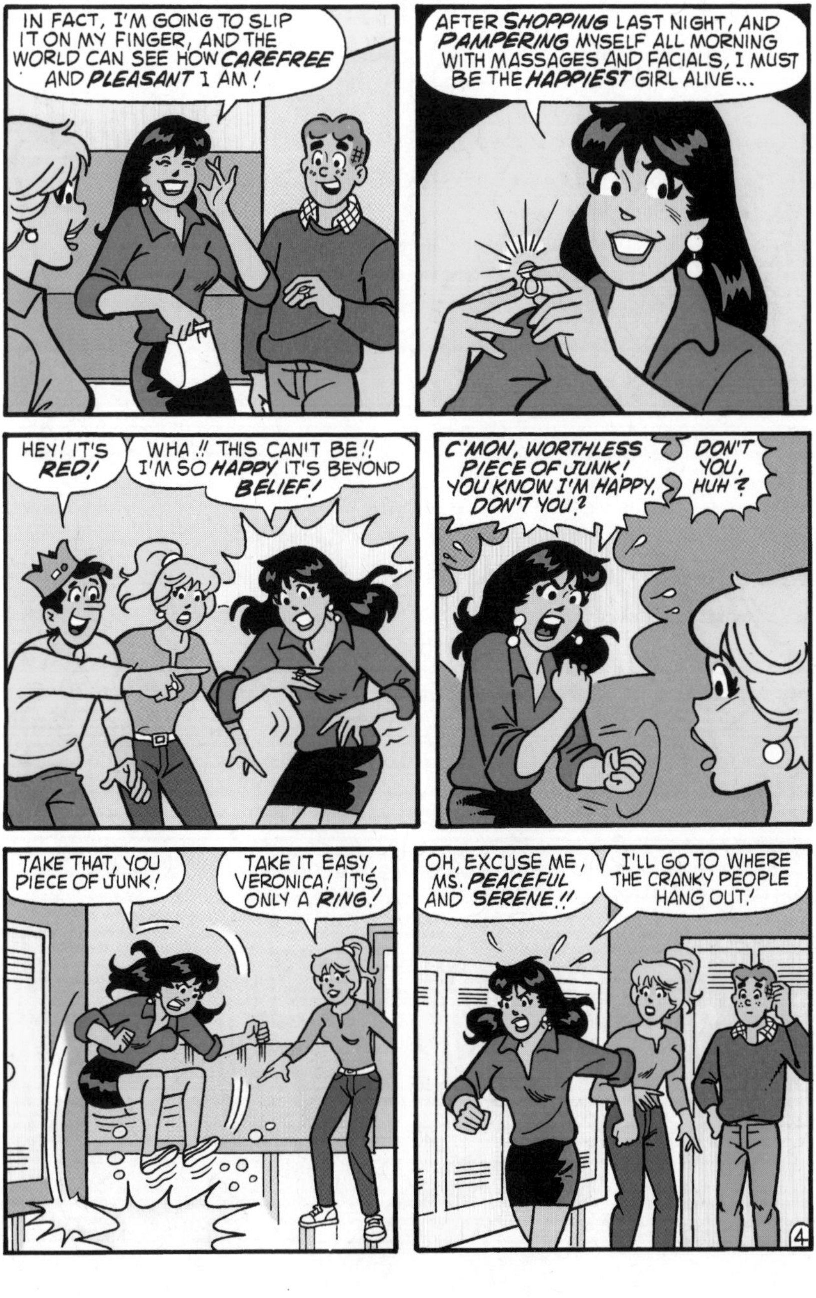
IN FACT, I'M GOING TO SLIP IT ON MY FINGER, AND THE WORLD CAN SEE HOW CAREFREE AND PLEASANT I AM!
AFTER SHOPPING LAST NIGHT, AND PAMPERING MYSELF ALL MORNING WITH MASSAGES AND FACIALS, I MUST BE THE HAPPIEST GIRL ALIVE...
HEY! IT'S RED!
WHA!! THIS CAN'T BE!! I'M SO HAPPY IT'S BEYOND BELIEF!
C'MON, WORTHLESS PIECE OF JUNK! YOU KNOW I'M HAPPY, DON'T YOU?
DON'T YOU, HUH?
TAKE THAT, YOU PIECE OF JUNK!
TAKE IT EASY, VERONICA! IT'S ONLY A RING!
OH, EXCUSE ME, MS. PEACEFUL AND SERENE!!
I'LL GO TO WHERE THE CRANKY PEOPLE HANG OUT!
4

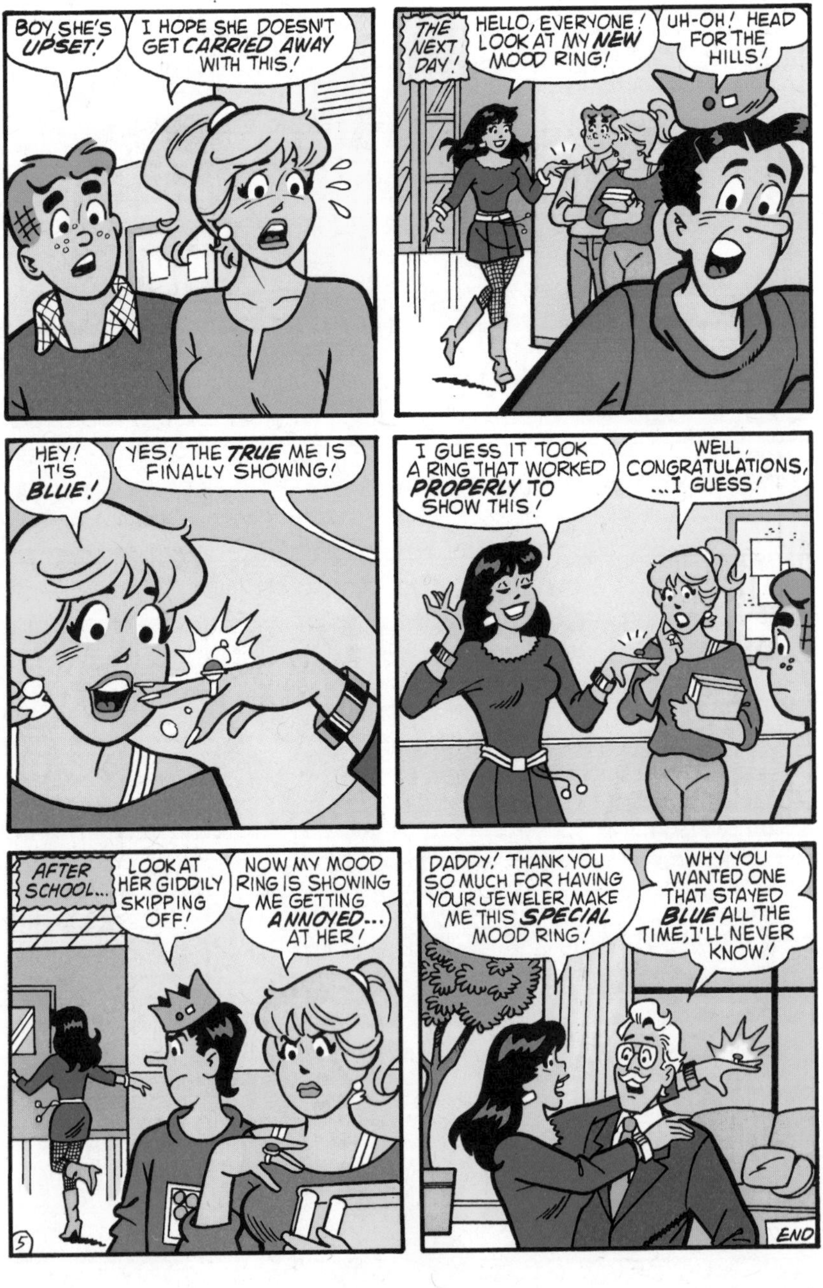
BOY, SHE'S UPSET!
I HOPE SHE DOESN'T GET CARRIED AWAY WITH THIS!
THE NEXT DAY!
HELLO, EVERYONE! LOOK AT MY NEW MOOD RING!
UH-OH! HEAD FOR THE HILLS!
HEY! IT'S BLUE!
YES! THE TRUE ME IS FINALLY SHOWING!
I GUESS IT TOOK A RING THAT WORKED PROPERLY TO SHOW THIS!
WELL, CONGRATULATIONS, ...I GUESS!
AFTER SCHOOL...
LOOK AT HER GIDDILY SKIPPING OFF!
NOW MY MOOD RING IS SHOWING ME GETTING ANNOYED... AT HER!
5
DADDY! THANK YOU SO MUCH FOR HAVING YOUR JEWELER MAKE ME THIS SPECIAL MOOD RING!
WHY YOU WANTED ONE THAT STAYED BLUE ALL THE TIME, I'LL NEVER KNOW!
END

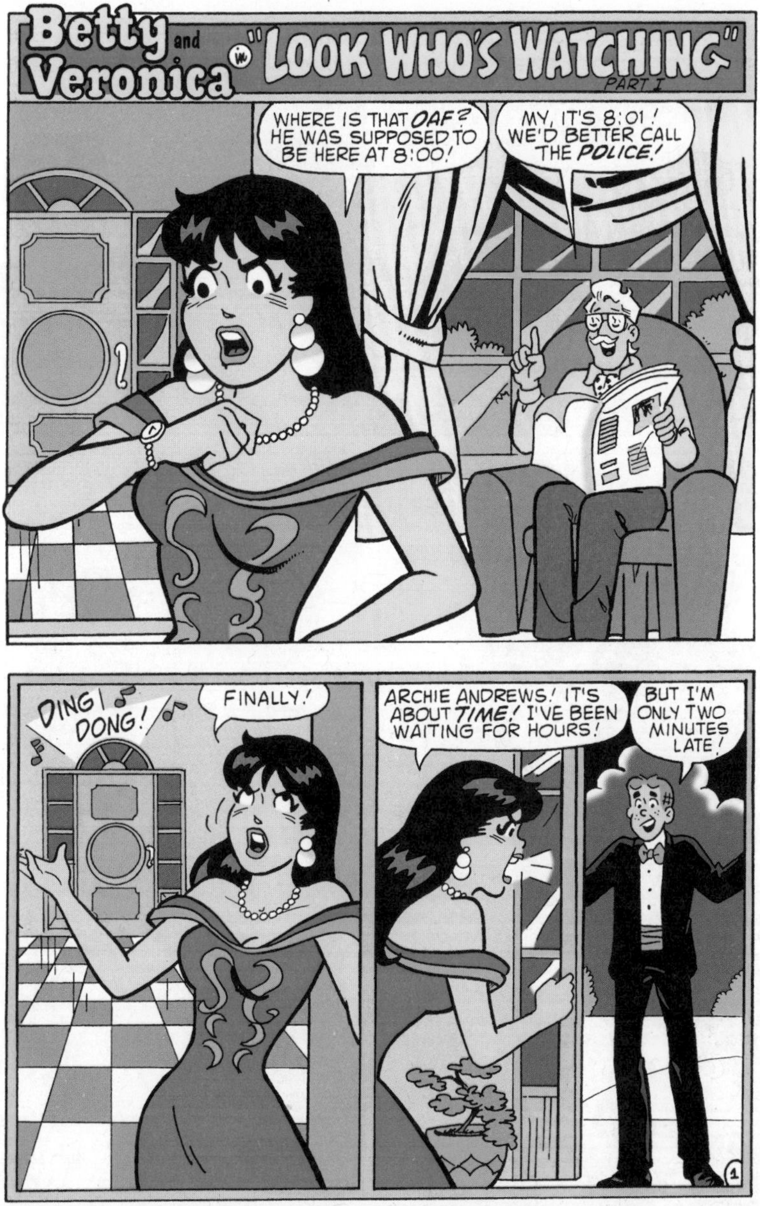
Betty and Veronica in "LOOK WHO'S WATCHING"
PART I
WHERE IS THAT OAF? HE WAS SUPPOSED TO BE HERE AT 8:00!
MY, IT'S 8:01! WE'D BETTER CALL THE POLICE!
DING DONG!
FINALLY!
ARCHIE ANDREWS! IT'S ABOUT TIME! I'VE BEEN WAITING FOR HOURS!
BUT I'M ONLY TWO MINUTES LATE!
1

Story & Pencils: Dan Parent

Inks: Henry Scarpelli Letters: Bill Yoshida Colors: Barry Grossman

Originally printed in BETTY & VERONICA SPECTACULAR #9, July 1994

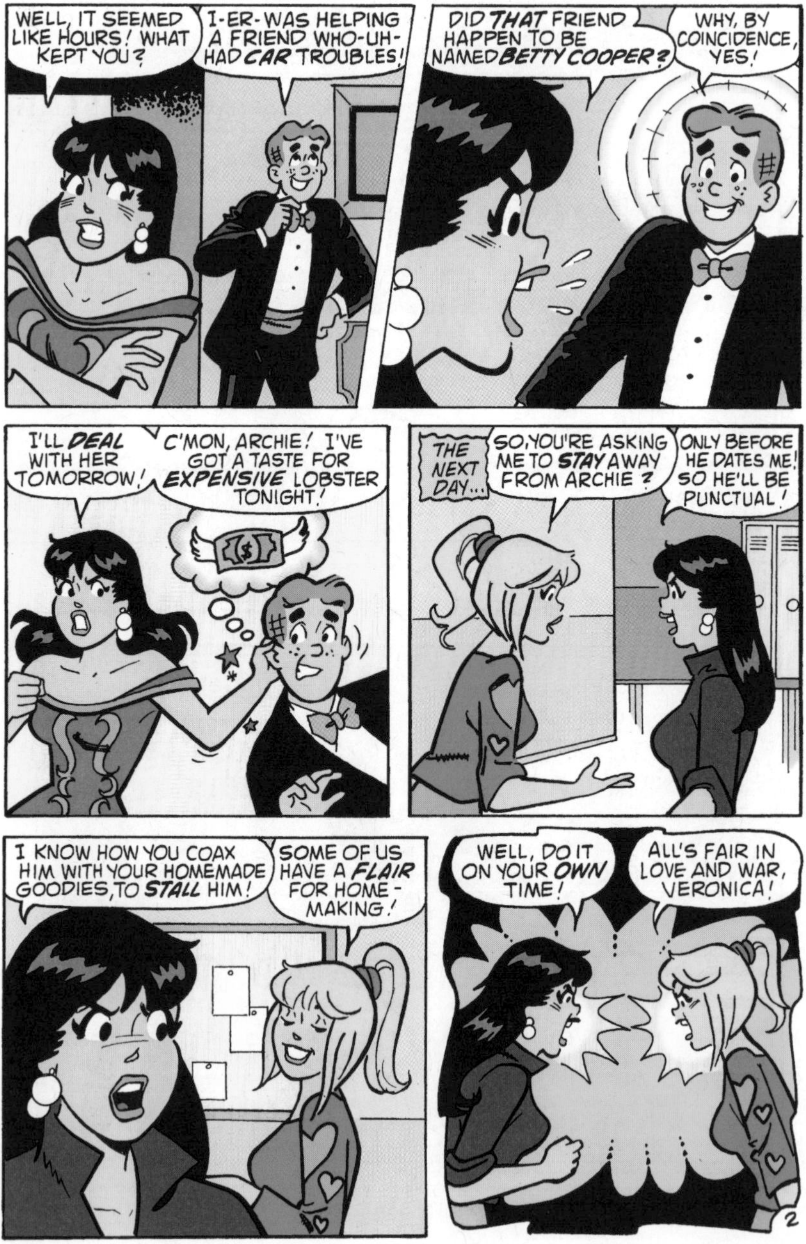
WELL, IT SEEMED LIKE HOURS! WHAT KEPT YOU?
I-ER-WAS HELPING A FRIEND WHO-UH-HAD CAR TROUBLES!
DID THAT FRIEND HAPPEN TO BE NAMED BETTY COOPER?
WHY, BY COINCIDENCE, YES!
I'LL DEAL WITH HER TOMORROW!
C'MON, ARCHIE! I'VE GOT A TASTE FOR EXPENSIVE LOBSTER TONIGHT!
THE NEXT DAY...
SO, YOU'RE ASKING ME TO STAY AWAY FROM ARCHIE?
ONLY BEFORE HE DATES ME! SO HE'LL BE PUNCTUAL!
I KNOW HOW YOU COAX HIM WITH YOUR HOMEMADE GOODIES, TO STALL HIM!
SOME OF US HAVE A FLAIR FOR HOME-MAKING!
WELL, DO IT ON YOUR OWN TIME!
ALL'S FAIR IN LOVE AND WAR, VERONICA!
2

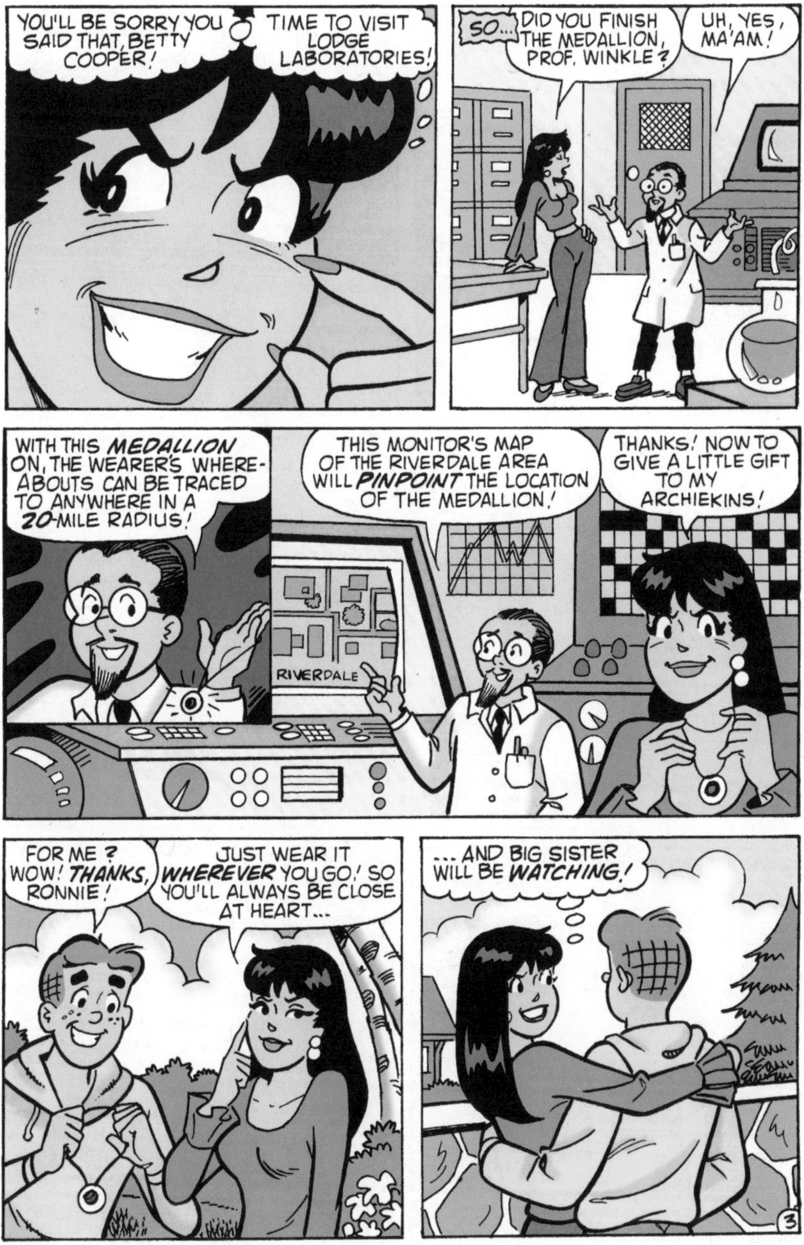
YOU'LL BE SORRY YOU SAID THAT, BETTY COOPER!
TIME TO VISIT LODGE LABORATORIES!
SO...
DID YOU FINISH THE MEDALLION, PROF. WINKLE?
UH, YES, MA'AM!
WITH THIS MEDALLION ON, THE WEARER'S WHEREABOUTS CAN BE TRACED TO ANYWHERE IN A 20-MILE RADIUS!
THIS MONITOR'S MAP OF THE RIVERDALE AREA WILL PINPOINT THE LOCATION OF THE MEDALLION!
RIVERDALE
THANKS! NOW TO GIVE A LITTLE GIFT TO MY ARCHIEKINS!
FOR ME? WOW! THANKS, RONNIE!
JUST WEAR IT WHEREVER YOU GO! SO YOU'LL ALWAYS BE CLOSE AT HEART...
... AND BIG SISTER WILL BE WATCHING!
3

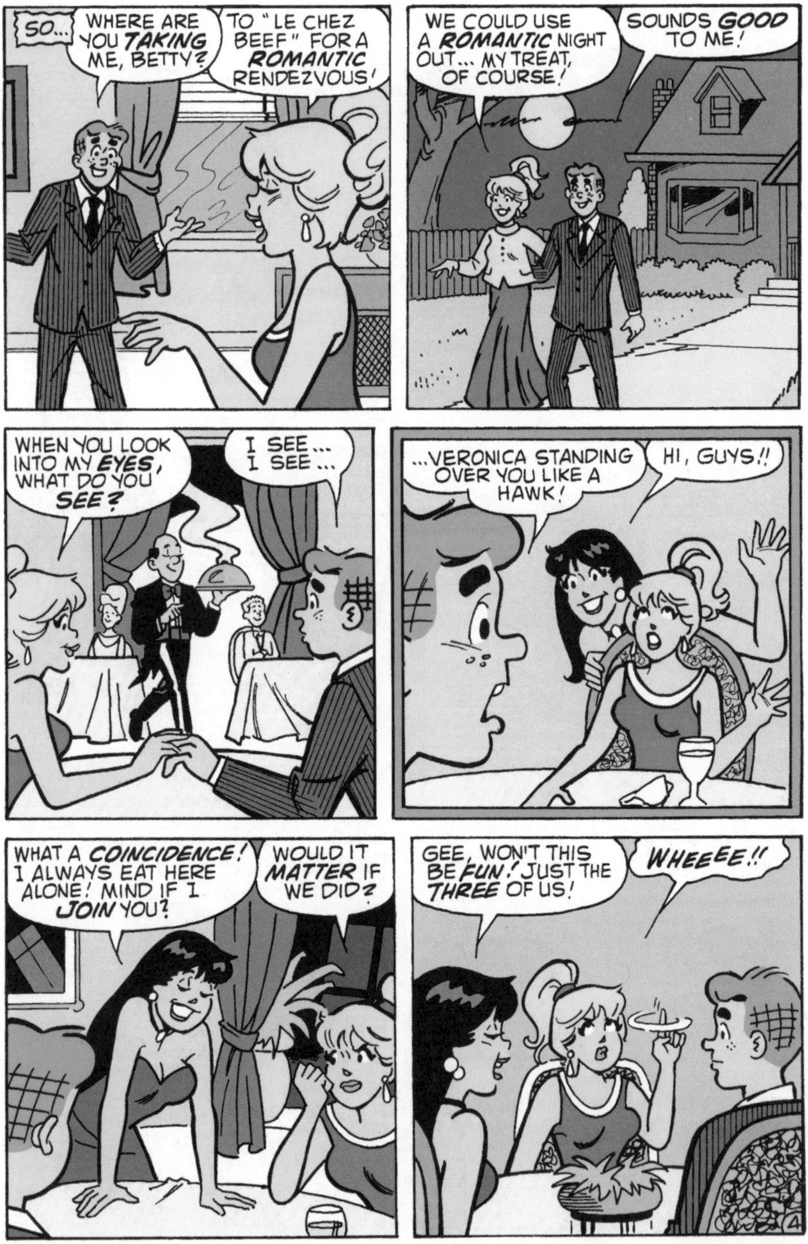
SO...
WHERE ARE YOU TAKING ME, BETTY?
TO "LE CHEZ BEEF" FOR A ROMANTIC RENDEZVOUS!
WE COULD USE A ROMANTIC NIGHT OUT... MY TREAT, OF COURSE!
SOUNDS GOOD TO ME!
WHEN YOU LOOK INTO MY EYES, WHAT DO YOU SEE?
I SEE... I SEE...
...VERONICA STANDING OVER YOU LIKE A HAWK!
HI, GUYS!!
WHAT A COINCIDENCE! I ALWAYS EAT HERE ALONE! MIND IF I JOIN YOU?
WOULD IT MATTER IF WE DID?
GEE, WON'T THIS BE FUN! JUST THE THREE OF US!
WHEEEE!!
4

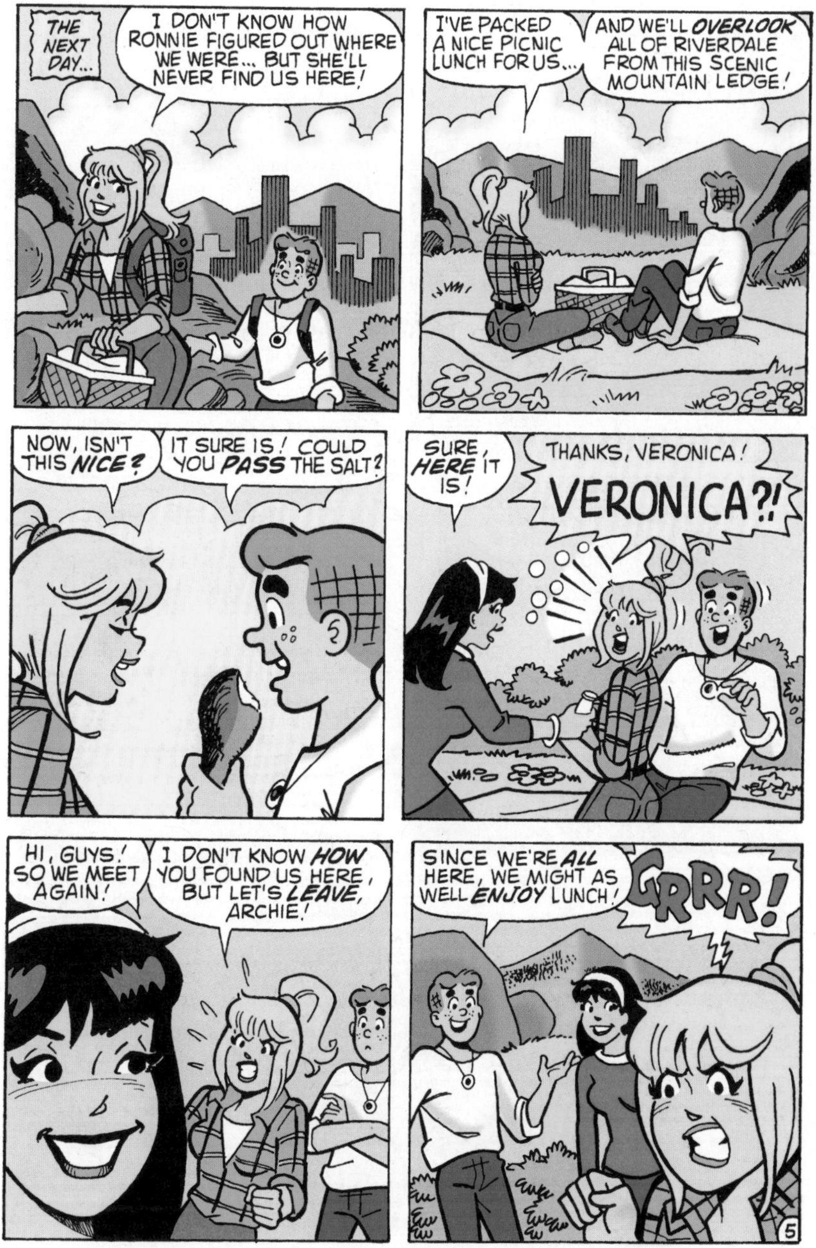
THE NEXT DAY...
I DON'T KNOW HOW RONNIE FIGURED OUT WHERE WE WERE... BUT SHE'LL NEVER FIND US HERE!
I'VE PACKED A NICE PICNIC LUNCH FOR US...
AND WE'LL OVERLOOK ALL OF RIVERDALE FROM THIS SCENIC MOUNTAIN LEDGE!
NOW, ISN'T THIS NICE?
IT SURE IS! COULD YOU PASS THE SALT?
SURE, HERE IT IS!
THANKS, VERONICA!
VERONICA?!
HI, GUYS! SO WE MEET AGAIN!
I DON'T KNOW HOW YOU FOUND US HERE, BUT LET'S LEAVE, ARCHIE!
SINCE WE'RE ALL HERE, WE MIGHT AS WELL ENJOY LUNCH!
GRRR!
5

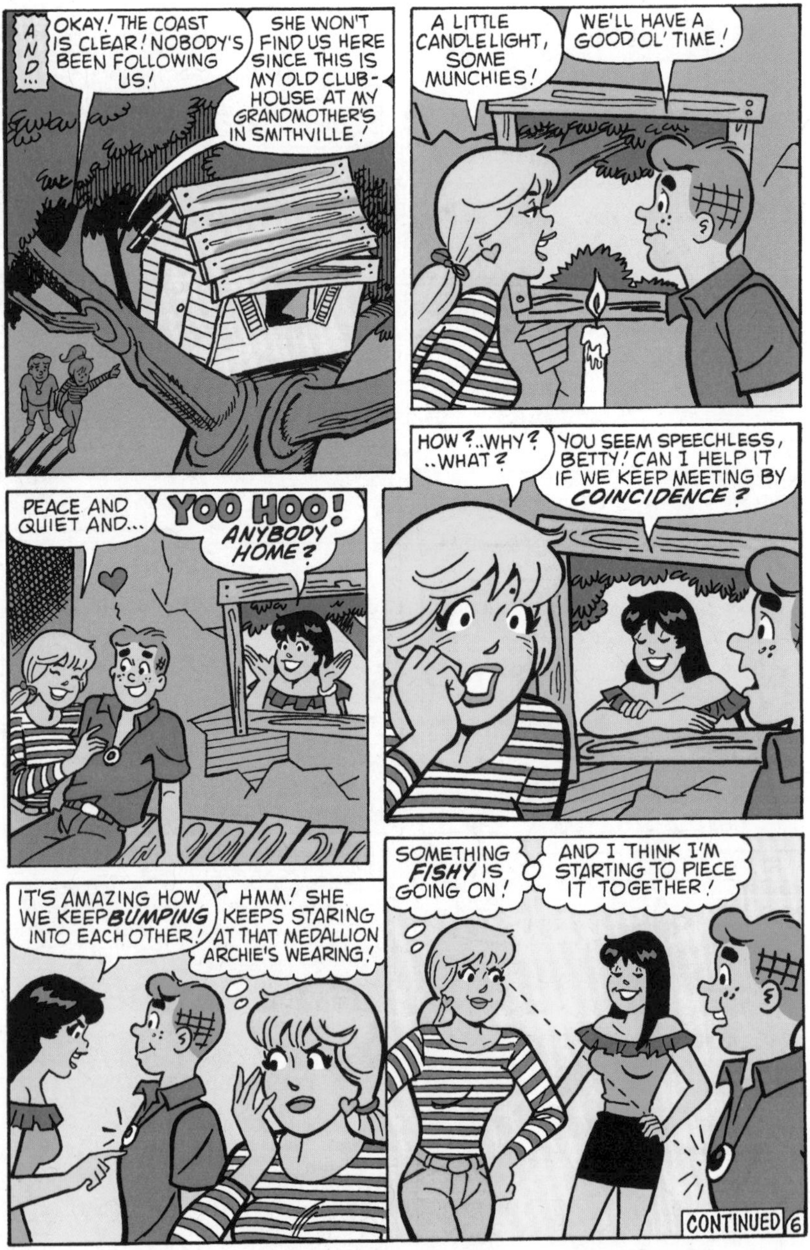
AND...
OKAY! THE COAST IS CLEAR! NOBODY'S BEEN FOLLOWING US!
SHE WON'T FIND US HERE SINCE THIS IS MY OLD CLUB-HOUSE AT MY GRANDMOTHER'S IN SMITHVILLE!
A LITTLE CANDLELIGHT, SOME MUNCHIES!
WE'LL HAVE A GOOD OL' TIME!
PEACE AND QUIET AND...
YOO HOO! ANYBODY HOME?
HOW?..WHY? ..WHAT?
YOU SEEM SPEECHLESS, BETTY! CAN I HELP IT IF WE KEEP MEETING BY COINCIDENCE?
IT'S AMAZING HOW WE KEEP BUMPING INTO EACH OTHER!
HMM! SHE KEEPS STARING AT THAT MEDALLION ARCHIE'S WEARING!
SOMETHING FISHY IS GOING ON!
AND I THINK I'M STARTING TO PIECE IT TOGETHER!
CONTINUED 6

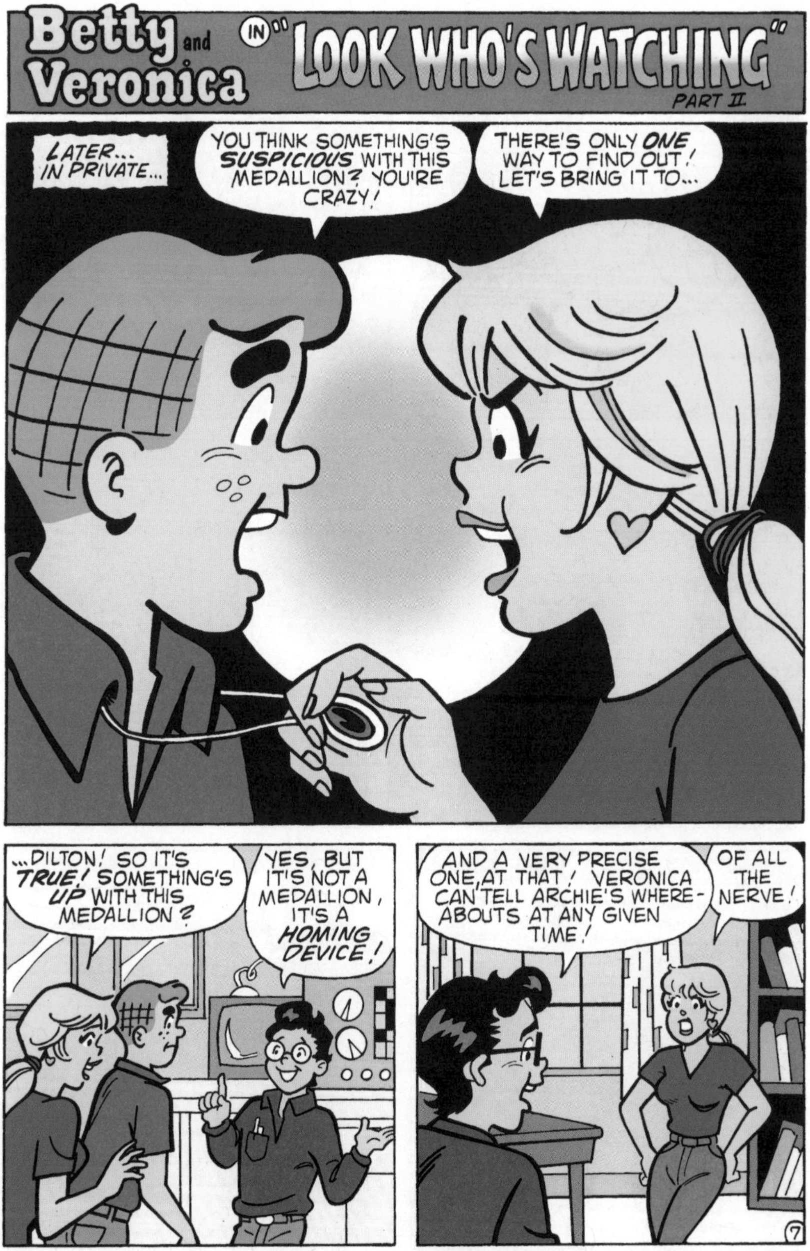
Betty and Veronica
IN "LOOK WHO'S WATCHING"
PART II
LATER... IN PRIVATE...
YOU THINK SOMETHING'S SUSPICIOUS WITH THIS MEDALLION? YOU'RE CRAZY!
THERE'S ONLY ONE WAY TO FIND OUT! LET'S BRING IT TO...
...DILTON! SO IT'S TRUE! SOMETHING'S UP WITH THIS MEDALLION?
YES, BUT IT'S NOT A MEDALLION, IT'S A HOMING DEVICE!
AND A VERY PRECISE ONE, AT THAT! VERONICA CAN TELL ARCHIE'S WHEREABOUTS AT ANY GIVEN TIME!
OF ALL THE NERVE!
7

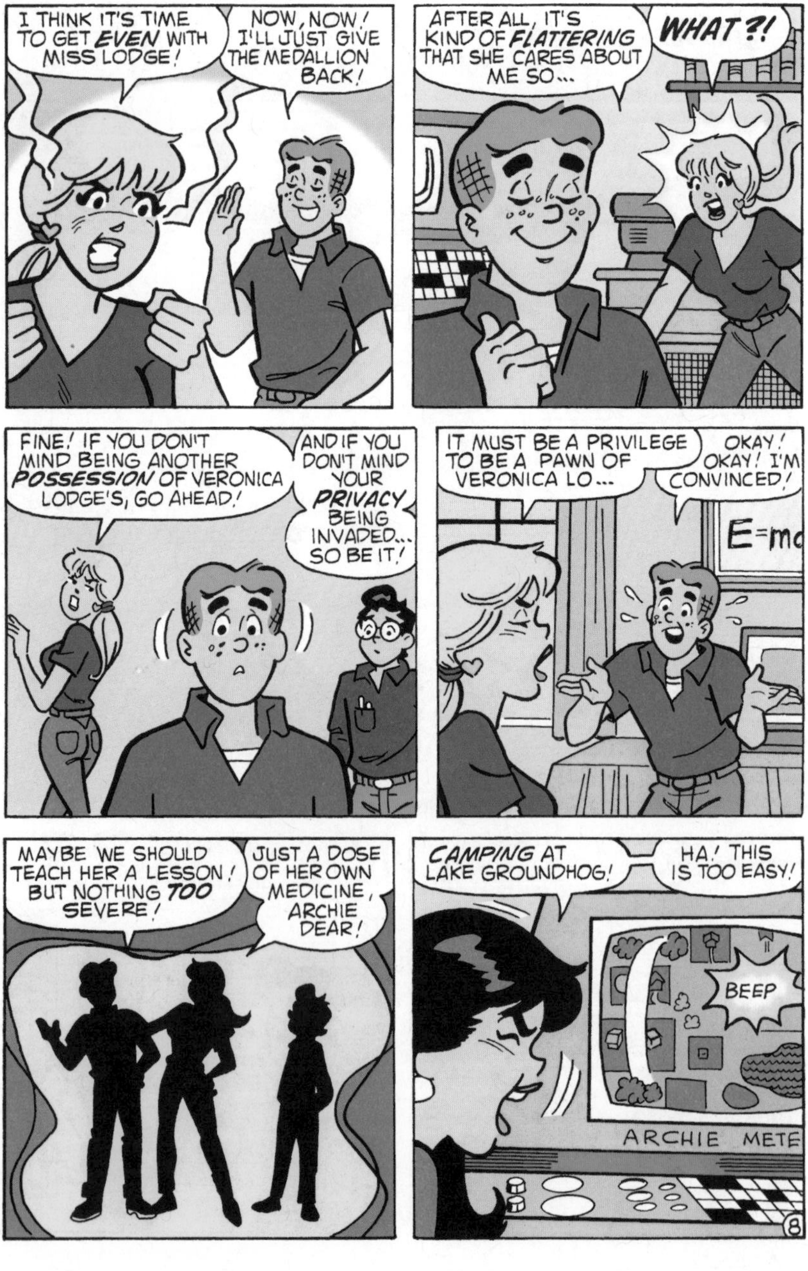
I THINK IT'S TIME TO GET *EVEN* WITH MISS LODGE!
NOW, NOW! I'LL JUST GIVE THE MEDALLION BACK!
AFTER ALL, IT'S KIND OF *FLATTERING* THAT SHE CARES ABOUT ME SO...
WHAT?!
FINE! IF YOU DON'T MIND BEING ANOTHER *POSSESSION* OF VERONICA LODGE'S, GO AHEAD!
AND IF YOU DON'T MIND YOUR *PRIVACY* BEING INVADED... SO BE IT!
IT MUST BE A PRIVILEGE TO BE A PAWN OF VERONICA LO...
OKAY! OKAY! I'M CONVINCED!
E=mc
MAYBE WE SHOULD TEACH HER A LESSON! BUT NOTHING *TOO* SEVERE!
JUST A DOSE OF HER OWN MEDICINE, ARCHIE DEAR!
CAMPING AT LAKE GROUNDHOG!
HA! THIS IS TOO EASY!
BEEP
ARCHIE METE
8

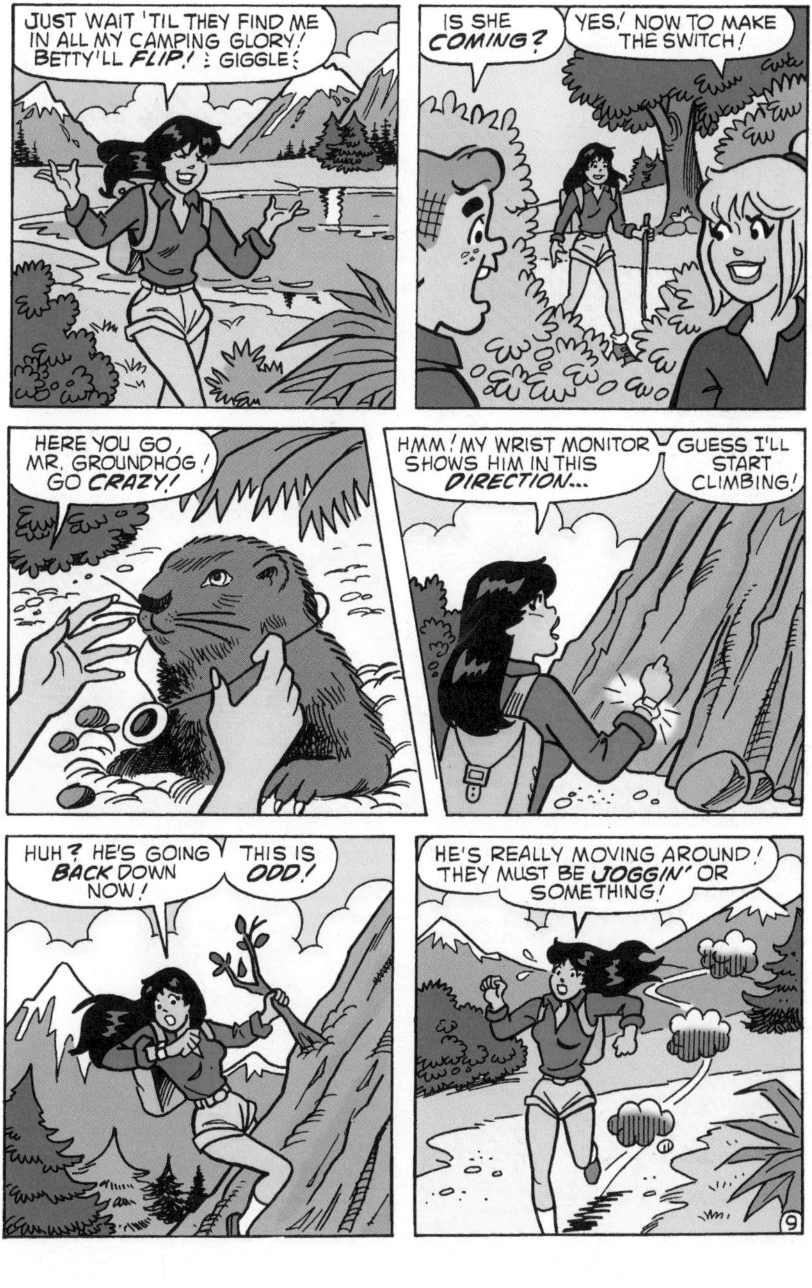
JUST WAIT 'TIL THEY FIND ME IN ALL MY CAMPING GLORY! BETTY'LL FLIP! :GIGGLE:
IS SHE COMING?
YES! NOW TO MAKE THE SWITCH!
HERE YOU GO, MR. GROUNDHOG! GO CRAZY!
HMM! MY WRIST MONITOR SHOWS HIM IN THIS DIRECTION...
GUESS I'LL START CLIMBING!
HUH? HE'S GOING BACK DOWN NOW!
THIS IS ODD!
HE'S REALLY MOVING AROUND! THEY MUST BE JOGGIN' OR SOMETHING!
9

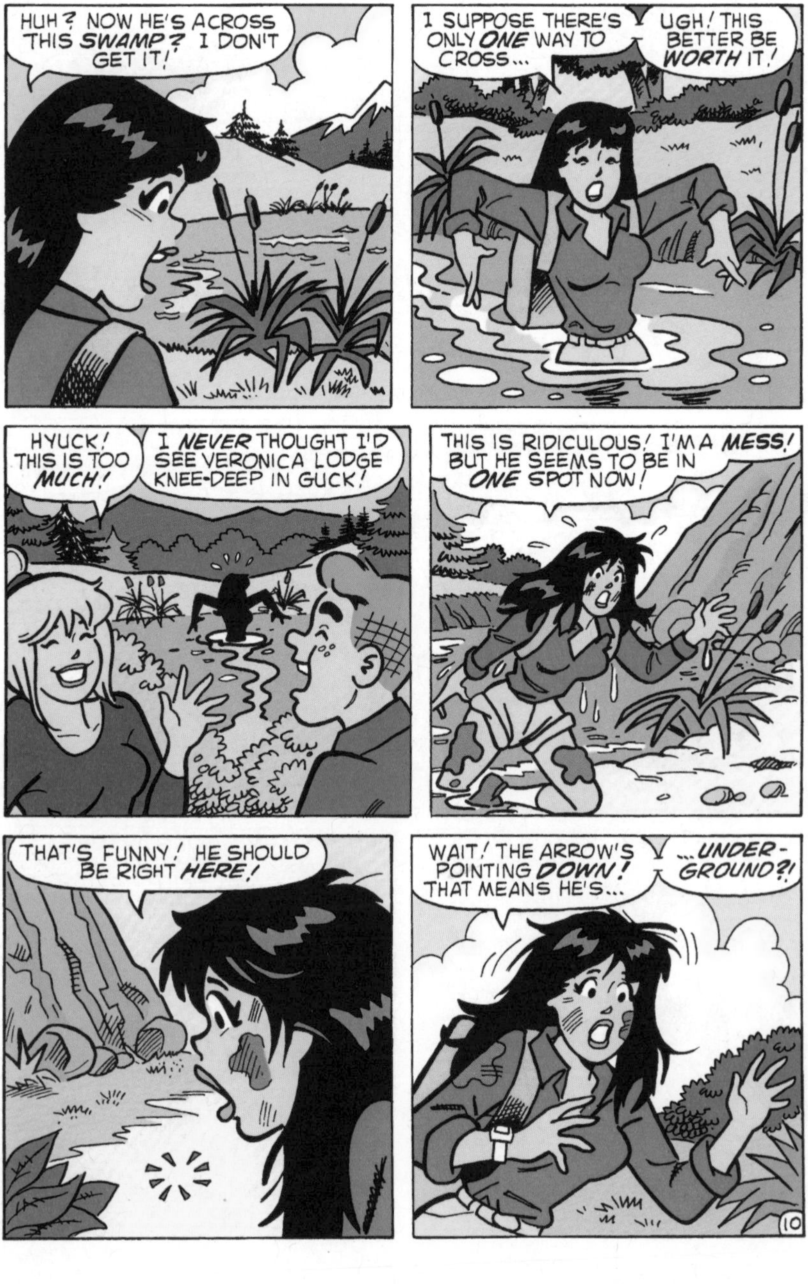
HUH? NOW HE'S ACROSS THIS SWAMP? I DON'T GET IT!
I SUPPOSE THERE'S ONLY ONE WAY TO CROSS...
UGH! THIS BETTER BE WORTH IT!
HYUCK! THIS IS TOO MUCH!
I NEVER THOUGHT I'D SEE VERONICA LODGE KNEE-DEEP IN GUCK!
THIS IS RIDICULOUS! I'M A MESS! BUT HE SEEMS TO BE IN ONE SPOT NOW!
THAT'S FUNNY! HE SHOULD BE RIGHT HERE!
WAIT! THE ARROW'S POINTING DOWN! THAT MEANS HE'S...
...UNDER-GROUND?!
10

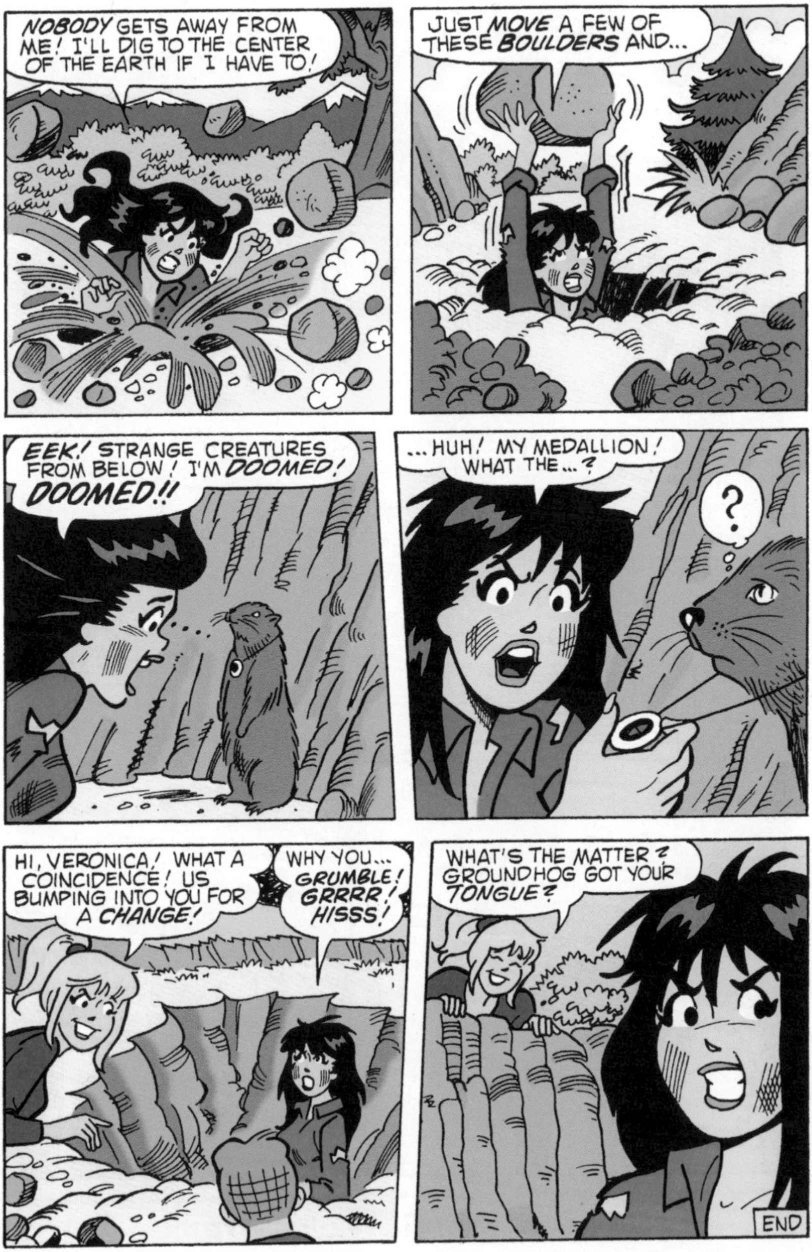
NOBODY GETS AWAY FROM ME! I'LL DIG TO THE CENTER OF THE EARTH IF I HAVE TO!
JUST MOVE A FEW OF THESE BOULDERS AND...
EEK! STRANGE CREATURES FROM BELOW! I'M DOOMED! DOOMED!!
...HUH! MY MEDALLION! WHAT THE...?
?
HI, VERONICA! WHAT A COINCIDENCE! US BUMPING INTO YOU FOR A CHANGE!
WHY YOU... GRUMBLE! GRRRR! HISSS!
WHAT'S THE MATTER? GROUNDHOG GOT YOUR TONGUE?
END

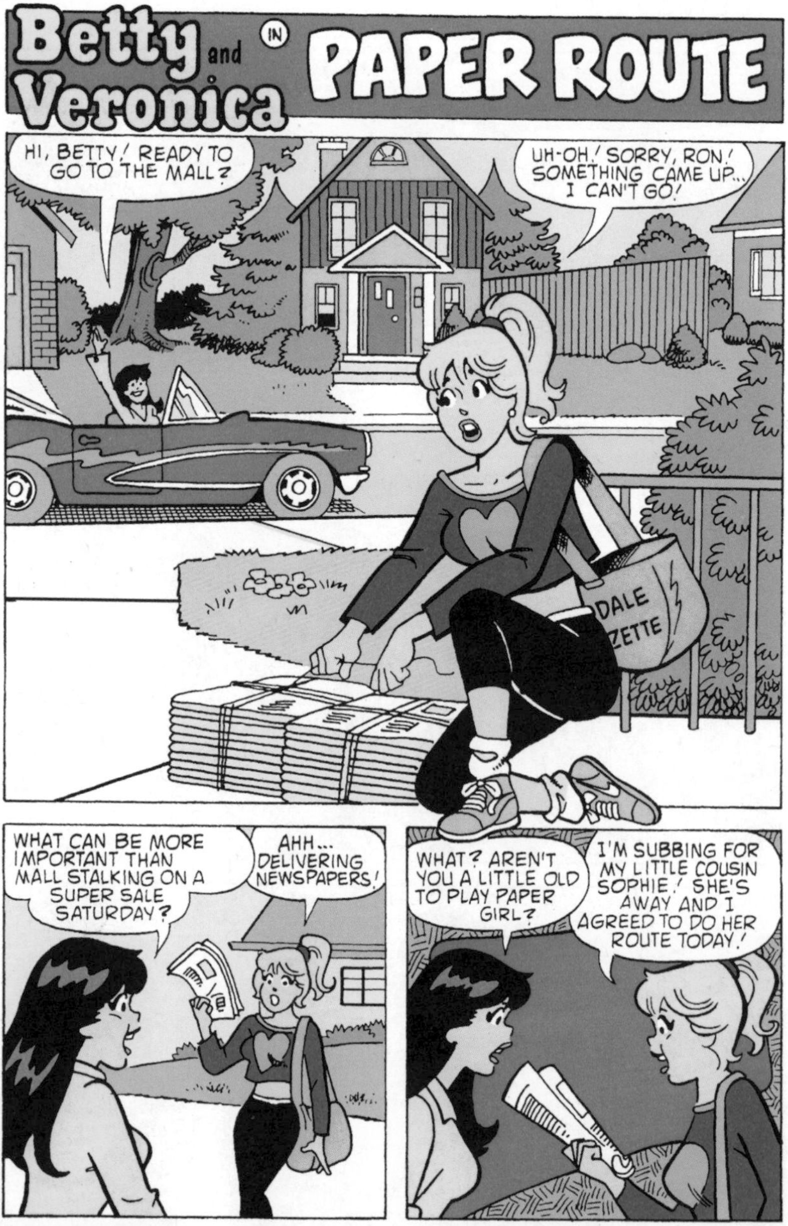
Betty and Veronica in PAPER ROUTE
HI, BETTY! READY TO GO TO THE MALL?
UH-OH! SORRY, RON! SOMETHING CAME UP... I CAN'T GO!
DALE ZETTE
WHAT CAN BE MORE IMPORTANT THAN MALL STALKING ON A SUPER SALE SATURDAY?
AHH... DELIVERING NEWSPAPERS!
WHAT? AREN'T YOU A LITTLE OLD TO PLAY PAPER GIRL?
I'M SUBBING FOR MY LITTLE COUSIN SOPHIE! SHE'S AWAY AND I AGREED TO DO HER ROUTE TODAY!

Story: Mike Pellowski Pencils: Dan Parent
Inks: Henry Scarpelli Letters: Bill Yoshida Colors: Barry Grossman

Originally printed in BETTY & VERONICA SPECTACULAR #9, July 1994

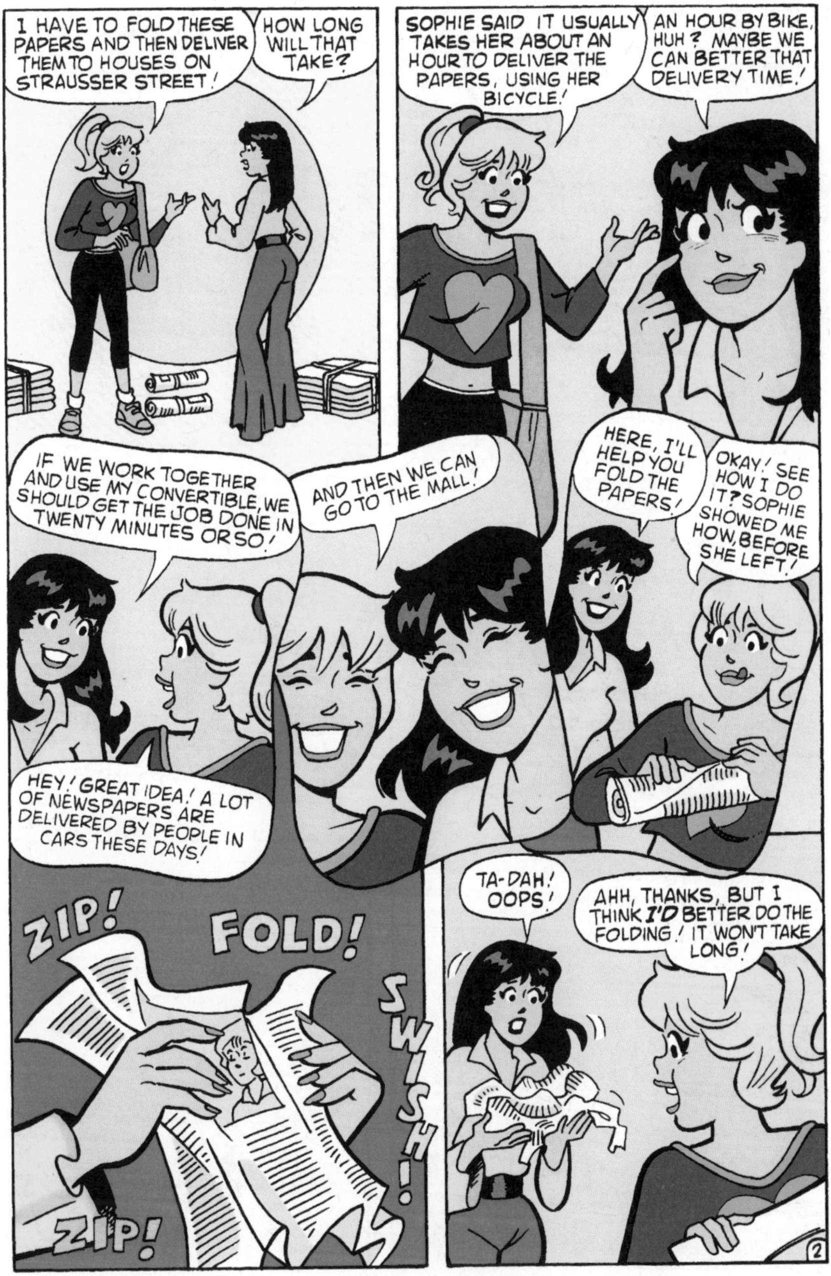
I HAVE TO FOLD THESE PAPERS AND THEN DELIVER THEM TO HOUSES ON STRAUSSER STREET!
HOW LONG WILL THAT TAKE?
SOPHIE SAID IT USUALLY TAKES HER ABOUT AN HOUR TO DELIVER THE PAPERS, USING HER BICYCLE!
AN HOUR BY BIKE, HUH? MAYBE WE CAN BETTER THAT DELIVERY TIME!
IF WE WORK TOGETHER AND USE MY CONVERTIBLE, WE SHOULD GET THE JOB DONE IN TWENTY MINUTES OR SO!
HEY! GREAT IDEA! A LOT OF NEWSPAPERS ARE DELIVERED BY PEOPLE IN CARS THESE DAYS!
AND THEN WE CAN GO TO THE MALL!
HERE, I'LL HELP YOU FOLD THE PAPERS!
OKAY! SEE HOW I DO IT? SOPHIE SHOWED ME HOW, BEFORE SHE LEFT!
ZIP!
FOLD!
SWISH!
ZIP!
TA-DAH! OOPS!
AHH, THANKS, BUT I THINK ***I'D*** BETTER DO THE FOLDING! IT WON'T TAKE LONG!
2

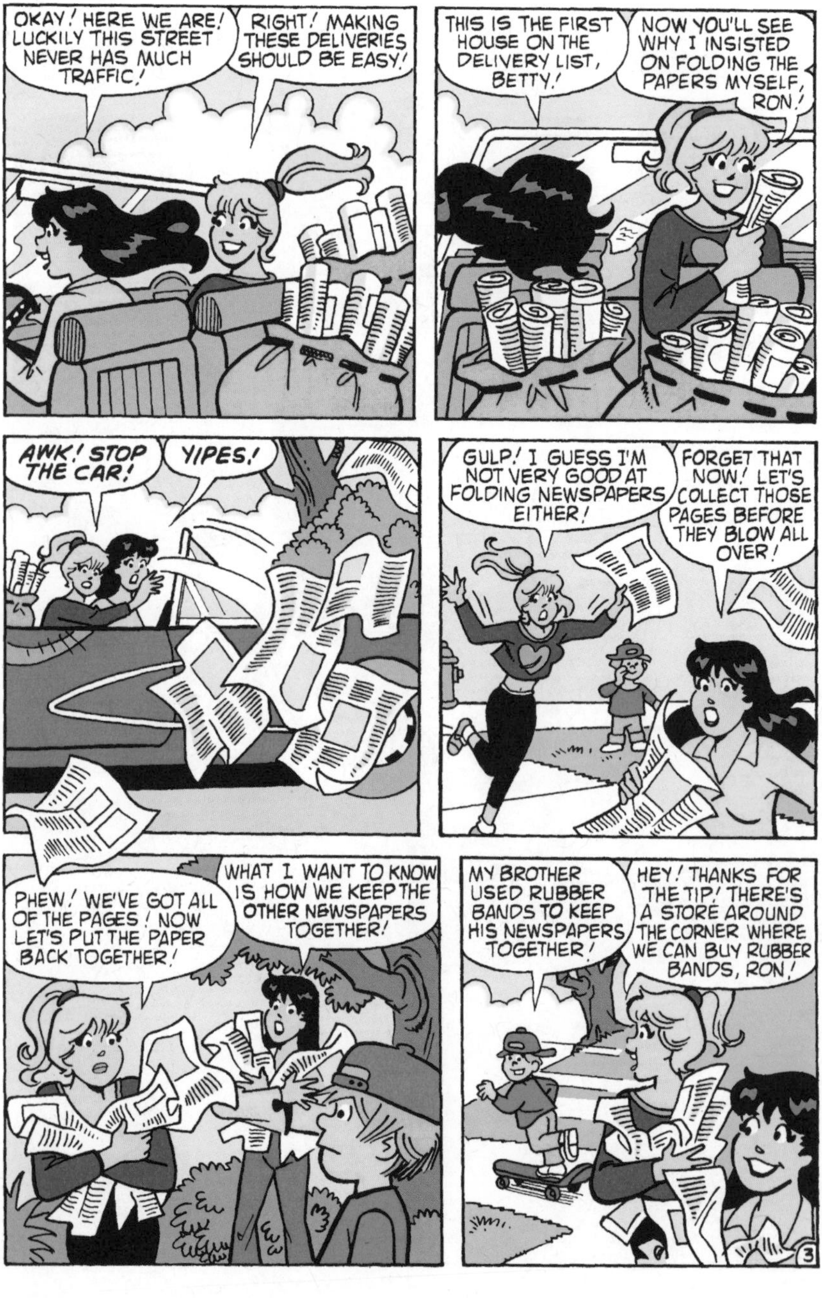
OKAY! HERE WE ARE! LUCKILY THIS STREET NEVER HAS MUCH TRAFFIC!
RIGHT! MAKING THESE DELIVERIES SHOULD BE EASY!
THIS IS THE FIRST HOUSE ON THE DELIVERY LIST, BETTY!
NOW YOU'LL SEE WHY I INSISTED ON FOLDING THE PAPERS MYSELF, RON!
AWK! STOP THE CAR!
YIPES!
GULP! I GUESS I'M NOT VERY GOOD AT FOLDING NEWSPAPERS EITHER!
FORGET THAT NOW! LET'S COLLECT THOSE PAGES BEFORE THEY BLOW ALL OVER!
PHEW! WE'VE GOT ALL OF THE PAGES! NOW LET'S PUT THE PAPER BACK TOGETHER!
WHAT I WANT TO KNOW IS HOW WE KEEP THE OTHER NEWSPAPERS TOGETHER!
MY BROTHER USED RUBBER BANDS TO KEEP HIS NEWSPAPERS TOGETHER!
HEY! THANKS FOR THE TIP! THERE'S A STORE AROUND THE CORNER WHERE WE CAN BUY RUBBER BANDS, RON!
3

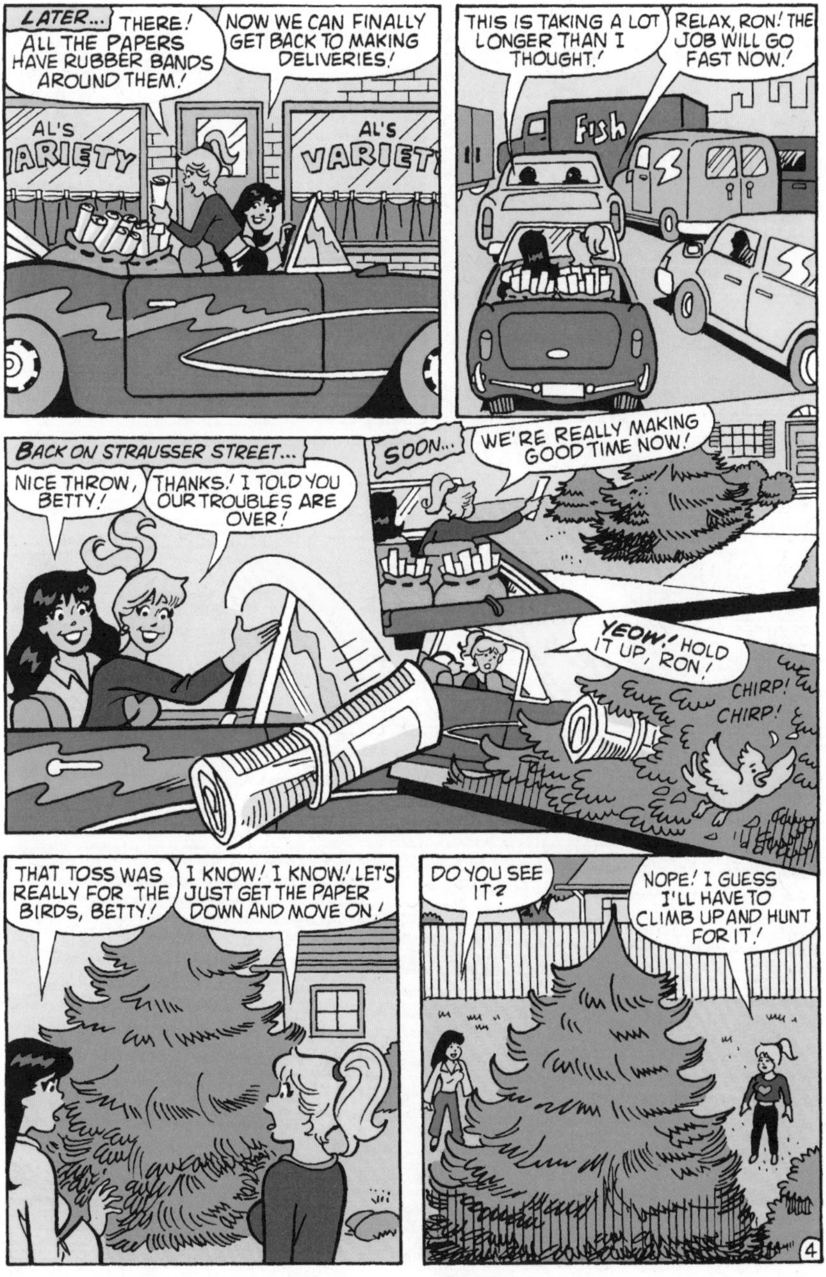
LATER...
THERE! ALL THE PAPERS HAVE RUBBER BANDS AROUND THEM!
NOW WE CAN FINALLY GET BACK TO MAKING DELIVERIES!
AL'S VARIETY
AL'S VARIETY
THIS IS TAKING A LOT LONGER THAN I THOUGHT!
RELAX, RON! THE JOB WILL GO FAST NOW!
Fish
BACK ON STRAUSSER STREET...
NICE THROW, BETTY!
THANKS! I TOLD YOU OUR TROUBLES ARE OVER!
SOON...
WE'RE REALLY MAKING GOOD TIME NOW!
YEOW! HOLD IT UP, RON!
CHIRP! CHIRP!
THAT TOSS WAS REALLY FOR THE BIRDS, BETTY!
I KNOW! I KNOW! LET'S JUST GET THE PAPER DOWN AND MOVE ON!
DO YOU SEE IT?
NOPE! I GUESS I'LL HAVE TO CLIMB UP AND HUNT FOR IT!
4

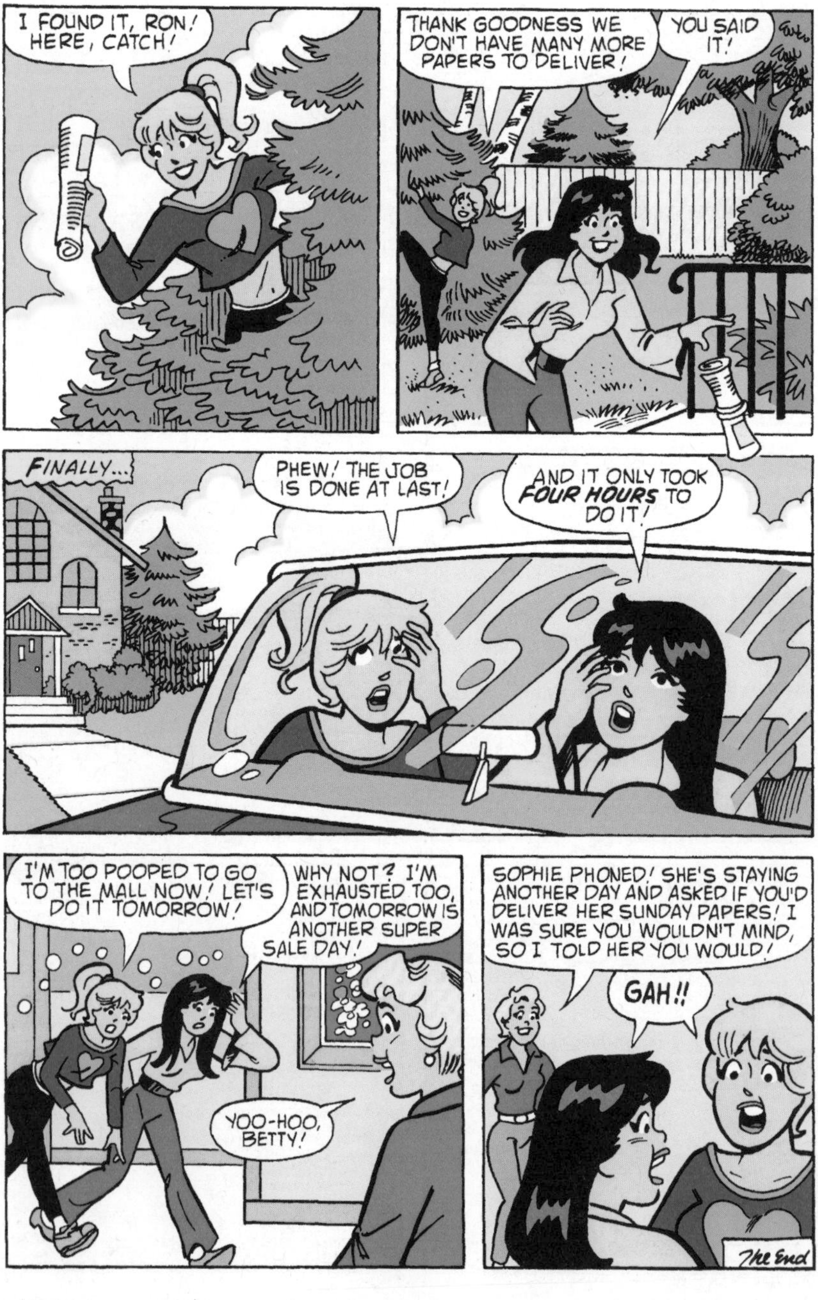
I FOUND IT, RON! HERE, CATCH!
THANK GOODNESS WE DON'T HAVE MANY MORE PAPERS TO DELIVER!
YOU SAID IT!
FINALLY...
PHEW! THE JOB IS DONE AT LAST!
AND IT ONLY TOOK FOUR HOURS TO DO IT!
I'M TOO POOPED TO GO TO THE MALL NOW! LET'S DO IT TOMORROW!
WHY NOT? I'M EXHAUSTED TOO, AND TOMORROW IS ANOTHER SUPER SALE DAY!
YOO-HOO, BETTY!
SOPHIE PHONED! SHE'S STAYING ANOTHER DAY AND ASKED IF YOU'D DELIVER HER SUNDAY PAPERS! I WAS SURE YOU WOULDN'T MIND, SO I TOLD HER YOU WOULD!
GAH!!
The End

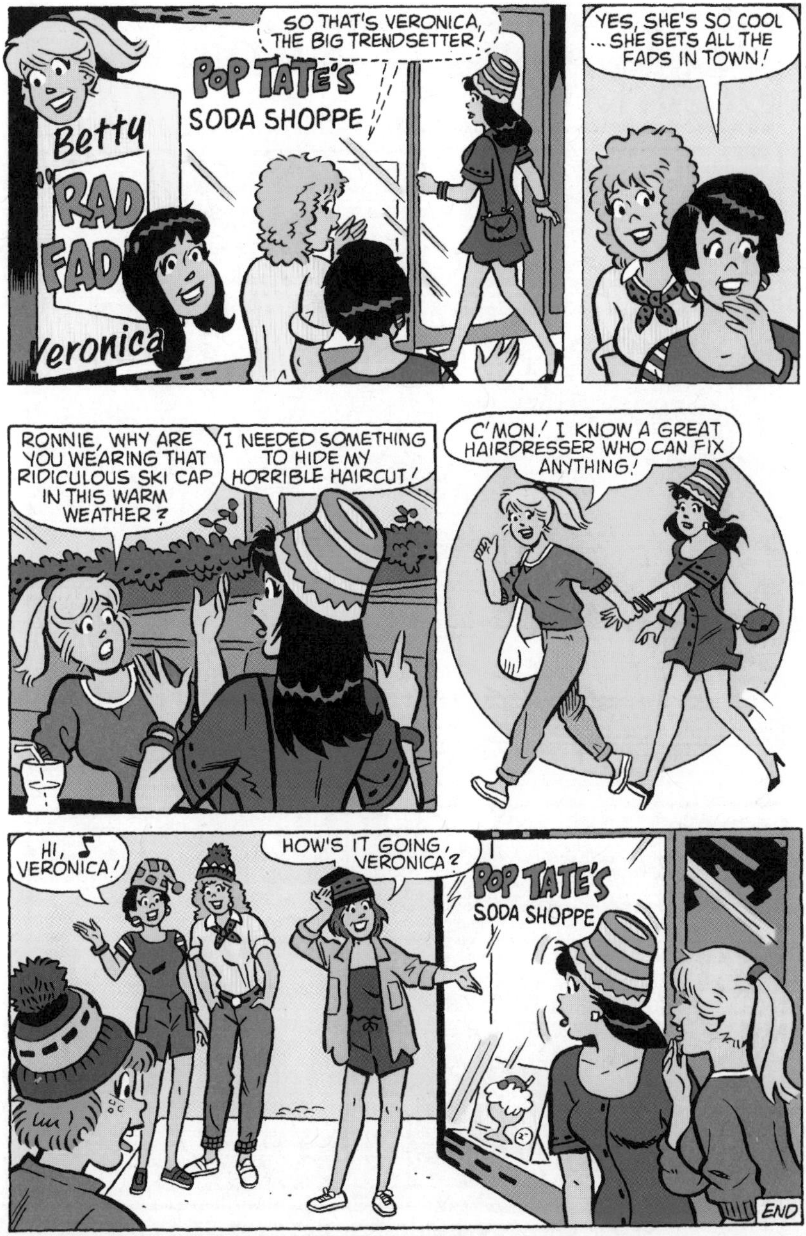
Betty
"RAD FAD"
Veronica
SO THAT'S VERONICA, THE BIG TRENDSETTER!
POP TATE'S
SODA SHOPPE
YES, SHE'S SO COOL ...SHE SETS ALL THE FADS IN TOWN!
RONNIE, WHY ARE YOU WEARING THAT RIDICULOUS SKI CAP IN THIS WARM WEATHER?
I NEEDED SOMETHING TO HIDE MY HORRIBLE HAIRCUT!
C'MON! I KNOW A GREAT HAIRDRESSER WHO CAN FIX ANYTHING!
HI, VERONICA!
HOW'S IT GOING, VERONICA?
POP TATE'S
SODA SHOPPE
END

Story: George Gladir Pencils: Stan Goldberg Inks: Rudy Lapick

Originally printed in BETTY & VERONICA SPECTACULAR #9, July 1994

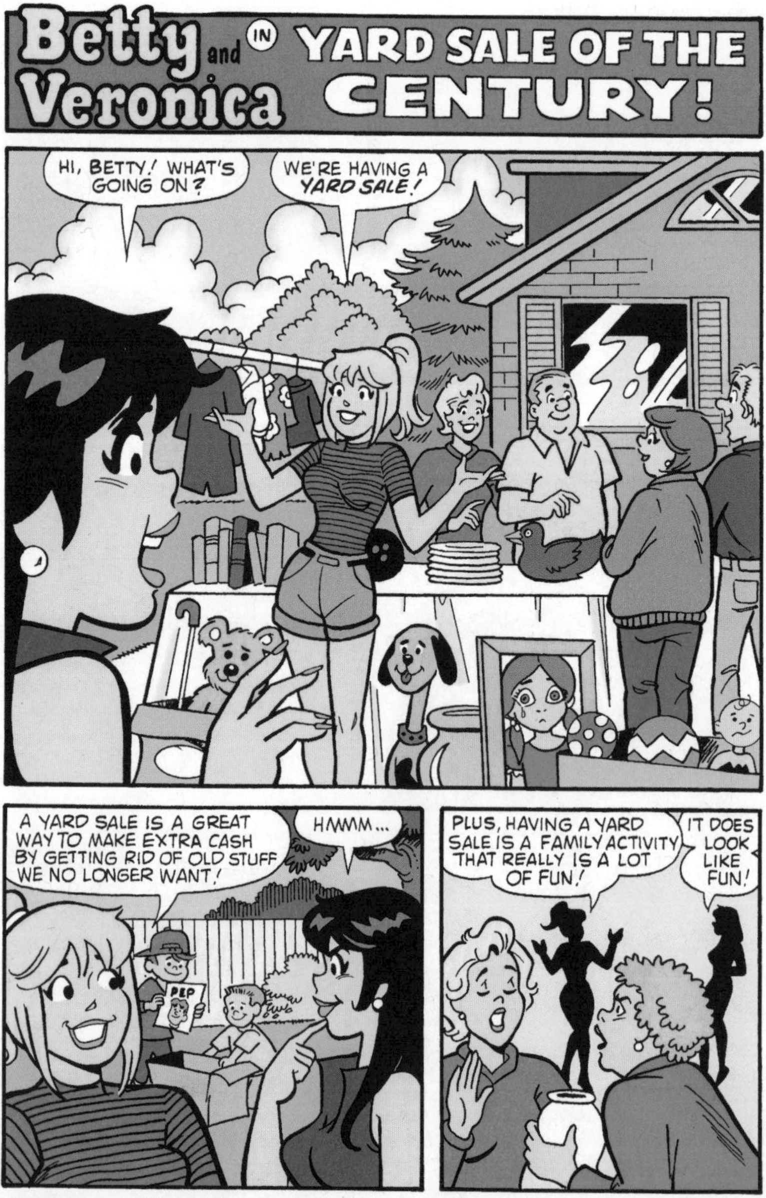
Betty and Veronica
IN
YARD SALE OF THE CENTURY!
HI, BETTY! WHAT'S GOING ON?
WE'RE HAVING A YARD SALE!
A YARD SALE IS A GREAT WAY TO MAKE EXTRA CASH BY GETTING RID OF OLD STUFF WE NO LONGER WANT!
HMMM...
PEP
PLUS, HAVING A YARD SALE IS A FAMILY ACTIVITY THAT REALLY IS A LOT OF FUN!
IT DOES LOOK LIKE FUN!

Story: Mike Pellowski   Pencils: Dan Parent

Inks: Henry Scarpelli   Letters: Bill Yoshida   Colors: Barry Grossman

Originally printed in BETTY & VERONICA SPECTACULAR #9, July 1994

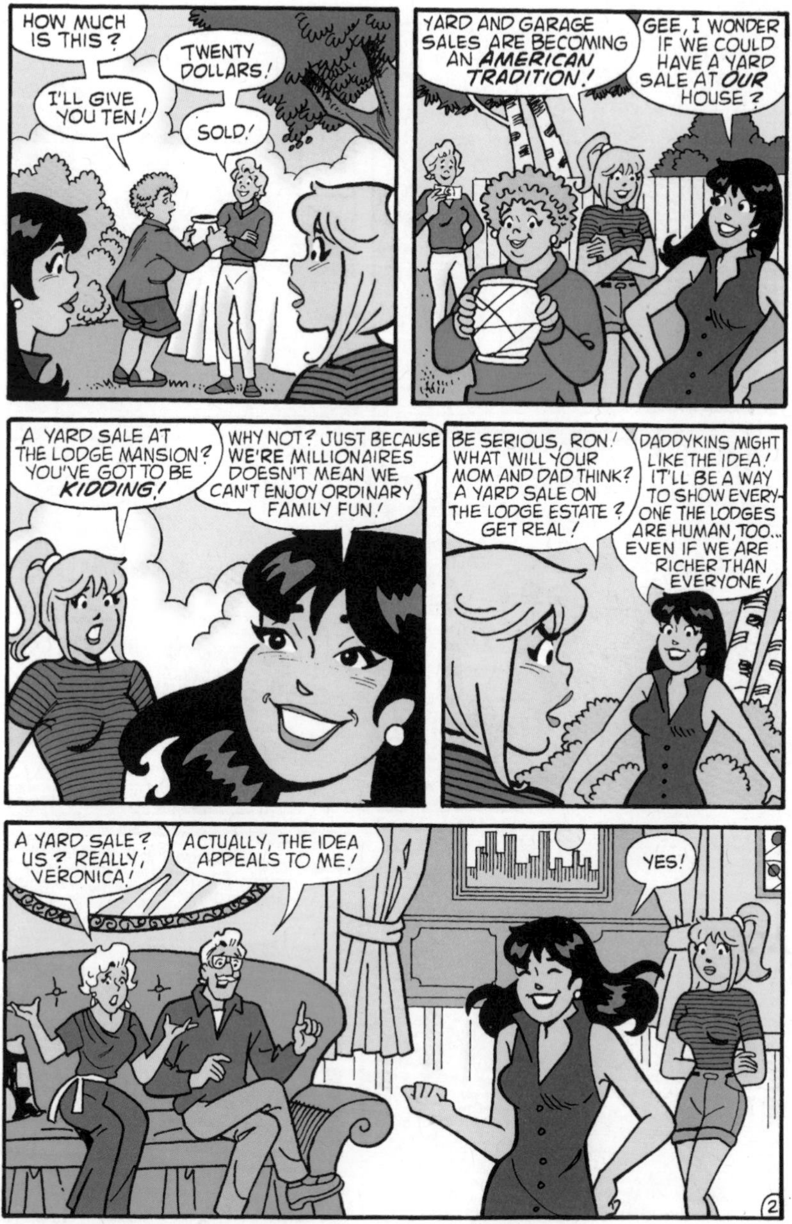
HOW MUCH IS THIS ?
TWENTY DOLLARS!
I'LL GIVE YOU TEN!
SOLD!
YARD AND GARAGE SALES ARE BECOMING AN AMERICAN TRADITION!
GEE, I WONDER IF WE COULD HAVE A YARD SALE AT OUR HOUSE ?
A YARD SALE AT THE LODGE MANSION? YOU'VE GOT TO BE KIDDING!
WHY NOT? JUST BECAUSE WE'RE MILLIONAIRES DOESN'T MEAN WE CAN'T ENJOY ORDINARY FAMILY FUN!
BE SERIOUS, RON! WHAT WILL YOUR MOM AND DAD THINK? A YARD SALE ON THE LODGE ESTATE ? GET REAL!
DADDYKINS MIGHT LIKE THE IDEA! IT'LL BE A WAY TO SHOW EVERYONE THE LODGES ARE HUMAN, TOO... EVEN IF WE ARE RICHER THAN EVERYONE!
A YARD SALE? US ? REALLY, VERONICA!
ACTUALLY, THE IDEA APPEALS TO ME!
YES!
2

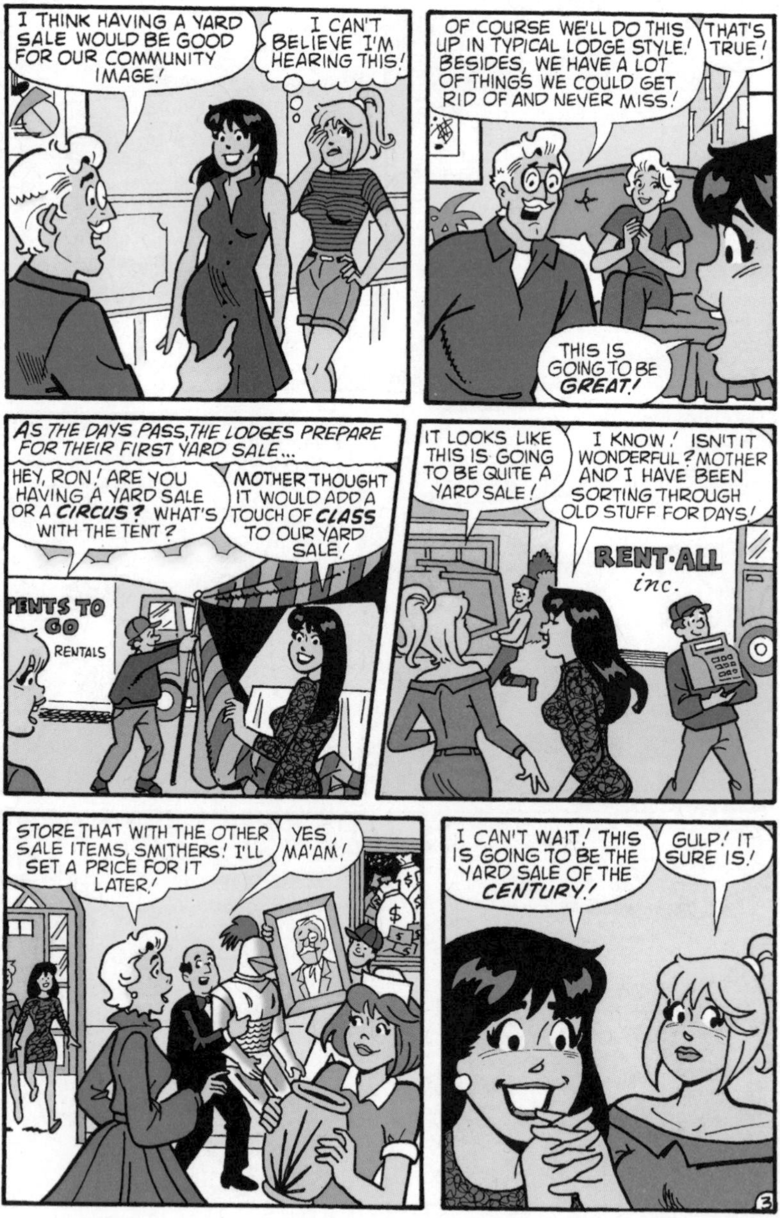
I THINK HAVING A YARD SALE WOULD BE GOOD FOR OUR COMMUNITY IMAGE!
I CAN'T BELIEVE I'M HEARING THIS!
OF COURSE WE'LL DO THIS UP IN TYPICAL LODGE STYLE! BESIDES, WE HAVE A LOT OF THINGS WE COULD GET RID OF AND NEVER MISS!
THAT'S TRUE!
THIS IS GOING TO BE GREAT!
AS THE DAYS PASS, THE LODGES PREPARE FOR THEIR FIRST YARD SALE...
HEY, RON! ARE YOU HAVING A YARD SALE OR A CIRCUS? WHAT'S WITH THE TENT?
MOTHER THOUGHT IT WOULD ADD A TOUCH OF CLASS TO OUR YARD SALE!
TENTS TO GO
RENTALS
IT LOOKS LIKE THIS IS GOING TO BE QUITE A YARD SALE!
I KNOW! ISN'T IT WONDERFUL? MOTHER AND I HAVE BEEN SORTING THROUGH OLD STUFF FOR DAYS!
RENT·ALL inc.
STORE THAT WITH THE OTHER SALE ITEMS, SMITHERS! I'LL SET A PRICE FOR IT LATER!
YES, MA'AM!
I CAN'T WAIT! THIS IS GOING TO BE THE YARD SALE OF THE CENTURY!
GULP! IT SURE IS!
3

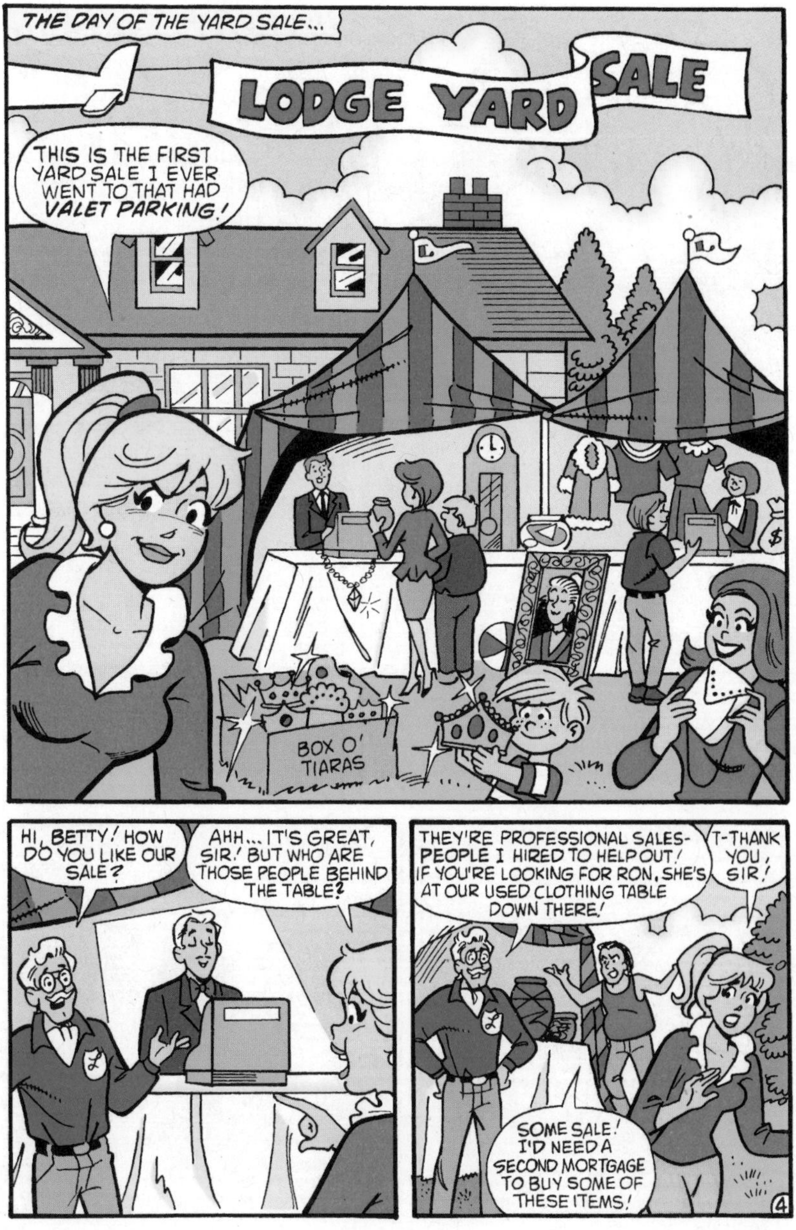
THE DAY OF THE YARD SALE...
LODGE YARD SALE
THIS IS THE FIRST YARD SALE I EVER WENT TO THAT HAD VALET PARKING!
BOX O' TIARAS
HI, BETTY! HOW DO YOU LIKE OUR SALE?
AHH... IT'S GREAT, SIR! BUT WHO ARE THOSE PEOPLE BEHIND THE TABLE?
THEY'RE PROFESSIONAL SALES-PEOPLE I HIRED TO HELP OUT! IF YOU'RE LOOKING FOR RON, SHE'S AT OUR USED CLOTHING TABLE DOWN THERE!
T-THANK YOU, SIR!
SOME SALE! I'D NEED A SECOND MORTGAGE TO BUY SOME OF THESE ITEMS!
4

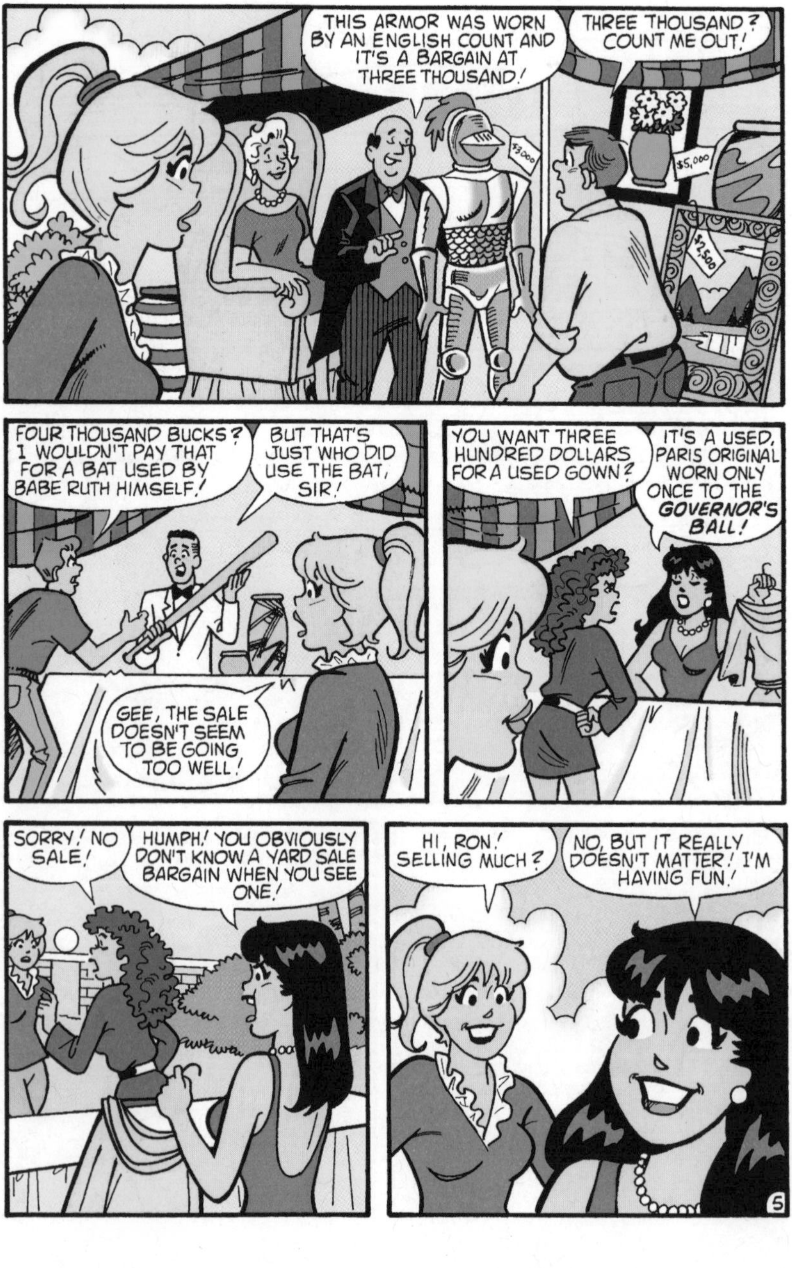
THIS ARMOR WAS WORN BY AN ENGLISH COUNT AND IT'S A BARGAIN AT THREE THOUSAND!
THREE THOUSAND? COUNT ME OUT!
$3000
$5,000
$2,500
FOUR THOUSAND BUCKS? I WOULDN'T PAY THAT FOR A BAT USED BY BABE RUTH HIMSELF!
BUT THAT'S JUST WHO DID USE THE BAT, SIR!
GEE, THE SALE DOESN'T SEEM TO BE GOING TOO WELL!
YOU WANT THREE HUNDRED DOLLARS FOR A USED GOWN?
IT'S A USED, PARIS ORIGINAL WORN ONLY ONCE TO THE GOVERNOR'S BALL!
SORRY! NO SALE!
HUMPH! YOU OBVIOUSLY DON'T KNOW A YARD SALE BARGAIN WHEN YOU SEE ONE!
HI, RON! SELLING MUCH?
NO, BUT IT REALLY DOESN'T MATTER! I'M HAVING FUN!
5

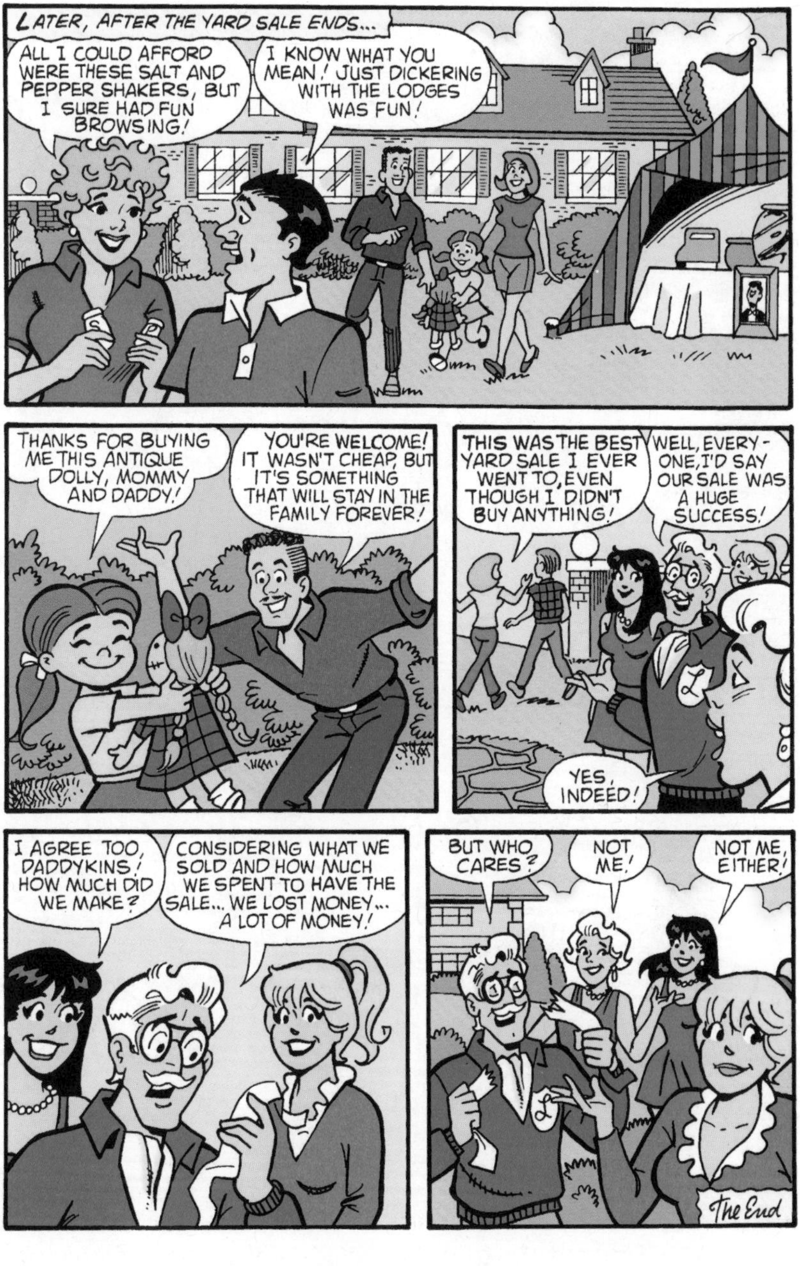
LATER, AFTER THE YARD SALE ENDS...
ALL I COULD AFFORD WERE THESE SALT AND PEPPER SHAKERS, BUT I SURE HAD FUN BROWSING!
I KNOW WHAT YOU MEAN! JUST DICKERING WITH THE LODGES WAS FUN!
THANKS FOR BUYING ME THIS ANTIQUE DOLLY, MOMMY AND DADDY!
YOU'RE WELCOME! IT WASN'T CHEAP, BUT IT'S SOMETHING THAT WILL STAY IN THE FAMILY FOREVER!
THIS WAS THE BEST YARD SALE I EVER WENT TO, EVEN THOUGH I DIDN'T BUY ANYTHING!
WELL, EVERY-ONE, I'D SAY OUR SALE WAS A HUGE SUCCESS!
YES, INDEED!
I AGREE TOO, DADDYKINS! HOW MUCH DID WE MAKE?
CONSIDERING WHAT WE SOLD AND HOW MUCH WE SPENT TO HAVE THE SALE... WE LOST MONEY... A LOT OF MONEY!
BUT WHO CARES?
NOT ME!
NOT ME, EITHER!
The End

Betty and Veronica in "HERE'S SAND IN YOUR FACE!" PART I

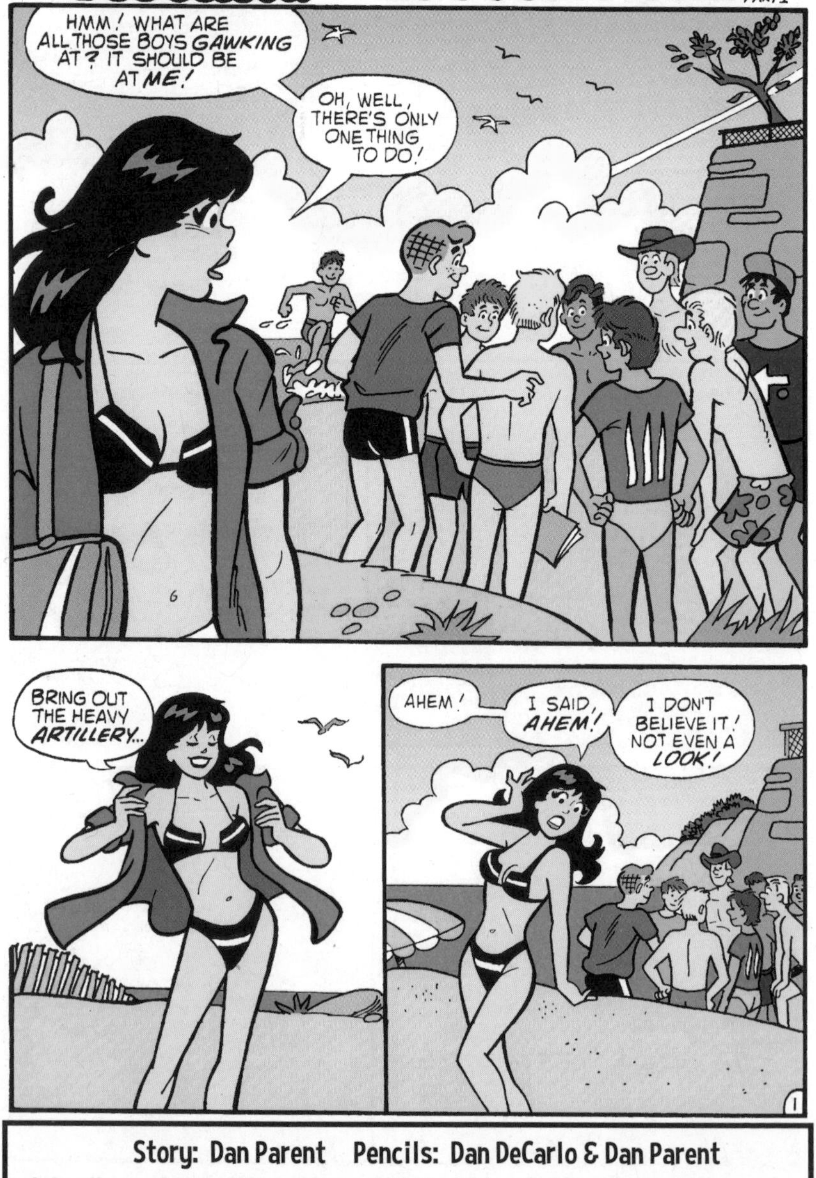
HMM! WHAT ARE ALL THOSE BOYS GAWKING AT? IT SHOULD BE AT ME!
OH, WELL, THERE'S ONLY ONE THING TO DO!
BRING OUT THE HEAVY ARTILLERY...
AHEM!
I SAID, AHEM!
I DON'T BELIEVE IT! NOT EVEN A LOOK!

Story: Dan Parent Pencils: Dan DeCarlo & Dan Parent
Inks: Henry Scarpelli Letters: Bill Yoshida Colors: Barry Grossman

Originally printed in BETTY & VERONICA SPECTACULAR #10, September 1994

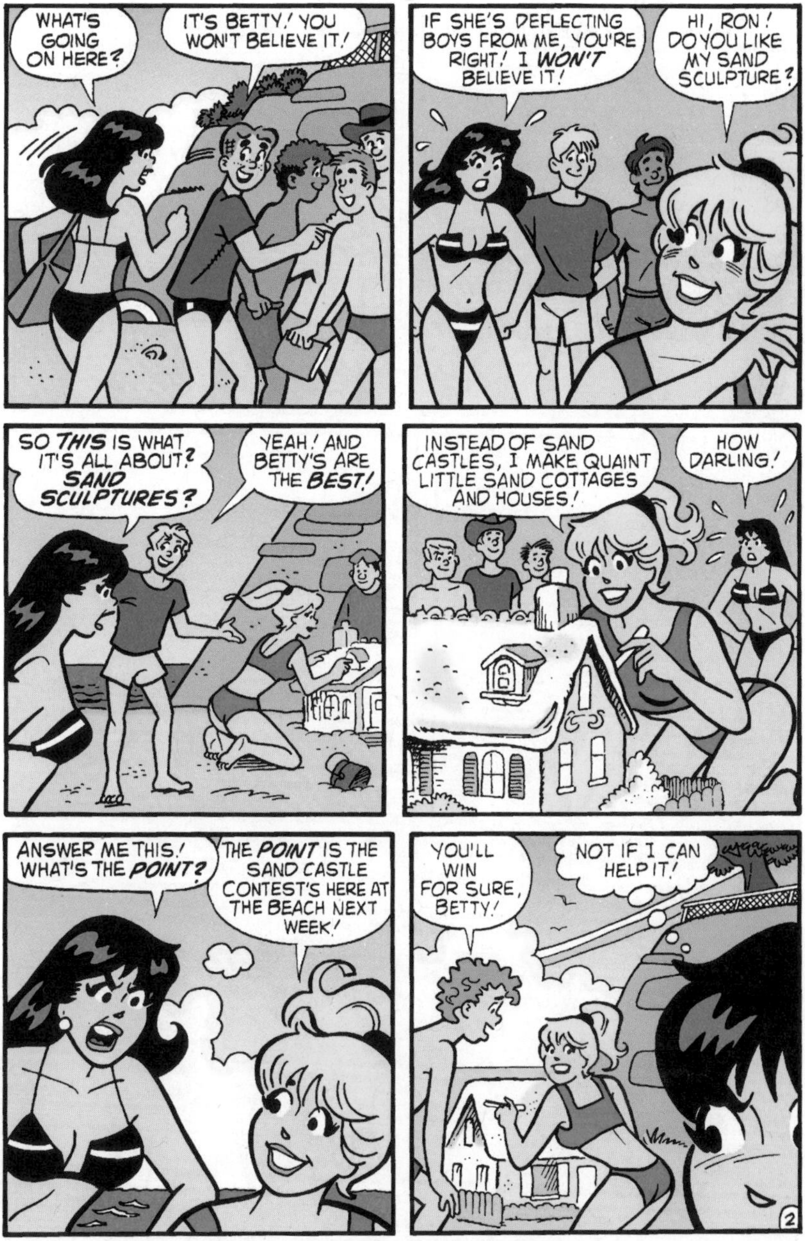
WHAT'S GOING ON HERE?
IT'S BETTY! YOU WON'T BELIEVE IT!
IF SHE'S DEFLECTING BOYS FROM ME, YOU'RE RIGHT! I WON'T BELIEVE IT!
HI, RON! DO YOU LIKE MY SAND SCULPTURE?
SO THIS IS WHAT IT'S ALL ABOUT? SAND SCULPTURES?
YEAH! AND BETTY'S ARE THE BEST!
INSTEAD OF SAND CASTLES, I MAKE QUAINT LITTLE SAND COTTAGES AND HOUSES!
HOW DARLING!
ANSWER ME THIS! WHAT'S THE POINT?
THE POINT IS THE SAND CASTLE CONTEST'S HERE AT THE BEACH NEXT WEEK!
YOU'LL WIN FOR SURE, BETTY!
NOT IF I CAN HELP IT!
2

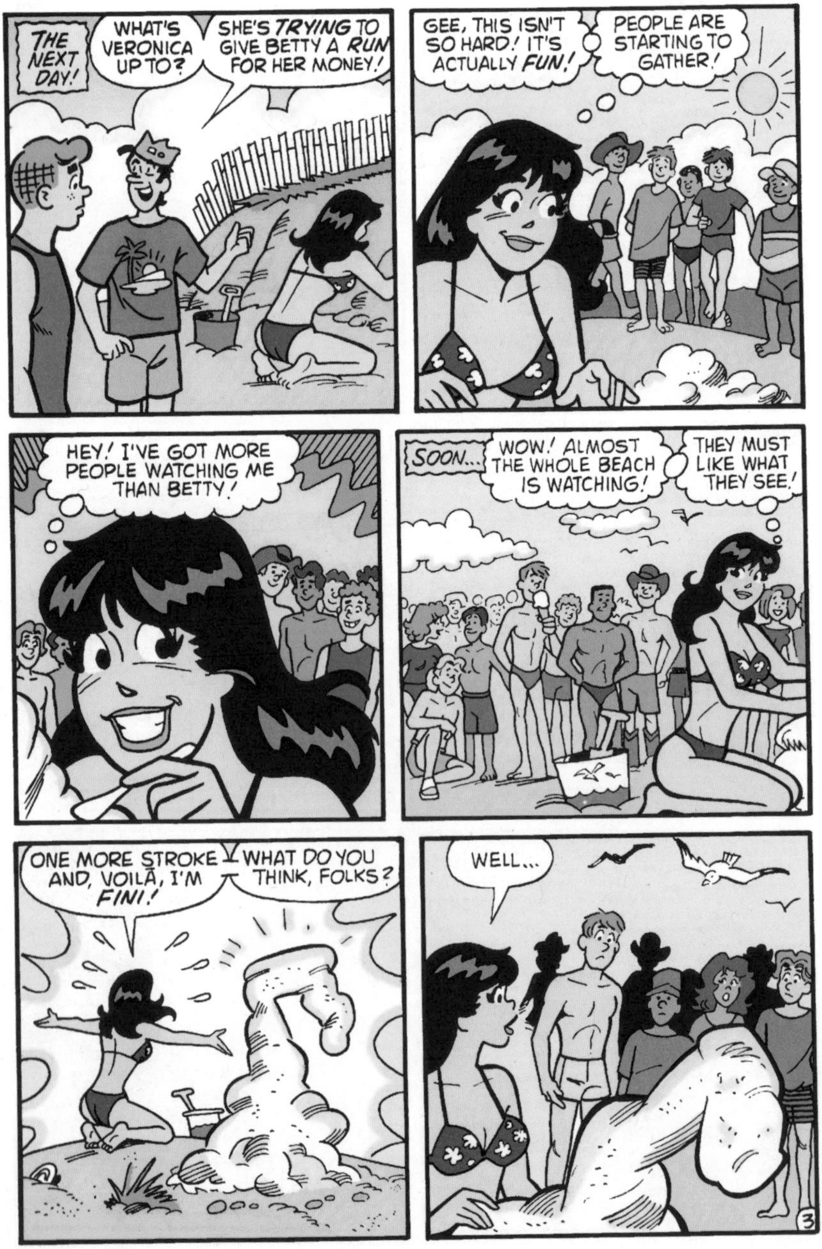
THE NEXT DAY!
WHAT'S VERONICA UP TO?
SHE'S TRYING TO GIVE BETTY A RUN FOR HER MONEY!
GEE, THIS ISN'T SO HARD! IT'S ACTUALLY FUN!
PEOPLE ARE STARTING TO GATHER!
HEY! I'VE GOT MORE PEOPLE WATCHING ME THAN BETTY!
SOON...
WOW! ALMOST THE WHOLE BEACH IS WATCHING!
THEY MUST LIKE WHAT THEY SEE!
ONE MORE STROKE AND, VOILÀ, I'M FINI!
WHAT DO YOU THINK, FOLKS?
WELL...
3

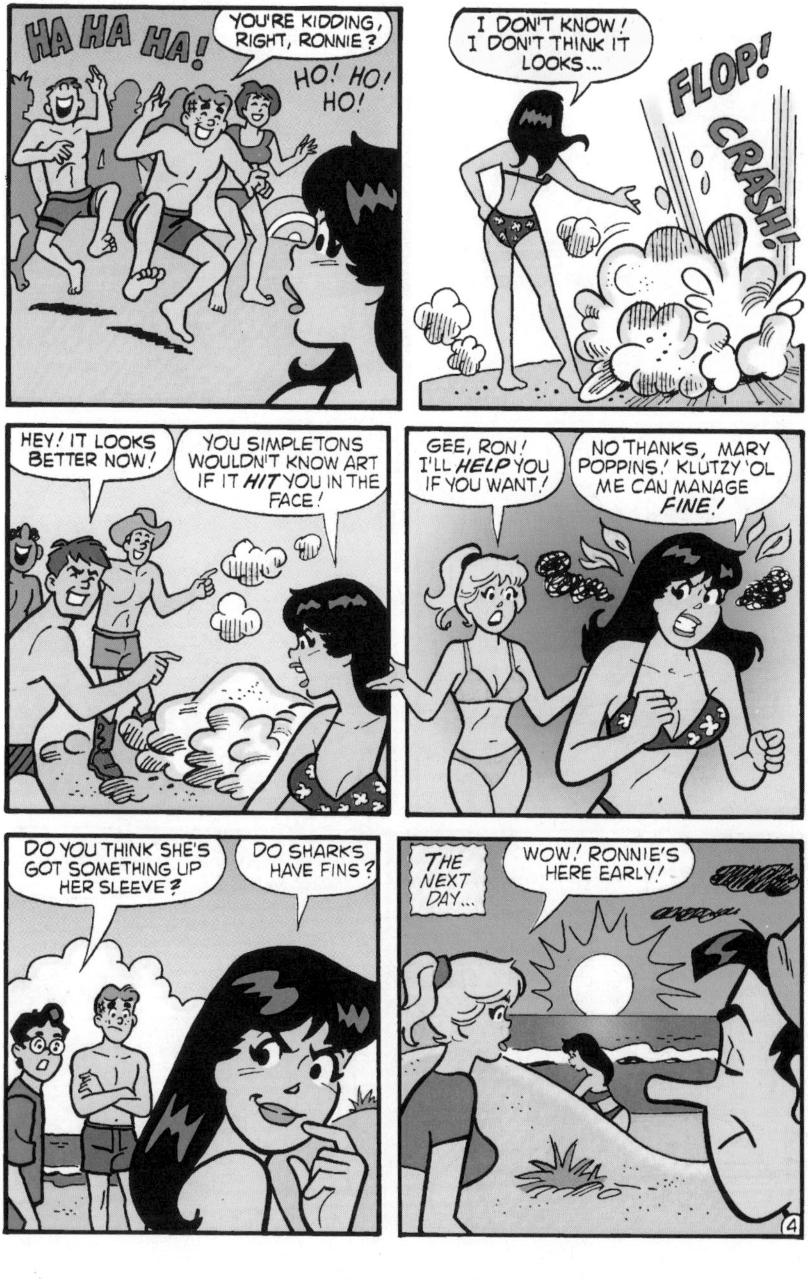
HA HA HA HA!
YOU'RE KIDDING, RIGHT, RONNIE?
HO! HO! HO!
I DON'T KNOW! I DON'T THINK IT LOOKS...
FLOP!
CRASH!
HEY! IT LOOKS BETTER NOW!
YOU SIMPLETONS WOULDN'T KNOW ART IF IT HIT YOU IN THE FACE!
GEE, RON! I'LL HELP YOU IF YOU WANT!
NO THANKS, MARY POPPINS! KLUTZY 'OL ME CAN MANAGE FINE!
DO YOU THINK SHE'S GOT SOMETHING UP HER SLEEVE?
DO SHARKS HAVE FINS?
THE NEXT DAY...
WOW! RONNIE'S HERE EARLY!
4

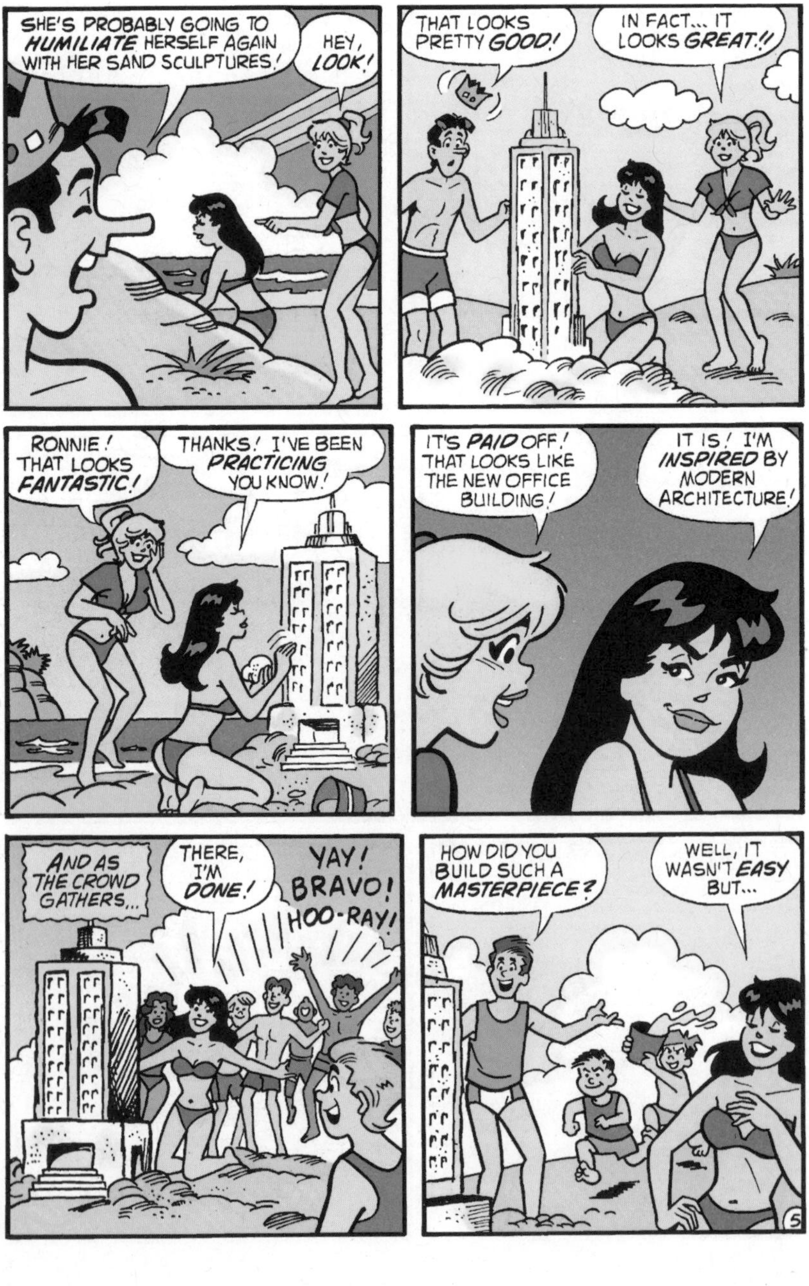

SHE'S PROBABLY GOING TO HUMILIATE HERSELF AGAIN WITH HER SAND SCULPTURES!
HEY, LOOK!
THAT LOOKS PRETTY GOOD!
IN FACT... IT LOOKS GREAT!!
RONNIE! THAT LOOKS FANTASTIC!
THANKS! I'VE BEEN PRACTICING YOU KNOW!
IT'S PAID OFF! THAT LOOKS LIKE THE NEW OFFICE BUILDING!
IT IS! I'M INSPIRED BY MODERN ARCHITECTURE!
AND AS THE CROWD GATHERS...
THERE, I'M DONE!
YAY! BRAVO! HOO-RAY!
HOW DID YOU BUILD SUCH A MASTERPIECE?
WELL, IT WASN'T EASY BUT...
5

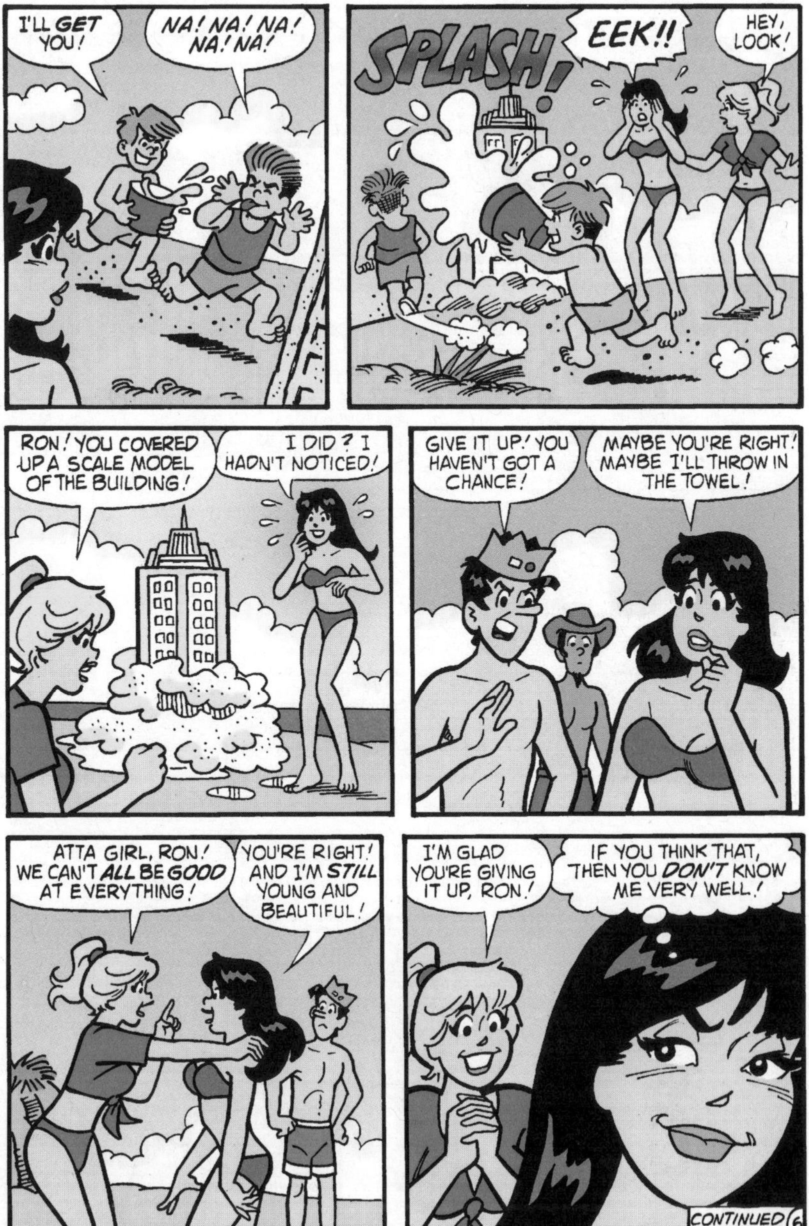
I'LL GET YOU!
NA! NA! NA! NA! NA!
SPLASH!
EEK!!
HEY, LOOK!
RON! YOU COVERED UP A SCALE MODEL OF THE BUILDING!
I DID? I HADN'T NOTICED!
GIVE IT UP! YOU HAVEN'T GOT A CHANCE!
MAYBE YOU'RE RIGHT! MAYBE I'LL THROW IN THE TOWEL!
ATTA GIRL, RON! WE CAN'T ALL BE GOOD AT EVERYTHING!
YOU'RE RIGHT! AND I'M STILL YOUNG AND BEAUTIFUL!
I'M GLAD YOU'RE GIVING IT UP, RON!
IF YOU THINK THAT, THEN YOU DON'T KNOW ME VERY WELL!
CONTINUED 6

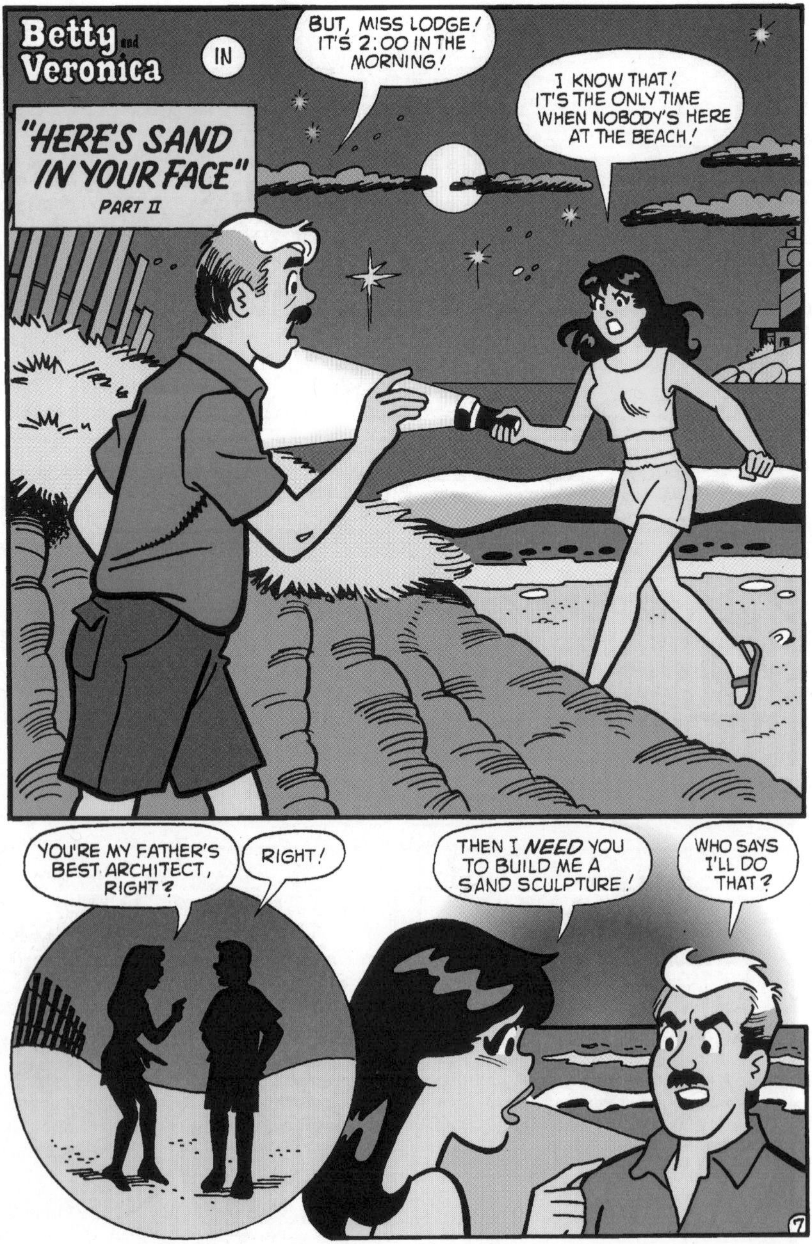
Betty and Veronica
IN
"HERE'S SAND IN YOUR FACE"
PART II
BUT, MISS LODGE! IT'S 2:00 IN THE MORNING!
I KNOW THAT! IT'S THE ONLY TIME WHEN NOBODY'S HERE AT THE BEACH!
YOU'RE MY FATHER'S BEST ARCHITECT, RIGHT?
RIGHT!
THEN I *NEED* YOU TO BUILD ME A SAND SCULPTURE!
WHO SAYS I'LL DO THAT?
7

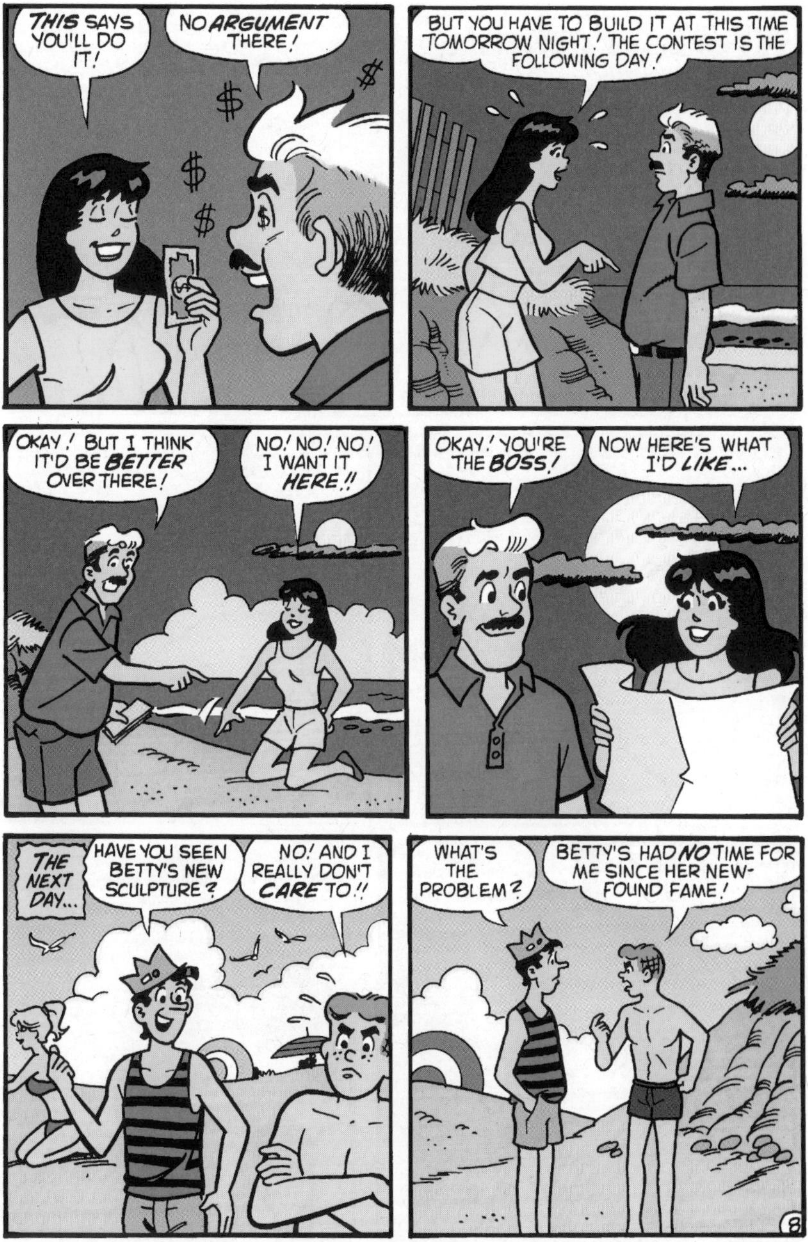
THIS SAYS YOU'LL DO IT!
NO ARGUMENT THERE!
$
$
$
$
BUT YOU HAVE TO BUILD IT AT THIS TIME TOMORROW NIGHT! THE CONTEST IS THE FOLLOWING DAY!
OKAY! BUT I THINK IT'D BE BETTER OVER THERE!
NO! NO! NO! I WANT IT HERE!!
OKAY! YOU'RE THE BOSS!
NOW HERE'S WHAT I'D LIKE...
THE NEXT DAY...
HAVE YOU SEEN BETTY'S NEW SCULPTURE?
NO! AND I REALLY DON'T CARE TO!!
WHAT'S THE PROBLEM?
BETTY'S HAD NO TIME FOR ME SINCE HER NEW-FOUND FAME!
8

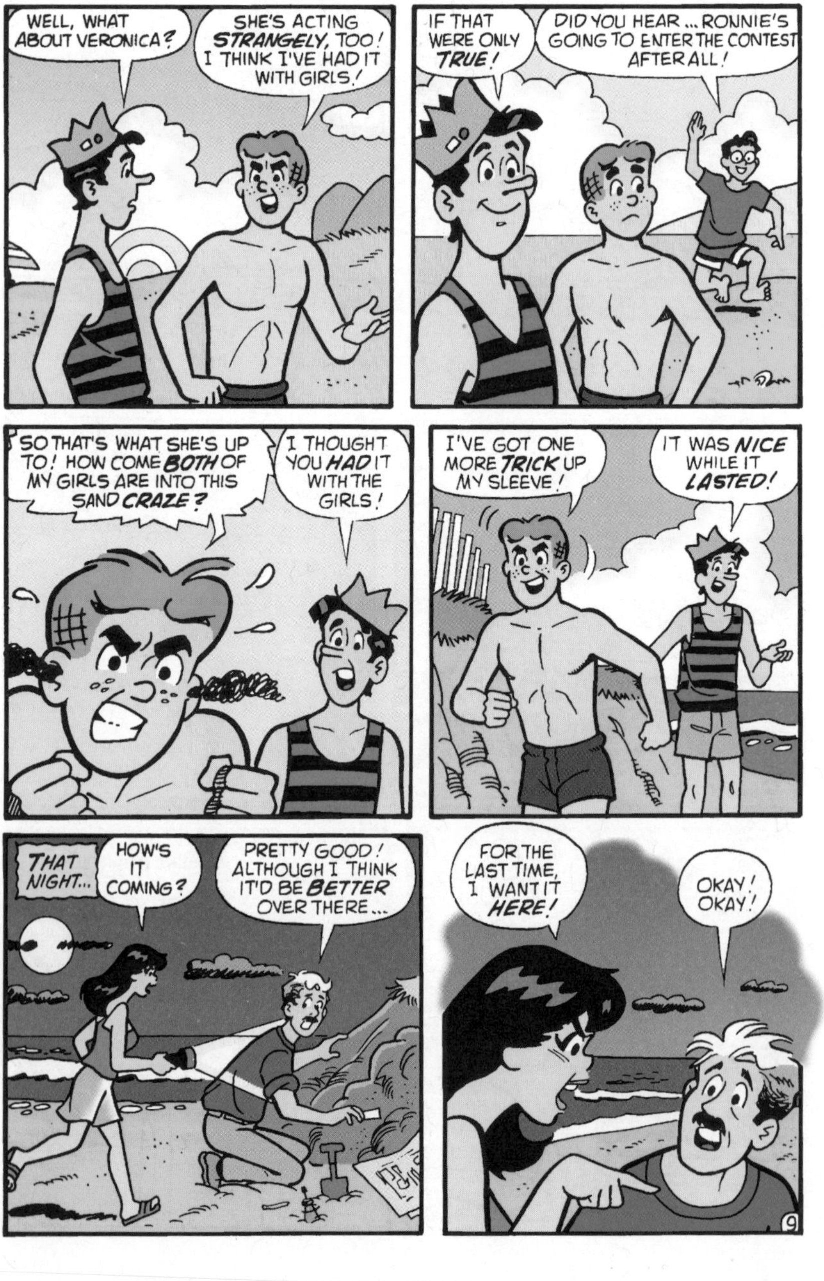
WELL, WHAT ABOUT VERONICA?
SHE'S ACTING STRANGELY, TOO! I THINK I'VE HAD IT WITH GIRLS!
IF THAT WERE ONLY TRUE!
DID YOU HEAR ... RONNIE'S GOING TO ENTER THE CONTEST AFTER ALL!
SO THAT'S WHAT SHE'S UP TO! HOW COME BOTH OF MY GIRLS ARE INTO THIS SAND CRAZE?
I THOUGHT YOU HAD IT WITH THE GIRLS!
I'VE GOT ONE MORE TRICK UP MY SLEEVE!
IT WAS NICE WHILE IT LASTED!
THAT NIGHT...
HOW'S IT COMING?
PRETTY GOOD! ALTHOUGH I THINK IT'D BE BETTER OVER THERE...
FOR THE LAST TIME, I WANT IT HERE!
OKAY! OKAY!
9

THE BIG DAY!

OH! RON'S *EARLY* AGAIN!

THIS OUGHT TO BE *GOOD!*

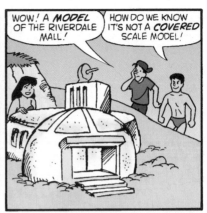

WOW! A *MODEL* OF THE RIVERDALE MALL!

HOW DO WE KNOW IT'S NOT A *COVERED* SCALE MODEL!

HEY, IT'S NOT! I THINK SHE *REALLY* DID THIS!

GEE! COULD SHE ACTUALLY HAVE *TALENT?*

THAT'S RIGHT, NEEDLENOSE! I *DO!*

HI, GUYS! G-GEE! WHAT'S *THIS?*

HOW DO YOU LIKE IT, BETTY? I'M SORRY TO PUT YOU *OUT* OF THE CONTEST!!

WHAT DO YOU MEAN? I PLAN ON *WINNING* THIS CONTEST! I'LL *SHOW* YOU HOW, LATER TODAY!

LATER...

YOUR MALL'S UNDER-WATER! YOU OBVIOUSLY FORGOT ABOUT *HIGH TIDE!*

SO *THAT'S* WHY HE WANTED TO BUILD IT OVER THERE!

10

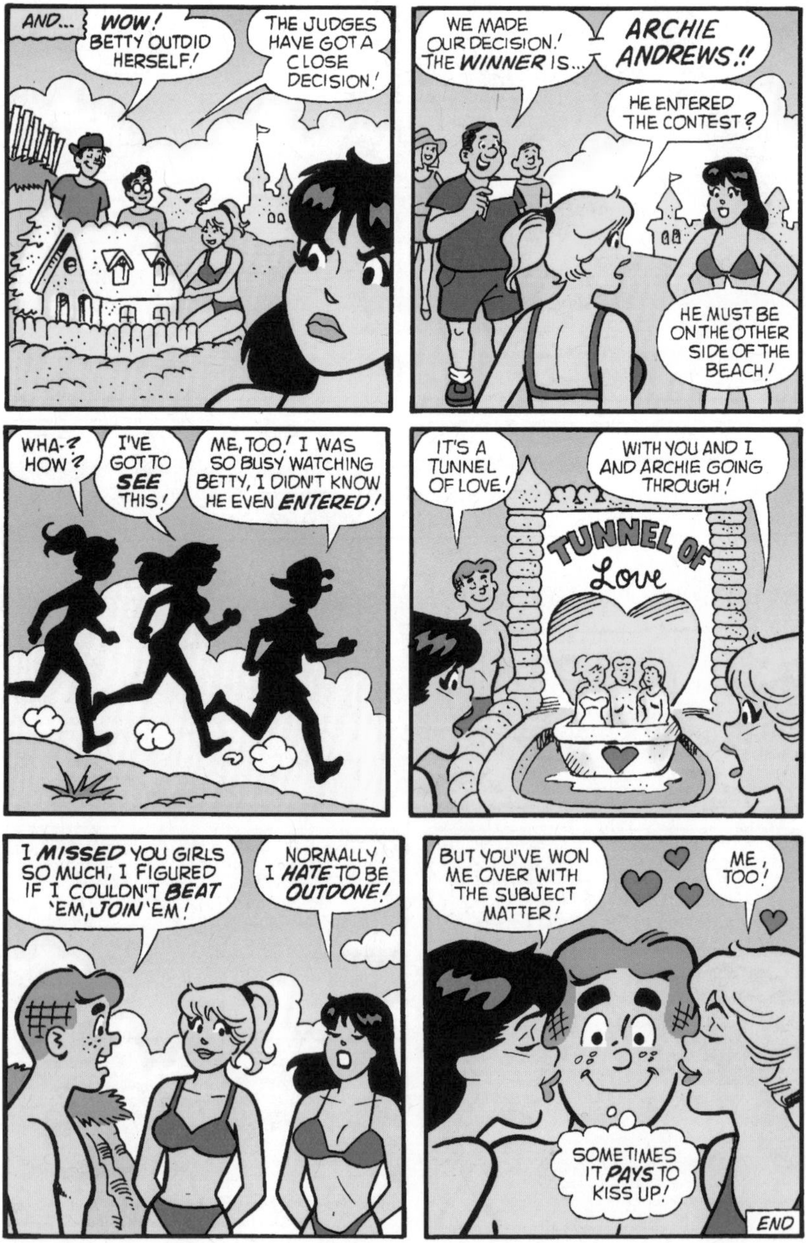
AND...
WOW! BETTY OUTDID HERSELF!
THE JUDGES HAVE GOT A CLOSE DECISION!
WE MADE OUR DECISION! THE WINNER IS...
ARCHIE ANDREWS!!
HE ENTERED THE CONTEST?
HE MUST BE ON THE OTHER SIDE OF THE BEACH!
WHA-? HOW?
I'VE GOT TO SEE THIS!
ME, TOO! I WAS SO BUSY WATCHING BETTY, I DIDN'T KNOW HE EVEN ENTERED!
IT'S A TUNNEL OF LOVE!
WITH YOU AND I AND ARCHIE GOING THROUGH!
TUNNEL OF Love
I MISSED YOU GIRLS SO MUCH, I FIGURED IF I COULDN'T BEAT 'EM, JOIN 'EM!
NORMALLY, I HATE TO BE OUTDONE!
BUT YOU'VE WON ME OVER WITH THE SUBJECT MATTER!
ME, TOO!
SOMETIMES IT PAYS TO KISS UP!
END

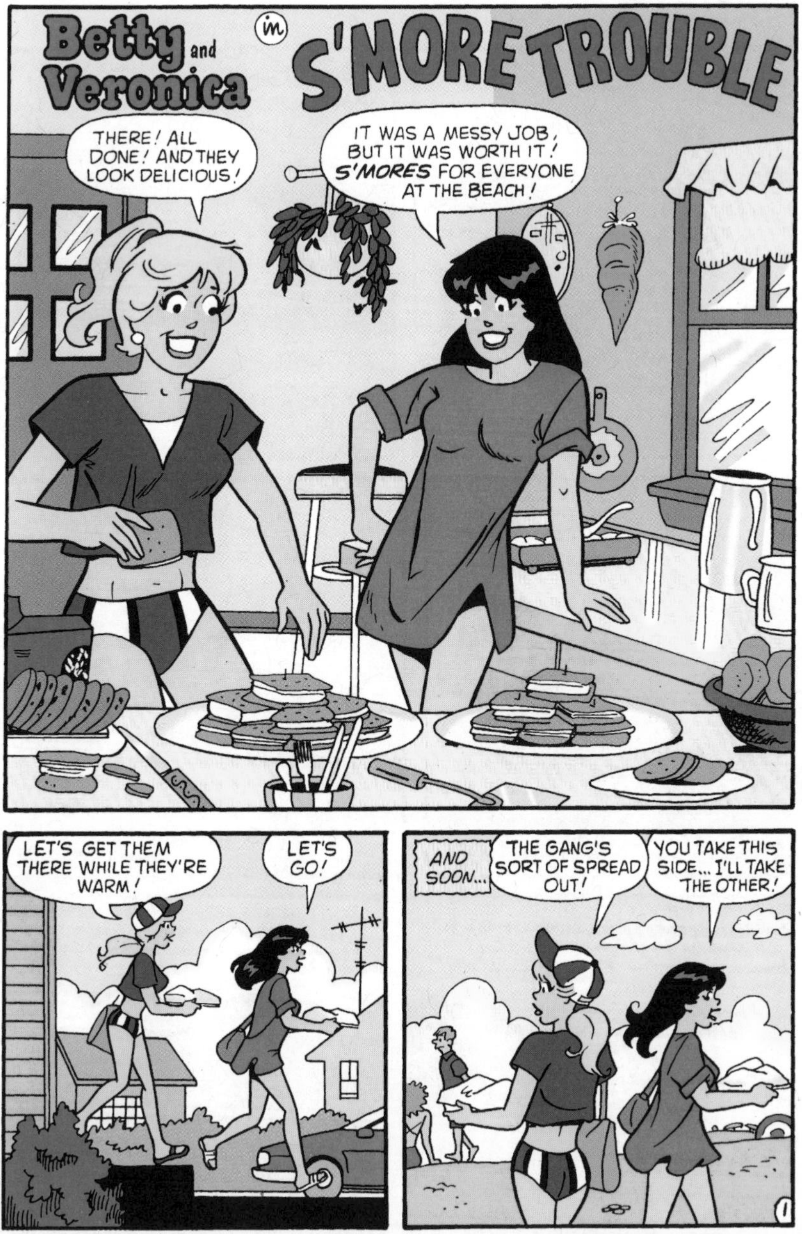
Betty and Veronica in
S'MORE TROUBLE
THERE! ALL DONE! AND THEY LOOK DELICIOUS!
IT WAS A MESSY JOB, BUT IT WAS WORTH IT! S'MORES FOR EVERYONE AT THE BEACH!
LET'S GET THEM THERE WHILE THEY'RE WARM!
LET'S GO!
AND SOON...
THE GANG'S SORT OF SPREAD OUT!
YOU TAKE THIS SIDE... I'LL TAKE THE OTHER!
1

Story: Bill Golliher Pencils: Dan DeCarlo & Dan Parent
Inks: Alison Flood Letters: Bill Yoshida Colors: Barry Grossman

Originally printed in BETTY & VERONICA SPECTACULAR #10, September 1994

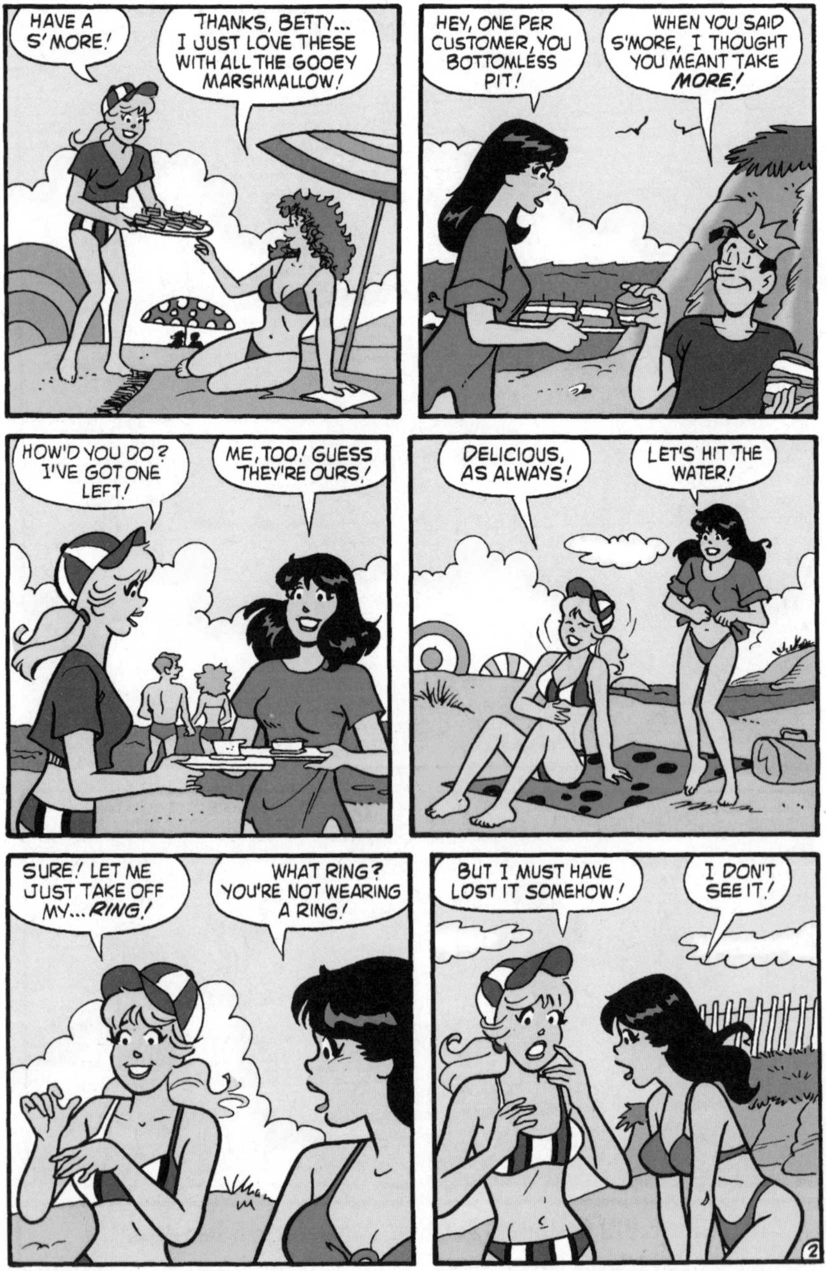
HAVE A S'MORE!
THANKS, BETTY... I JUST LOVE THESE WITH ALL THE GOOEY MARSHMALLOW!
HEY, ONE PER CUSTOMER, YOU BOTTOMLESS PIT!
WHEN YOU SAID S'MORE, I THOUGHT YOU MEANT TAKE MORE!
HOW'D YOU DO? I'VE GOT ONE LEFT!
ME, TOO! GUESS THEY'RE OURS!
DELICIOUS, AS ALWAYS!
LET'S HIT THE WATER!
SURE! LET ME JUST TAKE OFF MY... RING!
WHAT RING? YOU'RE NOT WEARING A RING!
BUT I MUST HAVE LOST IT SOMEHOW!
I DON'T SEE IT!
2

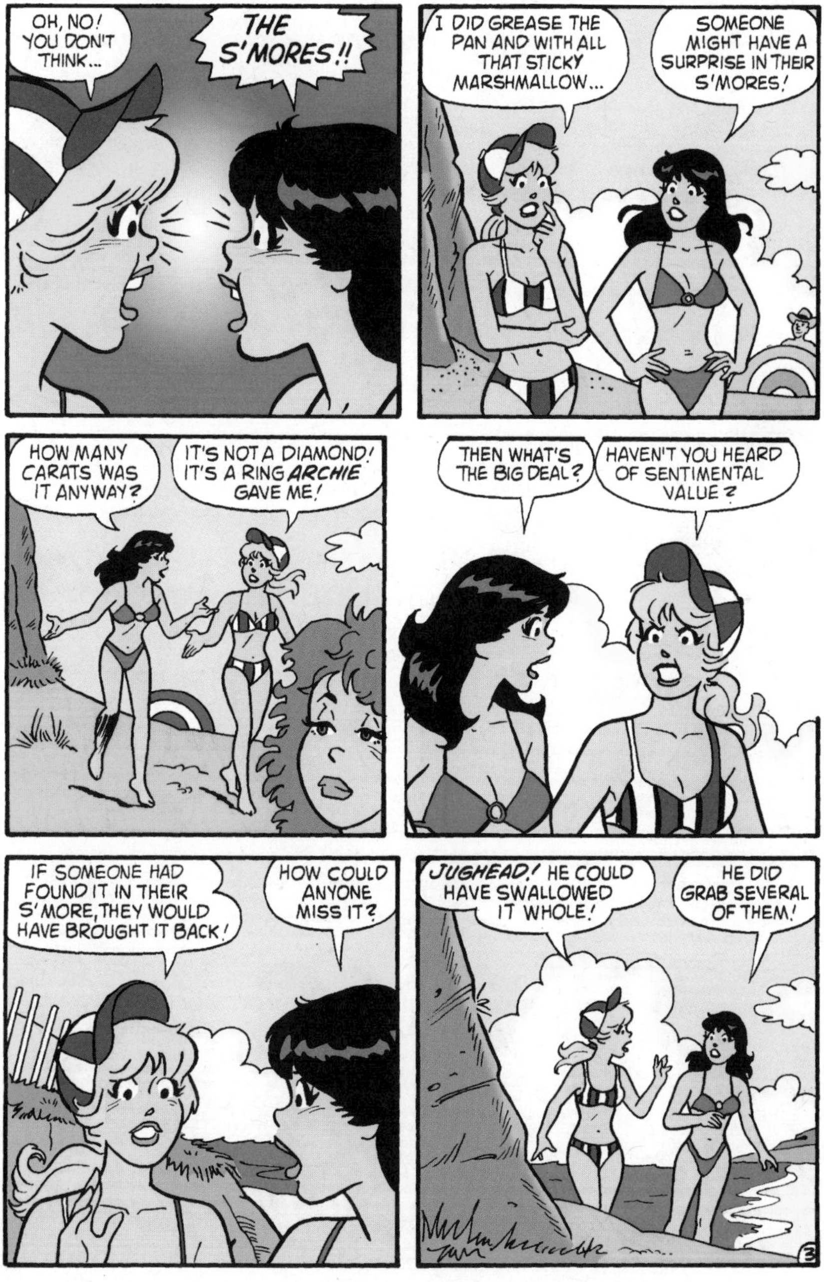
OH, NO! YOU DON'T THINK...
THE S'MORES!!
I DID GREASE THE PAN AND WITH ALL THAT STICKY MARSHMALLOW...
SOMEONE MIGHT HAVE A SURPRISE IN THEIR S'MORES!
HOW MANY CARATS WAS IT ANYWAY?
IT'S NOT A DIAMOND! IT'S A RING ARCHIE GAVE ME!
THEN WHAT'S THE BIG DEAL?
HAVEN'T YOU HEARD OF SENTIMENTAL VALUE?
IF SOMEONE HAD FOUND IT IN THEIR S'MORE, THEY WOULD HAVE BROUGHT IT BACK!
HOW COULD ANYONE MISS IT?
JUGHEAD! HE COULD HAVE SWALLOWED IT WHOLE!
HE DID GRAB SEVERAL OF THEM!
3

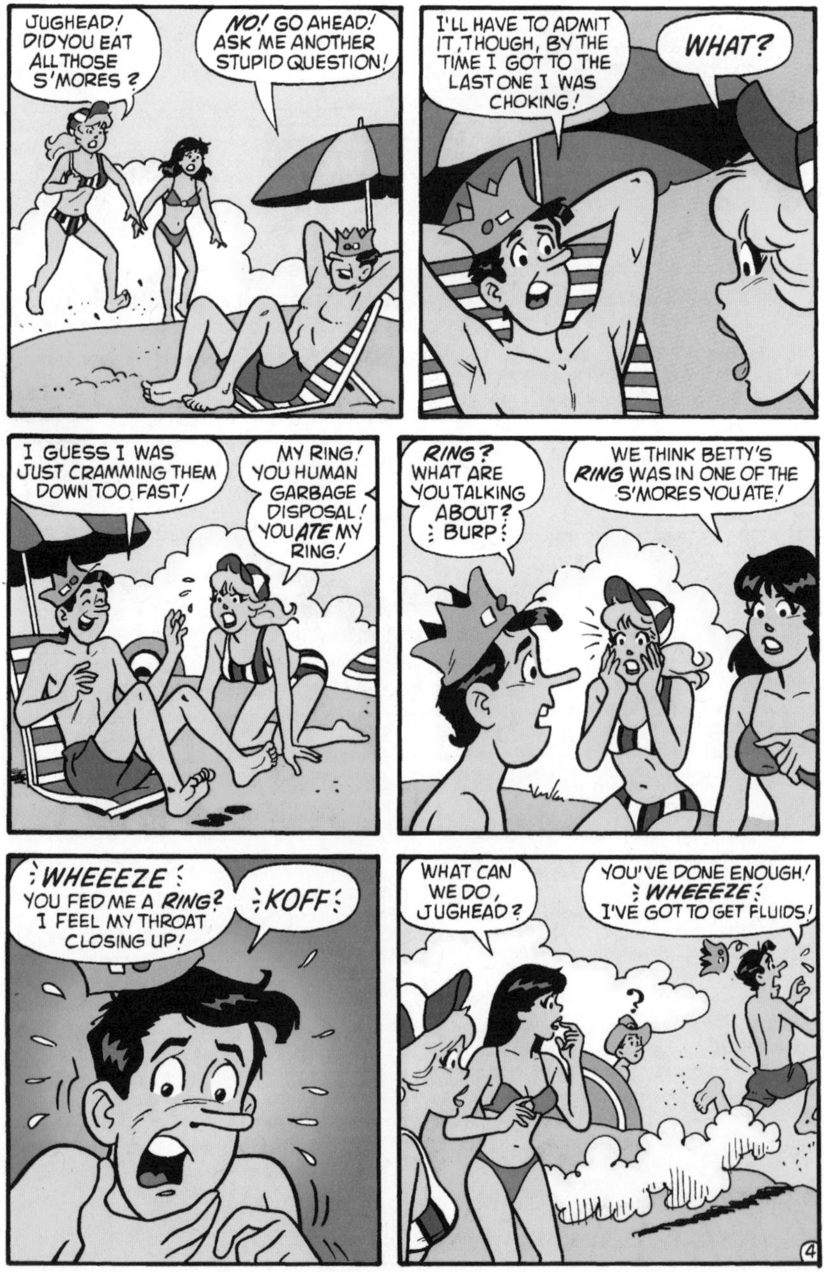
JUGHEAD! DID YOU EAT ALL THOSE S'MORES?
NO! GO AHEAD! ASK ME ANOTHER STUPID QUESTION!
I'LL HAVE TO ADMIT IT, THOUGH, BY THE TIME I GOT TO THE LAST ONE I WAS CHOKING!
WHAT?
I GUESS I WAS JUST CRAMMING THEM DOWN TOO FAST!
MY RING! YOU HUMAN GARBAGE DISPOSAL! YOU ATE MY RING!
RING? WHAT ARE YOU TALKING ABOUT? BURP
WE THINK BETTY'S RING WAS IN ONE OF THE S'MORES YOU ATE!
WHEEEZE YOU FED ME A RING? I FEEL MY THROAT CLOSING UP!
KOFF
WHAT CAN WE DO, JUGHEAD?
YOU'VE DONE ENOUGH! WHEEEZE I'VE GOT TO GET FLUIDS!
?
4

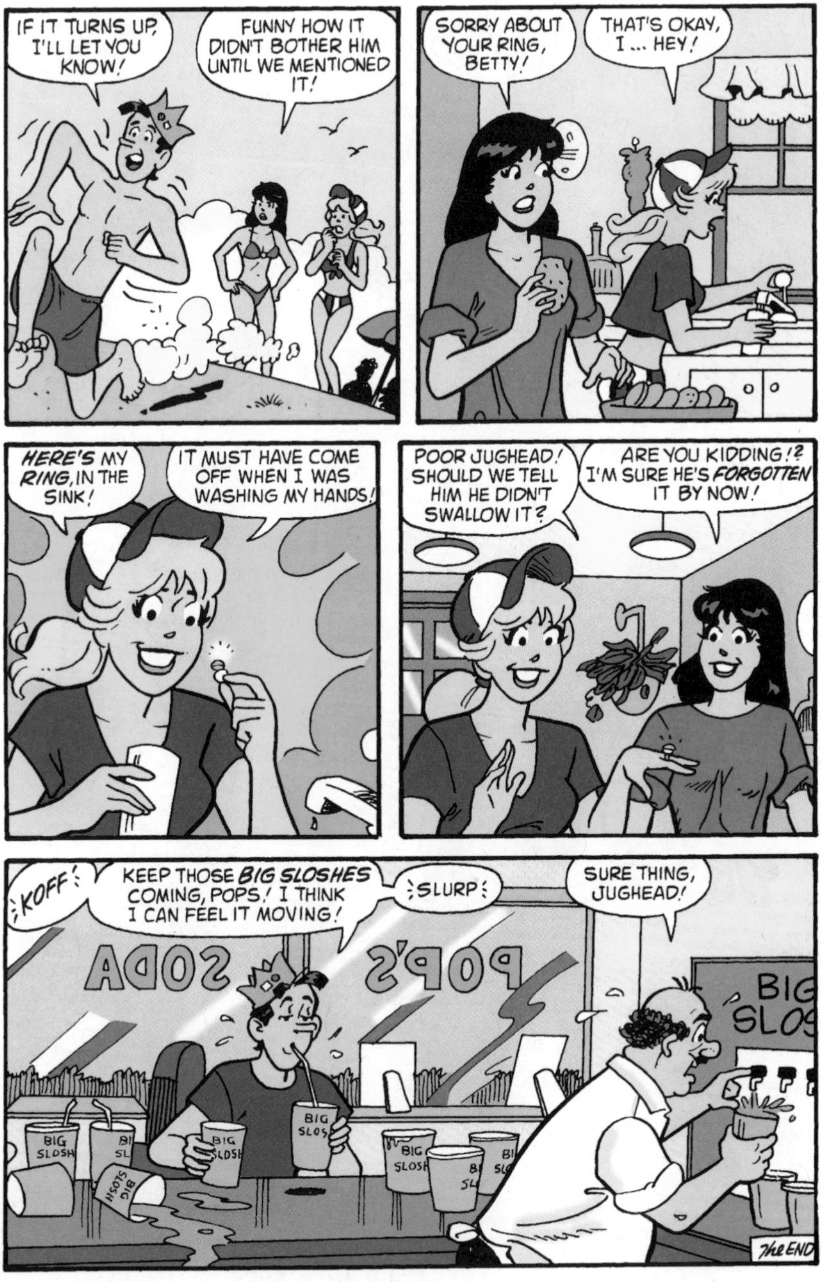
IF IT TURNS UP, I'LL LET YOU KNOW!
FUNNY HOW IT DIDN'T BOTHER HIM UNTIL WE MENTIONED IT!
SORRY ABOUT YOUR RING, BETTY!
THAT'S OKAY, I ... HEY!
HERE'S MY RING, IN THE SINK!
IT MUST HAVE COME OFF WHEN I WAS WASHING MY HANDS!
POOR JUGHEAD! SHOULD WE TELL HIM HE DIDN'T SWALLOW IT?
ARE YOU KIDDING!? I'M SURE HE'S FORGOTTEN IT BY NOW!
KOFF
KEEP THOSE BIG SLOSHES COMING, POPS! I THINK I CAN FEEL IT MOVING!
SLURP
SURE THING, JUGHEAD!
POP'S SODA
BIG SLOSH
The END

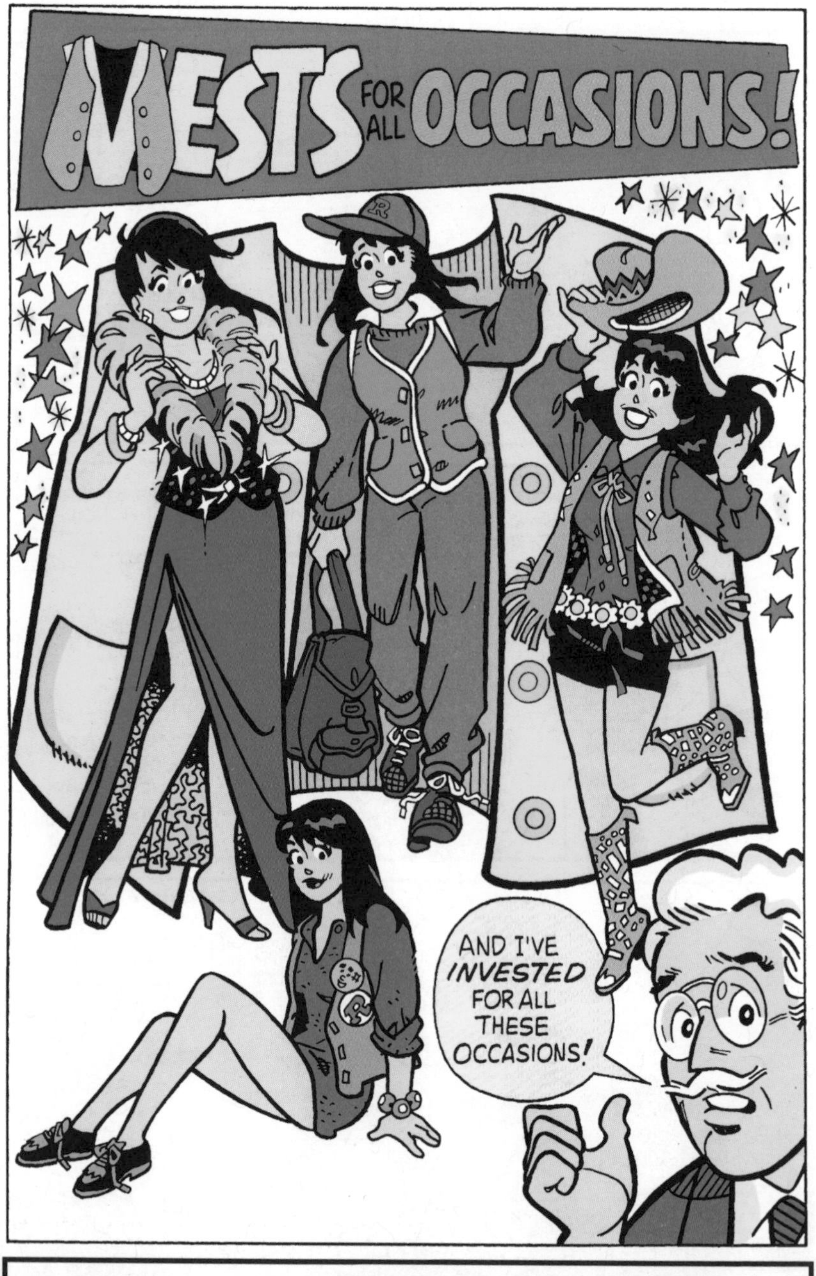
VESTS FOR ALL OCCASIONS!
AND I'VE *INVESTED* FOR ALL THESE OCCASIONS!

Art: Stan Goldberg Inks: Henry Scarpelli Colors: Barry Grossman

Originally printed in BETTY & VERONICA SPECTACULAR #10, September 1994

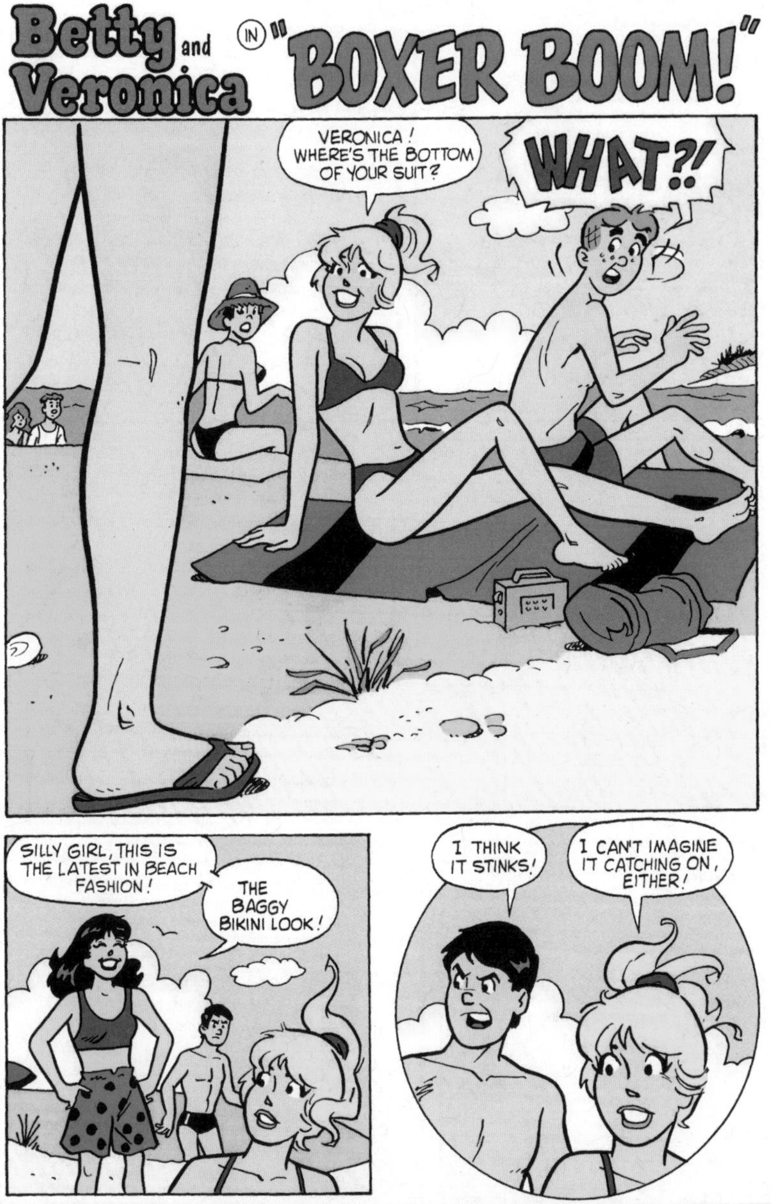
Betty and Veronica IN "BOXER BOOM!"
VERONICA! WHERE'S THE BOTTOM OF YOUR SUIT?
WHAT?!
SILLY GIRL, THIS IS THE LATEST IN BEACH FASHION!
THE BAGGY BIKINI LOOK!
I THINK IT STINKS!
I CAN'T IMAGINE IT CATCHING ON, EITHER!

Story: Bill Golliher Pencils: Dan DeCarlo
Inks: Alison Flood Letters: Bill Yoshida Colors: Barry Grossman

Originally printed in BETTY & VERONICA SPECTACULAR #10, September 1994

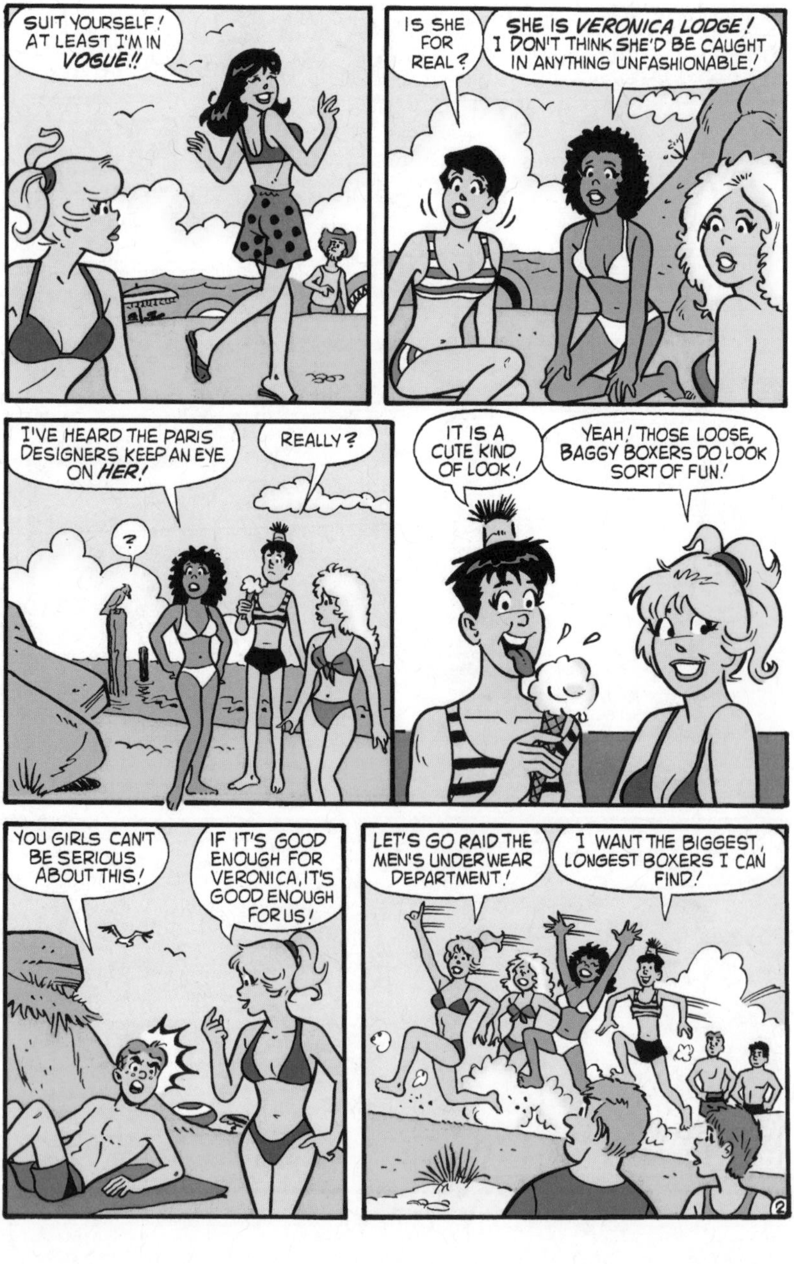
SUIT YOURSELF! AT LEAST I'M IN VOGUE!!
IS SHE FOR REAL?
SHE IS VERONICA LODGE! I DON'T THINK SHE'D BE CAUGHT IN ANYTHING UNFASHIONABLE!
I'VE HEARD THE PARIS DESIGNERS KEEP AN EYE ON HER!
REALLY?
?
IT IS A CUTE KIND OF LOOK!
YEAH! THOSE LOOSE, BAGGY BOXERS DO LOOK SORT OF FUN!
YOU GIRLS CAN'T BE SERIOUS ABOUT THIS!
IF IT'S GOOD ENOUGH FOR VERONICA, IT'S GOOD ENOUGH FOR US!
LET'S GO RAID THE MEN'S UNDERWEAR DEPARTMENT!
I WANT THE BIGGEST, LONGEST BOXERS I CAN FIND!
2

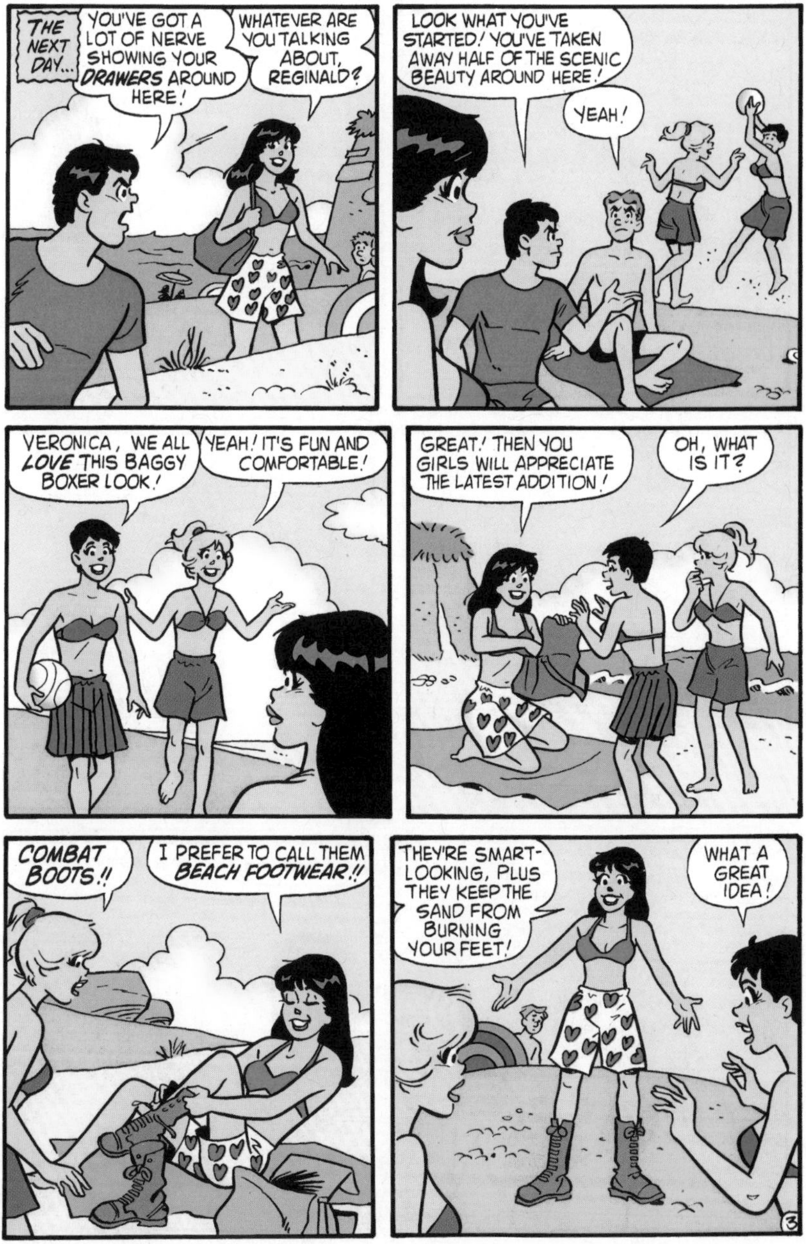
THE NEXT DAY...
YOU'VE GOT A LOT OF NERVE SHOWING YOUR DRAWERS AROUND HERE!
WHATEVER ARE YOU TALKING ABOUT, REGINALD?
LOOK WHAT YOU'VE STARTED! YOU'VE TAKEN AWAY HALF OF THE SCENIC BEAUTY AROUND HERE!
YEAH!
VERONICA, WE ALL LOVE THIS BAGGY BOXER LOOK!
YEAH! IT'S FUN AND COMFORTABLE!
GREAT! THEN YOU GIRLS WILL APPRECIATE THE LATEST ADDITION!
OH, WHAT IS IT?
COMBAT BOOTS!!
I PREFER TO CALL THEM BEACH FOOTWEAR!!
THEY'RE SMART-LOOKING, PLUS THEY KEEP THE SAND FROM BURNING YOUR FEET!
WHAT A GREAT IDEA!
3

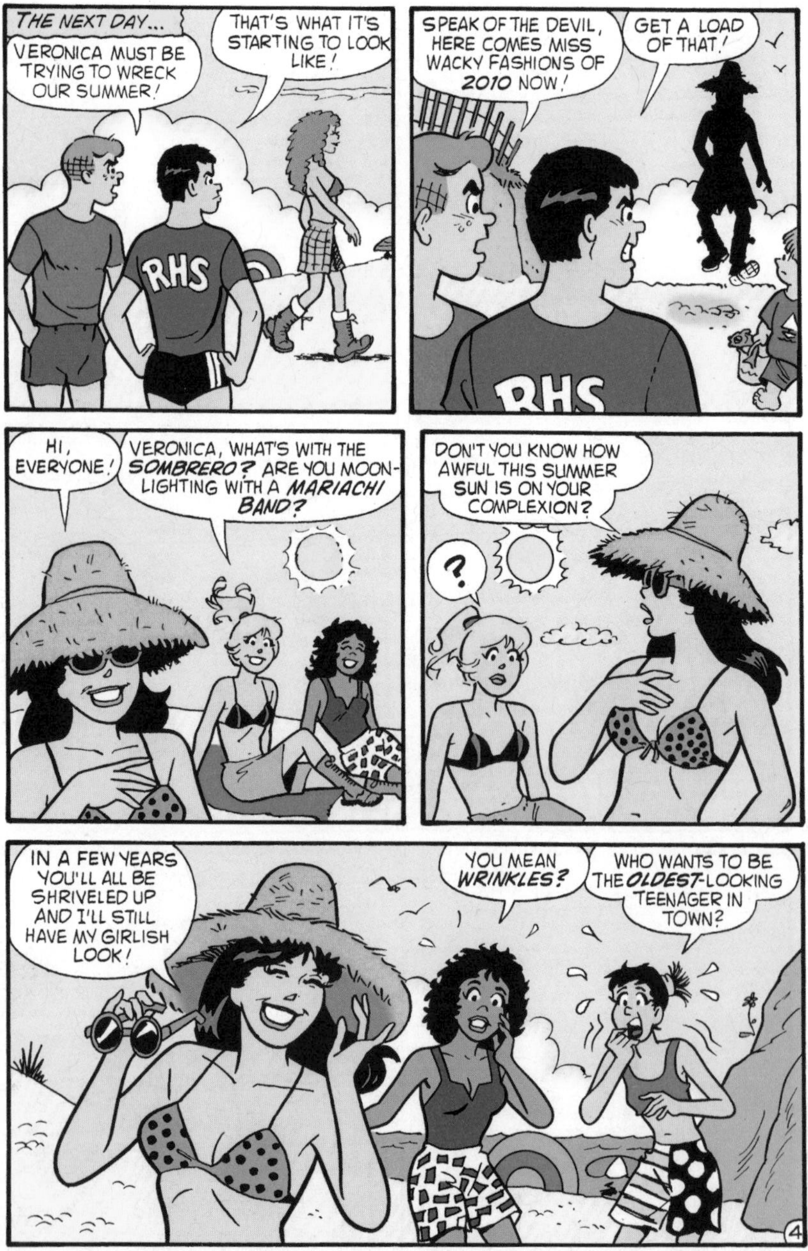
THE NEXT DAY...
VERONICA MUST BE TRYING TO WRECK OUR SUMMER!
THAT'S WHAT IT'S STARTING TO LOOK LIKE!
RHS
SPEAK OF THE DEVIL, HERE COMES MISS WACKY FASHIONS OF 2010 NOW!
GET A LOAD OF THAT!
RHS
HI, EVERYONE!
VERONICA, WHAT'S WITH THE SOMBRERO? ARE YOU MOON-LIGHTING WITH A MARIACHI BAND?
DON'T YOU KNOW HOW AWFUL THIS SUMMER SUN IS ON YOUR COMPLEXION?
?
IN A FEW YEARS YOU'LL ALL BE SHRIVELED UP AND I'LL STILL HAVE MY GIRLISH LOOK!
YOU MEAN WRINKLES?
WHO WANTS TO BE THE OLDEST-LOOKING TEENAGER IN TOWN?
4

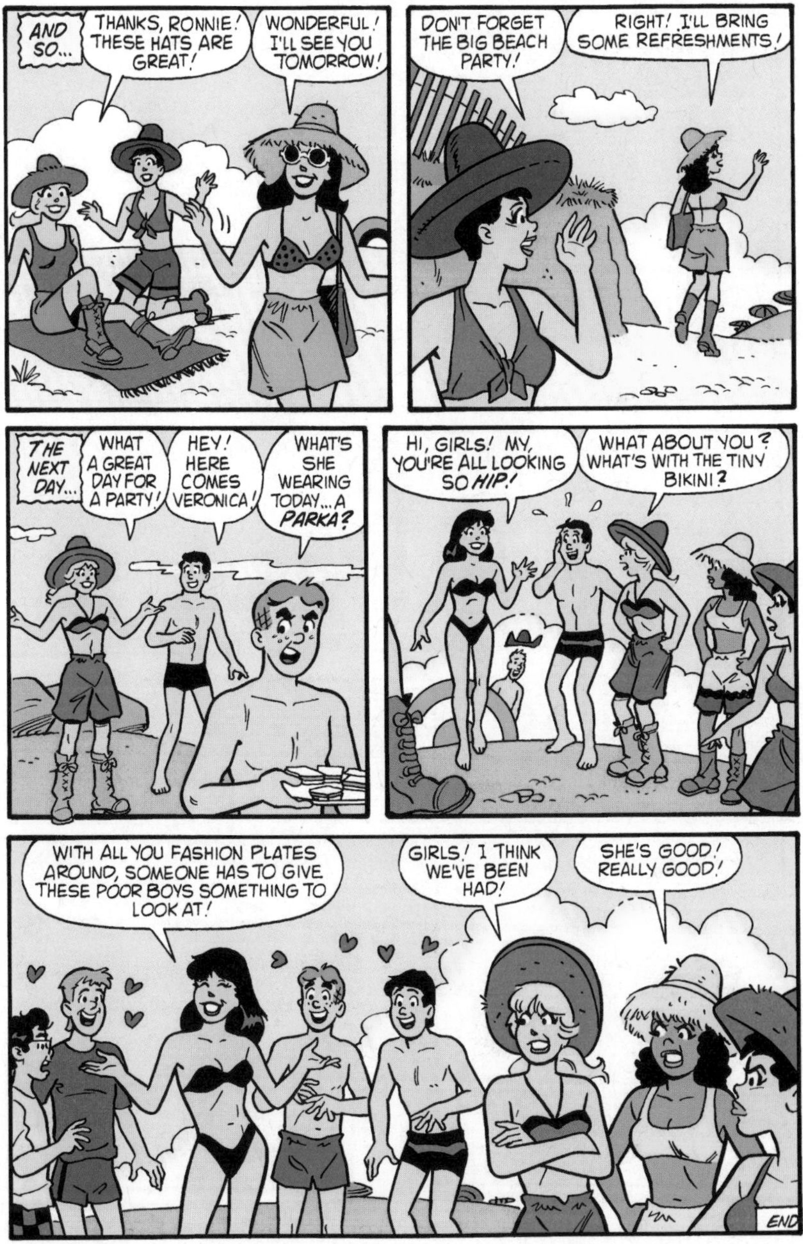
AND SO...
THANKS, RONNIE! THESE HATS ARE GREAT!
WONDERFUL! I'LL SEE YOU TOMORROW!
DON'T FORGET THE BIG BEACH PARTY!
RIGHT! I'LL BRING SOME REFRESHMENTS!
THE NEXT DAY...
WHAT A GREAT DAY FOR A PARTY!
HEY! HERE COMES VERONICA!
WHAT'S SHE WEARING TODAY...A PARKA?
HI, GIRLS! MY, YOU'RE ALL LOOKING SO HIP!
WHAT ABOUT YOU? WHAT'S WITH THE TINY BIKINI?
WITH ALL YOU FASHION PLATES AROUND, SOMEONE HAS TO GIVE THESE POOR BOYS SOMETHING TO LOOK AT!
GIRLS! I THINK WE'VE BEEN HAD!
SHE'S GOOD! REALLY GOOD!
END

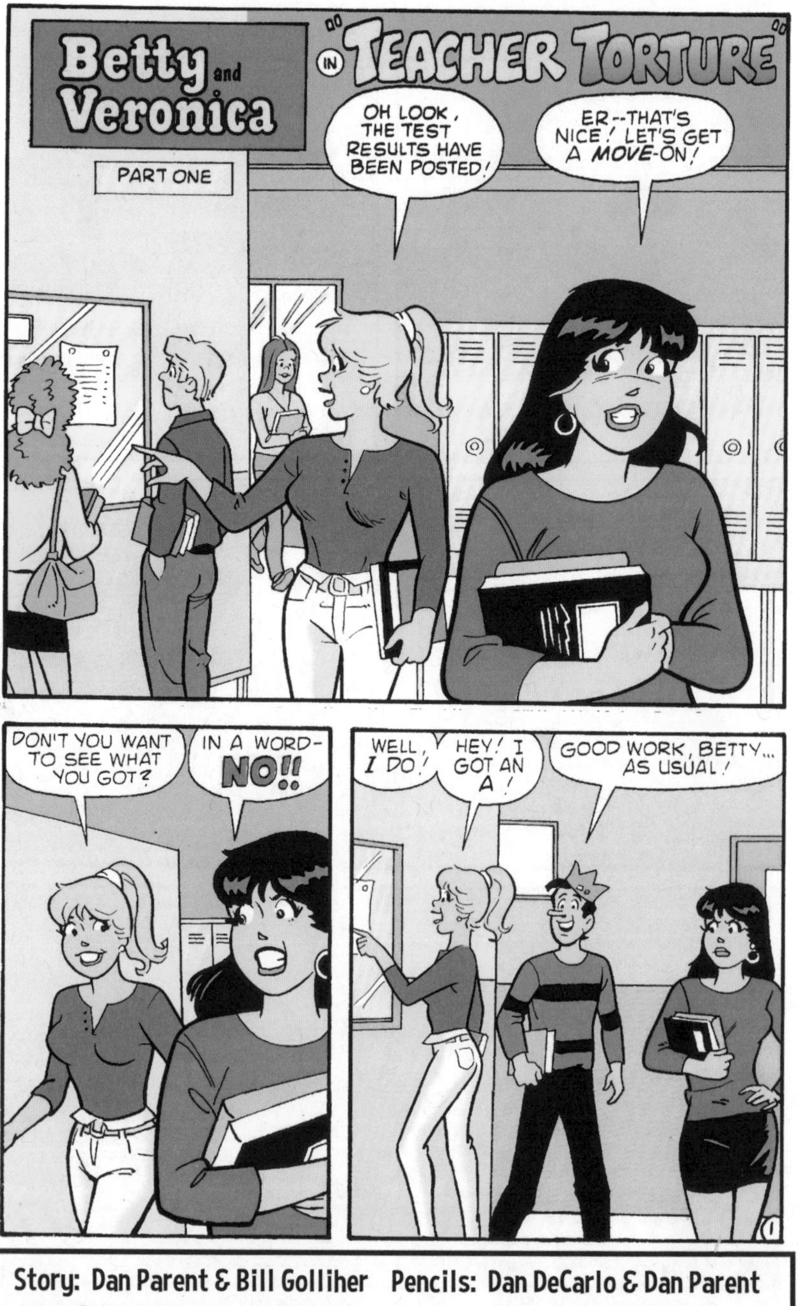
Betty and Veronica
in "TEACHER TORTURE"
PART ONE
OH LOOK, THE TEST RESULTS HAVE BEEN POSTED!
ER--THAT'S NICE! LET'S GET A MOVE-ON!
DON'T YOU WANT TO SEE WHAT YOU GOT?
IN A WORD-NO!!
WELL, I DO!
HEY! I GOT AN A!
GOOD WORK, BETTY... AS USUAL!
1

Story: Dan Parent & Bill Golliher **Pencils:** Dan DeCarlo & Dan Parent
Inks: Alison Flood **Letters:** Bill Yoshida **Colors:** Barry Grossman

Originally printed in BETTY & VERONICA SPECTACULAR #11, November 1994

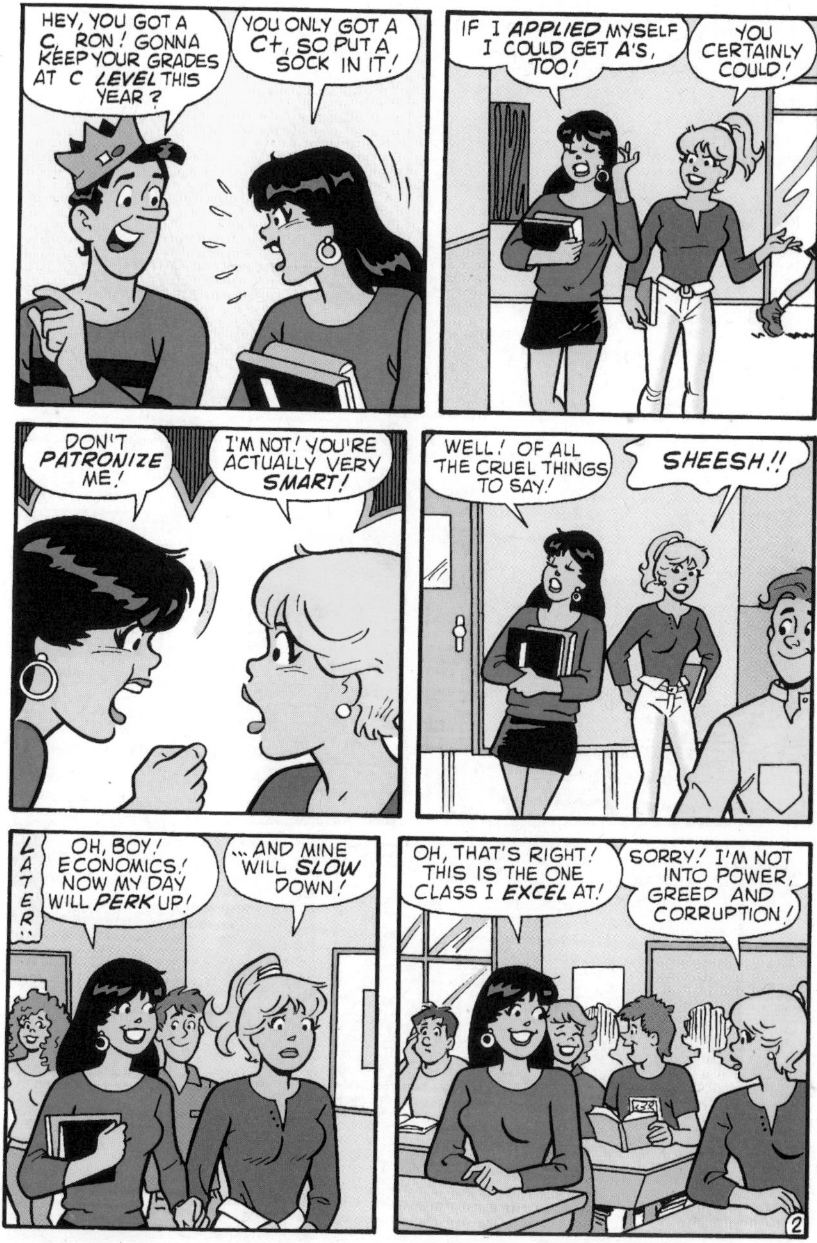
HEY, YOU GOT A C, RON! GONNA KEEP YOUR GRADES AT C LEVEL THIS YEAR?
YOU ONLY GOT A C+, SO PUT A SOCK IN IT!
IF I APPLIED MYSELF I COULD GET A'S, TOO!
YOU CERTAINLY COULD!
DON'T PATRONIZE ME!
I'M NOT! YOU'RE ACTUALLY VERY SMART!
WELL! OF ALL THE CRUEL THINGS TO SAY!
SHEESH!!
LATER..
OH, BOY! ECONOMICS! NOW MY DAY WILL PERK UP!
...AND MINE WILL SLOW DOWN!
OH, THAT'S RIGHT! THIS IS THE ONE CLASS I EXCEL AT!
SORRY! I'M NOT INTO POWER, GREED AND CORRUPTION!
2

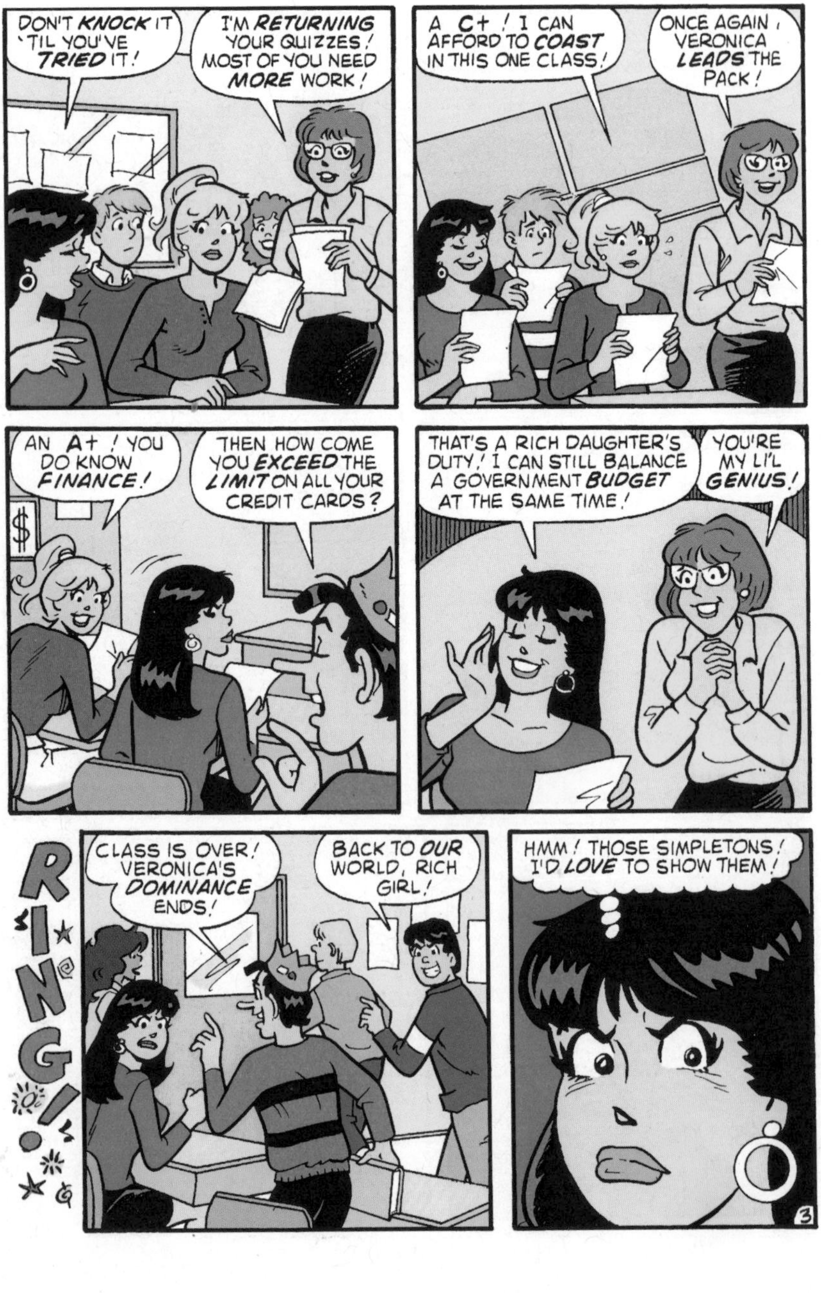
DON'T KNOCK IT 'TIL YOU'VE TRIED IT!
I'M RETURNING YOUR QUIZZES! MOST OF YOU NEED MORE WORK!
A C+! I CAN AFFORD TO COAST IN THIS ONE CLASS!
ONCE AGAIN, VERONICA LEADS THE PACK!
AN A+! YOU DO KNOW FINANCE!
THEN HOW COME YOU EXCEED THE LIMIT ON ALL YOUR CREDIT CARDS?
THAT'S A RICH DAUGHTER'S DUTY! I CAN STILL BALANCE A GOVERNMENT BUDGET AT THE SAME TIME!
YOU'RE MY LI'L GENIUS!
RING!
CLASS IS OVER! VERONICA'S DOMINANCE ENDS!
BACK TO OUR WORLD, RICH GIRL!
HMM! THOSE SIMPLETONS! I'D LOVE TO SHOW THEM!
3

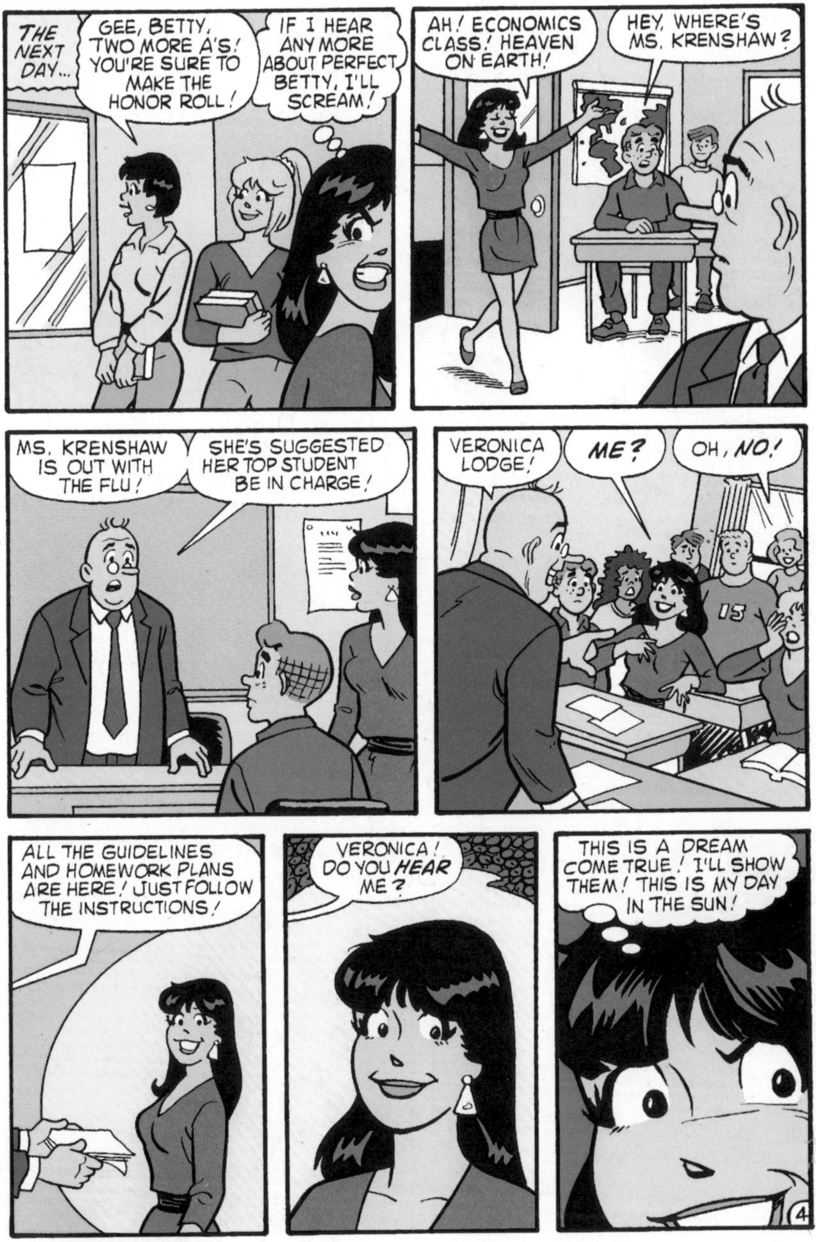
THE NEXT DAY...
GEE, BETTY, TWO MORE A'S! YOU'RE SURE TO MAKE THE HONOR ROLL!
IF I HEAR ANY MORE ABOUT PERFECT BETTY, I'LL SCREAM!
AH! ECONOMICS CLASS! HEAVEN ON EARTH!
HEY, WHERE'S MS. KRENSHAW?
MS. KRENSHAW IS OUT WITH THE FLU!
SHE'S SUGGESTED HER TOP STUDENT BE IN CHARGE!
VERONICA LODGE!
ME?
OH, NO!
15
ALL THE GUIDELINES AND HOMEWORK PLANS ARE HERE! JUST FOLLOW THE INSTRUCTIONS!
VERONICA! DO YOU HEAR ME?
THIS IS A DREAM COME TRUE! I'LL SHOW THEM! THIS IS MY DAY IN THE SUN!
4

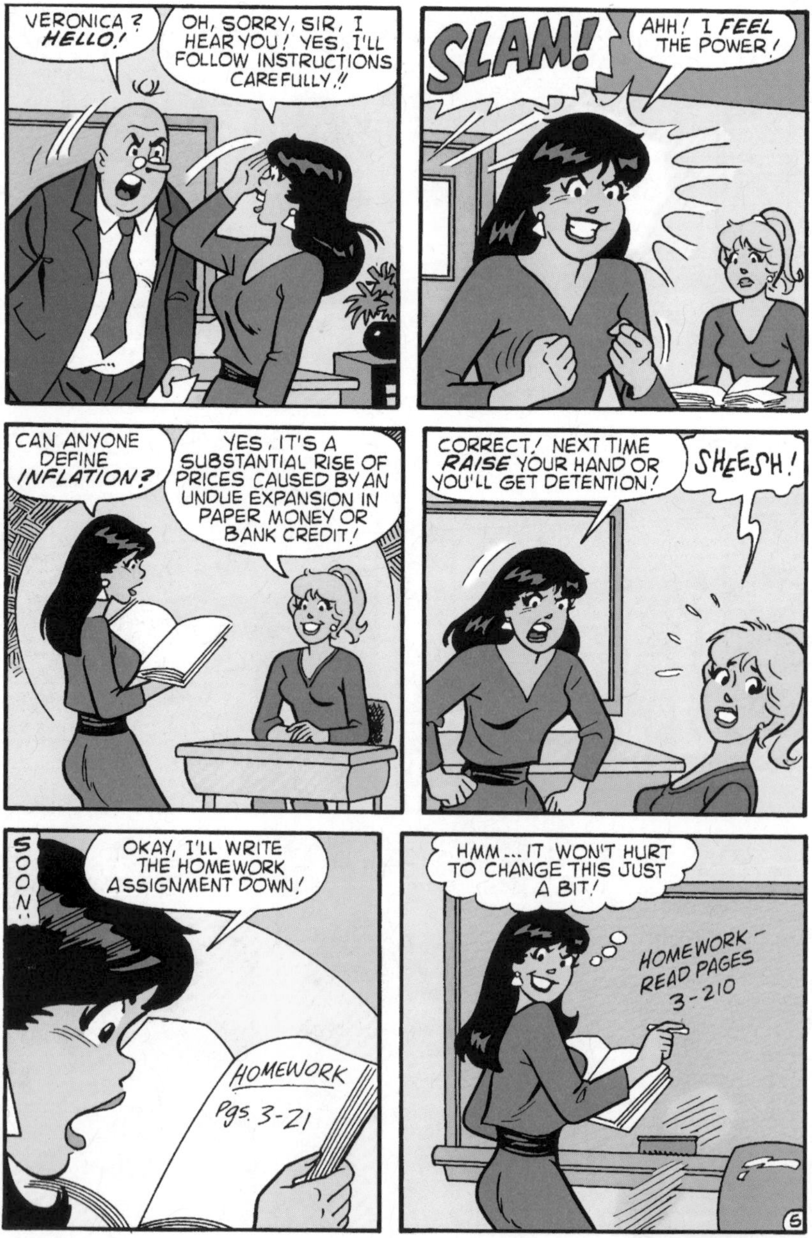
VERONICA? HELLO!
OH, SORRY, SIR, I HEAR YOU! YES, I'LL FOLLOW INSTRUCTIONS CAREFULLY!!
SLAM!
AHH! I FEEL THE POWER!
CAN ANYONE DEFINE INFLATION?
YES, IT'S A SUBSTANTIAL RISE OF PRICES CAUSED BY AN UNDUE EXPANSION IN PAPER MONEY OR BANK CREDIT!
CORRECT! NEXT TIME RAISE YOUR HAND OR YOU'LL GET DETENTION!
SHEESH!
SOON!!
OKAY, I'LL WRITE THE HOMEWORK ASSIGNMENT DOWN!
HOMEWORK
Pgs. 3-21
HMM... IT WON'T HURT TO CHANGE THIS JUST A BIT!
HOMEWORK - READ PAGES 3-210
5

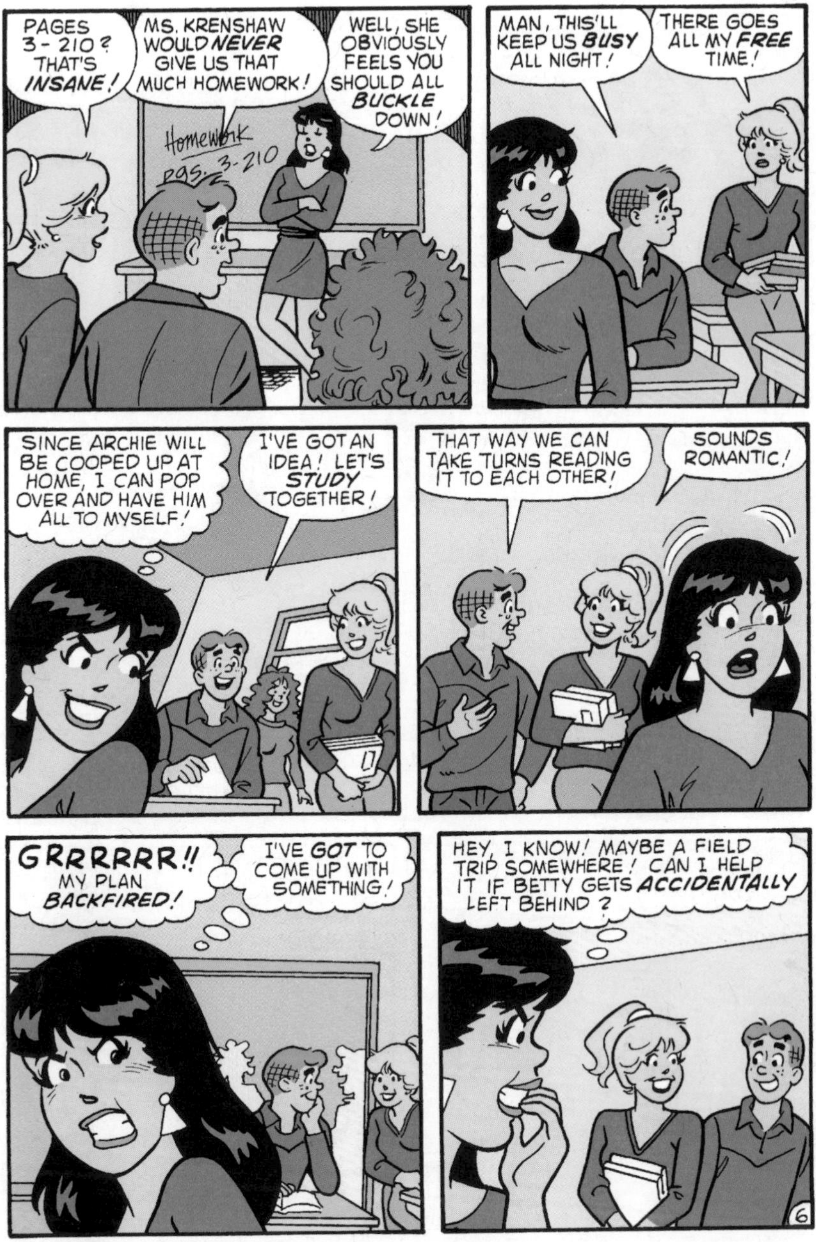
PAGES 3 - 210? THAT'S *INSANE*!
MS. KRENSHAW WOULD *NEVER* GIVE US THAT MUCH HOMEWORK!
Homework pgs. 3-210
WELL, SHE OBVIOUSLY FEELS YOU SHOULD ALL *BUCKLE* DOWN!
MAN, THIS'LL KEEP US *BUSY* ALL NIGHT!
THERE GOES ALL MY *FREE* TIME!
SINCE ARCHIE WILL BE COOPED UP AT HOME, I CAN POP OVER AND HAVE HIM ALL TO MYSELF!
I'VE GOT AN IDEA! LET'S *STUDY* TOGETHER!
THAT WAY WE CAN TAKE TURNS READING IT TO EACH OTHER!
SOUNDS ROMANTIC!
GRRRRRR!! MY PLAN *BACKFIRED*!
I'VE *GOT* TO COME UP WITH SOMETHING!
HEY, I KNOW! MAYBE A FIELD TRIP SOMEWHERE! CAN I HELP IT IF BETTY GETS *ACCIDENTALLY* LEFT BEHIND?
6

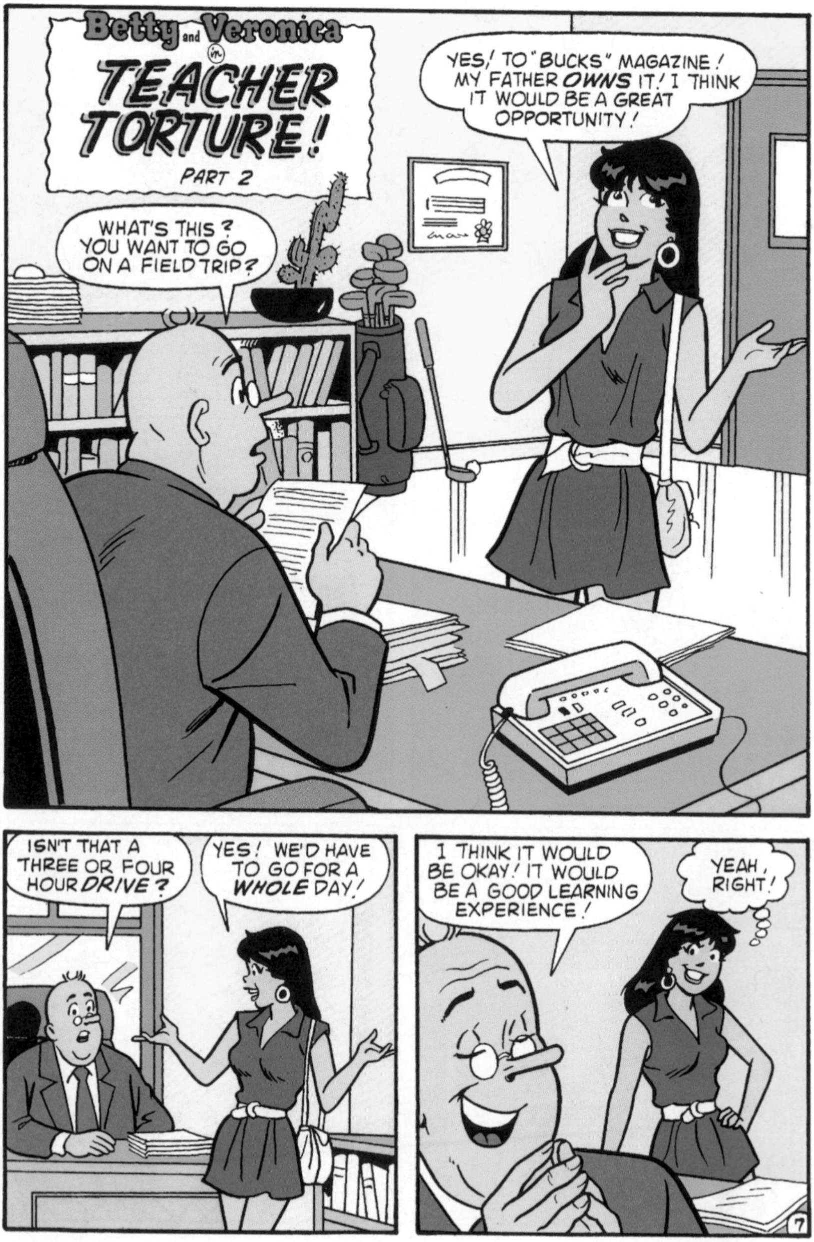
Betty and Veronica in
TEACHER TORTURE!
PART 2
WHAT'S THIS? YOU WANT TO GO ON A FIELD TRIP?
YES! TO "BUCKS" MAGAZINE! MY FATHER OWNS IT! I THINK IT WOULD BE A GREAT OPPORTUNITY!
ISN'T THAT A THREE OR FOUR HOUR DRIVE?
YES! WE'D HAVE TO GO FOR A WHOLE DAY!
I THINK IT WOULD BE OKAY! IT WOULD BE A GOOD LEARNING EXPERIENCE!
YEAH, RIGHT!
7

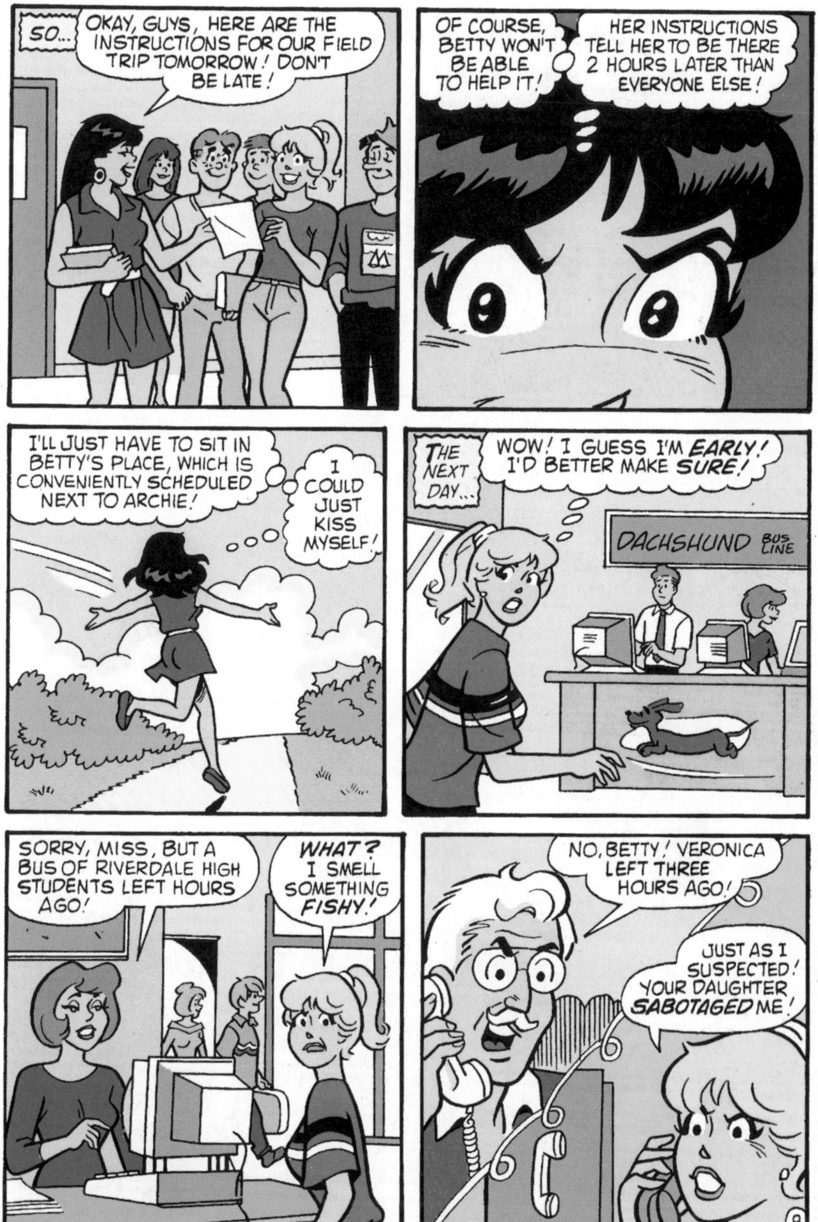
SO...
OKAY, GUYS, HERE ARE THE INSTRUCTIONS FOR OUR FIELD TRIP TOMORROW! DON'T BE LATE!
OF COURSE, BETTY WON'T BE ABLE TO HELP IT!
HER INSTRUCTIONS TELL HER TO BE THERE 2 HOURS LATER THAN EVERYONE ELSE!
I'LL JUST HAVE TO SIT IN BETTY'S PLACE, WHICH IS CONVENIENTLY SCHEDULED NEXT TO ARCHIE!
I COULD JUST KISS MYSELF!
THE NEXT DAY...
WOW! I GUESS I'M EARLY! I'D BETTER MAKE SURE!
DACHSHUND BUS LINE
SORRY, MISS, BUT A BUS OF RIVERDALE HIGH STUDENTS LEFT HOURS AGO!
WHAT? I SMELL SOMETHING FISHY!
NO, BETTY! VERONICA LEFT THREE HOURS AGO!
JUST AS I SUSPECTED! YOUR DAUGHTER SABOTAGED ME!
8

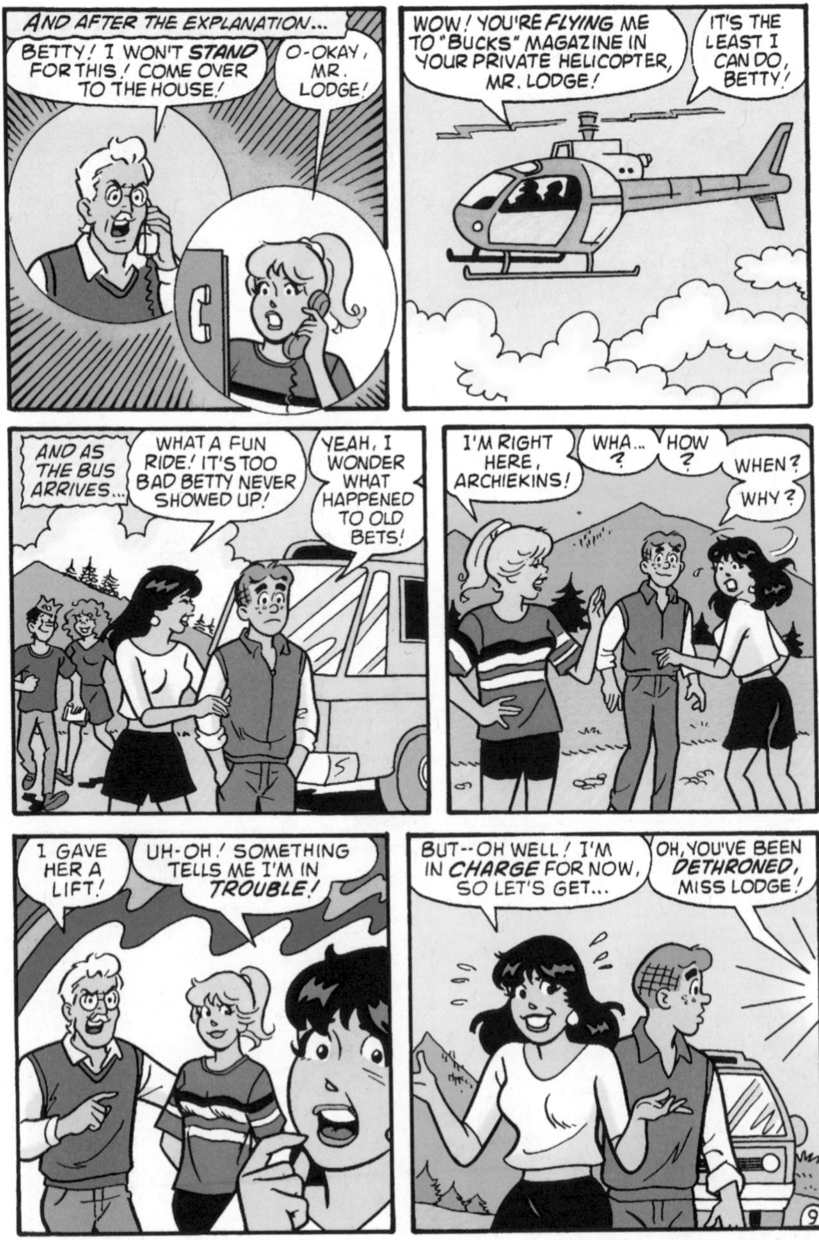
AND AFTER THE EXPLANATION...
BETTY! I WON'T STAND FOR THIS! COME OVER TO THE HOUSE!
O-OKAY, MR. LODGE!
WOW! YOU'RE FLYING ME TO "BUCKS" MAGAZINE IN YOUR PRIVATE HELICOPTER, MR. LODGE!
IT'S THE LEAST I CAN DO, BETTY!
AND AS THE BUS ARRIVES...
WHAT A FUN RIDE! IT'S TOO BAD BETTY NEVER SHOWED UP!
YEAH, I WONDER WHAT HAPPENED TO OLD BETS!
I'M RIGHT HERE, ARCHIEKINS!
WHA... ?
HOW ?
WHEN ?
WHY ?
I GAVE HER A LIFT!
UH-OH! SOMETHING TELLS ME I'M IN TROUBLE!
BUT--OH WELL! I'M IN CHARGE FOR NOW, SO LET'S GET...
OH, YOU'VE BEEN DETHRONED, MISS LODGE!
9

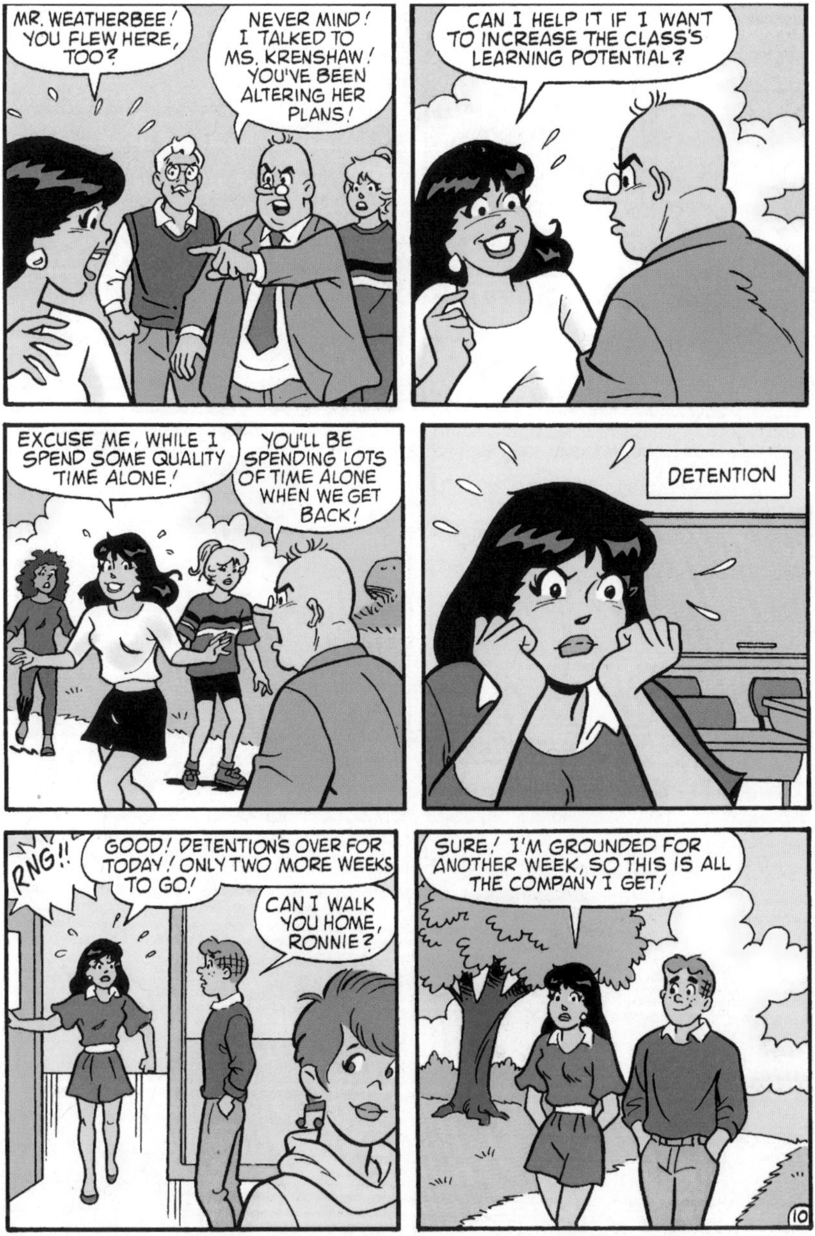
MR. WEATHERBEE! YOU FLEW HERE, TOO?
NEVER MIND! I TALKED TO MS. KRENSHAW! YOU'VE BEEN ALTERING HER PLANS!
CAN I HELP IT IF I WANT TO INCREASE THE CLASS'S LEARNING POTENTIAL?
EXCUSE ME, WHILE I SPEND SOME QUALITY TIME ALONE!
YOU'LL BE SPENDING LOTS OF TIME ALONE WHEN WE GET BACK!
DETENTION
RNG!!
GOOD! DETENTION'S OVER FOR TODAY! ONLY TWO MORE WEEKS TO GO!
CAN I WALK YOU HOME, RONNIE?
SURE! I'M GROUNDED FOR ANOTHER WEEK, SO THIS IS ALL THE COMPANY I GET!
10

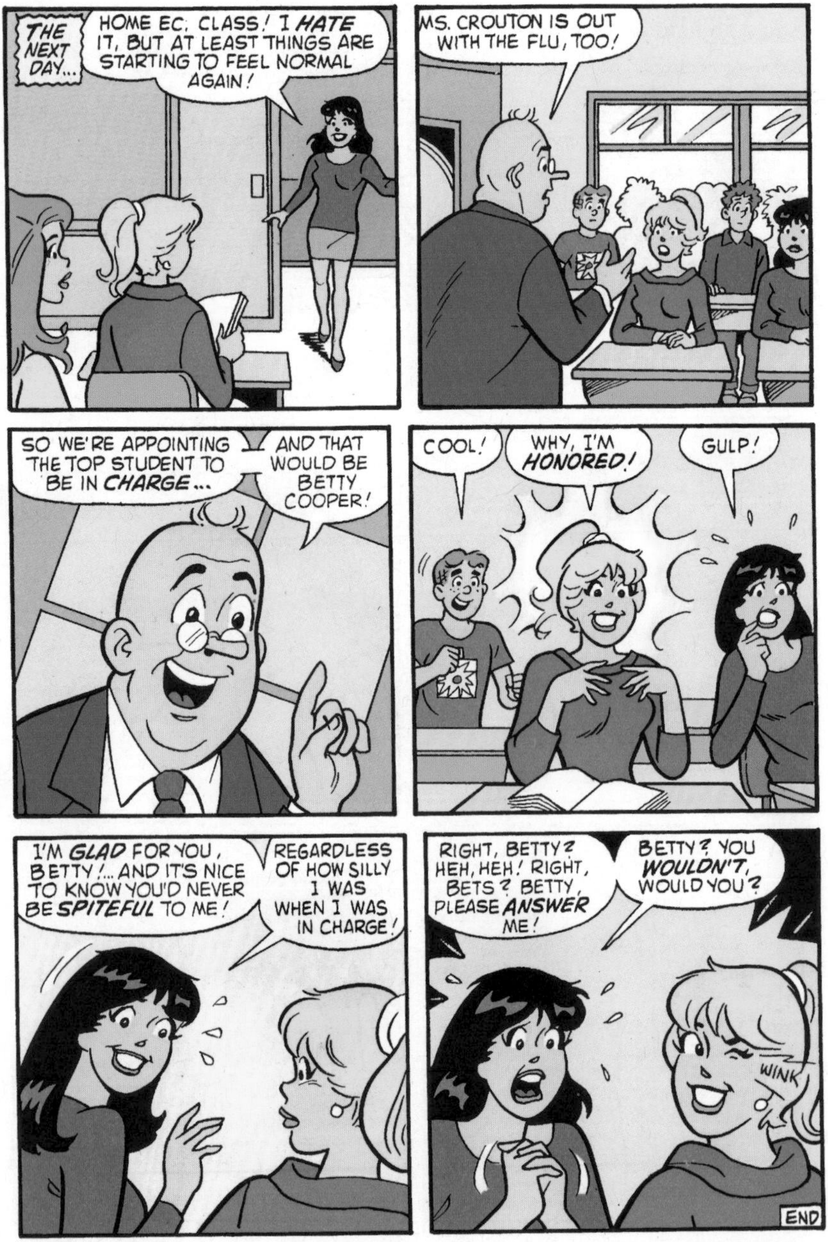
THE NEXT DAY...
HOME EC. CLASS! I HATE IT, BUT AT LEAST THINGS ARE STARTING TO FEEL NORMAL AGAIN!
MS. CROUTON IS OUT WITH THE FLU, TOO!
SO WE'RE APPOINTING THE TOP STUDENT TO BE IN CHARGE...
AND THAT WOULD BE BETTY COOPER!
COOL!
WHY, I'M HONORED!
GULP!
I'M GLAD FOR YOU, BETTY!... AND IT'S NICE TO KNOW YOU'D NEVER BE SPITEFUL TO ME!
REGARDLESS OF HOW SILLY I WAS WHEN I WAS IN CHARGE!
RIGHT, BETTY? HEH, HEH! RIGHT, BETS? BETTY, PLEASE ANSWER ME!
BETTY? YOU WOULDN'T, WOULD YOU?
WINK
END

Betty and Veronica in "PICTURE THIS!"

IT SURE WAS NICE OF JUGHEAD'S MOM TO LET US BRING JELLYBEAN TO THE MALL WITH US!

NICE? WE GOT JUGHEAD OUT OF AN AFTERNOON OF BABYSITTING!

DULLER IMAGE

OH, LOOK! THAT NEW GLAMOR PHOTO STUDIO IS OPEN! LET'S GET OUR PICTURE MADE!

I DON'T KNOW, VERONICA! I DON'T FEEL TOO GLAMOROUS!

GLAMOR PHOTO

NOT YOU, BETTY! I'M TALKING TO JELLYBEAN!

OH!

Story: Dan Parent & Bill Golliher   Pencils: Dan DeCarlo & Dan Parent
Inks: Alison Flood   Letters: Bill Yoshida   Colors: Barry Grossman

Originally printed in BETTY & VERONICA SPECTACULAR #11, November 1994

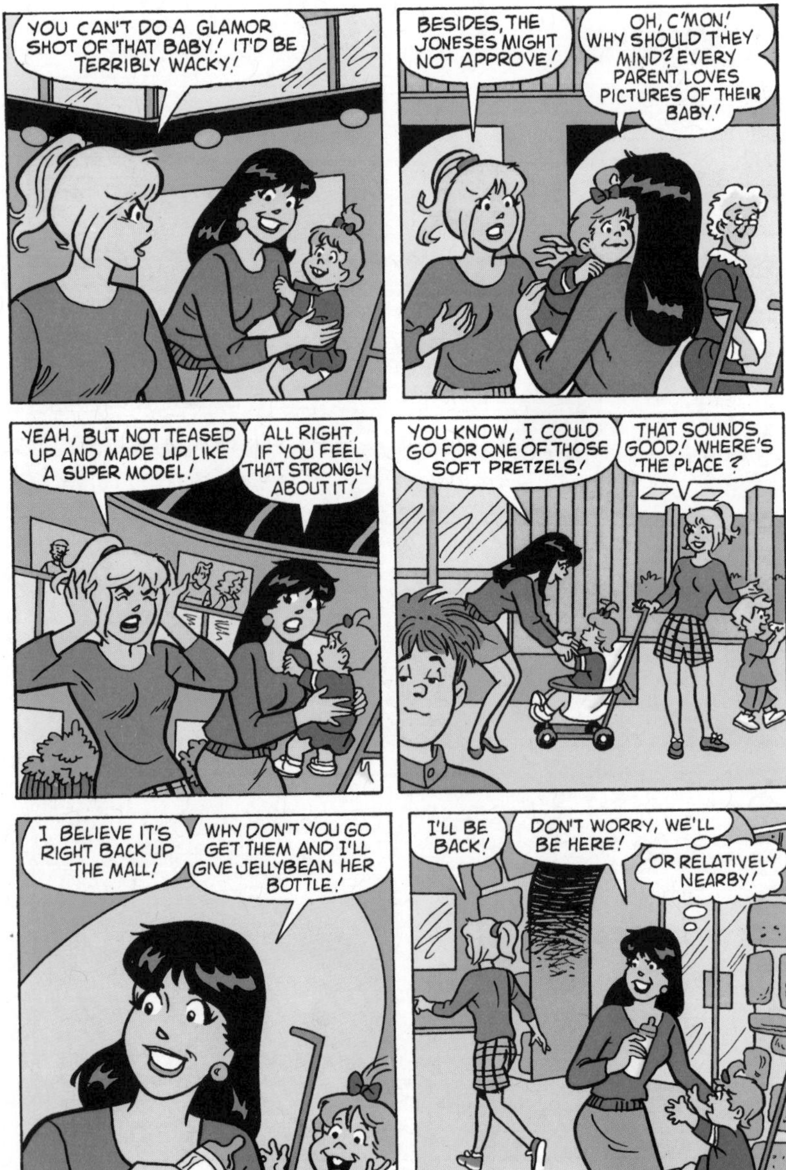
YOU CAN'T DO A GLAMOR SHOT OF THAT BABY! IT'D BE TERRIBLY WACKY!
BESIDES, THE JONESES MIGHT NOT APPROVE!
OH, C'MON! WHY SHOULD THEY MIND? EVERY PARENT LOVES PICTURES OF THEIR BABY!
YEAH, BUT NOT TEASED UP AND MADE UP LIKE A SUPER MODEL!
ALL RIGHT, IF YOU FEEL THAT STRONGLY ABOUT IT!
YOU KNOW, I COULD GO FOR ONE OF THOSE SOFT PRETZELS!
THAT SOUNDS GOOD! WHERE'S THE PLACE?
I BELIEVE IT'S RIGHT BACK UP THE MALL!
WHY DON'T YOU GO GET THEM AND I'LL GIVE JELLYBEAN HER BOTTLE!
I'LL BE BACK!
DON'T WORRY, WE'LL BE HERE!
OR RELATIVELY NEARBY!
2

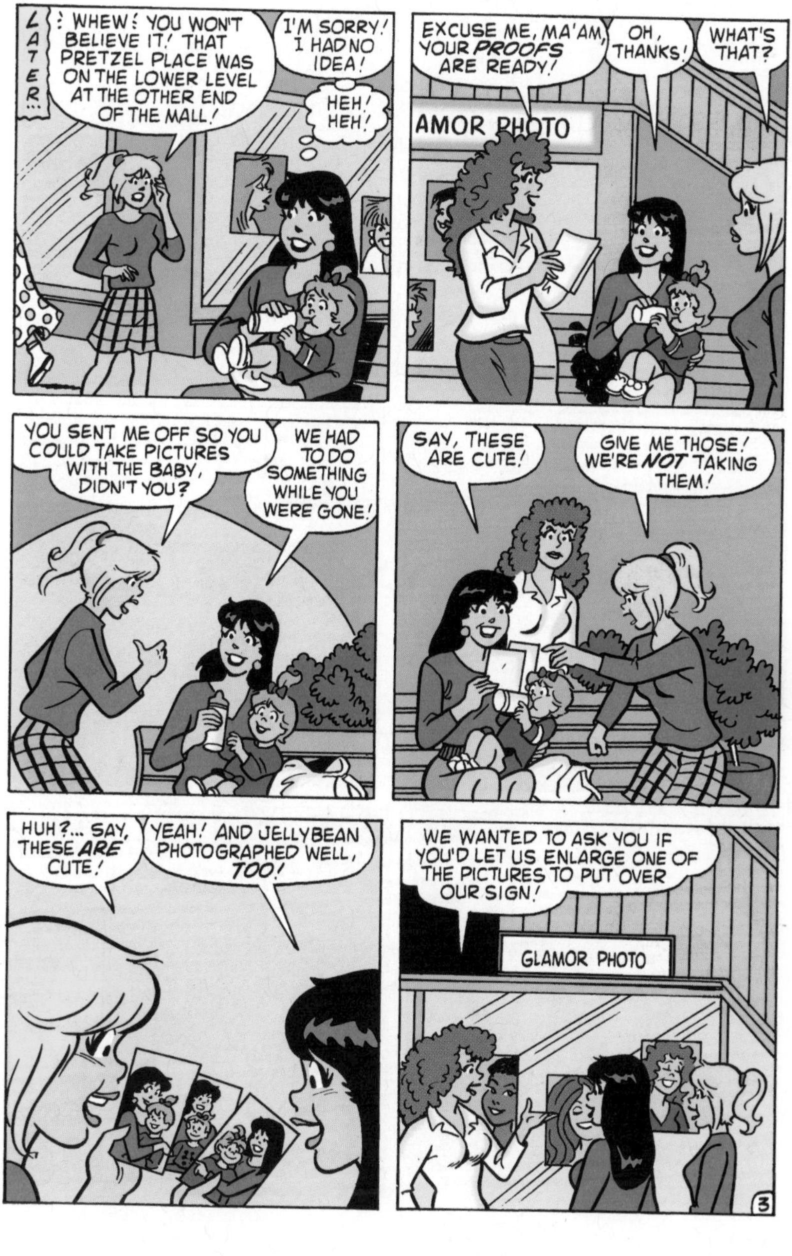
LATER...
WHEW! YOU WON'T BELIEVE IT! THAT PRETZEL PLACE WAS ON THE LOWER LEVEL AT THE OTHER END OF THE MALL!
I'M SORRY! I HAD NO IDEA!
HEH! HEH!
EXCUSE ME, MA'AM, YOUR PROOFS ARE READY!
OH, THANKS!
WHAT'S THAT?
AMOR PHOTO
YOU SENT ME OFF SO YOU COULD TAKE PICTURES WITH THE BABY, DIDN'T YOU?
WE HAD TO DO SOMETHING WHILE YOU WERE GONE!
SAY, THESE ARE CUTE!
GIVE ME THOSE! WE'RE NOT TAKING THEM!
HUH?... SAY, THESE ARE CUTE!
YEAH! AND JELLYBEAN PHOTOGRAPHED WELL, TOO!
WE WANTED TO ASK YOU IF YOU'D LET US ENLARGE ONE OF THE PICTURES TO PUT OVER OUR SIGN!
GLAMOR PHOTO
3

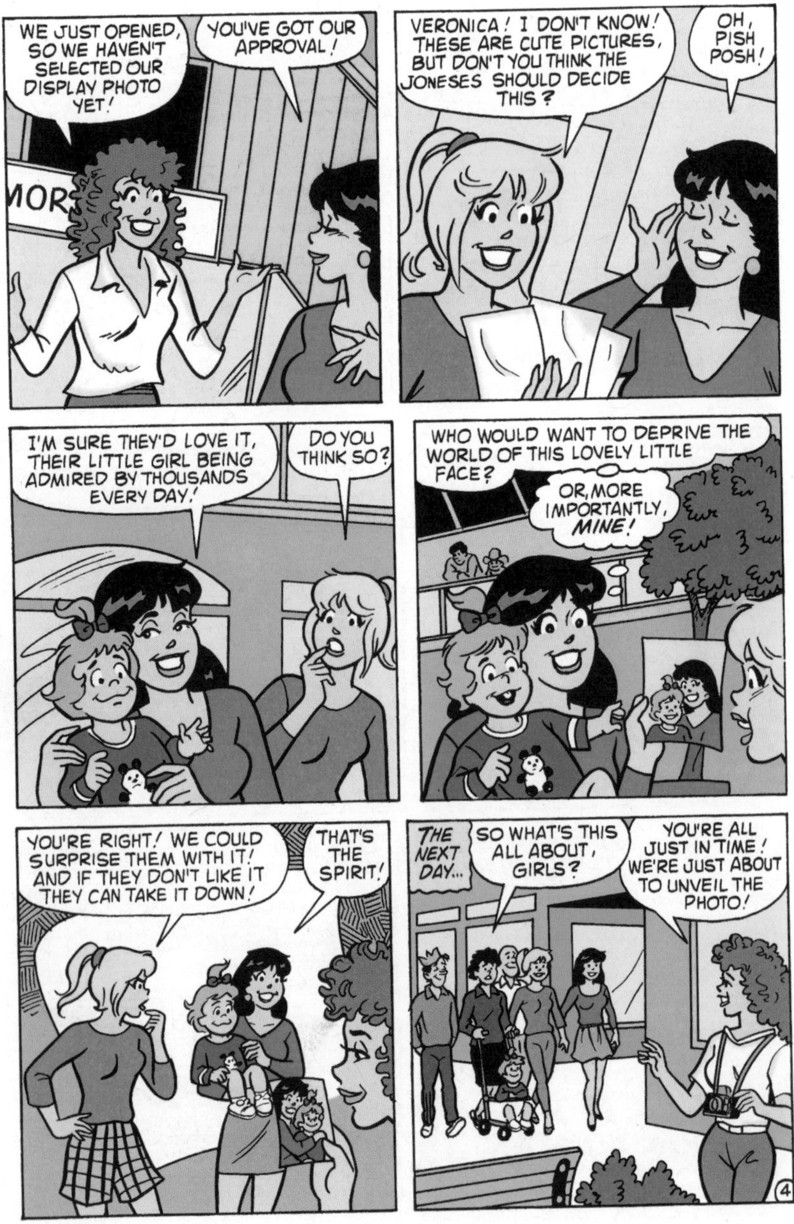
WE JUST OPENED, SO WE HAVEN'T SELECTED OUR DISPLAY PHOTO YET!
YOU'VE GOT OUR APPROVAL!
MORS
VERONICA! I DON'T KNOW! THESE ARE CUTE PICTURES, BUT DON'T YOU THINK THE JONESES SHOULD DECIDE THIS?
OH, PISH POSH!
I'M SURE THEY'D LOVE IT, THEIR LITTLE GIRL BEING ADMIRED BY THOUSANDS EVERY DAY!
DO YOU THINK SO?
WHO WOULD WANT TO DEPRIVE THE WORLD OF THIS LOVELY LITTLE FACE?
OR, MORE IMPORTANTLY, MINE!
YOU'RE RIGHT! WE COULD SURPRISE THEM WITH IT! AND IF THEY DON'T LIKE IT THEY CAN TAKE IT DOWN!
THAT'S THE SPIRIT!
THE NEXT DAY...
SO WHAT'S THIS ALL ABOUT, GIRLS?
YOU'RE ALL JUST IN TIME! WE'RE JUST ABOUT TO UNVEIL THE PHOTO!
4

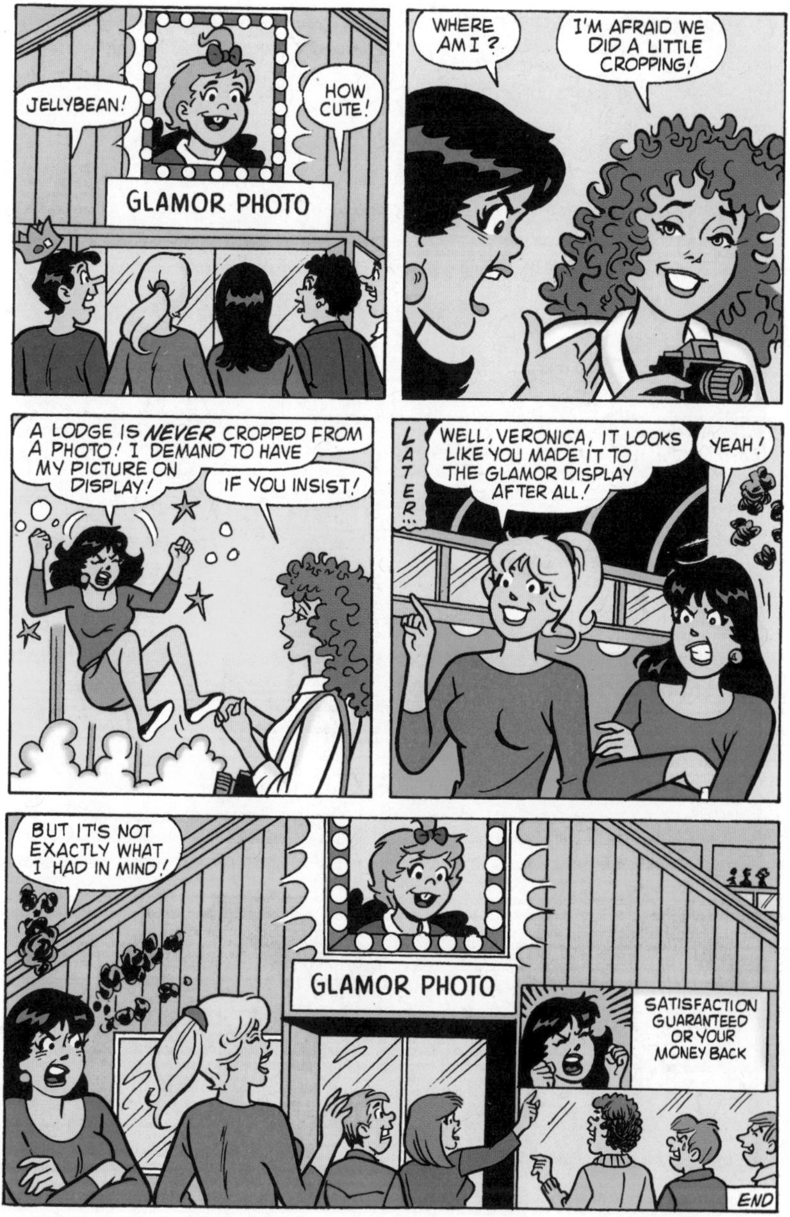
JELLYBEAN!
HOW CUTE!
GLAMOR PHOTO
WHERE AM I?
I'M AFRAID WE DID A LITTLE CROPPING!
A LODGE IS NEVER CROPPED FROM A PHOTO! I DEMAND TO HAVE MY PICTURE ON DISPLAY!
IF YOU INSIST!
LATER...
WELL, VERONICA, IT LOOKS LIKE YOU MADE IT TO THE GLAMOR DISPLAY AFTER ALL!
YEAH!
BUT IT'S NOT EXACTLY WHAT I HAD IN MIND!
GLAMOR PHOTO
SATISFACTION GUARANTEED OR YOUR MONEY BACK
END

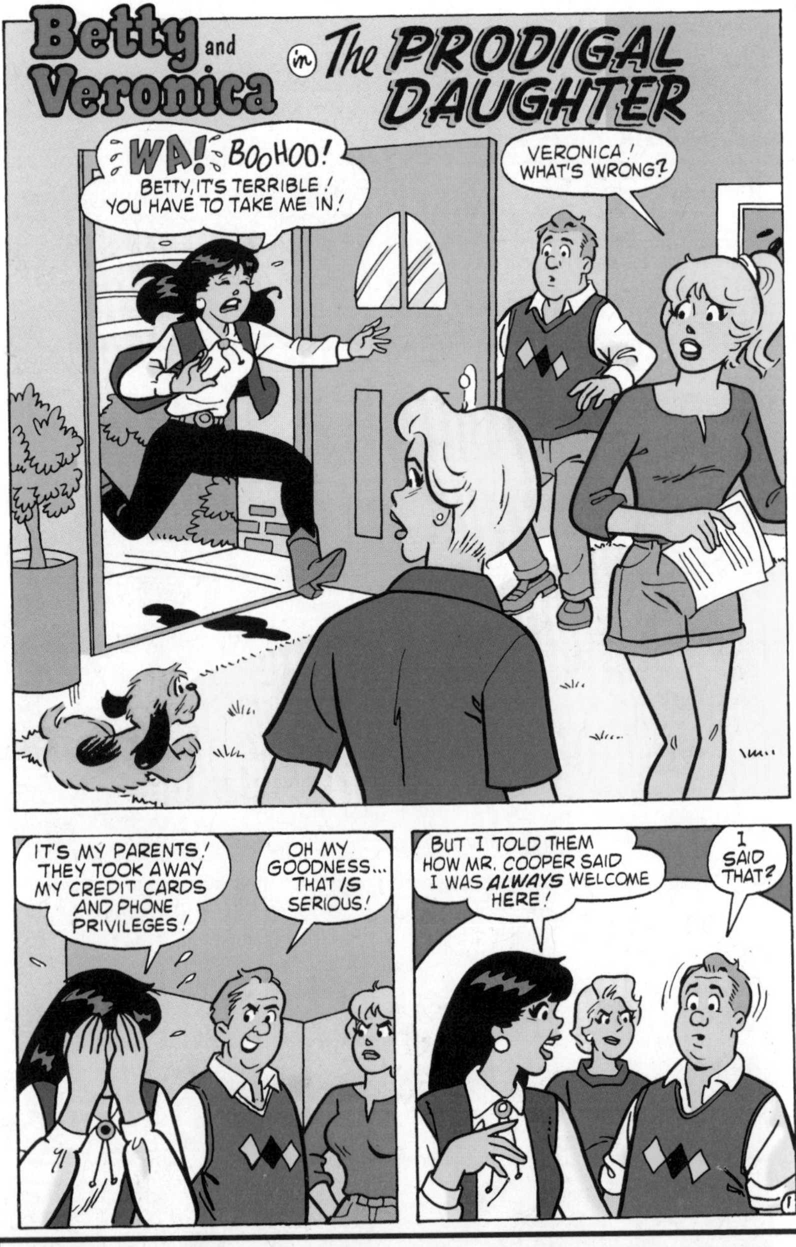
Betty and Veronica
in The PRODIGAL DAUGHTER
WA! BOOHOO! BETTY, IT'S TERRIBLE! YOU HAVE TO TAKE ME IN!
VERONICA! WHAT'S WRONG?
IT'S MY PARENTS! THEY TOOK AWAY MY CREDIT CARDS AND PHONE PRIVILEGES!
OH MY GOODNESS... THAT IS SERIOUS!
BUT I TOLD THEM HOW MR. COOPER SAID I WAS ALWAYS WELCOME HERE!
I SAID THAT?

Story: Dan Parent & Bill Golliher **Pencils:** Dan DeCarlo & Dan Parent
Inks: Alison Flood **Letters:** Bill Yoshida **Colors:** Barry Grossman

Originally printed in BETTY & VERONICA SPECTACULAR #11, November 1994

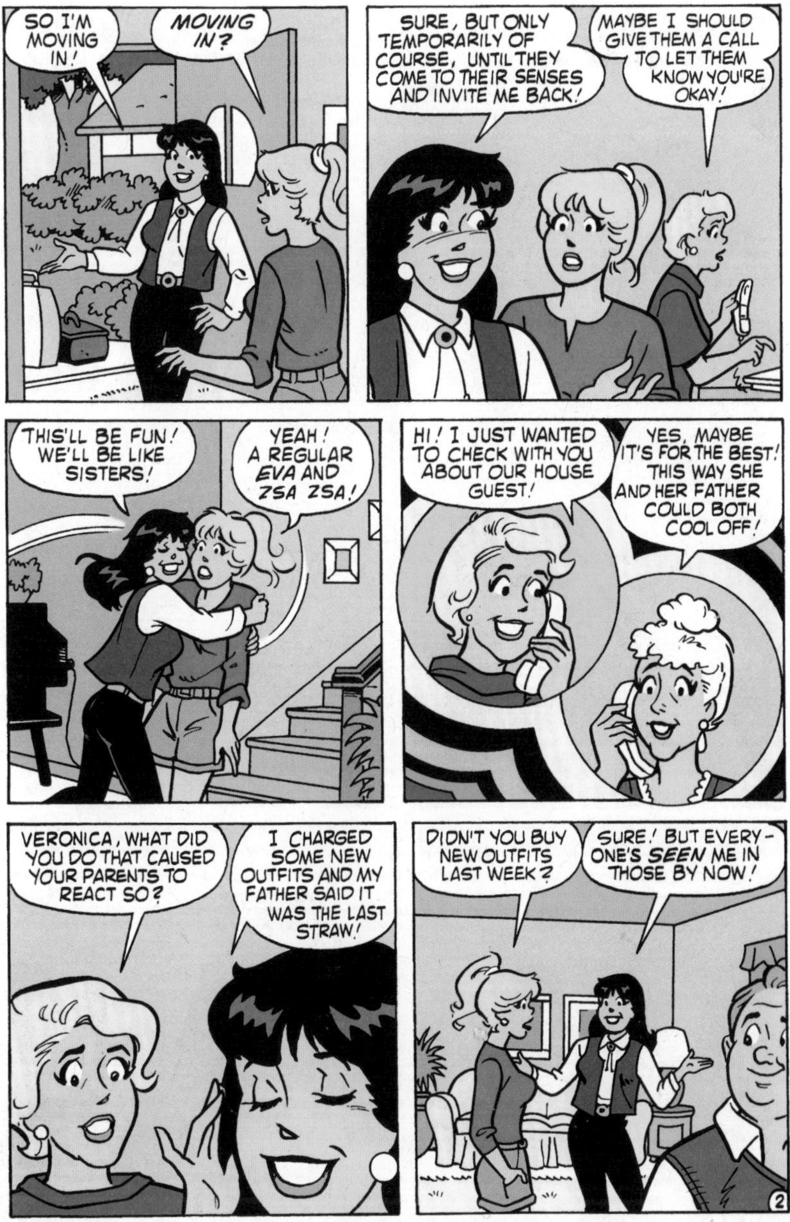
SO I'M MOVING IN!
MOVING IN?
SURE, BUT ONLY TEMPORARILY OF COURSE, UNTIL THEY COME TO THEIR SENSES AND INVITE ME BACK!
MAYBE I SHOULD GIVE THEM A CALL TO LET THEM KNOW YOU'RE OKAY!
THIS'LL BE FUN! WE'LL BE LIKE SISTERS!
YEAH! A REGULAR EVA AND ZSA ZSA!
HI! I JUST WANTED TO CHECK WITH YOU ABOUT OUR HOUSE GUEST!
YES, MAYBE IT'S FOR THE BEST! THIS WAY SHE AND HER FATHER COULD BOTH COOL OFF!
VERONICA, WHAT DID YOU DO THAT CAUSED YOUR PARENTS TO REACT SO?
I CHARGED SOME NEW OUTFITS AND MY FATHER SAID IT WAS THE LAST STRAW!
DIDN'T YOU BUY NEW OUTFITS LAST WEEK?
SURE! BUT EVERY-ONE'S SEEN ME IN THOSE BY NOW!
2

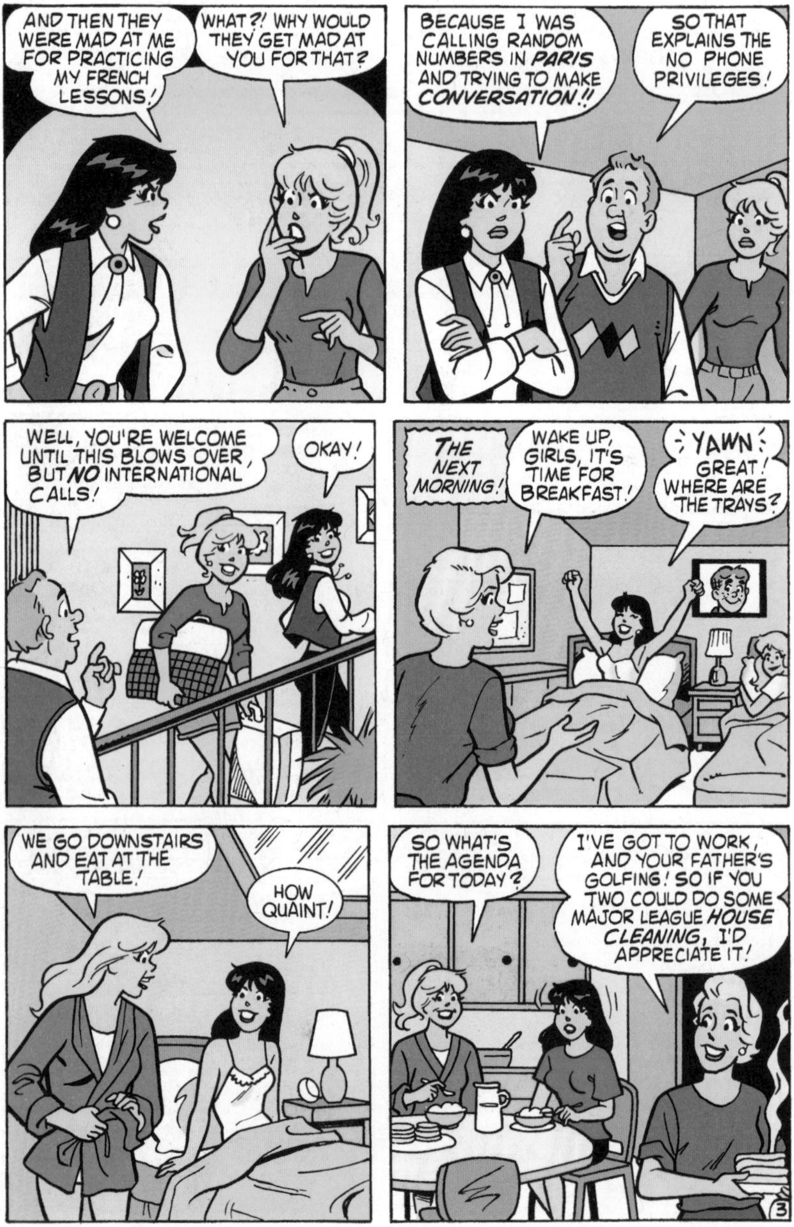
AND THEN THEY WERE MAD AT ME FOR PRACTICING MY FRENCH LESSONS!
WHAT?! WHY WOULD THEY GET MAD AT YOU FOR THAT?
BECAUSE I WAS CALLING RANDOM NUMBERS IN PARIS AND TRYING TO MAKE CONVERSATION!!
SO THAT EXPLAINS THE NO PHONE PRIVILEGES!
WELL, YOU'RE WELCOME UNTIL THIS BLOWS OVER, BUT NO INTERNATIONAL CALLS!
OKAY!
THE NEXT MORNING!
WAKE UP, GIRLS, IT'S TIME FOR BREAKFAST!
YAWN GREAT! WHERE ARE THE TRAYS?
WE GO DOWNSTAIRS AND EAT AT THE TABLE!
HOW QUAINT!
SO WHAT'S THE AGENDA FOR TODAY?
I'VE GOT TO WORK, AND YOUR FATHER'S GOLFING! SO IF YOU TWO COULD DO SOME MAJOR LEAGUE HOUSE CLEANING, I'D APPRECIATE IT!
3

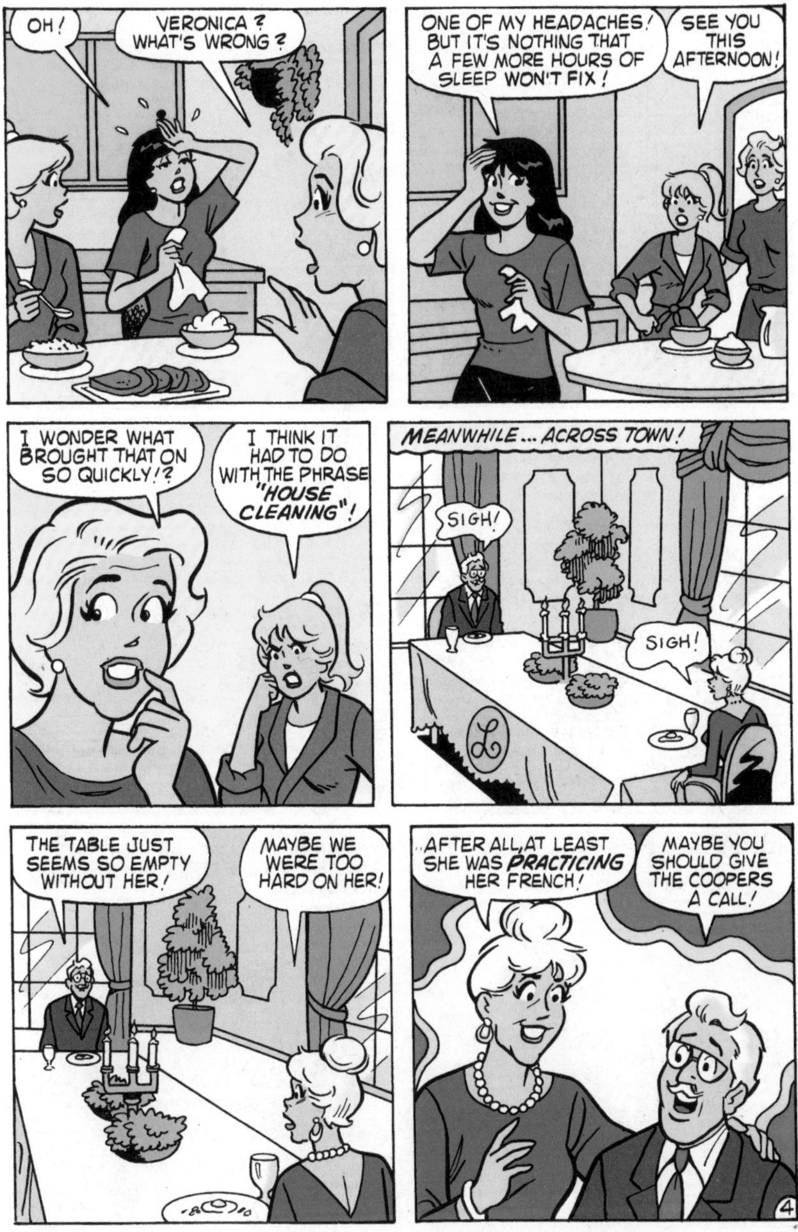
OH!
VERONICA? WHAT'S WRONG?
ONE OF MY HEADACHES! BUT IT'S NOTHING THAT A FEW MORE HOURS OF SLEEP WON'T FIX!
SEE YOU THIS AFTERNOON!
I WONDER WHAT BROUGHT THAT ON SO QUICKLY!?
I THINK IT HAD TO DO WITH THE PHRASE "HOUSE CLEANING"!
MEANWHILE... ACROSS TOWN!
SIGH!
SIGH!
THE TABLE JUST SEEMS SO EMPTY WITHOUT HER!
MAYBE WE WERE TOO HARD ON HER!
..AFTER ALL, AT LEAST SHE WAS PRACTICING HER FRENCH!
MAYBE YOU SHOULD GIVE THE COOPERS A CALL!
4

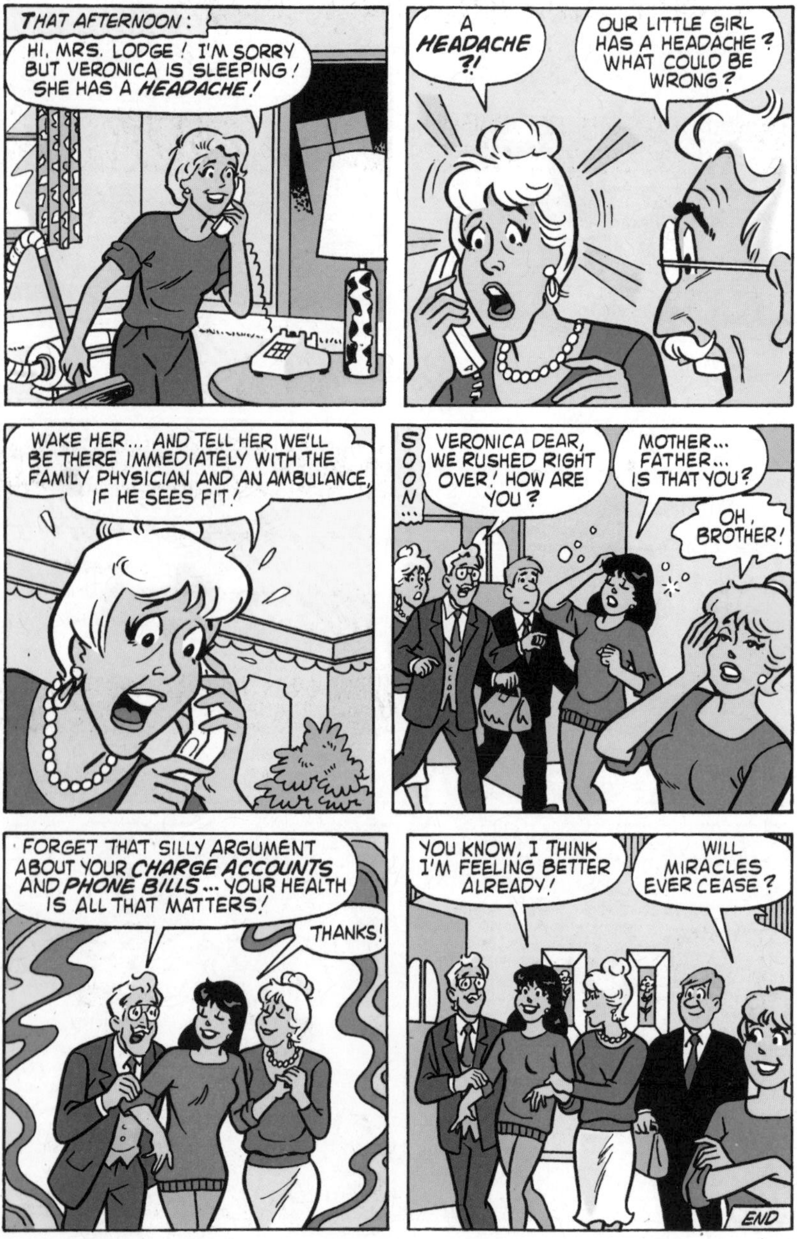
THAT AFTERNOON:
HI, MRS. LODGE! I'M SORRY BUT VERONICA IS SLEEPING! SHE HAS A HEADACHE!
A HEADACHE ?!
OUR LITTLE GIRL HAS A HEADACHE? WHAT COULD BE WRONG?
WAKE HER... AND TELL HER WE'LL BE THERE IMMEDIATELY WITH THE FAMILY PHYSICIAN AND AN AMBULANCE, IF HE SEES FIT!
SOON...
VERONICA DEAR, WE RUSHED RIGHT OVER! HOW ARE YOU?
MOTHER... FATHER... IS THAT YOU?
OH, BROTHER!
FORGET THAT SILLY ARGUMENT ABOUT YOUR CHARGE ACCOUNTS AND PHONE BILLS... YOUR HEALTH IS ALL THAT MATTERS!
THANKS!
YOU KNOW, I THINK I'M FEELING BETTER ALREADY!
WILL MIRACLES EVER CEASE?
END